KILLIGREW AND THE GOLDEN DRAGON

The Victorian Hornblower

1849, South China Sea. The burning clipper and her slaughtered crew bear all the hallmarks of the work of Zhai Jing-mu, China's most feared pirate. Kit Killigrew, second lieutenant of HMS *Tisiphone* captures the pirate and rescues Peri Dadabhoy, a beautiful Indian woman. After handing Zhai Jing-mu over to the police, Killigrew is free to enjoy the many pleasures Hong Kong has to offer, but then Zhai Jing-mu escapes. Killigrew races to recapture him before the pirate can wreak vengeance on those responsible for his imprisonment, and finds treachery and murder waiting around every corner...

KILLIGREW AND
THE GOLDEN DRAGON

Killigrew And The Golden Dragon

by

Jonathan Lunn

Magna Large Print Books
Long Preston, North Yorkshire,
BD23 4ND, England.

British Library Cataloguing in Publication Data.

Lunn, Jonathan
    Killigrew and the golden dragon.

    A catalogue record of this book is
    available from the British Library

    ISBN   0-7505-1803-0

First published in Great Britain in 2001 by Headline Book Publishing

Copyright © 2001 Jonathan Lunn

Cover illustration © G.B. Print

The right of Jonathan Lunn to be identified as the author of this work has been asserted by him in accordance with the Copyright, Designs and Patents Act, 1988

Published in Large Print 2002 by arrangement with Headline Book Publishing Ltd.

Magna Large Print is an imprint of Library Magna Books Ltd.

Printed and bound in Great Britain by
T.J. (International) Ltd., Cornwall, PL28 8RW

For Sam

I should like to thank the following for their invaluable assistance: James Hale, for agenting duties and for knowing exactly what to say when I was starting to lose my self-confidence; Sarah Keen for her excellent editing and suggestions; Yvonne Holland for a thorough job of copy-editing; Rosemarie Buckman for getting me into Europe and Alastair Wilson, whose astonishing breadth of knowledge enabled him to check the manuscript for errors both technical and historical (if you find any mistakes, I guarantee it's because I occasionally took liberties with strict historical accuracy for dramatic effect, rather than because he failed to set me straight).

I should also like to thank the following for providing inspiration: David Arnold, John Barry, Albert 'Cubby' Broccoli, William Laird Clowes, Michael Curtiz, Roald Dahl, James Robertson Justice, Jet Li, Basil Lubbock, Jan Morris, Tyrone Power, Frank Welsh, James Wong and John Woo.

I:

Pilongs

Commander Robertson gazed up to where Mr Strachan scanned the seas from the maintop of Her Majesty's paddle-sloop *Tisiphone* with a telescope pressed to his eye. 'Will someone please tell me what my assistant surgeon is doing?'

'Looking for the sea serpent, sir.' A faint smile played on Killigrew's lips.

Robertson gave his second lieutenant a withering glare. 'The sea serpent?' Sightings of a monstrous serpent had frequently cropped up in the press over the past two years, but few educated men took them too seriously.

'Yes, sir. He thinks it might be some kind of aquatic dinosaur, a species which wasn't wiped out by the Great Flood. If he can prove it he's going to name it *strachanosaurus*.'

'I'd've thought that *mass hysteriasaurus* would be a much better name,' snorted Robertson. A tall, burly man with a leonine head, he was old enough – and able enough – to have been promoted to captain long ago, but he lacked the necessary political connections; although rumour claimed he had been offered a promotion and turned it down. A captain could command nothing smaller than a frigate, and since the Royal

Navy did not have nearly enough ships to go round all its captains, such a promotion would have seen Robertson beached on half-pay. 'Don't tell me *you* believe in this dinosaur hoax, Second?'

'I've seen the skeletons in the Egyptian Hall, sir. I'm no expert, but they looked genuine enough to me. And Strachan tells me these things are taken very seriously indeed by both the Royal Society and the British Association for the Advancement of Science.'

'I suppose next you'll be telling me you believe in dragons?'

Killigrew grinned. 'Only the one my grand-father employs as a housekeeper, sir.'

Lean and tall, Kit Killigrew wore his peaked cap at a rakish angle, the hair beneath thick and dark. His saturnine complexion was the legacy of a Cornish father and a Greek mother who had met during the Greek War of Independence: Captain Jack Killigrew, an officer of the Royal Navy on half-pay, looking for adventure and a noble cause to serve, and Medora Bouboulina, a daughter of the great Laskarina Bouboulina, the lady admiral who had been the scourge of the Ottoman Navy. Killigrew's parents had died when he was three, and he had been brought up in Falmouth by his grandfather – another admiral in the family – until he was old enough to go to sea as a first-class volunteer. He had served against Barbary Corsairs, fought in the Syrian Campaign, and distinguished himself at the taking of Chingkiang-fu in the Opium War. Since then he had been fighting slavers on the

Guinea Coast, but he had never been able to get the Far East out of his heart. He was happy to be returning, and happier still that he was doing so in peacetime.

It was a glorious day, with hardly a cloud to be seen, and the breeze lifted the sea into a strong but steady swell. The *Tisiphone*, six days out of Singapore and bound for Hong Kong, sailed close-hauled on the starboard tack. The brig-rigged paddle-sloop was eight-score feet from stem to stern and thirty-two in the beam. Her figurehead, a representation of the snake-haired scourge of the damned, glowered beneath the bowsprit. A single black funnel rose between her two masts, and her armament consisted of two thirty-two-pounders abaft the paddle-boxes and a sixty-eight-pounder pivot gun on the forecastle. She was a relatively small ship, intended for inshore work rather than fleet actions, with a crew of a hundred. It was nearly three months since she had sailed from Portsmouth to join the South China Seas squadron in the suppression of the pirates who infested these waters.

At the maintop, Strachan stiffened as he peered through the telescope. For a moment Killigrew – who tried to keep an open mind – wondered if his friend had actually spotted the sea serpent. The assistant surgeon snapped the telescope shut and reached for the speaking trumpet, but in his excitement he merely knocked it off the platform. It fell to the deck with a clang, narrowly missing a seaman, who jumped aside with a yell.

'Hey! Watch what you're doing, you big, clumsy ... assistant surgeon, sir.' The seaman concluded more respectfully than he had started out when he realised whom he addressed.

'Sorry!' Strachan called back. He was in his mid-twenties, the same age as Killigrew, with blue eyes behind wire-framed spectacles and a tangle of light brown hair. 'But I see some ships!' He peered through the telescope again. 'Three of them!'

The seaman reported to the quarterdeck with the speaking trumpet which Strachan had dropped and held it out for Killigrew to inspect. There was a big dent in it where it had hit the deck.

'God preserve us from civilian officers!' Robertson snapped his fingers at the seaman and motioned to be given the trumpet, which he then raised to his lips. 'If you're going to stand in for my look-outs, Mr Strachan, be so good as to use the correct hails! In this case you should call: "Sail ho!" '

'Sorry, sir.' Strachan cupped his hands around his mouth. 'Sail ho!'

'Where away?' asked Robertson.

'What?'

The commander closed his eyes as if in pain. 'In which direction, Mr Strachan?'

'Oh! Over there.' The assistant surgeon pointed.

'Two points off the starboard bow,' deduced Robertson. 'I hope your friend knows more about dispensing medicines than he does about seamanship, Mr Killigrew. Be so good to lend him the benefit of your more expert eye.'

'Aye, aye, sir.'

Killigrew ascended the weblike ratlines and swung himself on to the maintop. Strachan was so startled he almost fell from the narrow platform, but Killigrew seized him by the arm with one hand and, with the other, caught the telescope as Strachan dropped it.

Killigrew balanced the heavy telescope with practised ease and held it to his eye, sweeping the horizon in the direction which Strachan indicated. He could see the sails of a three-masted clipper, hull-down below the horizon, and the mat-and-rattan sails of a large junk immediately alongside it, so close it was hard to tell where the junk ended and the clipper began. It took him a little longer to make out the sails of the second junk, on the far side of the clipper.

'Pilongs,' Killigrew said with gut certainty.

'Pilongs?' echoed Strachan. This was the first time he had visited the Orient.

'Chinese pirates,' explained Killigrew. He collapsed the telescope and handed it to the lookout, who had joined them on the maintop. 'Looks as if we've caught 'em in the act this time. Better get to the sick berth, Strachan.'

'All right.' Strachan climbed down through the lubbers' hole and descended the ratlines to the deck while Killigrew took the more flamboyant route of sliding down a backstay.

'Two small junks grappled to a clipper, sir,' he reported. 'Pilongs at work, without a doubt.'

Robertson ordered the boatswain to beat to quarters and sent a midshipman below to order the engineer to get steam up. As the hands cleared the decks for action, Lieutenant Lord

17

Endymion Hartcliffe joined Robertson and Killigrew on the quarterdeck. A younger son of the Duke of Hartcliffe, the first lieutenant was a stout, moon-faced man in his late twenties with curly hair and watery blue eyes.

'What've we got, Killigrew?' he asked, rubbing his hands together, more for something to do with them than as a show of eagerness.

'Two pilong junks grappled alongside a clipper.'

A call from the look-out at the masthead alerted them that the three ships were separating. Killigrew glanced through the telescope that Robertson handed him and saw that the two junks were indeed slipping away from the clipper. Even as he watched, smoke billowed up from the clipper's deck, already visible over the horizon, and a moment later the sails and rigging were ablaze.

He handed the telescope back to Robertson. 'The fiends have fired her.'

The commander nodded. 'They must've seen us.'

The clipper soon blazed fiercely. Killigrew guessed they had caught the pirates in the act of transferring the clipper's cargo of opium into the junks. It was all one to him if the opium was smuggled into China by Western traders or Chinese pirates; his main concern was the safety of the clipper's crew. They were probably dead already, he thought grimly. All that he and his colleagues could do was make sure that these particular pirates had hunted their last quarry.

Even with all sail crammed on her yards, the *Tisiphone* could manage no more than four knots in such light airs, barely enough to keep the two junks in sight. They were still barely halfway to where the clipper had burned down to the waterline and was already sinking, before a blast from the whistle signalled that steam was up, and a moment later the deck vibrated as the paddle-wheels churned into action. The sloop's speed trebled almost at once.

'Deck!' called the look-out. 'They're separating!'

'Clever,' said Killigrew, as Robertson levelled the telescope again. The junks could not hope to outrun a paddle-sloop under steam, but if they went their separate ways then at least one of them had a chance of escape.

'The larger one's holding her course,' said Robertson. 'Probably headed for the China coast. The other's veering off to starboard. The Paracels?'

Killigrew nodded. The Paracels were an archipelago of tiny islands and reefs, a deathtrap for any ship that did not know those waters. It was a fair bet that the master of the smaller junk knew them like the back of his hand.

'How far, Mr Yelverton?' Robertson asked the ship's master.

'To the Paracels?' As the *Tisiphone*'s master, Yelverton was responsible for navigation and was the most important officer on the ship – if not the most senior – after the commander. 'Eight miles, sir. If we go after them, we may just catch them first.'

'We ought to stop and lower a boat first,' said Killigrew, nodding to where what was left of the blazing clipper sank beneath the waves.

'I hardly think anyone is likely to have survived that fire,' snorted Robertson. 'Still, I suppose you're right, Second. It's our duty to check for survivors. Make ready the whaler, Bosun.'

The whale boat was the largest boat carried by the *Tisiphone*, apart from the thirty-foot pinnace stowed on deck above the engine room. The boatswain ordered the whaler's crew to assemble while one of the mates prepared to take command. It was swung out in its davits and lowered until it was just above the waves. Then the *Tisiphone* stopped just long enough for the hands to shin down the lifelines into the boat. The clipper's masts were the only part of her showing above the waves, now thick with flotsam: charred timbers, a sailor's sennit hat, a few cargo chests bobbing up and down forlornly.

Killigrew stood at the bulwark as the whaler's crew cast off. Here and there he could see bodies floating amongst the flotsam. Sharks' fins circled already. 'Remember, if you can't find any survivors, at least get a piece of wreckage; something to identify the clipper,' he said.

The mate saluted. 'Aye, aye, sir.'

The oarsmen pulled away from the *Tisiphone* and the engineer started up the sloop's paddle-wheels once more.

Lowering the boat had taken only minutes, yet the *Tisiphone* had lost more time in slowing down and speeding up again. But now the engines were at full steam the sloop quickly gained on the smaller of the two junks, which was only five miles away.

'Land ho!' cried the look-out at the masthead.

The boatswain lifted the speaking trumpet to his lips. 'Where away?'

'Dead ahead! Looks like an island ... no, several islands.'

'The Paracels,' said the master. 'If they make it to the reefs, we'll never catch them.'

'We might stand a chance if we went for the other junk,' said Hartcliffe. The larger junk was still visible on the horizon off the port bow. 'Nothing but clear water between here and China...'

'I think we should stick to our guns and stay with this one, my lord,' said Killigrew.

'Any particular reason, Second?' asked Robertson.

'They know we can catch the smaller junk, sir. So the larger one has to be the decoy.'

'Don't pilong chiefs always sail on their largest vessels?'

'That's what they want us to think, sir. If there's a pilong chief on board one of those junks, he'll be on the smaller one.'

'Is that what your ancestors would have done, Second?' In his gruff, sardonic way, Robertson liked to tease Killigrew about his piratical ancestors: his Cornish forebears had been notorious pirates in the sixteenth century.

The second lieutenant refused to give him the satisfaction of rising to the bait. 'It's what I'd do, sir.'

'*À bon chat, bon rat*, sir,' offered Hartcliffe.

'What's that?' demanded Robertson. Someone must at least have *tried* to teach him French once,

21

as befitted the position of navy officer, but Robertson refused to admit it now. If he possessed any social graces, Killigrew had seen no sign of them since he had rejoined the *Tisiphone* with her new commander. The hands called him 'Tommy Pipes' behind his back, a nickname usually reserved for the boatswain's mates whose bellows were relied upon to keep everything on board shipshape and Bristol fashion. There was little work for the boatswain's mates to do on board the *Tisiphone* now that Robertson was captain: he had a booming voice of his own and was never slow to use it.

'A loose translation would be: "Set a thief to catch a thief", sir,' explained Killigrew.

'I see,' Robertson remarked gruffly. 'And a descendant of pirates to catch pirates, I suppose?'

'I'm an officer of the Royal Navy first and foremost, sir.'

'That isn't good enough, Mr Killigrew. In my command I want only officers who are Royal Navy officers first, last and everything in between. I suppose you think we can catch the smaller one before she reaches the Paracels, and then go after the other?'

'In an ideal world, sir, yes.'

'In an ideal world, eh? It may have escaped your notice, Second, but we don't live in an ideal world. Don't fall into the trap of thinking these pilongs are nincompoops. They may be un-enlightened heathens without the benefits of steam and shell, but that doesn't make them imbeciles. While we're chasing the second junk, the first one will run for the horizon and change course the moment she's out of sight. We'll never catch her then.'

'Yes, sir. Shall I order the quartermaster to change course?'

'Never change horses in mid-stream, Second. We'll stand by your decision and see where it leads us.' He slapped the telescope against Killigrew's chest, his way of asking the lieutenant to hold it. 'Of course, if that junk reaches the Paracels before we can catch her and we end up losing both junks, you know I'll hold you responsible, don't you?'

'The thought had crossed my mind, sir.'

'We'll see,' harrumphed Robertson.

Killigrew checked on the junk they were chasing. She was barely five miles away now, but had less than three to cover before she reached the safety of the Paracels. He calculated the pilongs would be within range of the bow-chaser long before that; within the next twenty minutes, as things stood.

The *Tisiphone* rapidly gained on her quarry. A junk – even a pirate junk armed to the bulwarks – was no match for a Western ship in a fight, not even a mere sloop of war. A direct hit from a shell would blow a junk out of the water. Nonetheless there was a palpable air of excitement on board, as there was in any stern-chase; excitement, and tension. If it came to a fight the junk had no chance of winning, but there would always be a chance she would get a lucky hit before she went down, and even one round shot amidships would be enough to sweep the deck with splinters of wood and wreak bloody havoc amongst the crew.

'Attend to the bow-chaser, Second,' ordered Robertson. As second lieutenant, Killigrew was responsible for the guns, although the gunner – an officer by warrant rather than commission, and therefore subordinate – was perfectly capable. 'Give them a warning shot to begin with, if you please, though I doubt they'll pay it much heed. As Christians we owe them the chance of mercy, if nothing else.'

'Aye, aye, sir.' Killigrew made his way to the forecastle. 'Sixty-eight-pounder's crew close up,' he ordered. 'Call for silence!'

The boatswain's mate made the call to pipe down on his whistle and everyone stopped talking; not that there had been much chatter during the tense chase.

'Make ready!' ordered the gunner.

The gun crew slid the gun carriage on its racers towards one of the four gun ports in the prow. Every man of the gun crew had his number and his duties, and Killigrew had drilled them time and time again on the voyage from England. These were all able seamen who could do it blindfolded.

'One blank shot if you please, Guns,' Killigrew told the gunner.

'Aye, aye, sir. Remove tompion and search!'

One of the men checked that the gun had not been left loaded. It should not have been, but one could not take any chances.

'Load!'

A flannel cartridge was passed up from the magazine, slipped into the muzzle and rammed home.

'Run out!'

The gun crew hauled on the ropes to push the muzzle out through the gun port.

'Prime!'

A friction tube was inserted into the breech. There was no need to aim. The captain of the gun grasped the wooden toggle on the lanyard. Everyone else backed away. 'Ready!'

The gunner glanced at Killigrew, who nodded once.

'Fire!'

The captain of the gun jerked back the toggle. The gun boomed deafeningly and spewed a great plume of pale grey smoke from its muzzle.

'Are they heaving to?' Killigrew called to the look-out at the masthead.

'No, sir ... they're changing course, veering to port!'

'Running for the reefs,' snorted Killigrew. 'Range?'

''Bout a thousand yards, sir.'

'Right. We'll fire a shot across their bows. Round shot if you please, Guns.'

'Sponge!'

The barrel was wormed and sponged to clear the bore of any smouldering remains from the previous charge while one man went to fetch the next cartridge, along with a sixty-eight-pound round shot. The gun was loaded, primed once more and run out again.

'Point!' ordered the gunner. The captain of the gun lined up the bow-chaser until it pointed to a spot perhaps fifty yards ahead of the junk, to let its crew know they were within range. The *Tisi-*

phone was well out of range of the junk's archaic cannon.

'Elevate!'

The gun crew lifted the breech from the carriage and the number two of the gun crew slid the wedge back as far as it would go, to give the gun maximum elevation. 'Down!' he called.

'Ready!' said the captain of the gun.

The gunner waited until the pitching of the deck reached its zenith, and fired just before the gun was lined up with where he wanted the ball to fire. The gun boomed and shot back on its carriage. The shot screeched through the air and threw up a huge white plume close enough to the junk to drench the men standing on deck.

'Capital shooting, Guns,' said Killigrew. 'Any sign of them heaving to?' he called up to the lookout.

'No, sir! They ... they're putting out sweeps, sir!'

Killigrew could see that for himself as the crew of the junk lowered the large oars into the water, trying to give themselves that extra burst of speed they needed to carry them to safety.

'They've got sand, I'll say that for 'em,' opined the gunner.

'That's because they know we'll hang every last one of the jackals if we catch them,' said Killigrew. These men had murdered the crew of the clipper and he intended to see to it that those who were not killed in this fight would be hanged for their crimes. 'Reload.'

'Aye, aye, sir. Chain shot?' Chain shot to dismast them, slow them down enough to overhaul

26

them before they reached the reefs, and then get in close and pummel them into submission with round shot.

Killigrew was about to nod his acquiescence when he changed his mind. 'No, damn it. A shell. We'll blow the bastards out of the water.' If they could destroy this junk with one shot, they might still have time to catch the second junk.

'Aye, aye, sir!'

As the gun crew reloaded the bow-chaser, Killigrew studied the foe through a telescope. He could see them sweating at the sweeps, two men to an oar, pulling for their very lives. He knew the back-breaking agony of that kind of work over an extended period, and could have felt sorry for them if they had not been pirates, the scum of the seas. He had met Chinese the last time he had been in these waters and bore the race no ill will. He had been taught to treat all men as individuals, regardless of race, colour or creed. Indeed, of all the races he had encountered he had a particular fondness for the Chinese, with their fine art, cheerful nature and impeccable manners. But these men were criminals according to the Manchu Code as much as in British law. He would take as many alive as he could, to stand trial in Hong Kong as justice demanded, but he would not lose a wink of sleep over any that he had to kill in the process.

'Ready!' the captain of the gun announced.

Killigrew heard him, but was still searching the deck of the junk with the telescope, looking for the pirate chief who commanded her; perhaps wondering what kind of a man his adversary was.

27

Not that it mattered: in a few seconds he would go to join the great majority ...

'Shall I give the order to fire, sir?' prompted the gunner.

Killigrew was about to say 'yes' when he saw her.

She was pinioned between two burly pilongs – burly for Chinese, at least – on the high poop deck, and stood out by virtue of her emerald-green sari with gold brocade trimmings. Killigrew had not seen her until now and could only presume that she had been brought up from below that instant. A third pilong held a cutlass at her throat; to judge from his finery – a white silk tunic, pyjamy trousers and a crimson sash – he was the *lao-pan*, as the captains of pirate junks were known. He gazed straight back at Killigrew, grinning malevolently, as though he could see the lieutenant without the aid of a telescope, even at that distance.

'Hold your fire!' snapped Killigrew.

'Sir?'

'You heard me plain enough, Guns.' Killigrew turned the telescope to where the breakers that crashed over the reefs of the Paracels could now be seen less than a mile ahead of the junk. They only had a few more minutes to catch the junk before it reached safety.

'What's keeping you, Second?' Robertson's voice, amplified by his speaking trumpet – not that it was ever in need of amplification – boomed from the quarterdeck.

Killigrew snapped the telescope shut, tucked it under his arms, cupped his hands around his

28

mouth to reply, and then thought better of it. Instead he jogged briskly down the deck to where Robertson and Hartcliffe stood, and saluted smartly.

'Sir, it looks as if there's a hostage on board that junk. An Indian woman.'

'These pirates have doxies of all colours on board their boats,' Robertson snapped back. 'I don't care to make war on women any more than you do, Mr Killigrew, but I can't let a pilong junk get away just because there's a woman on board.'

'I agree, sir. But this one's a hostage, I'm certain of it. One of the pilongs is holding a cutlass to her throat.'

'A bluff.'

'I don't think so, sir.'

Robertson sighed. 'Very well, Killigrew. So there's a hostage on board. What do you want me to do about it? Let them get away?'

'No, sir. With your permission I'd like to take the first cutter, along with twenty men and try to board her.'

'Have you ever boarded a hostile vessel before, Mr Killigrew?'

'On occasion.' Killigrew and Robertson had been acquainted for just the few months since they had sailed from Portsmouth so the commander only really knew his Second Lieutenant by Rear-Admiral Napier's recommendation. Corsair galleys, pilong junks, Malay prahus, slave ships – Killigrew had boarded them all. But it never got any easier; if anything, the opposite. Once you had boarded a hostile vessel and thrown yourself on to a deck swarming with men

29

intent on slaughtering you, you knew that it was only good joss that kept you alive in the confusion of the bloody hand-to-hand combat, and each new experience only reinforced that knowledge as you saw more and more shipmates felled by blows which might just as easily have felled yourself.

'Then you'll know it's a damned tricky business. Not all of you will come back. How many of my men do you want me to risk, just to save one woman?'

'There's a difference, sir. All of the men are volunteers. They knew what they were signing up for when they joined us. That woman's an innocent; a passenger from the clipper, I'd guess.'

Robertson sighed. 'Very well. But we'll do it my way, Mr Killigrew. Lord Hartcliffe will take the first cutter with thirty men. The marines will stay on board to give covering fire as we pull alongside, keeping back enough to stop the cutter from being swamped by our wash...'

'With all due respect, sir, Killigrew's much better at this sort of thing than I am,' protested Hartcliffe.

'Pipe down, First. I haven't finished yet. You'll take the junk from the starboard side. Mr Killigrew will be in the second cutter with twenty men and approach the junk from port. They won't be able to keep up as heavy a fire if we attack them from both sides at once: they'll have to divide their forces. Well, don't just stand about like a couple of farts in a thunderstorm! Look lively, there!'

'Aye, aye, sir!' Killigrew ordered the boatswain to pick out the men for the boats – it was no good asking for volunteers: every man on board would step forward, if only to avoid accusations of cowardice from his shipmates – and went below to his cabin. He primed and loaded one of his six-barrelled 'pepperbox' revolving pistols, attached it to his belt with the hook on the butt designed for that purpose, and fastened on his cutlass and scabbard.

By the time he re-emerged on deck the hands the boatswain had chosen to man the cutters were ready with their own weapons; a motley array of muskets, pistols, hatchets and cutlasses. Most of the crew were old hands who had served on the *Tisiphone* before, on her previous commission with the West Africa Squadron. They had rushed to sign on again when they had heard that Commander Standish would no longer be captain. What they thought of Robertson, Killigrew had not yet divined; but then, he had not made his own mind up about the new captain.

Senior amongst the ratings in the second cutter's crew was Petty Officer Olaf Ågård, one of the *Tisiphone*'s quartermasters: a tall, blond giant who had been serving in the Royal Navy for so long he had lost all trace of his native Swedish accent. Next to him, and in sharp physical contrast, was Able Seaman Wes Molineaux. Barefooted and stripped to the waist beneath the tropical sun, with a single gold ring through one ear, Molineaux looked more like a corsair of the Barbary Coast than a seaman of the Royal Navy. His complexion was as dark as roasted Arabica

31

coffee beans, the features beneath his shaven head Nubian. He was not tall, but he had the broad shoulders and wiry physique of a true sailor. When he balled his fists on his hips and stood with arms akimbo to throw back his head and laugh his deep, fruity chuckle in some response to a shipmate's jest, he put Killigrew in mind of the Djinn of the Lamp: to hear was to obey, but only a fool would forget what a dangerous spirit he aspired to command.

The *Tisiphone* overhauled the junk to starboard. Hartcliffe and his men climbed into the first cutter on the starboard side of the sloop; on the port side, closest to the junk, Killigrew and his men got into the second. The engine was stopped and as the sloop slowed in the water the second cutter was lowered from the davits. As soon as Killigrew judged the *Tisiphone*'s headway to be negligible enough, he ordered the falls to be let go, and ten of the hands grasped the oars, the other ten readying their muskets.

'Shove off!' Killigrew ordered from the prow of the cutter.

The boat was pushed out from the *Tisiphone*'s side, well clear of the port-side paddle-wheel. 'Out oars!' ordered Ågård. The oars were eased into the rowlocks; the fenders were taken in. 'Give way together!'

Taking their stroke from the starboard after-oar, the oarsmen began to pull towards the junk. They were now close enough to see the breakers crashing over the reef with the naked eye, even from the height of the cutter. The boat soon gathered way as the oarsmen pulled mightily. The pilongs at the junk's sweeps would be growing weary by now, while the men in the cutter were rested and fit. The boat passed the *Tisiphone*'s prow and a moment later the first cutter emerged on the other side. Killigrew saw Hartcliffe in the bow and waved to him, before turning his attention to the junk.

'Pace yourselves,' he told the oarsmen. The junk might just be a few hundred yards ahead, but the cutters only had a knot or two's advantage and it might yet be a long chase. With Ågård at the tiller, the second cutter moved out across the junk's stern to overhaul it from port. To starboard, the first cutter paced them.

The junk's stern was ornamented with intricate Chinese carvings, and brightly painted to look like the face of a highly stylised grinning demon. When both boats were within a hundred yards of the junk, one of the demon's eyes swung up to reveal a gun port behind.

Ågård saw it too. 'Should we take evasive action, sir?' he called as the muzzle of a small bronze cannon – shaped like the mouth of a dragon – protruded.

Killigrew shook his head. 'Belay that, Ågård. There's one thing you can say for Chinese gunnery: their shots fall everywhere except where they're aimed.'

The dragon's mouth belched smoke and flames, and the shot screeched over their heads to plunge into the water about fifty yards abaft. Ågård grinned, relieved that Killigrew's coolheadedness had once again proved well founded. Killigrew looked more confident than he felt: for

33

a first shot, it had come a damned sight closer than he had expected. Unlike many pilongs, who might be fishermen or traders fallen on hard times, these knew their business.

The long barrels of *gingalls* – outsize Chinese matchlocks firing balls more than an inch in diameter – emerged through other ports, or were levelled over the bulwark on the junk's high poop. They fired in a ragged volley. Most of the shots went wide, kicking up frighteningly large spurts of water on all sides of the two boats. One of them smashed a large piece of wood from the upper strake of the second cutter's gunwales, and one of the oarsmen cried out.

'Anyone hurt?' demanded Killigrew.

'It's Dando, sir,' said Ågård.

'I'm all right,' the seaman said quickly. 'Just splinters, that be all.'

They enjoyed a few seconds' respite while the pilongs reloaded their *gingalls*. The long-barrelled matchlocks required two men to operate them and were slow and cumbersome, although if the half-pound balls found their target they could deliver a maiming wound. In the meantime the two boats crept closer and closer to the junk, while the *Tisiphone* crept by on the far side of the first cutter. The reefs were less than half a mile away now; the sloop would have to veer off if they did not catch the junk soon, or else risk ripping her keel out on the submerged rocks.

The *gingalls* fired again as soon as they were reloaded, even more sporadically than before. One of the men in the second cutter gasped and Killigrew glanced over his shoulder in time to see him slump with a great chunk torn out of his shoulder.

Seaman Molineaux levelled his musket. 'Belay that!' snapped Killigrew. 'Don't waste a shot.'

'I can get one from here, sir,' the seaman retorted truculently.

'I don't care. We'll need to make every shot tell when we get closer.'

Another shot from the cannon behind the demon's eye sent up a great plume of water only a few yards to starboard, and the men in the cutter were drenched with spray. They could only hope that the powder in their firearms had not got wet.

Then Killigrew heard the sergeant of the *Tisiphone*'s marines give the order to fire, and a smart volley crashed from the sloop's tops and bulwarks. Screams and cries sounded from the junk. Two men in the first cutter were hit by *gingalls*, one of them screaming in pain, and another man was wounded in the second. The narrower the gap became, the more the pilongs' fire told.

Killigrew's heart pounded. This was the worst time, waiting to grapple the enemy. Once they were on board there would be no time to be afraid, everything would happen too quickly; but until then all he could do was crouch in the cutter's bow and wait, while the *gingall* balls whistled past his head.

'Come on, my buckoes!' he yelled above the rattle of musketry. 'Just a few more yards ... one last effort...'

The cannon behind the demon's eye boomed

again, this time smattering the water between the two cutters with small shot. The second cutter's prow was level with the junk's stern, then past it. They were close against the junk's side, so close the oars almost scraped the hull on one side while becoming entangled with the sweeps on the other. Killigrew snatched up a hatchet, grabbed one of the sweeps with his left hand and hacked at it. Molineaux whirled a grappling iron above his head and flung it over the junk's bulwark, just forward of the raised stern. He pulled it tight before a pilong could snatch it up and fling it clear. Another grappling iron fell into place beside it.

'In bows!' ordered Killigrew. The rowers shipped their oars as the boat was pulled against the junk's side. A figure appeared on the poop deck above them, an iron shot held above his head in both hands, poised to fling it down and through the cutter's bottom boards. Killigrew flung the hatchet. It whirled over and over and embedded itself in the pilong's chest. He staggered back and dropped the heavy shot on his own head. Molineaux fired his musket and a pilong who had been aiming his *gingall* at Killigrew fell back with the top of his head missing.

There was no time for the lieutenant to thank Molineaux for saving his life. The cutter bumped against the side of the junk and two of the seamen made the ropes fast to cleats. Killigrew balanced on the cutter's gunwale while Ågård and the others covered him with their muskets. He had done this kind of thing enough times to know that hesitation could be fatal. Without pausing even for breath, he leaped for the junk's bulwarks.

II:

Lao-Pan

A pilong appeared at the bulwark above Killigrew with a sword raised above his head, ready to bring it down against his hand. A musket boomed in the cutter behind him and blood splashed across the man's tunic.

Killigrew pulled himself up and found he was staring into the barrel of an antiquated swivel gun, aimed by a grinning pilong, with the fuse burning in the touchhole. Holding on to the bulwark with one hand, his feet braced against the junk's side, Killigrew slapped the swivel gun's muzzle forcefully with his palm. The gun spun round and the barrel cracked against the side of the pilong's head. His eyes rolled up in his skull and he fell to the deck. A moment later the gun boomed and swept part of the deck with lead pellets.

Another pilong ran to where Killigrew clung to the side. The lieutenant swung his legs over the bulwark and kicked the pilong in the chest. As the pilong staggered back, Killigrew landed on his feet and drew his cutlass in his right hand and a pepperbox in his left. He got off a couple of shots from his pepperbox; there was no need to aim, the pilongs were all around him. Then they closed in.

If Killigrew had stopped to think about what he was doing, he would have realised how insane it was and panicked: a sure way of getting himself killed. He had seen that happen to other men, and it had come close to happening to him on more than one occasion. All you could do was fling yourself into the thick of it, unthinking, kill as many of them as you could as quickly as possible, and hope your shipmates were close behind you. The only advantage a man enjoyed at a moment like this was the fact that the enemy could be relied upon to be terrified. When one man with a gun faces a hundred men with guns, every one of the hundred thinks their opponent's weapon is levelled at himself. The odds were on the side of the pilongs, but they would have been less than human not to be overawed by a man who flung himself, roaring wildly, into the teeth of certain death.

Killigrew parried a sword blow with his cutlass, thrust the six muzzles of his pepperbox against a naked torso, and fired. He stabbed one man in the throat, shot another in the face, hacked and slashed again. Three more pilongs charged him. He shot one, hacked at the next and kicked the third in the crotch. There was a time and a place for gentlemanly fighting, and this was certainly not it.

Then Molineaux and the others had joined him on the deck of the junk, and Hartcliffe and the men from the first cutter swarmed over the far bulwark. Within seconds the bluejackets out-numbered the pilongs. The Chinese would not surrender, though: even when they must have realised defeat was inevitable, they fought to the bitter end, well aware that if they were captured the only fate they could expect was execution. Killigrew had heard fellow officers – men who had fought alongside him in the Opium War seven years earlier, men who should have known better – denigrate the fighting capabilities of John Chinaman. *Damned heathens*, they said; *no moral fibre*. Killigrew knew that was hogwash: the Chinese might be badly led in war, and lack modern Western armaments, but they could be as savage and courageous as the best.

He fought his way to where the halyards ran up the side of the mainmast to support the junk's mainsail. He slashed through one rope, and then a pilong thrust a billhook at him. A sweep of Killigrew's cutlass sliced the billhook from the shaft. The pilong was fast though, and strong: he slammed the shaft like a quarterstaff against Killigrew's chest and sent him staggering. As the lieutenant charged back to meet him, the pilong reached for a pistol tucked into his girdle. Killigrew slashed with his cutlass. The pilong ducked, and laughed when the blade passed several inches above his head. Oblivious to the halyard which the cutlass had parted, he pulled out his pistol and levelled it at the lieutenant with a smirk of triumph.

Killigrew backed away and glanced up. A descending shadow prompted the pilong to do likewise. A moment later the mainsail had peeled away from the mainmast to fold itself over Killigrew's opponent and another knot of half a dozen pilongs in the waist. Bluejackets swarmed over the matting sail, bashing the shapes which struggled beneath with belaying pins and cutlass hilts until they lay still.

The lieutenant looked around. There was no sign of the Indian woman, but he caught a glimpse of the *lao-pan* in the white tunic and crimson sash dashing through the portal which led into the cabin beneath the poop deck.

Killigrew went after him. He dashed into the cabin and tripped over an extended foot. His cutlass skittered into a corner as he sprawled on his front. He reached for it, but a slippered foot came down on his wrist and pinned his right arm to the deck.

He still had his pepperbox in his left hand. He shot the pilong under the jaw and blew his brains out. Footsteps sounded. Killigrew rolled on to his back as another pilong came at him, and shot him in the chest. Then he scrambled back into a corner to survey the cabin.

The *lao-pan* was in the far corner, with the muzzle of a flintlock pistol pressed behind the ear of the Indian woman, held in front of him as a human shield. For now Killigrew concentrated on the man. He was tall and blue-eyed, hinting at European blood, although there was no other trace of it in his sallow features. Even hiding behind a woman, he had a self-assurance Killigrew had never seen in a Chinese before. The most powerful mandarins carried themselves with Confucian humility, even when addressing those they clearly regarded as inferior, such as the Western barbarians. But here Killigrew could see he was facing a man who would bow to no

41

one, neither Queen Victoria nor the Daoguang Emperor in Peking.

Killigrew pushed himself to his feet and levelled his pepperbox at the *lao-pan*'s face, visible over the woman's right shoulder.

'Drop your gun, or I'll kill her,' the *lao-pan* said in tolerably good English.

Killigrew let the pepperbox fall to the floor. 'Surrender. We've taken the ship; you're not going anywhere.'

'We shall see.' The *lao-pan* gave the woman an almighty shove so that she fell into Killigrew's arms, and snatched up his cutlass. 'Barbarian fool! My pistol is empty!'

The *lao-pan* was about to hack at Killigrew's head when Molineaux came through the portal behind him and grabbed him by the wrist, staying the blow. The *lao-pan* whirled and punched the seaman in the stomach. Molineaux gasped and doubled up, but not before he had wrenched the cutlass from the *lao-pan*'s grip.

The Chinese snatched up the pepperbox and backed away, covering both Killigrew and Molineaux.

Killigrew relaxed and turned his attention to the woman. 'Do you speak English?' he asked her. 'Are you all right?' She merely nodded.

'With all due respect, sir, this is hardly the time!' protested Molineaux, with a jerk of his head at the *lao-pan*, who still clutched the pepperbox.

Killigrew sat the woman on a chair and turned his attention back to the *lao-pan*. He started to walk across the cabin towards him and held out his hand. 'My gun, if you please.'

The *lao-pan* levelled the pepperbox at Killigrew's head. 'Stay back!'

Killigrew continued to advance.

'I warned you...' The *lao-pan* pulled the trigger. The hammer fell on a spent percussion cap with a harmless click.

'Did you think you were the only one who could bluff with an empty pistol?' Killigrew demanded irritably.

The *lao-pan* threw the pepperbox at his face, but Killigrew had been expecting it, and ducked. He straightened in time to see the *lao-pan* lunge for the doorway. Killigrew caught him round the waist in a flying tackle and drove him against the bulkhead. The *lao-pan* rammed an elbow into his cheek and squirmed free. Still holding the cutlass, Molineaux got to the door first to bar his path. The *lao-pan*'s foot flashed out and connected with the seaman's wrist. The cutlass flew from his grip.

Then Hartcliffe appeared in the doorway. The *lao-pan* twisted away and snatched up the cutlass. 'Barbarian fools! You think you can cage Zhai Jing-mu like a songbird?' He backed towards one of the gun ports, his eyes flickering between Killigrew, Molineaux and Hartcliffe. He paid no attention to the Indian woman behind him, which was a mistake because she snatched up a decorated porcelain vase and smashed it over his head. The *lao-pan*'s eyes rolled up in his head and he measured his length on the deck with blood weeping from a scalp wound.

The woman slumped back into the chair, trembling.

'Are you all right, miss?' Killigrew asked her. 'Or is it ma'am?'

'Miss,' said the woman. 'Miss Peri Dadabhoy.' She stood up and bowed with her hands pressed palms together before her. Although a formal and thoroughly respectable garment among Indian women, the sari left a lot less to the imagination than the billowing gowns and blouses of Western women. Miss Dadabhoy was in her late teens or early twenties, with smooth skin the colour of *café au lait*, a straight nose, curly black hair, sensuous lips and dark brown, almond-shaped eyes above high cheekbones. Killigrew would have liked to have taken in more, but it was ungentlemanly to stare, so he returned her bow.

'Christopher Killigrew at your service, miss.' He had heard the name 'Dadabhoy' somewhere before, although he could not place it. 'And may I present Lord Hartcliffe? And not forgetting Able Seaman Molineaux, of course.'

'My friends call me Wes, miss,' said Molineaux.

'Take care of our friend there, Molineaux,' Killigrew said curtly, indicating Zhai Jing-mu, as Hartcliffe escorted Miss Dadabhoy out on deck. 'We'll take him to Hong Kong for trial.'

Molineaux found some rope and trussed up Zhai Jing-mu with a scowl which said: *Typical! The officers get to spoon with the blowers while the ratings get left to clear up the mess.*

Killigrew hesitated in the doorway. 'Molineaux?'

'Sir?'

'Well done.'

'Thank you, sir.' To judge from his truculent

44

tone, Molineaux was unmollified.

Killigrew could not blame him. 'You know how to handle yourself in a scrimmage, I'll say that for you.'

Molineaux finally grinned. 'Maybe I didn't go to school, sir, but even a misspent youth provides an education of sorts. What about you, sir? Don't tell me they taught you the old "Ringsend uppercut" at Eton.'

'I never went to school either, Molineaux, although unlike you I had the benefit of a private tutor. Two private tutors, if you include Jory Spargo.'

'Jory Spargo, sir?'

'A seaman on board my first ship. He taught me a few moves which might be looked down upon in polite company, but which have saved my life on more than one occasion. Well, be about your duties. We both have plenty of work to do.'

'Aye, aye, sir.'

Killigrew followed Hartcliffe and Miss Dadabhoy out on deck. The mess there was even worse, and Killigrew steered the young woman away so that she did not have to look at the carnage, leaving Hartcliffe – who was never at ease with the opposite sex – to supervise the rounding up of the other prisoners. None of the pilongs had surrendered: those that had been taken alive had been knocked unconscious, like their captain.

Some of the Tisiphones on deck had lowered the anchor and hauled down the foresail, bringing the junk to a halt barely a cable's length from where the breakers boomed over the reefs. The *Tisiphone* had pulled alongside and the first cutter was already being hauled back into its davits.

'We need a bosun's chair over here!' Killigrew called across to one of the boatswain's mates, and then turned back to Miss Dadabhoy. 'Are you injured in any way, miss? Do you require medical attention?'

She shook her head. 'There is no need for you to concern yourself on that account, Mr Killigrew. I was not subjected to "a fate worse than death".' She was almost mocking, a smile of amusement playing impishly on her lips. Killigrew found himself warming to her at once: she made a refreshing change from the simpering ninnies he usually met.

'We'll get you aboard the *Tisiphone*, you can have a cabin to yourself, some clean clothes, a brush and scrub up, whatever you require. We're headed for Hong Kong. You have family there?'

She nodded. 'My father.'

Killigrew had been trying to think of someone with the surname 'Dadabhoy'; now he remembered that Parsis did not have family names, but patronymics, taking their fathers' forenames as surnames.

'Not Sir Dadabhoy Framjee?' he guessed.

'You've heard of him?'

'Hasn't everyone in these parts?' Framjee was the foremost of the Parsi merchants engaged in the opium trade, a wealthy philanthropist so well liked he was one of the first Indians to be honoured with a knighthood. The number of schools, colleges, hospitals, Zarathustrian fire-temples, and other charitable concerns endowed by him bore testament to his generosity.

Killigrew had often heard the Parsis described as the Jews of India, succeeding in trade by dint of hard work and a reputation for honesty and integrity. The Parsis had come from Persia in the tenth century and settled in Gujerat in western India. Nowadays they spoke Gujerati, although they continued to pray in Persian. They were Zarathustrians, of the oldest monotheistic religion in the world, and the supposed similarity of their religion to Christianity, their willingness to adopt Western manners, and – Killigrew was ashamed as a European to admit it – the lightness of their skins had made them more acceptable to the British Raj, enabling them to thrive in the Bombay business community.

The son of a weaver, Dadabhoy Framjee had started out in life as a bottle-washer; half a century later, he was one of the richest men in the world, with agencies in India, China, Egypt and England, and a fleet of cargo ships. He had made his first fortune by the time he was twenty-three, lost it all when the Great Fire of Bombay had reduced his home to ashes, and worked hard to build an even larger one. But he had never forgotten his roots or his heritage. The ancient creed of Zarathustrianism demanded that the Parsis put back into the community what they had earned from it, and there could be no denying that Framjee's generosity was in proportion to his wealth.

'Begging your pardon, sir...' It was Petty Officer

47

Ågård, with a cut on his temple.

Killigrew realised he had been neglecting his duties to talk to the woman. Understandable, but unforgivable too. 'You'll have to excuse me, miss,' he told her, and turned to the petty officer. 'Better get back aboard the *Tisiphone* and get that looked at, Ågård.'

'Hmm?' The petty officer raised a hand to the cut and looked at the blood. 'Oh, that. It's not deep, sir. I'm not hurt as bad as some of the others.'

'How many dead?'

'Six, all told, sir. I reckon we got off lightly.' Ågård spoke briskly, in a matter-of-fact tone, his voice devoid of any accusation. The dead men had given their lives in a noble cause, and Miss Dadabhoy was alive and safe thanks to them. But part of Killigrew could not help wondering if it was a fair exchange: six good men for one woman. If his own life had been lost, he wondered if his ghost would have had the good grace to look down from above – or up from below – and still say he had only done his duty. He told himself they were dead, and blaming himself would not bring them back. Tomorrow they would be buried at sea, and their few personal effects auctioned before the mast at inflated prices, to raise money for any wives and children waiting for them back in Britain.

'Very well, Mr Ågård,' Killigrew said as Molineaux emerged from the cabin, pushing the now conscious *lao-pan* before him. 'Take the second cutter and return to the *Tisiphone*.'

'What do you want me to do with this one, sir?'

asked Molineaux.

'I'll take him.' Killigrew grasped the *lao-pan* firmly by the arm. 'I want you to see Miss Dadabhoy safely aboard the *Tisiphone*, Molineaux, then help Dando with the wounded.'

'Aye, aye, sir.'

The prisoners were put in irons in the sloop's lee waist with an armed guard of marines over them while the wounded went down to the sick berth for the surgeon, assistant surgeon and the sick berth attendant to tend to. It was traditional for the wounded to be treated according to the order in which they reached the sick berth, regardless of their rank, although those with minor cuts and sprains held back so that those in more urgent need of attention would be treated first.

Killigrew and Hartcliffe reported to Robertson on the *Tisiphone*'s quarterdeck.

'I suppose you expect me to congratulate you both, eh?' sniffed the commander. 'Damned young fools. Well, I'm as much to blame as you are. I gave you permission, after all. But don't think I'm going to thank you for doing no more than your duty. If you'd done any less, on the other hand ... well, then I'd have something to say to you, of that you may be sure!'

'I don't feel like being congratulated, sir,' said Killigrew. 'We lost six men, and another dozen wounded.'

'Seven,' Robertson corrected him. 'Private Evans was careless enough to get in the way of a stray *gingall* ball.'

Losing any man was bad enough, but Evans

had been detailed to act as Killigrew's 'servant' in the wardroom, keeping his glass replenished during dinner, doing his laundry, polishing his boots and bringing him a cup of tea every morning. When a man who did all that was killed, the loss became more personal.

'I'm very sorry to hear that, sir,' Killigrew said with feeling. The one consolation was that he knew Evans had been a bachelor, without a wife or child, but he had been popular amongst the crew – no easy feat for a marine – and he would be missed by his friends.

'I believe you are,' Robertson allowed grudgingly. 'But don't think that means I'm giving you permission to mope around the rest of the way to Hong Kong. You said it yourself: the men who died were volunteers who knew the risks. The Indian woman was an innocent who got caught up in this business through no choice of her own. It was a fair exchange. And if anyone should take the blame, it should be me. I'm captain of this vessel, which means I take full responsibility for anything that happens under my command. And with young rapscallions like you on my hands, that's a heavier burden than you can possibly imagine. Where is the woman, anyway?'

Killigrew noticed Molineaux loitering at the edge of the quarterdeck and remembered that he had last seen Miss Dadabhoy in his care. 'Molineaux?'

'I took the liberty of putting the blower in the captain's cabin, sir.'

'The what?' demanded Robertson, only half turning towards him.

'The lady, sir. Miss Dadabhoy, I mean.'

'I'll thank you not to use slang expressions when you address an officer, Molineaux. You're not in your London rookery now. So, you took the liberty of putting her in my cabin, did you? That's quite a liberty, I must say. You might have asked me first. Still, I don't see where else we can put her. That means I shall have to move into your cabin, First. You can share a cabin with Mr Killigrew here. I take it Miss Dadabhoy is having all her feminine wants attended to?'

Robertson's misogyny was evident in the sneering way he said the word 'feminine'. As far as he was concerned, women had no function other than to satisfy a man's sexual urges, and that was that. Since ladies of genteel families were generally unavailable for such assignations, he had even less use for them.

'Your steward's fetching her some hot water and towels now, sir, so she can have a scrub up before tea,' reported the seaman.

'Very good, Molineaux.' Robertson turned to Hartcliffe. 'I want you to pick a dozen men from the port watch and take command of the junk, First. Search it from top to bottom, make sure there aren't any more pilongs hiding below decks. Then wait here while we go back to pick up the whaler. The other junk seems to be long gone, and I don't propose we waste any time looking for it. When we get back we'll take you in tow. At least we'll get some prize money out of this.' He gave the junk a disparaging glance. 'Perhaps even enough to buy a round of drinks at the Hong Kong Club.'

The *Tisiphone* sailed back to where the whaler waited.

'No survivors, sir,' the mate reported grimly as soon as he was back on deck. He reported to Killigrew; he was terrified of the gruff commander, and flinched every time Robertson addressed him. 'The pilongs did a dashed thorough job.'

'What are those crates?' Killigrew gestured to the chests which bobbed in the water all around.

'Tea, sir,' said the mate. 'The clipper must've had a full hold.'

'That's queer.'

'I don't see what's queer about it, Second,' Robertson said pettishly. 'The clippers bring opium from Calcutta to exchange for tea in China, and then sail back to England with their cargoes. No point in sailing home with a hold that's only half full.'

'I'm aware of that, sir,' said Killigrew. 'What I don't understand is, why did the pilongs attack the clipper when she was obviously on the return voyage? Isn't that rather like Esquimaux stealing snow?'

Peri Dadabhoy was her father's daughter. She knew many women her own age, both European and Indian, who would have had a fit of the conniptions on being captured by pirates. She did not despise such women – it was not in her nature – and she understood that they were merely products of the culture in which they had been raised. But her father believed in the rights of woman and had raised his daughter the same

52

as her brothers, making sure she was given the education he had never had, and that she was fit for something more in life than embroidery and music. When Queen Victoria had married Prince Albert, Framjee had held a ball to celebrate the momentous occasion, inviting not only his Parsi friends but also Muslim, Hindu and Christian business associates. Although the Parsis did not believe in keeping their women in purdah, nevertheless it was unheard of for Parsi women to be present at such a heterogeneous gathering; yet Framjee had insisted that all his daughters attend alongside their brothers, to the astonishment of his Parsi friends and to Peri's secret mortification. She was proud of her heritage and she clung fiercely to her Zarathustrian beliefs, yet in spite of herself, once she had overcome her initial shyness, she had enjoyed the ball immensely.

She had not yet been born when her father had lost everything in the Great Fire of Bombay, but she had often heard the stories. Once she had asked where her father had found the courage to go on and continue in business. 'If Zarathustrianism teaches us nothing else, my child, it teaches us that life goes on and one must learn to smile in the face of adversity and have faith in the undying benevolence of God.'

A knock on the day-room door startled her out of her reverie. 'Come in,' she called.

Lord Hartcliffe entered and bowed. She returned his bow, which seemed to confuse him; he was probably more used to women curtsying, she reflected. 'My lord,' she said, smiling in a vain attempt to put him at his ease.

'Miss Dadabhoy ... um ... I was wondering whether you wished to join myself and the other senior officers for supper in the wardroom tonight, or if you preferred to dine alone in here.' Hartcliffe clasped his hands together, then seemed to realise he was unconsciously aping her and thrust them in the pockets of his pantaloons. 'Of course, if you don't feel up to a formal supper we shall all quite understand...'

'I shall be delighted, my lord.'

'Are you quite sure?' Hartcliffe remembered that a gentleman did not put his hands in his pockets in front of a lady and took them out again, patting them together before him. 'Don't think that we'll be put out if you decline. After the ordeal you've been through...'

She was careful to keep a straight face as he clasped his hands behind his back. 'No, it will be my pleasure. Unless there is some reason you feel it would be unfitting...?'

'Good Lord, no!' He wrung his hands. 'No, no, no! We should be delighted. Ah ... supper at five?'

'I shall look forward to it.' She held out a hand, and after some hesitation he shook it.

'If there's anything you need before then...?'

She shook her head. He bowed awkwardly and went out.

The wardroom was an elegantly furnished compartment seventeen feet by twelve, a mahogany table dominating the room. There were three upright upholstered chairs down either side of the table and one at either end. There were no windows: by day the light came from a skylight in the deck head, but now the blinds were drawn under the skylight, and illumination was provided by two oil lamps which swung from the deck head, and the silver-plated candelabra which formed the centrepiece on the table. Crystal decanters stood on a sideboard with the crockery. There were three doors in the bulkhead on the far side of the room, marked 'First Lieutenant', 'Second Lieutenant' and 'Surgeon'.

There were six men in the room when Peri entered at five, plus the white-coated wardroom steward. A white linen cloth had been laid on the table, and seven places set. The steward pulled out the chair at the far end, opposite Hartcliffe, who sat at the head of the table.

'Miss Dadabhoy,' said Hartcliffe, 'you've met Killigrew and Mr Westlake, our surgeon. May I introduce Mr Yelverton, the ship's master; Mr Vellacott, our purser and paymaster; and Mr Muir, our chief engineer? Gentlemen, this is Miss Dadabhoy.'

They murmured greetings and waited for her to be seated before resuming their places.

'Is Commander Robertson not joining us?' asked Peri.

'The captain usually dines alone,' explained Hartcliffe. 'As it happens, this evening he's been good enough to stand in for me as officer of the watch.'

'Have I done something to offend him?' asked Peri. 'I am sure I am mistaken, but I cannot help but get the impression he is avoiding me.'

'The captain of a vessel usually has to adopt a

somewhat aloof attitude to those under his command,' said Killigrew.

'Am *I* under his command?' asked Peri, amused.

'Only in so far as the ultimate responsibility for the lives of all on board rests with him,' Killigrew replied, offhand.

Peri had known plenty of British officers, soldiers of the Honourable East India Company's army in Bombay and naval men in Hong Kong. Broadly speaking, they seemed to fit into two categories: corpulent, red-faced men who drank too much and ate too much and damned the servants and the weather continually; and quieter, more intense men, usually either on their way to or returning from the latest troubles on the North-West Frontier and determined not to discuss their experiences. Killigrew seemed to belong to the latter category, but it was an uneasy fit: the presence of a young woman did not make him uncomfortable and he seemed to accept her being there as casually as did his fellow officers. Encounters with English gentlemen in Bombay and Hong Kong had taught her they were just as frightened of her as she had been of them; she had learned to make the most of this, although tonight, out of gratitude, she was more concerned to put them at ease.

Not that Killigrew needed to be put at ease, she guessed. Here was a man who would have been as much at home at a royal garden party as he evidently was throwing himself over the bulwarks of a hostile vessel.

Hartcliffe said a brief grace and the steward

started to serve the first course: crimped salmon *en matelot Normandie.* 'We tend to avoid soup at sea, for obvious reasons,' said Hartcliffe.

'Really?' Peri could not resist asking impishly. 'What are those?'

'Well, if the weather gets rough it tends to...' began Hartcliffe, and then realised that she was teasing him. He grinned good-naturedly, and the others chuckled. 'On a larger ship we'd each have a personal servant to serve our food – one of the marines – but in a wardroom this size, it's cramped enough with just the six of us, without having half a dozen marines clumping about the place. Mr McBride manages to do us very nicely, though,' he added as the steward made his way round the table with a bottle of Chablis. 'You, er ... you do partake, don't you?'

'In moderation,' she replied, holding down the neck of the bottle when it looked as though the steward might only half fill the glass. She had enjoyed drinking competitions with her brothers, and usually won.

'Ah. I wasn't sure if ... you know...'

'I believe you are thinking of Muslims, my lord.'

'To be sure, to be sure.' Hartcliffe stared at his plate, bit his lip for a moment, and then picked up his fish knife and fork, his tureen of small talk exhausted.

'You are on your way to Hong Kong?' asked Peri.

Hartcliffe nodded eagerly. 'Your father lives there?'

'Sometimes in Hong Kong, sometimes in

Bombay,' said Peri. 'Wherever his business takes him.'

'What line of work is your father in, Miss Dadabhoy?' piped up Vellacott.

'Shipping,' Hartcliffe said quickly.

Peri smiled thinly. 'You've no need to be embarrassed on my account, my lord,' she said, and turned back to the purser and paymaster. 'My father deals in opium, Mr Vellacott. Oh, he trades all manner of things, to be fair. But the bulk of his wealth is made from shipping opium from the Honourable East India Company's estates in Bengal to China, in exchange for tea, which he ships to England. Please believe me, gentlemen, I am not proud of how my father has earned his fortune.'

'There's no law against shipping opium,' said Killigrew. 'No British law, at any rate. Speaking for myself, I've always been a believer in free trade.'

'Except where slaves are concerned,' said Hartcliffe.

'Slaves, my lord?' asked Peri.

'Killigrew distinguished himself against the slavers on the Guinea Coast a couple of years ago.'

She turned back to the second lieutenant with renewed interest. 'How was that, Mr Killigrew?'

'It's a long story.' Killigrew gestured dismissively, and Hartcliffe started in his chair, as if someone had kicked him in the shin. 'I wouldn't want to bore you. Besides, we have a strict rule in the wardroom: no talking shop.'

'Well,' said Peri, a little disappointed. 'Your

free-trade principles extend to opium, but stop short of slavery. May I ask why there should be any difference?'

'People aren't goods. Opium is.'

'Yet both trades ruin lives.'

'True. But the principle is different. It's a question of liberty.'

'I am not sure I follow you.'

'The slaves are taken against their will, deprived of their liberty. That's wrong, isn't it?'

'Of course.'

'Well, opium users aren't forced to take opium...'

'Perhaps not to begin with,' said Peri. 'But there is new evidence to suggest that drugs such as opium are addictive.' Her father had encouraged her to learn about the family business along with her brothers; but he had not expected her to study the debilitating effects of opium quite so enthusiastically. 'Once a person starts using opiates, he finds it very difficult to live without them. Is this not so, Mr Westlake?'

'Humbug,' snorted the surgeon.

'Mr Westlake...' Hartcliffe said chidingly.

'I beg your pardon, miss,' said Westlake. 'But there's absolutely no evidence whatsoever to suggest that opium is addictive.'

'Mr Strachan – our assistant surgeon,' Killigrew added in an aside for Peri's benefit – 'says he refuses to prescribe any opiates on the grounds that he finds his patients become dependent on them.'

'Mr Strachan,' Westlake said scathingly, 'has a theory that malaria is somehow transmitted by

59

mosquito bites!'

'Mr Strachan – and Miss Dadabhoy here – may be right about opium, though,' said Hartcliffe. 'Remember Lieutenant Jardine? He went down with pneumonia and the quack prescribed Godfrey's Cordial. Well, he recovered from his pneumonia, but when he tried to stop taking his medicine, he fell prey to a range of new symptoms.'

'An entirely different illness, doubtless brought about by his weakened condition after his bout of pneumonia,' insisted Westlake.

'Yes, that's what his quack told him,' said Hartcliffe. 'No prizes for guessing what was prescribed as a cure.'

'An opiate?' asked Peri.

Hartcliffe nodded. 'Godfrey's Cordial. The problem was, every time he stopped taking the cordial, the symptoms returned.'

'Must have been something chronic,' said Westlake.

Hartcliffe ignored the interruption. 'And the more cordial he took, the less effect it seemed to have in ameliorating his symptoms, so he had to take larger and larger doses. In the end it quite debilitated him, until he was unable to carry out his duties and dismissed the service. A terrible shame: he was a promising young officer.'

'People should be informed of the dangers of taking opiates before it's prescribed,' said Killigrew. 'If they still want to wreck their lives, that's their look-out. The freedom to ruin oneself is merely the other side of the coin which is the freedom to get on in life. You can't have one without the other.'

'That's all very well for educated people like us, Mr Killigrew,' said Westlake. 'But the Chinese are ignorant—'

'*If* that is so, then we should educate them. Those who sneer at the people of China for smoking opium might do well to take a glance inside the gin palaces of Britain.'

'Then perhaps we should stop the gin trade, too.'

'Why stop the gin trade and not the wine trade? Because the people who drink gin are poor and therefore too ignorant to know any better? I find that a rather patronising attitude, Westlake. Just because a man was born into a poor family that does not make him a fool, no more than a man born into the gentry can be assumed to be a genius.'

'Then why do the poor ruin their lives through drink?'

'Their lives were already ruined the day they were born in poverty. They drink gin to help themselves forget that fact. Perhaps if you found yourself living with that kind of despair you too might take to drinking gin. That would be your choice. Take port, for instance. No one likes a glass of port or two after supper more than I. Perhaps I'm condemning myself to the misery of gout in later life, but that is my decision. Do you think it would be right for the government to forbid people to drink port?'

The surgeon shrugged. 'If it were for their own good.'

Killigrew shook his head. He turned to Peri, as

if he had higher hopes of making her understand his principles than he did of Westlake. 'I believe in a little thing called liberty, Miss Dadabhoy, the freedom to make my own choices in life. I do not believe it is the duty of the government to tell me what I may and may not do, so long as my actions harm none but myself. And if I have the right to make such decisions for myself, then so should the labouring classes be permitted their gin and the Chinese their opium. Instead of worrying about the fact that these people indulge in such vices, perhaps we should concern ourselves with the conditions that drive them to seek oblivion. If your father did not smuggle opium into China, there are plenty of others who would be keen to get their hands on his client list. At least Sir Dadabhoy spends much of his profits on philanthropic works in Gujerat, putting money back into the community. I suspect there are plenty of other China traders who are less charitable.'

'It is kind of you to say so.'

He shrugged. 'It's only the truth. And at least your father didn't put pressure on the British government to go to war with China. Selling opium to a willing client is one thing. Forcing him to buy it at the point of a gun is another.'

'Steady on, Killigrew,' said Vellacott. 'The China War was fought in defence of the rights of British merchants trying to trade with the Chinese. What they buy once that trade is established is their own affair. There's a demand for tea in Britain. We've offered the Chinese our manufactures and they've turned their noses up at them. So it has to be opium.'

'Why should they buy British cotton, when they manufacture their own perfectly good silk? And it doesn't have to be opium: there's a massive deficit of silver bullion in China. But I don't see the China traders rushing to offer it in place of opium.'

'A bullion deficit brought about because the Chinese have spent so much of it on opium.'

'Forgive me for saying so, Vellacott, but you're missing the point. Let's look at it from the point of view of the Chinese, shall we? Suppose our positions were reversed. Now let's say the British government made the selling of gin illegal. I wouldn't approve, for the reasons I've already stated: it would be an infringement of the liberties of British subjects. But there are many other laws in Britain which I consider infringements of the liberties of British subjects; yet I respect them, because they are the law.'

'Such as?' asked Peri, intrigued.

'Well, for one thing, the political franchise needs to be widened.'

'Here he goes again,' said Yelverton, rolling his eyes, and turned to Peri. 'Killigrew thinks everyone in Britain should have a vote, instead of just those who occupy a house of ten pounds' annual rental.'

'Even that's too radical, if you ask me,' grunted Westlake. 'They should never have done away with the forty-shilling freehold rule. Only the people with a property stake in the country can be judged fit to make such momentous decisions.'

'The rich look after the poor, you mean?'

Killigrew asked with amusement. 'You should take a walk through Bluegate Fields some time, Mr Westlake. They're not doing a very good job of it.'

'Ha! This from a man who'd let women have the vote!'

'And why should they not, Mr Westlake?' Peri asked sweetly.

'Women's brains are smaller than men's—' began the surgeon.

'Not in proportion to their body weight,' she countered.

'That's neither here nor there. They have a lower mental capacity. Stands to reason. Give women the vote, next thing you know, they'll be running the country.'

'With a lower mental capacity?' Peri asked, with a straight face. Glancing at Killigrew, she saw him stifle a smile, although her irony was wasted on Westlake.

'If you ask me, the country's already run by an old woman,' said Hartcliffe.

'That's no way to talk about Lord Russell!' protested Vellacott.

'Lord Russell doesn't have a mind of his own,' said Hartcliffe. 'That's why he needs Trevelyan and Grafton to do all his thinking for him.'

'Who's Trevelyan?' Peri asked Killigrew in a whisper.

'Permanent Head of the Treasury,' he murmured back. 'Not a nice man.'

'Trevelyan and Grafton say it's the Paddies' own fault they're starving – when any fool can see it's the fault of their landlords – and lo, the dead are lying in heaps in the country lanes of Ireland,' continued Hartcliffe.

'That's your free trade for you, Killigrew,' Westlake said triumphantly.

'Not free trade, Mr Westlake,' Killigrew responded tightly. 'Callous inhumanity. Where was I?'

'You were asking us to suppose the government outlawed the sale of gin in Britain, Mr Killigrew,' said Peri.

'Thank you,' he said with a smile. 'Now, suppose the Chinese started smuggling gin into Britain, ignoring our laws. Naturally our government protests. So the Chinese go to war with us – and win.'

'Not likely,' said Vellacott.

'It's merely a hypothetical supposition,' said Killigrew. 'The Chinese going to war with us to force us to accept their breaking of our laws. Hardly what you'd call a moral crusade, is it, gentlemen? Well, I put it to you that's exactly what we did to the Chinese back in thirty-nine.'

'What exactly happened in the Opium War?' asked Peri. 'I tried to follow the reports in the newspapers, but I'm afraid I could not make much sense of what was going on.'

Killigrew smiled thinly. 'Neither could I – and I was right in the thick of it.'

'Hark at him!' Hartcliffe jibed good-naturedly. 'His ship didn't arrive until the last few months. Some of us who were there from the outset, however–'

'And a proper hash you'd been making of it until then,' Killigrew retorted. 'God knows, that war should never have been started – a ridiculous, patchy affair between two arrogant empires which had failed to understand one another and failed to appreciate the merits of one another – but if it had been done when 'twas done, then 'twere well it had been done quickly.'

Hartcliffe nodded in agreement. 'We failed to prosecute the war thoroughly – I think even Rear-Admiral Elliot sensed the ignobility of our crusade – but a decisive blow early on might have convinced the Chinese they weren't dealing with barbarians but with an industrially more advanced opponent whom their junks could not match. It might even have preserved lives by bringing the war to a swift conclusion instead of allowing it to drag on for as long as it did.

'The problem was the Emperor refused to deal directly with us. When his troops suffered reverses, his subordinates were too afraid to report their failure; our reluctance to press home victories only made it easier for the mandarins to conceal their defeats from the Emperor. After nearly three years of blockades, punitive attacks, muddled negotiations, the expeditionary force finally arrived from home waters, including HMS *Dido* with a certain Midshipman Killigrew on board. We seized the city of Chingkiang-fu – on the vital crossroads of the Yangtze River and the Grand Canal – and threatened the great city of Nanking. That forced the Chinese to come to terms. You probably know the rest.'

Peri nodded. The Treaty of Nanking had opened five ports – Amoy, Canton, Foochow, Ningpo and Shanghai – to Western trade, demanded that the Chinese pay an indemnity of twenty-one million dollars, and decreed that Hong Kong be ceded to the British. As a British possession separate from the mainland, the island of Hong Kong was a safer place for Western merchants to conduct their trade, free from interference from the Chinese authorities.

An awkward silence ensued and once again it was left to Peri to break it. 'What are your politics, my lord?' she asked Hartcliffe. She recalled that the Duke of Hartcliffe was a mainstay of the Tory Party. 'Are you a Tory, like your father?'

'Good Lord, no!' Hartcliffe replied with a grin, more relaxed now he had a couple of glasses of wine inside him. 'I'm a communist. "Working men of all countries unite," what?'

'I'll drink to that,' said Killigrew, raising his glass.

'Before or after the loyal toast?' Yelverton asked sardonically.

'In place of,' Killigrew asserted with mock gravity.

'*Aux barricades!*' declared Hartcliffe. '*Les aristocrates à la lanterne!*'

Westlake turned to Peri. 'Of course, you realise they're both stark, raving mad?'

She smiled. 'Yes. I noticed that this afternoon.'

'Roll on, thou deep and dark blue Ocean – roll!
Ten thousand fleets sweep over thee in vain;
Man marks the earth with ruin – his control
Stops with the shore.'

67

Able Seaman Wes Molineaux was rarely happier than when he took a trick at the *Tisiphone*'s helm, and the lines of verse came almost unconsciously to his lips. As a kinchin, barely more than a toddler, he had helped to supplement his mother's meagre wages as a charlady by 'mudlarking': searching the mudflats of the Thames at low tide for salvage – a copper nail here, a lump of coal there, it all added up. On cold winter mornings he and the other river urchins had warmed their feet in the run-off from the steam-powered manufactories on the south bank, and as the sensation had slowly returned to his numbed dew-beaters he had watched the tall ships come and go from the Pool of London, bearing cargoes from exotic lands, never once imagining that one day he would make a living as a sailor and get to see such lands for himself.

In those days he had known only cold and hunger. He had been the youngest of three siblings and the harsh life of the slums around Seven Dials had inevitably forced him into a life of crime. For twelve years he had prospered, becoming the toast of the flash mob, until one day a job had turned sour and he had been forced to flee to Ireland, hiding up in Cork and eventually taking ship on HMS *Powerful* as the cook's mate.

The voice of the officer of the watch startled Molineaux out of his reverie. 'Poetry, Mr Molineaux?' asked Killigrew, lighting his first cheroot of the day.

'Byron, sir. *Childe Harold's Pilgrimage*.'

'I keep forgetting your intellectual taste in poetry. I thought you said you never went to school? Who taught you to read?'

'An old pal of mine, sir.' Molineaux had often wondered what had happened to the man who, amongst other things, had taught him everything he had ever needed to know about breaking and entering, and thought about going to Australia to see if he could find him. But from what he had heard, some who were transported to the colonies did well for themselves once they became ticket-of-leave men; besides, knowing his old mentor, he had probably made leg-bail years ago and was in lavender somewhere. 'He taught me how to read, using *The Police Gazette* as a primer.'

'*The Police Gazette?*'

'Where they print the notices of stolen goods,' Ågård said drily.

'Ah!' Killigrew was well aware of Molineaux's felonious past, and discreetly left it at that.

'Sail ho!' cried the look-out at the masthead.

'Where away?' demanded the boatswain.

'Two points on the port quarter!'

Killigrew took the telescope from the binnacle to see for himself. 'Opium clipper coming up fast astern,' he reported to no one in particular a few moments later. 'One point to starboard, Ågård. We'll exchange flags of courtesy as she passes.'

'Aye, aye, sir. One point to starboard, Molineaux.'

'One point to starboard it is Mr Ågård.' On the crowded mess-deck, Molineaux and Ågård knew one another as Wes and Olly; but here on the quarter-deck, it was 'Molineaux' and 'Mister'; just one of the navy's little foibles which Molineaux had had to get used to.

Staying in the service had never been part of the plan. He had only joined the *Powerful* for one commission, until the hue and cry in London had died down. But one commission had lasted three hard years in the Mediterranean. Molineaux had chafed under navy discipline, earned himself a flogging through insubordination, and had promised himself he would jump ship at the first opportunity, when the commodore had been knocked overboard by a careless hand. Jumping after him to save his life had just seemed like the natural thing to do. The commodore had rewarded Molineaux with a singularly inappropriate gift, a volume of poetry by some cove called Andy Marvell. Molineaux had been seated on the head one day, on the verge of using the pages for a purpose for which they had never been intended, when he had chanced to read some of the lines.

He had been hooked at once. Afterwards he had sometimes wondered if the gift had been so inappropriate after all. From then on he had devoured poetry hungrily. He did not always comprehend the classical allusions, but that did not matter: what was important was the beauty of the language. A seaman on a man-o'-war did not get much time to himself, but even a few hours snatched here and there added up over voyages which lasted for months. His new shipmates aboard the *Tisiphone* had mocked him when they had first caught him reading poetry, so he had started reading aloud *The Rime of the Ancient Mariner* from a Coleridge anthology: after the first five stanzas the barracking had stopped; at the end of Part the Third he had closed the book, climbed into his hammock and bid them goodnight, turning a deaf ear to their entreaties to learn what happened next. Before the week had ended every rating on board had begged him to read them the rest, and he had finally relented.

Sailing close-hauled under full canvas, it was not long before the merchantman effortlessly overhauled the paddle-sloop. With favourable winds, a fast clipper could sail from Calcutta to Canton in about three weeks. A handsome East Indiaman with a low, sleek, double-decked hull, three raking masts and delicate rigging, the clipper's sides were painted in a chequered black-and-white pattern, perhaps to fool pilongs into thinking she was a man-o'-war. The sun was just below the horizon, yet its rays struck the clipper's upper masts and made her gleaming white royals and topgallant sails glow like spun gold. The men scrubbing the *Tisiphone*'s deck before breakfast paused in their work to admire the clipper's fine lines.

Miss Dadabhoy emerged from the after hatch, looking refreshed and lovely in her emerald-green sari. Molineaux could not help thinking that she had a few lines worthy of admiration herself. Not that he entertained any ambitions in that direction; he had once been the fancy of the hour for a well-to-do lady who was curious about the negro anatomy, and he had been happy to satisfy her curiosity. Both of them had been pleasantly surprised by the experience, while it lasted: some of these well-bred ladies could be no better than they ought to be. In those days Molineaux had been young and foolish enough to fall in love, but the lady in question had had no hesitation in reminding him of his place when he had told her of his undying devotion. Now he was an older and wiser man: it was not that he was not good enough for the likes of them; his mother had raised him to believe he was just as good a man as any gentry cove. But a black raised on the back streets of Seven Dials could have little in common with a lady more used to the genteel salons of Mayfair.

'Now that's what I call a beautiful sight,' said Killigrew.

Miss Dadabhoy turned. 'Mr Killigrew!'

He met her gaze with innocent brown eyes and indicated the clipper with a nod, although Molineaux was not convinced that was the direction the young officer had been looking in when he had spoken. The seaman grinned. Some of these officers were no better than they ought to be, either.

III:

Hong Kong

Peri Dadabhoy climbed the rest of the way on to the quarterdeck and gave the passing clipper a cursory glance. 'I must confess I have never been able to understand why some men are so enthusiastic about sailing ships.'

'When I was a boy, I used to spend hours sitting on the quayside at Falmouth,' said Killigrew. 'I used to watch the ships come and go, and listened to the old salts spinning yarns about the wonderful things they'd seen and the exotic lands they'd visited. I think that even if my family hadn't been naval officers for generations, I'd still have gone to sea.'

'It is a dangerous way of life, though, is it not?' she asked.

'That depends how one looks at it. Only landlubbers think of the oceans as a barrier to be crossed. I've always seen the sea as a path to faraway places.'

She shook her head. 'Why do you do it, Mr Killigrew? Risk your life to save people you have never met from pirates and slavers?'

'Someone has to.'

'Why you?'

He sighed, and moved away from the two seamen who stood at the helm. 'If you must know ... I suppose it all goes back to when I was in my first ship: HMS *Dreadful*, a frigate on the Mediterranean station. I was twelve when I joined the navy. One grows up swiftly in the service. Hardly a day went by in the *Dreadful* without someone getting a flogging. The captain was a good man, but weak; the first lieutenant manipulated him. He ran everything, and he was a fiend.'

'Were *you* ever flogged?'

'No. They don't flog the young gentlemen; although I was caned a few times,' he added with a rueful grin. 'But that doesn't mean that the snotties have a soft life. I suppose one expects a little rough and tumble to go on in the cockpit: youthful high-spirits, skylarking – it all helps to toughen up the character. But sometimes it goes too far. The oldsters in the cockpit – the older midshipmen and the mates – used to bully us remorselessly.'

'Somehow I cannot imagine you allowing anyone to bully you.'

'Don't think of me as Lieutenant Kit Killigrew. Think of First-Class Volunteer Christopher Killigrew, twelve years old and away from home for the first time, with no one to turn to and no one to trust.' He grimaced. 'It builds character, all right. The first lesson I learned was never to cry. The more you cried, the more they picked on you. So you kept your mouth shut and knuckled down. There was one boy who never learned that lesson, so the bullies picked on him especially. I used to listen to them tormenting him as I lay in my hammock and pretended to be asleep, and do you know what I was thinking?'

'"Thank heavens it's not me"?'

He looked at her in surprise. This was the first time he had ever told anyone this story, because he had been afraid they would laugh at him or despise him. But she seemed to understand. 'Exactly.'

She reached out to him tenderly and put one of her hands on his. 'It was a natural reaction; certainly not anything to be ashamed of.'

'Oh, but you haven't heard the best of it yet. I hated those oldsters for bullying my friend. I used to lie awake and dream about how one day I would teach them a lesson. But I never did because I was afraid that I would only bring trouble on myself. So I did nothing, while each day his spirit became more and more crushed. He was coming apart at the seams, right before my eyes, but I did nothing because I was simply glad it wasn't me.'

'Did the bullies get their comeuppance?'

'Eventually. But by then it was too late. One day as I was coming off duty, I stepped into the cockpit and there he was, swinging from a beam on the deck head. He'd decided he couldn't take it any more, so he'd hanged himself.'

'And you blamed yourself.'

'I still do. Wouldn't you?'

'I cannot say. I have never been in such a situation.'

He nodded. 'I was so upset, for a while I thought about leaving the navy at the first opportunity.'

'Why didn't you?'

It was a question Killigrew had asked himself many times in those dark days on board HMS *Dreadful*. 'Two reasons, I suppose. First, I didn't want to prove my grandfather right. He'd always said I was spineless, useless – a white-livered bookworm – and that I wouldn't last five minutes in the service.'

'Your grandfather said that?' she asked in astonishment. She had already learned from Hartcliffe that Killigrew had been raised by his grandfather after the death of his parents. Peri had never known her grandfather, but her father had never shown her anything but love and support.

'In a way I'm glad he did,' said Killigrew. 'If he hadn't, I'd never have had anything to prove.'

'Perhaps that was what he intended all along,' she suggested shrewdly.

Killigrew glanced at her, his eyebrows raised in surprise. 'Perhaps.'

'And the other reason?'

'About a fortnight after my friend hanged himself, I went into battle for the first time. I say "battle" – more of a skirmish, really – but it was terrifying enough at the time. We were patrolling off the Barbary Coast when we cornered a corsair galley in a bay. We chased them back to their fortress, there was a fight and ... well, to cut a long story short, we won. In the dungeons of the fortress we found prisoners captured from merchant vessels. The corsairs had been planning to sell them into slavery. When we released them... In the days after my friend's death, I'd been asking myself what it was all for, what purpose the navy served. I had my answer in the faces of those people when they were freed. I saw a way to atone for having stood by while a friend of mine was driven to suicide.'

'And have you not yet atoned for that, after all these years?'

'That's not for me to say. But a wise man once said: "It is necessary only for the good man to do nothing for evil to triumph." ' Then, as if afraid he was sounding pompous, he grinned boyishly. 'Besides, the danger is half the appeal.'

She studied him thoughtfully. He looked very dashing in his pea jacket and pilot cap, a cheroot wedged in the corner of his mouth. He made no attempt to dispose of it in the presence of a lady. At first she wondered if he did not consider her to be a lady on account of the colour of her skin, but she dismissed the thought as unworthy. He had treated her attentively and gallantly from the moment they had met. It was simply that he was something of what Miss Fothergill – her English governess – would have called a 'fast' man.

She remembered the first time she had seen him, the day before yesterday, leaping over the side of the pilong junk with a pistol in one hand and a cutlass in the other. He had been grinning. At the time she had assumed it was a grimace of terror; now she was not so sure. 'Life is too precious to be treated lightly, Mr Killigrew.'

He blushed and looked thoughtful. 'It's difficult to explain,' he said, and wandered over to the taffrail.

She followed him. 'I should like you to try, nonetheless.'

He gave her a penetrating glance and then he looked away. 'It's the queerest thing,' he admittedly softly. 'But when one jumps over the bulwarks of a hostile ship, or over the battlements of an enemy fortress ... when one knows one may be slain at any moment ... that's when I feel most alive. You say that life is precious; but you can have no idea how precious life is until you've stared into Death's eyes – and stared him down.'

'Perhaps. But surely once would be enough?'

He laughed. She did not mind; she had the feeling he was laughing at himself as much as at her. 'You'd think so, wouldn't you? But after you've done it once, everything else becomes dull by comparison.'

'You make danger sound like a drug.'

'Perhaps, in a way, it is.'

A pilot cutter came out to meet the *Tisiphone* when the steam-sloop entered Victoria Harbour and guided her to her berth in the anchorage. Robertson sent the pilot back to Harbour Master's Wharf with two messages: one for Sir Dadabhoy Framjee to the effect that his daughter was on board and in good health; and another to the Hong Kong Police, explaining that they had prisoners on board who needed to be taken into custody.

On the north side of Hong Kong Island, the town of Victoria faced across the sheltered waters of the harbour to the fishing village of Kowloon on the Chinese mainland. There were far more buildings in Victoria these days compared to when Killigrew had first visited the colony seven years earlier at the end of the war, and pale stone had begun to replace the temporary wooden shelters in earnest. Most of the buildings straggled for a mile or so along the waterfront, but here and there a few bungalows and rich merchants' houses had been built amongst the steep, treeless hills which formed a dramatic backdrop to the scene, with Victoria Peak rising to a height of over sixteen hundred feet. The stone buildings were constructed in the neo-classical style, giving the waterfront an appearance that was more Mediterranean than Oriental, but there were still plenty of wooden buildings, mat-sheds and godowns belonging to the various companies which traded out of Hong Kong.

The town was dominated by the new three-storey barracks, but there were other notable buildings. Missionaries of various denominations had wasted no time in using Hong Kong as a beachhead in the Celestial Kingdom from which to convert the heathen Chinese, and already there was a Roman Catholic cathedral, a Union chapel, an American Baptist chapel, a Chinese temple, and even a Muslim mosque. Only the Church of England cathedral remained unfinished. At East Point, on the furthermost extremity of the settlement, stood the trading factory of Grafton, Bannatyne & Co., the company's golden dragon ensign flying from the roof. A two-masted paddle-steamer was anchored in the harbour close to the factory, and Killigrew studied it through his telescope and saw it had a stylised oriental dragon painted gold for a figurehead.

Amongst all the companies which traded with China, Grafton, Bannatyne & Co. was pre-eminent. George Grafton had retired to England a little over ten years previously, leaving his junior partner behind in Canton to act as general manager of the company: *tai-pan*, 'great manager', as the Chinese referred to him. In London, Grafton had purchased himself a seat in the House of Commons, using his new-found influence to defend the interests of the China traders, and it had been his lobbying which had encouraged the British government to go to war with China over the opium issue.

The bumboats homed in on the *Tisiphone* from all directions, like half-pay post-captains swarming around a flag-officer entering the waiting room at the Admiralty. The mess-cooks crowded the bulwarks, looking to purchase local delicacies that would provide some variation from the standard navy fare of salt beef and weevil-infested biscuits. There were wash-boats too, crewed by cheerful washerwomen and seamstresses who knew Jack Tar was a dandy at heart and that laundry facilities on board navy ships were primitive at best.

'I'm going across to the *Hastings* to present my compliments to Rear-Admiral Collier,' Robertson told his officers. 'Second, I want you to take the pilongs and hand them over to the local authorities. You can take Miss Dadabhoy ashore while you're about it; see to it that she gets safely back to her father's house.'

Killigrew coughed into his fist. 'With all due respect, sir, I think it would be more tactful to minimise any contact between Miss Dadabhoy and her would-be kidnappers...'

'Hmph? Oh, all right, I suppose so. Take the pilongs ashore in one of the cutters. Lord Hartcliffe can take Miss Dadabhoy ashore with him in the dinghy.'

The pilongs were placed in the cutter under the muskets of the marines. Killigrew climbed down after them, keeping a watchful eye on his charges, and the cutter's crew rowed them ashore.

There were already three warships in the harbour: the seventy-two-gun ship of the line HMS *Hastings*, wearing the flag of Rear-Admiral Sir Francis Collier; the paddle-sloop HMS *Fury*; and an American sloop of war, the eighteen-gun USS *Preble*. There were other vessels, too: lorchas with Western-style hulls and Oriental sails and rigging; American whalers; and Chinese 'scrambling dragons', known to Westerners as 'fast boats' because of their speed or 'smug boats' because of their usefulness in smuggling opium on to the mainland. They looked like Venetian galleys, with banks of oars and masts bearing mat-and-rattan oblong sails three times taller than they were wide.

Perhaps the most eye-catching vessel in the harbour was a houseboat. A hundred feet from stem to stern, she was a floating palace, three storeys piled one above the other like a wedding cake, with the roof curled up at the eaves in the oriental manner and a pagoda-like tower amidships rising up two storeys more.

Innumerable sampans crowded the waterfront, along with junks of all sizes with mat-and-rattan sails and high, beautifully painted sterns, as well as countless *yolos*: small sampans, almost square, with curved matting roofs. These last were crewed by Tanka women in blue trousers and smocks, their plaited hair decorated with ribbons and flowers, sometimes with one child tied to their backs and another at their breasts, disarmingly young and cheerful, smiling with big, white, gleaming teeth. The boats served as homes and places of trade for the Tanka people. They crowded so thickly against the dockside it seemed as if one could walk a hundred feet out into the harbour without getting one's feet wet.

Yet apart from the chatter of Chinese voices and the occasional passing tramp of soldiers' boots as they marched along the waterfront, the harbour was oddly quiet and far from being a bustling port. Trade at Victoria had not yet taken off the way its founders had hoped; with the five treaty ports open now, Hong Kong had been robbed of its *raison d'être*. There were no noisy steam cranes on the wharf – what trade did come to Hong Kong was actually transshipped at the Cap-sing-mun Passage, a dozen miles or so to the west.

By the time the cutter had nosed through this crowd to the wharf, a detail of sepoys in dark green uniforms already waited amongst the bustling crowds of coolies hurrying on errands, Chinese hawkers selling goods from the panniers of their pack horses, merchants being carried on sedan chairs. Under the command of a young European officer and accompanied by a civilian in a black frock coat, top hat, and extravagant side-whiskers, the sepoys waited outside a noisy waterfront tavern to take the pilongs into custody.

Killigrew saluted. 'Lieutenant Killigrew, HMS *Tisiphone*.'

The officer returned his salute. 'Lieutenant Dwyer, Ceylon Rifles.' Dwyer was a young man, red-haired, freckle-faced and snub-nosed. 'This is Assistant Superintendent Cargill of the Hong Kong Police,' he added, indicating the whiskery civilian.

'Welcome to Hong Kong, Mr Killigrew,' said Cargill. 'Glad to see you've not wasted any time,' he added with a broad smile, indicating the prisoners.

'All right, Havildar, let's take these men into custody,' Lieutenant Dwyer told his sergeant. 'Some of Zhai Jing-mu's men, do you think, Mr Cargill?'

'Either his, or Yao Ping-han's. I don't suppose we'll be able to get them to talk, though.'

'Did you say Zhai Jing-mu?' asked Killigrew.

'Ah,' said Cargill. 'You've heard of him, then?'

'That fellow there referred to himself as Zhai Jing-mu when we arrested him.' Killigrew indicated the *lao-pan*, whose white coat was looking decidedly grubby after three days on the deck of the *Tisiphone* without a chance to change.

Dwyer stared down his snub nose at Killigrew, and then Cargill burst out laughing. 'I believe Mr Killigrew is kidding you, Dwyer. You know what these salts are like, always spinning a yarn.'

Killigrew frowned. 'If I've said something to amuse you, Mr Cargill, I fear I did so in all innocence.'

'Come now, Mr Killigrew. Don't tell me you

83

don't know who Zhai Jing-mu is?'

'A pilong captain, I suppose...'

'Captain!' snorted Dwyer. 'Admiral would be closer to the mark. He's said to have a fleet of over a hundred pirate junks under his command.'

Cargill nodded. 'We've been after him for over two years now. The most notorious pirate in these waters; and believe you me, that's saying something. He's believed to be responsible for the disappearance of five clippers last year.'

'Seven,' said Zhai Jing-mu.

Both Cargill and Dwyer stared at him with renewed interest. 'Good God, Cargill ... you don't suppose this could be him, do you?'

The assistant superintendent brushed his whiskers thoughtfully. 'He's about the right age, according to my reports. Blue eyes, too. Rare in a Chinaman.'

Dwyer put a hand under the pilong's jaw and tilted his head back to study his face. 'Speakee English, eh? You Zhai Jing-mu?'

The *lao-pan* jerked his head away with a contemptuous sneer. 'I will be a free man one week after the tiger moon is down,' he said in Cantonese. 'And you will be dead.' He turned to Killigrew. 'And you and Miss Dadabhoy – before the end of the first week in the rabbit moon, you will all have been dispatched to the Hell of Ten Thousand Knives.'

'You've got that the wrong way round,' Cargill replied in the same language. 'If you *are* Zhai Jing-mu – and I'm starting to believe it myself – then you'll be hanged along with the rest of your crew.'

'What did he say?' asked Dwyer.

'Big talk,' said Cargill. 'Just hot air.'

Dwyer's men took the pilongs in custody and led them off in the direction of the gaol. Cargill lingered on the wharf and studied Killigrew with a speculative expression. 'Aren't you curious to know what that fellow just said to you, Mr Killigrew?'

'I speak a little Cantonese. I was on board the *Dido* during the China War.'

Cargill nodded. 'Before I came out. So, you're *that* Killigrew, eh? I take my hat off to you, sir.' He raised his topper.

'You think he really is this Zhai Jing-mu?'

'After that little display of defiance? If you were here during the war then you'll know the Chinese: all grovelling humility after they've been bested, and as often as not before. But not that one. No, Mr Killigrew, I believe you've captured the man I've been chasing these past two years.' He laughed suddenly. 'I suppose I ought to resent the fact that you've succeeded where I've failed, but, by George, I can't! If you'd heard some of the stories about the atrocities he's said to have committed ... not all of them without foundation, I can tell you. I'm just glad that devil's finally under lock and key.'

'I just hope you'll be able to keep him there.'

'Oh, don't you worry about that, Mr Killigrew. I intend to keep a very close guard on our friend. He'll be tried at the earliest opportunity, before any of his friends can effect a rescue attempt; although to tell you the truth, I rather hope they do. Then we'll snap them up, too. Zhai Jing-mu may be the worst of the pirates in these parts, but

85

he's not the only one.'

Killigrew smiled. 'I'm glad to hear it. For a moment there you had me thinking our work in these waters was over and done with before we'd even started.'

'Ever been to Hong Kong before?'

'Not since forty-three.'

Cargill nodded. 'As you can see, it's changed a great deal in the past six years...'

Before the policeman could finish his sentence, the door of the waterfront tavern burst open and a Chinese in European clothes came haring out. He dodged past Killigrew and raced down the waterfront.

Another figure emerged behind him, a tall, barrel-chested man with a huge, unkempt beard. Killigrew watched in astonishment as the man raised his hand with a pistol in it – his massive fist made the gun seem puny – and fired. Already thirty yards away, the Chinese cried out and fell. He rolled in the dust of the unpaved street and clutched his wounded leg.

'Capital shot, Captain Ingersoll,' Cargill remarked to the pistoleer.

Ingersoll scowled at him. 'I were aiming for his back,' he snarled with a West Country accent. 'Sonuvabitch stole fifty dollars off me!' He pocketed the pistol and strode over to reclaim his money.

Cargill turned back to Killigrew. 'What was I saying?'

'Just that Hong Kong's changed in the past six years. It's certainly a good deal livelier than I remember.'

Cargill grinned. 'Welcome back to the Orient, Mr Killigrew.'

As the horses thundered around the oval track at the Happy Valley racecourse, Killigrew gazed through his pocket telescope. It was not the horses he was studying, however, but the other race-goers. Just about everyone who was anyone in Hong Kong society was present: Samuel George Bonham, Her Majesty's Governor, Plenipotentiary and Superintendent of Trade; Rear-Admiral Collier and the officers of the other ships in the harbour; missionaries; and the owners and representatives of all of the great trading houses.

Unlike most of the military men there, resplendent in their uniforms, Killigrew was fashionably but unobtrusively dressed in a morning coat and top hat, as befitted attendance at a race meeting. He saw Miss Dadabhoy, ravishing in a sapphire-blue sari, but there was no sign of anyone who might have been her father. Her curly black hair was done up and crowned with a garland of flowers. There were no two ways about it, she was a damned fine-looking woman. And intelligent, too, unafraid to speak her own mind.

He had been thinking about her a great deal in the week since the *Tisiphone* had arrived at Hong Kong. That worried him. He had had plenty of female friends, and while it would not have been fair to say they meant nothing to him, certainly they meant no more to him than he did to them. Usually it was an equitable arrangement. Only

87

once had he made the mistake of becoming emotionally attached to a woman, and it had turned out unhappily for both of them. He could not blame the woman in question for that: he had put her on a pedestal and built her up in his mind into something she had not been. The disappointment had been inevitable, but hurtful nonetheless. He had promised himself he would never make that mistake again. But that did not mean that he should never fall in love; he would just have to be more careful.

He was about to go and talk to Peri Dadabhoy when a half-familiar voice called out behind him. 'Kit? Long time no see!'

Killigrew turned and saw a handsome young man of roughly his own age, dressed in civilian clothing. There was something vaguely familiar about the man's face, but Killigrew could not instantly place it. But since only a select band was accorded the honour of being allowed to address him as 'Kit', he pasted an uneasy smile on his face as he struggled to remember where he had met this fellow. 'Good afternoon!' he said with false enthusiasm.

The man grinned. 'You don't remember me at all, do you?'

Killigrew shook his head. 'I'm sorry...'

'Well, it *was* over nine years ago. In those days you couldn't see my face for the pimples.' He thrust out his hand. 'Jago Verran.'

The name was the trigger which brought all the memories back. Jago Verran had been one of his fellow midshipmen on board HMS *Dreadful*. They had been shipmates for four years, and looking at him again Killigrew was amazed he had not recognised his old friend earlier. He clasped Verran's hand and pumped it vigorously.

'Jago! Look at you, you old sonuvagun!'

'And you're looking as well as ever. When did you arrive?'

'A week ago. What about you? What have you been doing since we parted?'

'I spent three years on the *Alecto*, mostly cruising in the Med., but things were much quieter after Syria. I made it to mate but when I saw my career wasn't going anywhere I quit the Andrew Miller and joined the merchant service. I've got my own vessel now.'

'I'd heard that the problem with the merchant service was that the mess bills were even bigger than in the navy.'

Verran laughed. 'Nothing could top your mess bills, Kit. Anyway, Mr Bannatyne pays his captains well – damned well.'

'You're working for Bannatyne now?'

Verran nodded. 'That's my flapper down in the harbour now: the *Golden Dragon*.'

'What about that rather splendid houseboat opposite Governor's Wharf?'

'That belongs to Commissioner Tan. A bit of an embarrassment to Governor Bonham, actually, but it has its uses.'

'I'm not sure I follow you.'

'The Chinese still think they own Hong Kong but they're letting us use it out of the goodness of their hearts.'

Killigrew nodded. He was well aware that the Chinese believed the whole world owed obeisance to the Daoguang Emperor in Peking, and that when the British had gone to war with China ten years earlier they had been no more than uncivilised barbarians rebelling against the celestial authority of the Son of Heaven.

'So Tan's been appointed prefect for Hong Kong?'

'Strictly unofficial, from our point of view. The plenipo' won't let him set foot on the island, except by invitation. That's why Tan lives on the houseboat. We're still trying to make the Celestials understand they've ceded Hong Kong to us in perpetuity, and their government has no authority over this island. But I suspect Bonham finds it damned useful having a representative of the Emperor so close at hand; although I dare say the Emperor finds it equally useful having one of his mandarins in a place where he can spy on everything that goes on in the colony. Still, never mind that. What about you, Kit? No need for me to ask what you've been doing these past few years: Chingkiang-fu, Borneo, the Guinea Coast...' Verran grinned. 'You never were one for taking it easy, were you? Even when we were snotties.'

Killigrew shrugged. 'I wear the uniform and take the pay. I've always felt I might as well earn it.'

'Earn it! What are they paying you these days? Let's see, what are you now? Still a junior lieutenant? A hundred and eighty a year?'

'Plus prize money.'

'Which is never in short supply when you're on board, I seem to recall. All the same, it's a poor

90

reward for risking your life on a frequent basis.'

'Queen and country, Jago,' replied Killigrew, his tone self-mockingly offhand.

'Gammon! I get two hundred and fifty a year from Mr Bannatyne, and no nonsense from any damned admirals that haven't seen any fighting since the Treaty of Paris. Five hundred a year, Kit. You could be earning that. Bannatyne is always looking for captains for his clippers.'

'You've met him, then?' Killigrew had heard that the *tai-pan* of Grafton, Bannatyne & Co. was something of a recluse.

'Of course! I take my orders directly from him. Oh, don't believe the stories you hear. He's just an ordinary chap.'

'One of the richest ordinary chaps in the world.'

Verran laughed again. 'Oh, he's a downy cove, I'll grant you that.'

'That's one way of putting it. They say he and his partner put pressure on the government at home to go to war with China, simply so they could trade more freely with the Chinese.'

'I thought a free-trader like you would approve of expanding commerce?'

'Not if the price has to be paid in human lives.'

Verran chuckled. 'You make him sound like some kind of monster. He's all right. A bit stiff-necked, I'll grant you, but if you ask me that's just because he's a little shy. He has me up at his house for dinner every night I'm in Hong Kong.'

'Sounds ghastly,' Killigrew said with a smile.

'Oh, it has its compensations. Mrs Bannatyne, for instance.'

'Good company?'

'A regular stunner.'

'Young?'

'Same age as us. She's John Keane's daughter.'

'John Keane? As in, Keane and Co.?'

Verran nodded. 'Just between the two of us –
although to tell you the truth, I think everyone in
Hong Kong must have guessed it – Bannatyne
only married her as part of a business trans-
action. He got a thousand shares in Keane and
Co. as his dowry, and when Keane died what he
inherited through his wife made Bannatyne the
majority shareholder. Within six months Keane
and Co. was no more, subsumed within Bannatyne's empire.'

'I didn't think Keane was that old. What did he
die of?'

'A terrible accident... Don't look at me like
that, Kit. It *was* an accident. I was there when it
happened. He was on board the *Golden Dragon*,
we got caught in a typhoon and he was washed
overboard... There was nothing anyone could
have done. His body was found a week later by
some Chinese fishermen. Mrs Bannatyne
blamed me...' Verran looked glum for a moment.
'Sometimes I blame myself.' Then he pasted a
smile on his face. 'Ah, well. She'll come round in
due course.'

'A little dangerous, wouldn't you say? Making
eyes at your employer's wife? Especially when
your employer is a man as rich and powerful as
Blase Bannatyne.'

'A little danger only spices things up.'

Killigrew smiled thinly. 'You always did have a

penchant for mischief.'

Verran did not seem to have heard him. 'Not that there's much danger of Bannatyne noticing,' he continued, lowering his voice discreetly. 'He's completely obsessed with his work; he neglects her dreadfully. When they went on honeymoon to Macao, he took his annual accounts with him, and I can tell you for a fact that he spent as much time in business meetings as he did in the nuptial bed. No, Kit, there's something missing from Mrs Bannatyne's married life. And I intend to give it to her,' he added with a wink. Then he raised his voice again. 'Anyway, what about you? Any ladies in your life at the moment?' He nudged Killigrew and nodded to where Miss Dadabhoy was now talking to – or rather, being talked at by – another face Killigrew recognised, that of the Reverend Werner Ultzmann. 'Was Miss Dadabhoy suitably grateful to her rescuer?'

'She thanked me, if that's what you mean. Not that one expects thanks for doing one's duty.'

Verran laughed. 'You know damned well what I mean. You can't tell me you haven't boarded her?'

'There's nothing between myself and Miss Dadabhoy,' said Killigrew, although he might have added: 'yet'.

'"I believe you, my boy!"' Verran quoted a catch-phrase of the London stage that had been doing the rounds for the past few months; Killigrew was disappointed to discover it had reached as far as Hong Kong. 'You must be losing your touch, Kit. You'd better stick an oar in, old boy, otherwise Ultzmann might ruin your chances.

93

Have you met the reverend? He's definitely one of the great characters of this colony.'

'Oh yes,' Killigrew said heavily. 'We've met.'

Ultzmann was somewhere in his late forties, dressed in clothes that had probably been fashionable in his native Pomerania when he had left it many years ago, including a Dutch bargee's cap of the kind worn by German students. It was not that he was unable to afford new clothes; it was widely known that the Lutheran missionary was well paid by the firm of Grafton, Bannatyne & Co. for his services as an interpreter and adviser.

The reverend had been in China for many years, and it was said that despite his bulk, the Chinese cast to his features – an accident of nature, since both his parents had been Prussians – had enabled him to travel on the mainland disguised as a Chinese, so long as he wore rose-tinted tea-stone spectacles to disguise his blue eyes. He professed a horror of the opium trade in which his employers were engaged, but had agreed to work for Grafton, Bannatyne & Co. on the condition that the company distributed free Bibles with its opium.

Ultzmann was enjoying the sound of his own voice so much that he did not notice Miss Dadabhoy give Killigrew a pleading glance over his shoulder. The lieutenant took his leave of Verran and went swiftly to her rescue. He bowed low.

'Miss Dadabhoy, may I say that you are looking exceptionally ravishing today, even by your usual standards?'

'You are too kind,' she replied mechanically, as if bored by the commonplace gallantry. Most young women Killigrew knew either sneered at him for being too poor, or regarded him with a ridiculous adoration which only embarrassed him. There was something refreshing about the way Peri mocked him playfully. Sometimes he feared his greatest sin was taking himself too seriously; a person like Peri was just what he needed to prick his pomposity.

Ultzmann was evidently annoyed at the interruption. 'I don't believe we have been introduced, Mr...?'

'Then your memory betrays you, Reverend. We *have* met. The twenty-first of July 1842. Killigrew's the name, Lieutenant Christopher Killigrew. Of course, in those days I was just a midshipman.'

'I do not have much of a memory for dates.' Ultzmann's English was so accented, and if he successfully passed himself off as a Chinese Killigrew could only assume that his Cantonese was more fluent.

'Neither do I, usually. But that date is one I'm not likely to forget in a hurry. Chingkiang-fu, Reverend. Surely you remember? You told Lord Saltoun the city would be undefended.'

'Ah, yes.' Ultzmann's face became grave. 'A most unfortunate happenstance. Man proposes, God disposes. But all turned out for the best, did it not? Had we not taken Chingkiang-fu, would the Chinese have acceded so readily to the Treaty of Nanking?'

'I'm sure that thought must be a great comfort

to the widows and orphans of the men who died in that attack.'

Ultzmann shrugged. 'One cannot make an omelette without breaking eggs.'

'But it shouldn't require six eggs to make a three-egg omelette.' Killigrew turned to Peri. 'Is your father here today, Miss Dadabhoy?'

'Yes, I'll take you to him. If you'll excuse us, Reverend?' She led the way across the greensward, and as soon as they were out of earshot of the missionary she turned to Killigrew with a smile. 'Thank you for rescuing me. That is the second time now, is it not?'

He grinned. 'All in the day's work for the Royal Navy, miss.'

'You do not care for the reverend, I think.'

'Whatever gave you that idea?' Killigrew asked innocently, and she flicked her fan chidingly against his shoulder. 'I don't hate Ultzmann. You have to respect someone before you can hate them properly, and the reverend's too much of a buffoon.'

'So. Are you going to tell me what happened at Chingkiang-fu?' she asked. 'Or are you just going to put on a manly expression and tell me modesty forbids; a phrase which often leads me to wonder if it is not *honesty* which forbids?'

'It was during the war. I was serving on board the *Dido* at the time under Captain Keppel. I was a midshipman then, only eighteen. Keppel hurt himself in a fall and while he was laid up I managed to slip away and join the naval brigade which took part in the attack on the city. As I said, Ultzmann told us the city would be undefended. It wasn't. A good many men died that day finding out. But you don't want to hear about that.'

'Too grisly for a delicate lady's sensibilities, you think?'

'Too grisly for anyone's sensibilities, man or woman. You are fully recovered from your ordeal, I trust?'

'Which one? Being a captive aboard Zhai Jing-mu's junk, or being subjected to the reverend's tedious attempts to convert me from my deplorable heathenism?'

'Which was worse?'

'Oh, definitely the reverend. What do you think, Mr Killigrew? Shall I burn in Hell for eternity because of my beliefs?'

He joined in the game at once. 'Oh, indubitably. But if Heaven is full of men like Ultzmann, wouldn't you prefer Hell?'

'Was it not Machiavelli who said he would prefer to go to Hell after he died because the company would be more interesting than in Heaven?'

'Either him, or Benjamin Disraeli.'

'Is there any news on when Zhai Jing-mu will go on trial? I have been following the reports in the newspapers, but there is no word of when the trial is to take place. I had thought the chief justice would have called on me to be a witness.'

'Commander Robertson and I spoke to Admiral Collier and we agreed there was no need to put you through reliving your ordeal in the witness box.'

'I am grateful for your consideration, Mr

97

Killigrew. But if it means I can be certain that he will be convicted...'

'He'll be convicted. We caught him red-handed, and the weapons we found on board his junk are material evidence of his piracy. That, and the testimony of myself and Lord Hartcliffe will be more than sufficient to convict him. You have my word on it.'

'All the same, is there not a danger his defending counsel will not dredge up some loophole through which he can escape? How did Swift put it? "Laws are like cobwebs, which may catch small flies, but let wasps and hornets break through." My father says that lawyers can be dangerous, easily twisting the words of an honest naval officer unversed in their tricks.'

'You needn't have any fears on that account. Lord Hartcliffe and I have plenty of experience of dealing with land-sharks in court from the Guinea Coast. Besides, I don't imagine they'll find a lawyer in Hong Kong who's prepared to defend Zhai Jing-mu with too much enthusiasm.'

They watched the horses pass the finishing post and Peri sighed. 'Fourth place.'

'One of your father's horses?' asked Killigrew. She nodded. 'He'll have to have a word with his trainer.'

'With me, you mean.'

'You train your father's horses?' he asked in astonishment.

'Until we can find someone better qualified. You seem surprised?'

'I was just wondering how best to extricate my foot from my mouth.'

'Blame the jockey, Mr Killigrew. I keep telling him that Shibdiz always runs best when she gets out in front and stays there, but he will hold her back in the first few furlongs. Did you have a wager, Mr Killigrew?'

He shook his head. 'I don't gamble.'

She regarded him coolly. 'Not with money, at any rate.'

'I can't get passionate about horse-racing. If I had a personal stake in the race, perhaps – if I was the jockey, for instance, or the trainer, I could feel I'd made a personal contribution to the victory – that would be another matter entirely.'

'Is winning important to you?'

'It's the second best feeling in the world. I'm not like Shibdiz, I'm afraid. I'm usually slow off the mark, but I have been known to come from behind in the final straight. Would you feel insulted if I told you that when I asked to be introduced to your father it was more than just a ruse to get away from Ultzmann?' he asked, changing the subject.

'Yes. But I might be persuaded to forgive you,' she added with a smile.

'Oh, I can be very persuasive, miss.'

'I am sure you can. There is my father. I know he wants to meet you.'

'Me? Why on earth would the great Sir Dadabhoy Framjee wish to meet a mere naval lieutenant?'

'He wishes to thank you. He seems to think you saved his daughter's life.'

'I hope you didn't give him that impression.'

'Heaven forbid, Mr Killigrew.'

Sir Dadabhoy Framjee was in his sixties, a short man with pronounced cheekbones and a thrusting, pointed jaw which seemed to dominate his whole face, even below a wide, white moustache which made him look more Turkish than Indian. He wore a white coat, *pahgris* headdress and oriental slippers which turned up at the toes. To Killigrew he looked like the fierce Sultan Schariar from the Arabian Nights, but even in those hard eyes which had built up a massive trading empire, there was a twinkle of humour and kindness which suggested even his heart might be melted by the storytelling of a Scheherezade.

Framjee was talking to a young Chinese man of average height and build, with a face that was handsome in a smooth-cheeked, effeminate way, his limpid brown eyes full of a beguiling innocence. The Chinese wore a loose-fitting sky-blue tunic and his hair was in the style that all his race were required to adopt by Manchu law: shaven at the front and tied in a long queue at the back. The Tartar Manchus had invaded China two hundred years ago and the relationship between them and China's native Han people was not unlike that between the Normans and the Anglo-Saxons must have been in the days of Robin Hood.

As Killigrew and Peri approached, Framjee turned to his youngest daughter and beamed. She bowed with her palms pressed together before her in the Indian manner. Killigrew sensed something in the formality of that greeting: not hostility, perhaps, but a sense of unease between father and daughter.

'Father, may I present Mr Killigrew, the *Tisiphone*'s second lieutenant? Mr Killigrew, this is my father, Sir Dadabhoy Framjee.'

Killigrew bowed. 'It's an honour to meet you, sir.'

'Likewise, Mr Killigrew.' Framjee's accent was pure Cambridge, although Killigrew knew the merchant had never had a formal education; that was perhaps the reason he endowed so many schools in Gujerat, so that others might gain the advantages in life which he had never had. Like many Parsi merchants Killigrew had met, Framjee was more English than the average Englishman. 'My daughter has told me a great deal about you.'

'None of it true, I hope,' said Killigrew.

Framjee chuckled. 'All of it flattering, I assure you.' Killigrew gave Miss Dadabhoy a sidelong glance as she tried to conceal her smile behind her fan. 'This is my comprador, Li Cheng,' added the merchant, indicating the Chinese, who bowed in the Oriental style, with his left fist clasped in his right hand. 'Mr Li handles the Chinese side of my business.'

Killigrew mirrored the comprador's bow. Li smiled, but Killigrew was not fooled. He was well aware the Chinese considered outward displays of emotion impolite in the presence of strangers, and often used a smile to conceal whatever they were really feeling: nervousness, anger, disgust or astonishment; all the emotions which the 'barbarians' managed to provoke in the Chinese on a regular basis.

'If you will excuse me now, Mr Li?' said

Framjee. 'And remember what I told you to tell Wu-qua. Seventeen thousand cattis of gunpowder tea, but it must be of the finest quality. And do not just check the samples: make a random check from the rest of the consignment.'

'*Hai.*' Li Cheng bowed and hurried away.

'You need to tell your comprador how to do his job?' Killigrew asked in some surprise.

'He is new. But he seems jolly clever.'

'Can you trust him?'

Framjee smiled. 'Ask me again in twenty years' time. I am afraid my business is not one which engenders trust. My rivals will tell you that their word is their bond, but you should trust a cobra sooner than you should trust them. Their greed knows no bounds.'

'Whereas you are the epitome of honesty, Father,' Peri said ironically.

Framjee was unperturbed. 'Where would I be without you, my conscience, my darling daughter?'

'The very place you stand now, Father, and every bit as wealthy. If you will excuse me, Mr Killigrew? I need to talk to our jockey.' The lieutenant bowed and Peri wandered off.

'You will have to forgive my Peri, Mr Killigrew. She does not approve of the way I earn my living; though she spends the money freely enough,' he sighed.

'You surprise me, sir. She does not strike me as the kind to have extravagant tastes.'

'No, you are right. I am not being fair to her. I am jolly glad to have this opportunity to thank you in person for saving her life, Mr Killigrew. If

102

I had to choose between her and my riches, it would be an easy decision, believe me.' He looked glum. 'Sometimes I wonder if she is not right to disapprove of the opium trade. I have tried to find alternative goods to import into China, believe me I have. But there is nothing else they will buy. They regard everything the West has to offer as inferior, the work of barbarians. Did you know that is what they call us? *"Fan kwae."* "Foreign Devils".'

'Pardon me for contradicting you, sir, but a more accurate translation would be "ocean ghosts". It's just their way of describing us as a pale-skinned people who come from beyond the seas. The Chinese often give people nicknames based on some unusual physical characteristic; they intend no insult.'

'You speak Cantonese, Mr Killigrew?'

'I've picked up a smattering. I was here during the war.'

'A terrible business ... oh! I do not mean to give offence...'

'None taken, sir, I assure you. I'm not proud of having fought in that war. When I joined the navy I thought that if I ever did have to fight in a war it would be against a ruthless tyrant like Napoleon. Instead I found myself slaughtering the Chinese because they wouldn't buy our opium.'

'You blame merchants like myself for that.' Framjee sounded as though he blamed himself.

'I blame men like Sir George Grafton, who used their influence to bring the war about. You were not such a man, as far as I am aware.'

103

'Perhaps not. But I still profit from the results of that war. But listen to us both, wearing metaphorical hair shirts for what happened ten years ago, when we should be putting those events behind us and trying to build a new relationship with the Chinese. Theirs is a noble culture, Mr Killigrew, with much to teach us.'

'As we have much to teach them, if only they'll admit it.'

'Ours are two very different cultures, are they not? Perhaps that is why our relations have been so troubled?'

'I sometimes wonder if the problem isn't that we're so very different as that we're so very alike.'

'I am not certain that I follow you, Mr Killigrew.'

'Two powerful empires, both convinced that we are pre-eminent in the world, and that all other cultures should bow down and accept our way of life as superior.'

Framjee laughed. 'That is very true, sir. I had not thought of it that way before.'

Killigrew lit a cheroot and offered one to the Parsi, who shook his head. 'I'm sorry about the loss of your clipper, sir.'

Framjee made a dismissive gesture. 'It was not the first clipper I have lost to Zhai Jing-mu and his pilongs. Thanks to you and your colleagues it should be the last.'

'Your own daughter played a part in capturing him, sir. I think if it had not been for her he might yet have escaped.'

The Parsi chuckled. 'I am afraid she is a spirited girl.'

'No need to apologise, sir. So many women these days are raised to be simpering ninnies, it's refreshing to meet a girl with both sense and backbone. You've brought her up well.'

'Her mother deserves the credit for that. I was always too bound up in my work to pay much attention to either of them; until my wife succumbed to malaria in the early days of this colony. Losing her taught me to appreciate the things that really matter in this life: the ones you love. The ship I lost and her cargo were insured; what you rescued for me, no insurance company could put a price on.'

'No. But Zhai Jing-mu could.'

'I do not understand.'

'Pilongs attack clippers when they're on their way to Hong Kong with a cargo full of opium; but your ship was attacked as it was sailing for Bombay. My guess is that Zhai Jing-mu knew exactly who was on board.'

Framjee nodded. 'I would have paid any amount of money for Peri's safe return.'

'And Zhai Jing-mu knew that. Someone must have told him that your daughter would be sailing on that ship.'

'That would not surprise me. He has spies everywhere. There are many in China who are opposed to the Manchu government in Peking. Here in Hong Kong, they are safely beyond Chinese jurisdiction. Since this colony was established, it has acted as a magnet for the worst scum of China, who use it as a refuge, a base for their criminal enterprises. I am not one who believes that all the Chinese in Hong Kong are criminals – to the contrary, I would say most of them are honest, honourable, hard-working people. But there are enough criminals to make their presence felt. You have heard of the Brotherhood of Heaven, Earth and Man?'

'The Triads, you mean? I've heard rumours.'

'The Triads have close links with the pilongs. Many of the pilongs are members of the Brotherhood.'

'I thought the Triads were political organisations rather than criminal ones? Doesn't their watchword – *fan Ch'ing, fu Ming* – translate as "overthrow the Ch'ing dynasty and restore the Ming"?'

'Treason is as much a crime in China as it is in England, Mr Killigrew. Revolutionaries need money, and rarely have scruples about how they get it. The Triads are happy to work with the pilongs, as long as the pilongs restrict their attacks to Western shipping.'

'All the same, the attack on your daughter's ship took planning, foreknowledge. Could the Triads have provided the pilongs with that kind of information?'

'The Brotherhood of Heaven, Earth and Man has spies in all sorts of surprising places,' warned Framjee. 'That is the key to its power.'

IV:

Triads

Hollywood Road was all hustle and bustle when Killigrew, granted a couple of hours leave by Robertson, made his way to the Chinese shantytown of Tai-ping-shan the next day. Pale-faced, languid Chinese gentlemen fluttered fans at their faces as they were pushed on wheel-barrows, seated on one side of the huge wheel while their luggage acted as a counterbalance on the other. Wealthier merchants were carried on palanquins, covered litters, which on mainland China were reserved for the use of mandarins. Coolies hurried back and forth carrying buckets of water slung from bamboo poles on their shoulders. A pair of grubby, cheerful children rode through the crowd on the back of a water buffalo.

When the British had colonised Hong Kong in 1842 it had been little more than a rock with a few small fishing villages on it. A census taken five years ago, not counting the troops of the garrison, had put the island's population at 23,872. Of these, 618 had been European. The vast majority of the rest were Chinese. Many of them were opponents of the Ch'ing Dynasty who had come to the island to be beyond Manchu jurisdiction, but that did not mean they had any great love for the British; others were merely criminals with a price on their heads. Europeans generally avoided Tai-ping-shan, so it was with a devil-may-care sense of recklessness that Killigrew wandered down the narrow, crowded streets.

In fact there was surprisingly little sense of menace in the shantytown. The Chinese avoided his gaze, but then they found casual eye-contact abhorrent so he did not take it personally. Certainly there were no menacing glares. Killigrew had found that a little politeness went a long way with the Cantonese.

He wandered about aimlessly – keeping a weather eye open for trouble, but needlessly so – losing himself in the atmosphere: the pleasantly exotic sound of a Chinese band playing in the upper storey of an open-fronted building, the sing-song jabber of cheerful Cantonese voices, the heady aroma of unfamiliar scents and spices. There were animals everywhere – pigs, dogs, hens, goats, ducks – sometimes secured in pens, sometimes just wandering the streets every bit as aimlessly as Killigrew.

He found an eating stall and ordered *gum chen kai*: soft, succulent chicken livers and crisp pork fat eaten with wafers of orange-flavoured bread. There were plenty of places to eat in Victoria, but they provided stolidly English food. Even if it had not been in his nature to sample as much foreign culture as he could in the course of his travels, Killigrew would still have gone to great lengths to escape the monotonous fare of mutton and boiled vegetables that seemed to be the staple of every chop-house from Falmouth to Shanghai.

He sat down at one of the communal tables. The other customers – all of them Chinese – eyed him uncertainly until he wished them hearty eating and rubbed his chopsticks together to remove any splinters like a seasoned Chinese gourmet. They smiled and nodded, and returned to their conversations. He ate his *gum chen kai* with a bowl of fried rice and was washing it down with delicious rice wine when he saw a vaguely familiar face in the crowd. It took him a moment to place the man: Li Cheng.

There was no reason why Framjee's comprador should not pay a visit to Tai-ping-shan, of course – he probably had relatives there, perhaps even lived there himself – yet some instinct made Killigrew wonder. Someone had tipped off Zhai Jing-mu in advance as to which ship Peri Dadabhoy would be travelling on; who was better placed to be privy to such information than the Parsi's new and untried comprador?

Killigrew drained the last of his rice wine hurriedly and paid the chef before following the comprador. He was conscious that his Western face and clothes must have stuck out like a brig in a fleet of junks as he trailed Li through the crowds, but the comprador never once glanced over his shoulder. Wherever he was going, he was headed there with a purpose.

A short distance down the road they came to a joss house with two stone lions, carved in the Oriental fashion – with stone balls in their mouths skilfully carved from the same rock so they could not be removed – on guard on either side of the door. The only other sentinel was an old Chinese monk who smiled and bowed as Li mounted the broad flight of half a dozen steps leading up to the door. After the briefest hesitation, Killigrew followed him. The monk made no attempt to stop him, smiling and bowing just the same as he had for Li.

Killigrew paused just inside the open door until his eyes grew accustomed to the gloom. Various gaudy statues of Taoist immortals, about twelve feet high, towered along the back wall, and the air was heady with the scent of perfumed sandal-wood joss sticks being burned as offerings. There was no sign of Li amongst the supplicants kneeling before the numerous altars, but a rattling sound drew Killigrew's attention to a side door. He ducked through and saw Li on his knees, shaking a porcelain canister full of bamboo sticks until one of them fell out. He picked up the stick, handed the canister to an attendant, and took the stick through another door.

The attendant saw Killigrew. 'You wantchee savvy joss, missee?'

'Why not?' He stepped forwards and the attendant handed him the canister. He kneeled down as Li had done and shook the canister until a stick fell out. It had a Chinese character inscribed on it in red ink, but Killigrew had never mastered the art of reading Chinese script.

He passed the canister back and the attendant gestured for him to go through the same door as Li. Killigrew emerged into bright sunlight and found himself in a courtyard where a paved path led between ponds full of goldfish. The courtyard was deserted except for Li, who was disappearing through a door on the far side. As soon as he was out of sight, Killigrew crossed the courtyard briskly and then peered cautiously through the door.

The room beyond was another shrine, windowless, again heavy with the scent of joss sticks. Cones formed by successions of bamboo rings, with strips of lucky red papers hung inside them, dangled from an array of bamboo poles which formed a false ceiling suspended from the real one. Before an altar where another Taoist idol glowered, Killigrew saw Li hand his bamboo stick to an elderly priest dressed in ornate brocaded robes.

'Fan Ch'ing, fu Ming,' said the comprador.

The priest nodded and pulled aside a silk curtain. Li passed through.

Killigrew crossed the threshold and the priest beckoned him forward with impossibly long fingernails. The lieutenant held out his bamboo stick but the priest shook his head. 'English?'

Killigrew nodded.

'When were you born?' The priest spoke surprisingly good English.

'The fifteenth of October,' said Killigrew, and grinned. 'Birth date of great men.'

The priest shook his head irritably. 'What year?'

'The year of...' Killigrew was about to say 'Our Lord' when it occurred to him that speaking of Christ in a Taoist temple might be considered blasphemous by the priest, and he had no wish to give offence. 'Eighteen hundred and twenty-four.

111

I don't know what date that is in the Chinese calendar.'

The old man clearly had enough experience of dealing with Westerners to be able to work it out in his head; either that, or he was making it up as he went along. But Killigrew was not overly superstitious so he did not mind either way. 'You were born in the Year of the Monkey, in the Dog Moon. In the Celestial Kingdom, the monkey is the king of all the animals.' The priest gestured expansively. 'A man born in the Year of the Monkey is intelligent, resourceful and adaptable. He is master of many skills and greatly enjoys being busy, loves travel, and seeks difficult challenges to test himself. He takes great pride in fighting for noble causes but does not take kindly to criticism.'

'How dare you say such a thing?' snarled Killigrew. The priest stepped back in fear until the lieutenant gestured calmingly. 'It's all right, I'm joking.'

The priest scowled. 'He is also fond of teasing people. A man born in the Year of the Monkey is rarely troubled by ill health and has very powerful *yang*. He is also capable of much deceit.' Finally the priest took the bamboo stick from Killigrew and glanced at the Chinese character inscribed on it. 'There are many dangers on the path to your karma. The greatest lies within yourself. Two spirits, always opposed, like two battling dragons fighting for control of your heart.' The priest clenched his fists and knocked the knuckles together in front of his chest. '*Yin* and *yang*: two people you will never

112

meet again but who will always be with you. When these two dragons are reconciled, you will be at one with yourself; not before.'

Which was all very interesting mumbo-jumbo, but not what Killigrew had come to learn. He decided to take another chance. *'Fan Ch'ing, fu Ming,'* he told the priest.

There was not a flicker of a reaction on the priest's face. 'The consultation is concluded,' he said with a bow.

Killigrew made for the door Li had passed through, but the priest moved quickly to block his path. 'You go through that door,' he said firmly, indicating the one the lieutenant had entered by.

Killigrew was tempted to force the issue there and then, but after what he had heard he knew he would be able to come back with a search warrant and a large contingent of the Hong Kong police at a later date. He smiled and bowed in the Oriental manner, and re-emerged into the courtyard.

Two large Chinese men dressed in black pyjamas, crimson sashes and turbans awaited him in the middle of the courtyard. One carried a large scimitar and had two shorter curved swords tucked in his sash, the other a flail made from two rods connected to either end of a third by a short length of chain.

Killigrew stopped about ten yards away. 'I don't know what the Taoist tradition is, but in the West it's considered bad joss to spill blood in a holy place.'

Smiling, the two killers bowed as one. Returning their smiles thinly, Killigrew did likewise.

Then they charged.

The man with the flail came first, whirling the iron rods skilfully about his head until they blurred. Killigrew backed up the path to receive him, forcing the man to lunge further than he had anticipated. He was already off balance when Killigrew ducked beneath the whirling rods, side-stepped as far as he could on the narrow path and extended a foot. The man tripped and fell headlong into a fishpond.

The other man came at Killigrew at once, swinging his scimitar. Killigrew caught him by the wrist, whirled him around and plucked one of the short swords from his belt. The swordsman rammed an elbow into the lieutenant's stomach and broke free. Winded, Killigrew staggered back, clutching the short sword. The swordsman advanced, grinning, while the man with the flail climbed out of the fishpond, sopping wet and cursing in Cantonese.

Killigrew backed up the path until he was between two more ponds, so they could only attack him one at a time. The swordsman came first, charging with a wild cry. He hacked at Killigrew's head. The lieutenant parried the blow with the short sword but his arm was jarred so badly he was barely able to defend himself against the next. He continued to back up until he felt one of the wooden posts supporting the veranda at the edge of the courtyard against his back.

The swordsman swung at his neck. Killigrew ducked, heard a splintering sound behind him and glanced over his shoulder to see the wooden post had been cut clean in two. The swordsman grinned. Killigrew stared at him in amazement, and then recollected himself and stabbed the man in the stomach.

As the swordsman staggered away with the short sword embedded in him, Killigrew snatched up the scimitar he had dropped and braced himself to meet the man with the flail. The killer whirled his flail until one of the chains wrapped itself about the scimitar's hilt. He pulled on the flail and Killigrew, refusing to relinquish his grip, was almost jerked off his feet. The killer flicked the other end of the flail and a blow to the back of Killigrew's head nearly robbed him of his senses. His legs crumpled and he sank to his knees. He twisted on to his back and pulled the killer down on top of him. Then he let go of the sword and gripped the central rod of the flail in both hands. The two of them rolled over and over, gripping the flail between them. The killer rolled on top and pushed the rod hard against Killigrew's throat, throttling him. As his consciousness faded, Killigrew lifted a knee into the killer's crotch. The killer relaxed enough for Killigrew to smash the rod against the bridge of his nose and throw him off.

Gripping the flail, the lieutenant rose to his feet. The killer lunged for the fallen scimitar but Killigrew kicked it into one of the ponds. He tried to swing the flail at his opponent but his handling was clumsy and he succeeded only in clipping himself across the head. As he staggered forwards, the killer smashed a fist into his chest and tore the flail from his grip. He whirled it expertly about his head and shoulders, under one arm and over the other, creating a fence of blurred steel between himself and the lieutenant. Killigrew held up a warning finger. The killer frowned in bewilderment, and Killigrew turned and ran.

At the far side of the courtyard he jumped on to the wooden handrail at the edge of the veranda, gripping a wooden support post for balance. The killer swung the flail at Killigrew's legs. He jumped over the bar, swung himself round the support post and kicked the man in the face. Then he jumped down and retreated into the shrine.

There was no sign of the old priest. Killigrew turned back to face the door and jumped up to grab hold of one of the bamboo cones. He intended to kick the killer in the chest with both feet as he came through the door, but his weight was too great and the cone broke away from the array from which it had been suspended. Killigrew landed on his feet as the killer charged through the door, whirling the flail. The lieutenant dropped the bamboo cone over his head like a cage and side-stepped.

The killer dropped the flail and drove a fist through the hoops of bamboo. Killigrew caught him by the wrist and swung him against a wooden pillar. The hoops splintered and Killigrew rammed the killer's head against the pillar until he lost consciousness.

The lieutenant was dusting his hands off when two Sikh police constables – one with a turban, the other bare-headed – charged through the door.

'Who says you can never find a bobby when you need one?' asked Killigrew.

To his astonishment, the burly constables seized him and clapped a pair of handcuffs over his wrists.

Killigrew was taken to the police office in Victoria and made to wait, still handcuffed, while one of the constables sat across the table from him with his brawny arms folded and a grim expression on his face.

'If I'm under arrest, you have to tell me what the charge is,' Killigrew told him.

Assistant Superintendent Cargill strode briskly through the door with a sheaf of papers under one arm. 'How about murder, to be going on with?'

'I acted in self-defence. Those two men attacked me without provocation.'

'Without provocation!' Cargill laughed harshly. 'You wander alone and unarmed into Tai-ping-shan and, as if that were not foolhardy enough, you blunder into a Chinese joss house and insult them by making a mockery of their religion. My job's difficult enough as it is, without Europeans making things worse for me. I have over twenty-thousand Chinese in my jurisdiction. Half of them are Triads or criminals, and the other half have no faith in British justice. If we're ever going to win their trust they have to see that Westerners and Chinese get the same treatment. Can't have one law for Europeans and another for the yellow-bellies. What the deuce were you doing? Sight-seeing?'

'I was dining at an eating stall when I saw Sir Dadabhoy Framjee's comprador, Li Cheng. I followed him on a suspicion he was up to no good and he led me to that joss house.'

'There's no law against going to joss houses, Killigrew.'

'When he was there I overheard him say, *"Fan Ch'ing, fu Ming"* to a priest. You know what that means?'

Cargill's demeanour changed at once. '"Over-throw the Ch'ing and restore the Ming",' he said, brushing his whiskers thoughtfully. 'The Triads' watchword. Take off the darbies, constable.'

The constable unlocked the handcuffs and Killigrew rubbed his chafed wrists. 'How come your men arrived so quickly?'

'Sheer luck,' said Cargill. 'They were patrolling Hollywood Road when some damned yellow-belly decided to play knock the topper off the peeler, Hong Kong-fashion.'

None the wiser, Killigrew arched an eyebrow quizzically.

'He stole Constable Gopal's turban,' the assistant superintendent explained. 'They chased him into the joss house, where he disappeared. They were about to give up the chase when one of the attendants reported a disturbance in the courtyard.'

'What about the man I knocked unconscious?'

'Don't you worry about him. He's being brought in for questioning too.'

'And the joss house? It's obviously a Triad lair.

118

Aren't you going to raid it?'

'You haven't given me enough for a search warrant. But I can arrange for a watch to be maintained on it. I have Chinese informers who can be trusted. We'll see who comes and goes. Perhaps it may lead us somewhere very interesting indeed.'

'What about Li Cheng?'

'Did you see him talk to either of the men who attacked you?'

'No.'

'I can have him brought in for questioning, but there's nothing I can charge him with.'

'You could warn Sir Dadabhoy that his comprador is suspected of having links with the Triads, if not actually a Triad himself.'

Cargill grinned. 'I'll leave that to you. You seem to be in with our Parsi friend and his daughter. Once you've done that, I want you to steer clear of this whole business, apart from coming in to identify the man who attacked you. This is police matter. You let me worry about the Triads and I'll leave you to deal with any pilongs who think they can fill Zhai Jing-mu's boots.'

'Did it ever occur to you that the pilongs and the Triads might be working together?'

'You've been talking to Framjee, haven't you? I'm well aware of his pet theories about a link between Zhai Jing-mu and the Brotherhood of Heaven, Earth and Man. But I'm a police officer. That means I deal in facts I can prove, not vague theories. If you come up with hard and fast proof of any links, let me know. Until then, I'll worry about my jurisdiction and leave you to worry about yours.'

'By all means. Before I go, do you have somewhere where I can scrub up?' He held up his bloodied right hand.

'Of course.' Cargill showed him to a back room with a washstand and ordered a servant to bring a pail of water. Killigrew washed his hand and checked his reflection in the polished surface of his tin cheroot case. He still looked dishevelled after his bout with the two Triads, but after patting his hair back into place and hoiking his high collar a couple of inches higher to conceal the bruises on his throat, he looked presentable enough.

He returned to Cargill's office to take his leave, and at that moment Constable Gopal entered, looking agitated. 'Cargill Sahib? The Triad we arrested at the joss house...?'

'Put him in a cell on his own, Constable. I'll deal with him in due course.'

'That is just the problem, *sahib*. He's escaped.'

Cargill closed his eyes as if in pain.

Killigrew had the good grace not to smirk. 'Since you seem to have everything in hand, Assistant Superintendent...'

'One moment, Killigrew. Before you go, you might like to bear in mind that if everything you've told me is true, then you killed a Triad today. They won't take kindly to that. I suggest you watch your back.'

Killigrew nodded and left.

It was a short walk from the gaol to Caine Road, on the lower slopes of Victoria Peak: straight up the aptly named Ladder Street. It was tempting to ride on a Chinese wheelbarrow, but Killigrew had not spent two years fighting slavers on the Guinea Coast only to use his fellow human beings as beasts of burden. Caine Road was the residential area for most of Hong Kong Society – a term which was understood to mean the white fraction of the island's population. The Framjee residence was set back from the main road, up a winding path through a forest of bamboo and stunted Chinese pines. The house itself was surprisingly modest for the residence of one of the wealthiest men in the world, and looked more like one of the so-called villas that were springing up all over the suburbs of London.

Killigrew rang the bell and presently the door was opened by a Sikh butler with a broken nose who looked down at him snootily. 'Yes, *sahib*?'

'I'd like to speak to Sir Dadabhoy Framjee if I may, please.'

'Sir Dadabhoy is not at home, *sahib*. If you will leave your card I shall tell him you called.'

'Who is it, Gobinda?' Peri's voice called from somewhere inside.

'A gentleman calling to see your father, *memsahib*.'

'Is that you, Mr Killigrew? Show him in, Gobinda.' Peri stood halfway down the main staircase, wearing a saffron sari and with a book held in one hand at her side. 'Did you come on foot, Mr Killigrew? It is a steep climb; you must be exhausted. Can I offer you a glass of sherbet? Or perhaps you would prefer tea?'

'Sherbet sounds perfect, Miss Dadabhoy.'

121

'Father will be home soon. You might as well wait. We shall take the sherbet on the lawn, Gobinda.'

'Yes, Miss Peri.' The butler closed the door behind Killigrew before disappearing towards the back of the house.

If Killigrew had been expecting the interior of Framjee's house to resemble a sultan's palace he was disappointed. The hallway was decorated very much *à l'Anglais*: oil paintings on the wall, all manner of knick-knacks cluttering every surface – Staffordshire pottery vying for space higgledy-piggledy with jade horses (Tang Dynasty, unless Killigrew was very much mistaken) – and an elephant's foot umbrella stand just inside the door.

'You'll have to forgive Gobinda.' Peri led the way into the drawing room. 'He is a terrible snob, but he means well.'

'Has he been with the family long?'

'As long as I can remember. Why do you ask?'

'Oh, just making polite conversation.' Killigrew followed her through the French windows out on to the terrace at the side of the house. He waited for her to sit down at the cast-iron lawn table before taking his place opposite her. 'May I ask what you're reading?'

She held up the volume she had placed on the table so he could read the spine for himself. '*Marmion*. Sir Walter Scott.'

'You like Scott?'

'A little. I prefer Omar Khayyám.'

'I'm afraid I can't claim to be familiar with his work.'

'I do not think it has been translated into English.'

'Perhaps you should try to translate it yourself?'

'I?'

'Why not?'

She shook her head. 'I do not think I could do it justice.'

'Have you tried? You should have more faith in yourself.'

Gobinda emerged with a jug of sherbet and two crystal goblets, poured out the fruit drink, and retreated inside. Killigrew sipped his sherbet and gazed about the garden. 'This is a lovely spot.'

Peri smiled thinly. 'My father's idea of an English country garden.'

'I'll trade him this view for an English country garden any day of the week.'

She put her elbows on the table, interlinked her fingers and rested her chin on the backs of her hands. 'And of all the places you have seen in your travels, which would you say is your favourite?'

'Oh, it depends on what mood I'm in. And the time of day, of course.'

'The time of day?'

He nodded. 'My perfect day would start in the Levant, with the cry of the muezzin calling the faithful to prayer. Much better than those damned church bells we have in Britain. Then, a morning walk in China in spring, with the mist amongst the orange blossoms. For luncheon, a table outside a Greek *taverna* overlooking the Aegean with a plate of kebabs cooked over a charcoal fire, a side salad of crisp white chopped onions and flavoursome tomatoes, and a glass of properly chilled dry white wine...'

'I thought one drank only red wine with red meat?'

'Only if you're a snob. In the afternoon, home to the Cornish coast in high summer, where the sea breeze takes the bite out of the worst of the sun. Then to Java to watch the sunset. Have you ever been?' She shook her head. 'You haven't lived until you've seen the sun set over the Sunda Strait.'

'And in the evening?'

'Oh, it has to be London. The theatre – something light and witty, Sheridan or Molière for preference – and a little supper at Rules with the companion of my choice.'

'And who would that be?'

'If you're ever in London, I'd be honoured if you'd let me escort you around town.'

'I think I would like that.'

The clop of horses' hoofs and the rattle of a carriage sounded from the front of the house. 'That will be my father returning,' said Peri, and the two of them waited until Framjee emerged on to the terrace.

Killigrew rose to his feet and bowed. 'Sir Dadabhoy. Peri was merely keeping me entertained while we awaited your return.'

The Parsi glanced from Killigrew to Peri. 'Mr Killigrew. To what do I owe the pleasure?'

'I was wondering if I might have a word with you?'

'By all means.'

'In private?'

Framjee joined them at the table. 'There are no secrets between my daughter and me, Mr Killigrew. Anything you consider fitting enough for my ears you must also consider fitting enough for hers.'

Killigrew resumed his seat. 'It's about your comprador, Sir Dadabhoy. Li Cheng–'

'He is no longer my comprador.'

'Meaning?'

'When I arrived at my offices this morning I found his letter of resignation waiting on my desk. Effective as of midnight last night.'

'An abrupt departure. Could he have been a spy for the pilongs?'

'It is perfectly possible. Why do you ask?'

'I saw him in Tai-ping-shan this afternoon. Some instinct made me follow him into a joss house. I heard him use a Triad watchword, and then he disappeared. I tried to follow him, but I was attacked by a couple of Chinese thugs.'

Peri's hand flew to her mouth. 'Mr Killigrew! Why did you not say something sooner? Are you hurt?'

Killigrew shook his head. 'I'm quite unharmed, miss. Fortunately for me the police arrived. There's no need for concern, I assure you.'

'If you have earned the enmity of the Triads, Mr Killigrew, I fear there is every need for concern,' said Framjee.

'It's yourself I'm concerned for, Sir Dadabhoy. You and Peri. You should know Zhai Jing-mu vowed to be avenged on Lieutenant Dwyer of the Ceylon Rifles, as well as myself, Assistant Superintendent Cargill and–'

'Me, Mr Killigrew?' Peri suggested with equanimity.

'I'm afraid so, miss.'

Framjee looked worried. 'Perhaps you should return to Bombay, my dear,' he suggested.

She shook her head. 'I will not allow myself to be ruled by fear, Father. Am I to abandon you, simply because a defeated pirate makes a hollow threat? Besides, what can he do while he is locked up in the gaol, awaiting trial?'

'Nothing, himself,' said Killigrew. 'But if he has friends in the Triads, Sir Dadabhoy, and if Li Cheng is somehow involved with them, if not actually a member of their society–'

'That is a great many ifs, Mr Killigrew,' said Peri. 'And you have not convinced me that Mr Li is a Triad. He was always very civil to me when I met him.'

'I'm sure the spider was very civil to the fly when he invited him into his parlour,' said Killigrew.

She laughed. 'I am grateful for your concern on my behalf, Mr Killigrew, but I am sure it is quite unfounded. Would you not agree, Father?'

'They *did* try to take you hostage, my child.'

'But they did not try to harm me. And they failed, and now Zhai Jing-mu is in gaol, awaiting certain execution. I do not think they would be so foolish as to try any such thing again. What could they possibly gain from it?'

'She has a point, Mr Killigrew,' said Framjee. 'Are you quite certain you are not merely jumping at shadows? With all due respect, you do have a reputation for being ... how can I put this? Excitable?'

Killigrew grimaced. 'A legacy of my Greek mother.' He looked at them both in turn, smiling happily beneath the warm sun in the genteel surroundings of the garden. It was difficult to believe that anything so terrible as kidnapping could happen here. 'Perhaps you're right,' he admitted reluctantly. 'I just want to be cautious, that's all. At least promise me you'll be vigilant?'

'I always am, Mr Killigrew,' said Framjee, and the lieutenant saw a steely glint in the Parsi's eye that reminded him here was a man who had built up two commercial empires against stiff competition. 'And we are not entirely without protection here. All of my menservants have served the Honourable East India Company as sepoys, and they are loyal to me. If Mr Li should return here looking for trouble, I can assure you he will receive a very warm reception.'

Killigrew stayed for tiffin and then took his leave of them, feeling reassured. As he walked down to Harbour Master's Wharf he saw a vessel sailing into the harbour which took his mind off his earlier concerns: one of the biggest junks he had ever seen. Amidships she had more than twenty feet of freeboard between the waterline and the top of the bulwarks, the lowest part of the bulwark which curved up sharply towards the forecastle. The poop deck towered far higher than any three-decker of Nelson's day and the mainmast stretched so high that the yellow streamers which flew from it seemed to tickle the underside of the clouds. He took out his pocket telescope and counted a dozen gun ports in one broadside. He could tell from the three tigers' heads painted on the stern it was the flagship of an Imperial admiral. He frowned: if the Governor of Canton had sent an Imperial man-o'-war to Hong Kong it might mean trouble. He transferred his attention to the decks of the *Tisiphone* and the *Hastings*. Everything seemed quiet enough: their anchor watches were in place and there was no sign of any ships beating to quarters.

One of the guns on board the junk boomed. Killigrew saw a plume of smoke blossom from the junk's side, but there was no corresponding round shot strike. After about five seconds another gun boomed, and then another. The junk was firing blank shots in a salute. The junk fired fifteen guns in all, and after a pause the guns of the shore battery fired thirteen in response. He relaxed. Whatever the junk was doing there, it was expected by the port authorities.

Killigrew paid a Tanka woman to row him back to the *Tisiphone* in her *yolo*. When he climbed up the side-ladder he found Lord Hartcliffe talking to Yelverton on the quarterdeck.

'Hello, Kit. Pleasant day?'

'It had its moments.' Killigrew nodded to the massive junk. 'Trouble?'

'Your guess is as good as mine. Admiral Huang Hai-kwang, come to talk to Rear-Admiral Collier.'

'Huang Hai-kwang? Wasn't that the name of the only captain of a junk to get the better of a British vessel in the war?'

'For which he was duly promoted,' Hartcliffe

said grimly. 'By the way, this arrived for you this afternoon.' He produced a bamboo tube about ten inches long.

Killigrew checked the seal on the end and recognised the chop of Prince Tan Dian-ning. He broke it off and extracted the tightly rolled scroll within. To his surprise, it was written in English.

'Not bad news, I hope?' asked Hartcliffe.

'That depends on the quality of Prince Tan's chef. It's an invitation to dinner.'

'Dinner?' Robertson echoed quizzically.

'Yes, sir. It's a repast quite common in most parts of the world, often used as an opportunity for entertaining guests.'

'Spare me your feeble attempts at humour, Second. What I'd like to know is what you've done to be singled out for the honour of an invitation on board Prince Tan's houseboat.'

'I'm his son, sir. That is to say, his adopted son,' Killigrew added quickly.

'You never cease to astonish me, Second. And how did you get to be the adopted son of a Chinese mandarin?'

'We met after the Opium War, sir. I foolishly allowed myself to be enticed on board one of the flower boats on the Pearl River during a stay at Canton and almost had my throat slit for my pains. His excellency was being entertained in the next compartment and he intervened to save my life. According to Confucian ethics, if you save a man's life you become responsible for anything he does after that time.' It had been Prince Tan who had taught Killigrew so much

129

about Chinese culture and philosophy. 'I expect his excellency is keen to know if I've done anything to disgrace him in the last six years.'

'Let's hope he never learns the truth, then! You trust him?'

'I owe him my life, sir.'

'That's hardly the same thing. I may not be an old China hand like yourself, but I've been warned the Chinese never do anything without an ulterior motive.'

'You might say the same of any race on God's earth, sir. It could be the Chinese authorities' wish to pass on a message through unofficial channels.'

Robertson looked dubious for a moment, but made up his mind with a grimace. 'Oh, very well, then. I think we can spare you for a couple of hours. Perhaps you may be able to learn something from his excellency that will be useful to the governor. Just remember that relations between ourselves and the Chinese are poised on a knife edge. It wouldn't take much to spark off another war – there are plenty of people on both sides of Victoria Harbour who think that what was begun during the last war was left unfinished – so mind what you say.'

'Aye, aye, sir.'

Killigrew made his way down to his cabin, washed and changed into his full dress uniform. The crew of the dinghy rowed him across to Prince Tan's floating palace.

As he drew near he glimpsed a face at one of the windows on an upper storey: a Eurasian beauty, with wide blue eyes and skin like

130

porcelain stretched tight over an angular face beneath black hair piled high on her head. Her doll-like beauty was exquisite, and Killigrew found himself wondering if he would be invited to meet her once he was on board. Then a hand – too large to be hers – pulled down a blind and concealed her from view.

The guards on the houseboat's gallery had been instructed to expect him and they made no challenge when the dinghy approached. A Chinese houseboy emerged and bowed as Killigrew stepped on to the landing stage.

'Lieutenant Killigrew? His highness is expecting you.'

'You lads had better get back to the *Tisiphone*,' Killigrew told the crew of the dinghy. 'Come back for me at seven bells.' He had to be back on duty at eight, and there was no harm in letting Prince Tan's men know he would be missed. The dinghy's crew rowed away and the houseboy escorted Killigrew to one of the upper decks.

The interior of the houseboat was exquisitely decorated. There was not a single beam or bulkhead that was not intricately carved into landscapes, dragons, Chinese lions and flamingos. The houseboy ushered Killigrew into a room luxuriously furnished with silk cushions and hung with crimson silk.

'Please to wait here. His highness will join you presently.' The houseboy left and Killigrew, well acquainted with Chinese customs, kept his cocked hat on: the Chinese considered it bad manners to bare one's head. He whiled away the time by studying a hanging scroll painted with a

131

landscape of mountains and lakes, with a written scroll on either side of it. He could hear someone plucking delicate notes from a *pipa* somewhere upstairs and he wondered if it was the Eurasian beauty he had seen a few moments ago.

'Hands up!' a voice screeched behind him in English.

Killigrew whirled round and within an instant his dress-sword was in his hand. He searched the room for his would-be assailant but there was no one, just a bird in an ornate cage which hung from the ceiling. He moved closer to investigate and saw that it was a mynah bird.

'Jobbernowl!' the bird sneered in English.

Killigrew brushed the tip of his sword against the bars of the cage, so gently that the bird was not even alarmed. ' "Who's a pretty boy, then?" is more traditional,' he murmured.

'An amusing bird, is it not?' asked another voice.

Killigrew turned to see an old man in richly brocaded robes had entered the room behind him. His face was lined with age, his long, thin moustachios shot through with silver, and there were deep bags under his eyes which gave him a soulful look. When the old man saw the weapon in Killigrew's hand, alarm showed in his features for perhaps a fraction of a second before he composed himself once more.

Killigrew quickly sheathed his sword. 'I humbly offer you my most profound apologies, your highness,' he said. He did not offer to shake hands, knowing that the Chinese considered it an unhygienic barbarian custom, but bowed in the

Oriental manner. 'It was not my intention to dishonour myself by drawing my weapons in your exalted home.'

'Jobbernowl!' said the mynah bird. 'Hands up!'

Prince Tan returned the bow. 'I am to blame. The bird was a gift from a business acquaintance. I should have taught it better manners. It is only natural that you should seek to defend yourself upon hearing such importunate language.'

'Your apology is wholly unnecessary,' said Killigrew.

Prince Tan gestured to the table. 'Please be seated, my honoured barbarian son.'

They sat down facing one another at the table and an *amah* girl entered with a tea tray as if on cue, and started to go through the ritual of serving out tea.

'I'm still in your debt,' said Killigrew.

'As I told you seven years ago, in saving your life, I was trusting my own judgement in the belief that you would do nothing to dishonour that trust.'

'I hope that my actions since we last met have done honour to my Chinese father.'

'I am sure that they have; and that they will continue to do so in future. I trust my barbarian son is well?' asked the prince.

'Very well, your highness, thank you.'

'His virility undiminished?'

Killigrew smiled and exchanged glances with the *amah*, who lowered her eyes demurely. 'Not so you'd notice. And yours?'

Tan sighed. 'I am an old man now, alas. What is

133

it you barbarians say?'

'The spirit is willing, but the flesh is weak?'

'Quite so. Have some tea.'

'Jobbernowl!' squawked the mynah bird.

Tan smiled sadly. 'Since you are here, perhaps you could explain to me what "jobbernowl" means?'

'Oh, it's a colloquialism for a fool or an idiot,' said Killigrew. 'You used to hear it all the time when I was a younker. Seems to have gone out of fashion nowadays, though. I can't remember the last time I heard someone use it.'

'You see?' Tan asked the bird. 'Every time you use that barbarian word you insult one of my guests.'

'Be quiet! Jobbernowl!'

Tan turned back to Killigrew, who grinned.

'I understand my barbarian son recently distinguished himself by the capture of the notorious pirate Zhai Jing-mu?' asked Tan.

'I had the good joss to be in the right place at the right time.'

'Such is karma. But you must beware. Zhai Jing-mu has many powerful friends; and an enemy of his is an enemy of theirs. You have heard of the Brotherhood of Heaven, Earth and Man?'

'The Triads?' Killigrew nodded. 'Yes, I believe a couple of them introduced themselves to me this afternoon.'

'So I have heard.'

'News travels fast. What can you tell me about Admiral Huang?'

'Ah. I was wondering when you would ask me

134

that question. Admiral Huang is here to offer Rear-Admiral Collier a chance for barbarian vessels and vessels of his Imperial Majesty's navy to work together to wreak righteous destruction on the pilongs.'

'Sounds good to me. *If* that really is what the admiral wants.'

Tan smiled. 'You understand the subtleties of the civilised mind well for a barbarian. There are two factions in the Imperial Grand Council in the Forbidden City. The one which is in favour at the moment advises a policy of harmonious compromise with the barbarians. But there is another faction, foolish men who can only remember the loss of face which resulted from the barbarian affair.' The 'barbarian affair' was how the Chinese dismissively referred to the Opium War. 'These men are unable to see that a second war will be even more disastrous for the Celestial Kingdom than the first was. Admiral Huang is such a man. If he is proposing a policy of co-operation between our navies, then it would be foolish not to wonder if he had an ulterior motive for doing so. Perhaps you should ask what the price for such co-operation might be.'

Killigrew sipped his tea and studied Tan thoughtfully. 'What *is* the price for such co-operation?'

'That Zhai Jing-mu be handed over to the authorities in Canton for trial.'

Killigrew laughed. 'Governor Bonham would never agree to that. Besides, what difference does it make whether Zhai Jing-mu's tried in Victoria or Canton? The penalty for piracy is the same under British law as it is in the Manchu Code, if not the manner of its execution.'

'Admiral Huang has been pursuing Zhai Jing-mu for four years, and in that time never once came close to capturing him. Yet you captured him within days of reaching the South China Sea.'

'Sheer luck,' said Killigrew. 'The admiral thinks I made him lose face?'

Tan smiled humourlessly. 'Do you think the pilongs will sit back and allow you to execute Zhai Jing-mu without making any attempt to free him?'

'They'd never break him out of Victoria Gaol.'

'Agreed. It would be far easier to rescue him while he was *en route* to Canton.'

Killigrew was starting to see what his host was driving at. He knew Tan would never make such an accusation openly, but he was curious to see how far the mandarin was prepared to go. 'True. But the question is purely academic, as Bonham won't agree for Zhai Jing-mu to be tried anywhere but in Victoria.'

'Indeed. I was merely speculating concerning Huang's motives. Be wary of the admiral, my barbarian son. His faction may be out of favour at court at present, but that may not always be the case. And he is a dangerous man to have for an enemy.'

'That's fine by me,' Killigrew said coolly. 'So am I.'

136

V:

Yolo

Molineaux and Ågård put the two unconscious sailors on either side of the wheelbarrow outside the Britain's Boast, one of Victoria's many waterfront taverns.

'All right, take them down to the wharf,' Ågård told the coolie pushing the barrow.

'*Hai.*' The coolie ducked his head and pushed the barrow before him. Molineaux and Ågård sauntered along behind him. There were worse jobs in Her Majesty's navy than gathering up the drunks after a run ashore, but by and large Molineaux would have preferred to be one of the unconscious men on the barrow.

One of the boatswain's mates waited in the cutter tied up at the wharf. There was already a pile of drunk men amidships, snoring or groaning. 'Two more for you, Mr Fanning,' said Ågård, as Molineaux helped the coolie carry the drunks from the wheelbarrow to the cutter.

'We're still one shy,' said the boatswain's mate.

'Who is it?'

'Who do you think?'

'Jem Dando,' Molineaux sighed.

The boatswain's mate nodded. 'I've got to get this lot back aboard, but I don't have to report him run until the morning watch. If he's not back

137

by then, though ... then it'll be a matter for the corporal and the marines.'

'We could keep on looking for him,' suggested Ågård.

'If you think he's worth it,' agreed the boatswain's mate.

'We've tried everywhere. The Britannia, the Golden Tavern, the Britain's Boast, the British Queen, the Caledonian, the Eagle, the Commercial, the Waterloo...'

'What about Labtat's?' asked Fanning.

'Labtat's?'

'Labtat's Tavern.' The boatswain's mate laughed. 'I can tell you two ain't old China hands if you've never heard of Labtat's. A cable's length up the road, then hard-a-starboard. You can't miss it. Just keep an ear open for the sound of splintering furniture and breaking heads.'

'Labtat's it is, then.' Molineaux clapped Ågård on the shoulder. 'I'll look for him. No need for us both to lose sleep, Olly. You get back to the *Tizzy*; if I find Jem I'll hire a *yolo*.'

Ågård nodded and climbed into the cutter. As the boat pulled back to the *Tisiphone*, Molineaux paid the coolie off and made his way along the waterfront. Before he had gone a hundred yards he heard English voices and what sounded like a West Country lilt. The voices came from one of the *yolos* crowded in the harbour. Chickens clucked and squawked incongruously.

He stood at the edge of the dockside and peered into the darkness. 'That you, Jem?'

Whoever was in the *yolo* was too preoccupied to hear him. 'Hold her down, Zeke.'

138

'Let me go!' a Chinese woman squealed in English. 'You bloody bastard barbarian! Let me go!'

'Yeow! Damned hellspite bit me!'

The man with the West Country accent laughed. 'We'll soon learn her some manners...'

The woman screamed.

'Stow your gaff, bitch, or we really will give you something to scream about.'

That didn't sound like Dando. Molineaux heard the sound of material being ripped. A moment later he had jumped down on to the deck of the nearest *yolo* and was making his way across the tightly packed boats to the scene of the commotion. He was aware of dirty Oriental faces peering out at him from under awnings, but no one made any attempt to stop him. That was the problem with the Chinese: a child could get murdered under their noses, and most of the time none of them would lift a finger to stop it. Karma, they called it.

The small boats rocked under his weight, but he jumped nimbly from deck to deck until he had reached his destination. He stood in the *yolo*'s bow, next to the chicken coop where a couple of bantams clucked and flapped in agitation. Under the boat's awning, two men were holding down a young Tanka woman. One of them held a knife to her throat while the other forced her legs apart and kneeled between them.

Molineaux felt rage boil in his blood. 'Let her up,' he snarled.

The two men stared at each other and then slowly turned their heads to meet Molineaux's gaze. 'It's just some damned blackamoor,' sneered one.

'Walk away, shipmate,' growled the other.

'I ain't your shipmate,' said Molineaux. 'And as you old China hands are always so fond of saying: "no can do".'

'Get rid of him, Zeke.'

One of the men rose to his feet, hitched up his trousers, and swaggered across to where Molineaux stood, picking up a gaff-hook on the way. 'You got wax in your ears, boy? Get away from here!'

Molineaux motioned for the two men to precede him with a mockingly grandiloquent gesture. 'After you.'

'You're asking for it!' Zeke swung the gaff at Molineaux's head. The seaman ducked under the blow and drove a fist into the other's stomach. Zeke doubled up, Molineaux punched him on the jaw, and Zeke fell to the deck, dazed.

The other man left the woman and pushed himself to his feet to advance on Molineaux. 'You're making a big mistake, nigger. Do you know who I am?'

'Firstly, *you're* the one making a big mistake – by calling me "nigger". And secondly, you're asking the wrong question.'

The man furrowed his brow. In the faint glow from the distant harbour lights, Molineaux could see he was in his mid-thirties or thereabouts, with a face which was mostly covered by a greasy beard. He looked well-dressed, but he was clearly no gentleman. 'The wrong question...?'

Molineaux nodded. 'The question ain't: do I

know who you are? The question is: do I give a fish's tit?'

The man threw a punch at Molineaux's head. The seaman ducked, but the man's punch had been a feint and he caught Molineaux with a left hook. The seaman went down and fell on the chicken coop. It splintered under his weight and a hen flapped into the air. Molineaux caught it by the legs and threw it at the man's face. The man cried out in alarm and took a step back. He tripped over the gunwale and fell into the water between two *yolos* with a splash.

'Look out!' yelled the woman.

Molineaux turned to see the dim glint of light on the six barrels of a pepperbox which Zeke had produced from somewhere. The seaman launched himself at Zeke, but even the few feet which separated them might as well have been miles.

The gun went off, but not before the woman had kicked Zeke in the wrist so that the pistol discharged itself harmlessly into the gunwale.

'Bitch!' Zeke tried to pistol-whip her, but she scurried nimbly out of the way. A moment later Molineaux caught him by the wrist and forced him back down. As they rolled over and over on the cluttered deck, Molineaux glimpsed embers glowing through a gap in the door of a small stove. He forced Zeke's arm down until the back of his hand came into contact with the hot-plate on top of the stove. Zeke yelled and dropped the pistol. Molineaux punched him in the stomach, and jumped to his feet. He grabbed Zeke by the shirt-front, hoisted him up, and punched him in

141

the jaw. Zeke tottered back and fell over the gunwale, landing on the head of the other man who was trying to climb back aboard.

Molineaux retrieved the fallen pistol and stood over them both with one foot on the gunwale. The bearded man got one hand on the gunwale and glared up at Molineaux. 'I knows you. You'm the nigger sailor on the *Tisiphone.*'

Molineaux stamped viciously on his fingers and aimed the pepperbox at his head. 'If I hear you using that word one more time, mister, I'll blow a hole in your head so big we'll all be able to see what kind of shit you've got where most coves keep their brains.'

With a snarl, the bearded man began to swim between the *yolos* after Zeke as he made his way to the quayside. 'You bain't be hearing the last of this, matey!'

'You got me quaking in my boots,' sneered Molineaux. He dropped the pepperbox overboard and turned to the woman. 'You oh-kay, miss?' Molineaux had spent two years on a Yankee brig and his talk was laced with Americanisms; the Tanka girl must have met a few American sailors herself, for she seemed to understand him.

She nodded. '*Hai.* Yes. Thank you.' She glanced down at her torn clothes. 'Bloody bastard barbarians! They tearum my shirtee!' Unabashed by Molineaux's presence, she took off the tattered remains and tossed them aside to ferret for something else to wear. Even in the dim light Molineaux could see enough to remind him that he had not had a woman since Portsmouth.

She was fastening on a fresh shirt when she saw him staring at her. 'What matter? You no see cowchillo without clothe before?'

'Not one as cute as you.'

She unfastened her shirt once more to display her breasts to him. 'You takee alla look-see you wantchee. My no shamee.'

'Evidently not, miss. They're very fine.' He turned away to start tidying up the debris the fight had caused.

Pouting, she fastened her shirt once more. 'What for you helpee me?'

'I wouldn't want you thinking all barbarians are pigs.'

'You devil-slave. What for you carum?'

He stood up and rounded on her angrily. 'Hey! I ain't no devil, and I sure as hell ain't no slave.' He shook his head, and chuckled. 'First time I ever bashed a man with a chicken. Who were those coves, anyway?'

'Him Missee Ingersoll, him captainee of number-one opium hulk at Cap-sing-mun.'

'You think maybe he'll come back?'

'Him no savvy me. Alla China cow-chillo lookee alla same to barbarians.'

Molineaux grinned. 'I wish that were true. If all Chinese girls looked the same as you, I think I'd retire here.'

'Him savvy you, though. If I be you, I be plenty scarum. Him makee muchee trub for you.'

'He can try.' Molineaux became aware that he was being watched. He casually picked up the gaff-hook and whirled, but it was only the hen he had thrown at Ingersoll, perched on the gunwale

143

with its head cocked on one side as it glared accusingly at Molineaux. 'You still here?' he asked it. 'I'm surprised you didn't make a bid for freedom while you still had the chance, before you ended up in someone's cooking pot.'

The woman picked up the chicken and carried it back to the wrecked coop. The other chickens were also running loose on deck. 'They b'long here; they savvy they catchee plenty chow. What for you b'long here, devil-slave?'

'My name's Wes,' he told her irritably, as he started to jury-rig the chicken coop with a ball of twine he found.

'My namee Mei-rong.'

'Pleased to meet you, Mei-rong.'

'You no answer my question. What for you b'long here?'

'If I thought you could cook chicken the way my mum does, maybe I'd b'long here long time.'

'That not kind of hunger my thinkee you wantchee satisfy.' She crouched down next to him to help and put one hand on his.

He was tempted to lean forward and kiss her, but he shook his head. 'You don't owe me a thing, Mei-rong. If I took advantage of your gratitude I'd be no better than them two thugs we just chased away.'

'Is plenty different when cow-chillo willing,' she pointed out.

He stood up. 'Don't think I ain't tempted. But I've got to find one of my shipmates.'

'You no likee China cow-chillo?'

'I likee you very much, Mei-rong.'

'Then what trub?' She stood up on tip-toes to

144

put her arms around his neck. He dipped his head to kiss her and a moment later she had wrapped her lithe legs around his hips, giggling. Then the two of them fell to the deck.

'Ah, what the hell?' Molineaux growled between lingering kisses. 'Jem Dando can find his own way home.'

Killigrew was drilling the starboard watch in cutlass exercises the following morning when a boat came alongside from the shore and Assistant Superintendent Cargill climbed aboard. He conversed briefly with Hartcliffe on the quarterdeck and the first lieutenant nodded and directed one of the midshipmen to show the police officer down to Robertson's day room.

Killigrew concentrated on his work. 'Come on, Dando! Get that blade up! You're supposed to be swapping thrusts with a pilong, not doing petit point needlework!'

'Sorry, sir. Had a run ashore last night. I'm feeling a little the worse for wear.'

'If this were for real, Dando, do you think that excuse would wash with your opponent?'

'No, sir.'

'Have a heart, sir,' said Molineaux. 'You know how difficult it is to get your weapon up when you've got gallon distemper.'

The others laughed. Killigrew smiled tolerantly, but before he could reply Hartcliffe called him across to the quarterdeck. 'Keep them at it, Fanning,' Killigrew told the boatswain's mate. 'If any of these lads have the blue devils, we'll soon sweat it out of them.' He made his way across to where Hartcliffe stood. 'Which way does the wind lie?'

'The Old Man wants to see you in his day room. Seems one of the men in your watch assaulted a member of the public last night.'

'How do they know it was one of the men in my watch? Have they got a good description?'

'Well, he was black and wearing pusser's slops.' Killigrew sighed. 'Molineaux!'

The seaman broke off his cutlass drill and crossed to the deck at the double. 'Sir?'

'Accompany me to the captain's day room, if you please.'

'Aye, aye, sir.' Molineaux followed the lieutenant down the after-hatch. 'Am I in the rattle, sir?'

'That depends. Someone answering your description assaulted a member of the public last night.'

'Oh, that. I can explain everything, sir—'

'Save it for the captain, Molineaux.'

In the day room, Robertson stood by the window while Cargill sat in one of the chairs by the table. 'I understand you wanted to speak to me and Able Seaman Molineaux, sir?'

'Yes, Mr Killigrew. Mr Cargill here tells me that a gentleman was roughly assaulted on the waterfront last night by a black sailor. The gentleman has two fingers broken in his right hand—'

'He weren't no gentleman, Cap'n,' said Molineaux.

'Pipe down!' snapped Killigrew. 'You'll speak when spoken to. Hoist in?'

'Aye, aye, sir.'

'Well, Molineaux,' said Robertson, 'am I to take it that you are admitting to this crime?'

'I was the one what done it, sir, but it weren't no crime. It was self-defence. This cove Ingersoll and his mate were trying to do me in.'

'And why, may I ask, were they trying to do that?' asked Cargill.

'Maybe you should ask them what they were doing on the waterfront in the first place?' suggested Molineaux.

'The waterfront is a public highway, sailor,' said Cargill. 'They had as much right to be there as any man.'

'Yeah, except when I found them they weren't on the quayside itself, they was in one of the *yolos*, trying to rape a Tanka girl. I went to help her and that's when they turned on me.'

'Well!' said Robertson. 'I'd say that puts an entirely different complexion on things. Wouldn't you agree, Mr Cargill?'

'If this man is telling the truth.' Cargill nodded at Molineaux.

Killigrew could see another sharp retort welling up inside the seaman. He caught Molineaux's eye and shook his head infinitesimally. The seaman bit his tongue. 'Dismissed, Molineaux.'

'Aye, aye, sir.' Molineaux saluted Robertson and Killigrew, shot a disdainful glance at Cargill, and went out.

'Well?' said Robertson.

'Sir, barring occasional flashes of insub-ordination, Able Seaman Molineaux is one of our most reliable and honest hands. I might remind you that he's been twice mentioned in Admiralty dispatches. If he says this fellow Ingersoll was trying to rape a Tanka girl, I believe him.'

'I'm inclined to agree,' said Robertson. 'So, Mr Cargill, what do you want to do now? You needn't expect me to punish one of my hands for an act of chivalry, but if you want to take Able Seaman Molineaux into custody, I can't stop you. What I can do, however, is raise merry hell with your superiors, and believe me I shall if I have to.'

Cargill grimaced. 'I'm sure that won't be necessary, sir. I'll have a discreet word with Captain Ingersoll, make it clear to him that he's only likely to embarrass himself if he pushes the matter any further. I'm sure he'll see sense and let it drop.'

'Let it drop!' exclaimed Robertson. 'Aren't you going to charge him with attempted rape? Assault?'

'It was only a Tanka girl...'

'I see,' said Killigrew. 'What was it you said to me yesterday about having one law for Europeans and another for the Chinese?'

Cargill squirmed. 'I'm afraid it's not that simple, Mr Killigrew. Captain Ingersoll is the master of the *Buchan Prayer*, Mr Bannatyne's receiving ship, and Mr Bannatyne is an extremely influential man in these parts.'

'You mean when he says "Jump!" you ask: "How high?" ' said Killigrew.

'That's about the long and the short of it, sir, yes,' Cargill admitted with disarming candour. 'You know Bonham's predecessor left under

148

something of a cloud? Everyone in Hong Kong knows it was Bannatyne who swung that. The story is the two of them had a row over some matter of dealing with the Chinese and Sir John refused to take Bannatyne's advice. Six months later – as much time as it takes news to get to the Colonial Office and back – Sir John was forced to resign. And it was Bannatyne who recommended Bonham as his replacement. Now, if you gentlemen wish to take on the *tai-pan* of Grafton, Bannatyne and Co., that's your prerogative. But I'd be obliged if you'd keep me out of it.'

'Very well, Mr Cargill,' sighed Robertson. 'I can see you're in a difficult position. If Ingersoll's prepared to drop the matter, then so am I. Sounds to me like the damned scoundrel got his just desserts. Two fingers broken, eh?' The commander chuckled. 'Good for Molineaux.'

Killigrew escorted Cargill back up on deck. 'I'm given to understand that the trial of Zhai Jing-mu has been postponed yet again. Seeing that it's over a week since we arrested him, might I ask what the delay is?'

Cargill sighed with the air of a man who was weary of having to answer the same question over and over again. 'I've been gathering evidence...'

'Gathering evidence? We caught him in the act. I hardly see what further proof is needed.'

'I see your point of view, Killigrew. Now please see mine: Zhai Jing-mu has slipped through our fingers too many times in the past. I want to be one hundred per cent certain of a conviction before he goes to trial. Not ninety-seven per cent, not ninety-eight per cent, not even ninety-nine per cent. One hundred per cent. Over the past three years he's done thousands of pounds worth of damage to the China trade, not to mention the loss of life he's responsible for. We don't want another three years of his reign of terror because of some legal technicality.'

'When you put it like that... By the way, I spoke to Sir Dadabhoy Framjee yesterday. He tells me that Li Cheng resigned as his comprador yesterday morning, and hasn't been seen at the Framjee factory since.'

'Now that *is* interesting,' agreed Cargill, stroking his whiskers. 'I shall certainly have to have a word with this fellow Li.' He climbed down into the waiting boat. 'And I expect you to stay well clear of the whole thing, Mr Killigrew. If you see this fellow Li anywhere, send word to me. Understand?'

Killigrew nodded. 'I think I'm starting to understand how this colony works.'

For a moment it looked as if Cargill might reply, but then he scowled. 'All right, take me back ashore.'

Killigrew watched the boat for a moment and then turned to the boatswain's mate. 'Pass the word for Molineaux, Fanning.'

'Aye, aye, sir. Wes! Mr Killigrew wants a word.'

The lieutenant wandered over to the taffrail and Molineaux joined him there a moment later. 'Well, Molineaux, it looks like you managed to wriggle out of it this time.'

The seaman grinned. 'Don't I always?' he smirked, and then saw Killigrew's face. 'I mean, glad to hear it, sir. Thank you.'

As Killigrew gazed across to where Admiral Huang's junk was still at anchor, he saw a Chinese woman being lowered to a chop-boat tied up below. From her fine silk robes with rich brocade, it was obvious that she was a gentlewoman, or at least a courtesan at the peak of her career.

Molineaux saw her too. 'Cool the blower with the gammy dew-beaters, sir! She's a bit young to have gout, ain't she?'

'Golden lotus feet, Molineaux,' said Killigrew. 'The Chinese find small feet attractive in women, so they take the girls when they're young, break the bones in their feet, and then bind them tightly so they can't grow more than a few inches in length. I understand the Manchus are trying to ban the practice; you have to give them credit for that.'

Lord Hartcliffe snorted. 'Damnable savages! Subjecting their women to such an unhealthy, constricting torture merely to make them conform to some unnatural ideal of feminine beauty!'

'Pull!' urged Mrs Bannatyne. 'Pull harder!' She gripped one of the posts of her four-poster bed as her *amah* hauled on the stays of her corset. 'Tighter!'

'Is too tight!' protested the *amah*. 'I hurtee you!'

'I'll decide when it's too tight. It's supposed to be eighteen inches.'

'But your waist is not eighteen inches!'

Mrs Bannatyne glared at her.

The *amah* flushed. 'But you have got beautiful shape, Missee Bannatyne. Not like my poor, fat, pig-like lump of body.'

'Spare me your Oriental humility. I've seen skeletons with more flesh on them than you. Now are you going to pull, or do I have to get Mr Shen in here to do it for you?'

In the mirror over the dressing table, Mrs Bannatyne saw a trace of fear in the *amah*'s eyes. 'I do it, Missee Bannatyne.' She hauled on the stays again, but it was no good: any tighter and Mrs Bannatyne would be in danger of fainting halfway through the evening. Plenty of girls did, to give dashing young men a chance to catch them before they hit the floor, but at twenty-five Mrs Bannatyne considered herself too old for such games, even if she had not been a married woman. She was just going to have to accept that she was a fat and frumpy twenty-two inches around the waist and the days when she had been the belle of every ball were far behind her.

She finished dressing and the *amah* was helping her pin up her hair when there came a knock on the bedroom door. 'All right, Bai-ling,' she told the *amah*. 'You can go now. I can manage the rest.'

The *amah* bowed and went out. 'Come in,' Mrs Bannatyne called through the open door.

She expected her husband to come through the door, but it was Captain Verran. In the dresser mirror she saw him lean nonchalantly against the door lintel with his arms folded and an insouciant leer on his face. 'Good evening, ma'am. May I say you look as ravishing as ever?'

'You may,' she replied distantly, wishing she had not dismissed the *amah*. Captain Verran's attentions were all very flattering – there was no denying he was a handsome fellow – and if she had not been married she might have been tempted to encourage his advances. He had a roguish charm which both repelled and attracted her at the same time. 'Is my husband back yet?' she asked.

Verran shook his head. 'He's spending the night on board the *Buchan Prayer*. He asked me to give you his apologies.' Verran took a step into the room and kicked the door to behind him with his heel. 'So it's just you and I tonight.'

'And the servants.' She rose from her chair to face him. 'I think it would be more appropriate for you to spend the night on the *Golden Dragon*.'

'In my cramped cabin? When you have so many rooms in this big, fine house of your husband's? You could give the servants the night off, you know.'

'Captain Verran! I shan't report this conversation to my husband, but I think you had better leave at once.'

'Your husband!' Verran spat contemptuously. 'You think I don't know he neglects you?'

'If he does, that is between my husband and myself.' She did not fool herself into thinking that her marriage to her husband had been a fairy-tale romance; more in the way of a business arrangement between her father and her bridegroom. As the daughter of the great John Keane she had always been aware that she could not hope to marry for love. But her husband treated her with respect, albeit a respect marked with cold formality, even when he was fulfilling his marital duties: to him, love-making seemed a chore necessary to provide himself with an heir to his financial empire, rather than an opportunity to display any warmth or affection towards his wife. But as the wife of the *tai-pan* she lived in a state of luxury comparable with that of the lesser European royalty. She knew she had no cause for complaint. Besides, she had sworn to love, honour and obey her husband, and it was a vow she meant to keep.

Verran moved closer to her. 'I could make you happy. Happier than he's ever made you.'

'You could ruin us both. Please, Captain Verran. Do not make me ask you to leave a second time.'

He stared intensely into her eyes with a fervour that sent a chill down her spine – a chill which had nothing to do with desire and everything to do with fear – and for a moment she feared he might try to force himself on her there and then. She reached behind her and picked a brooch with a long pin off the dresser. But then his customary smile slipped greasily across his face and he backed off.

'You need time to think about it, I can tell. That's fine by me. You'll come round to my way of thinking sooner or later. You know you want it.'

'I think I am a better judge of what I do or do not want, Captain Verran,' she said tightly. 'Good night to you, sir.'

He grinned and touched the peak of his cap to her, before turning on his heel and heading for

154

the door. He was halfway through it when he stopped and turned. Her heart pounded with fear, but he stayed with one hand on the doorknob. 'Oh, I forgot to mention. Your husband asked me to tell you he wishes you to throw a ball at the factory next month. On the twenty-fourth.'

'A ball?' she echoed in astonishment. Her husband never threw balls.

Verran nodded. 'The finest this colony's ever known.'

'It's short notice, I must say. The twenty-fourth ... that's less than four weeks away!'

'The invitations are to go out before the end of the week.'

'Who's to be on the guest list?'

'Why, everyone who's anyone. Mr and Mrs Bonham, naturally, and General Staveley and his family. The other traders, of course, and the officers of the garrison. Oh, and the officers of any navy ships in the harbour. I dare say Mr Bannatyne will let you have the full guest list at his earliest convenience.' Verran touched the peak of his cap again, and went out.

Mrs Bannatyne sat down with her head swimming. The news that her husband intended to host a ball had put all thoughts of Verran's unwelcome advances from her mind. When she had been a child, in the old days before Sir George Grafton had retired to Britain, the balls at the factory in Canton had been the finest in all Hong Kong. Social entertainments were a vital part of the China trade, a chance for the tea merchants to show off their wealth and opulence. In China, appearances were everything. Perception was more important than reality. If a man appeared to be bankrupt, then he might as well *be* bankrupt. But since Bannatyne had taken over the day-to-day running of the company, balls had become a thing of the past. It was Bannatyne's way of saying that Grafton, Bannatyne & Co. was far too successful to need to impress anyone.

She wondered if her husband *was* bankrupt. If he was, she would be the last person to find out. He never let her know anything about the business. At the beginning she had wanted to become involved, not for power or for riches, but simply so that she would have something to talk about with a man with whom she had nothing in common. She had chosen his work because nothing else seemed to interest him, but he insisted on keeping her at arm's length.

She sighed. As the hostess, she would be expected to make all the arrangements. Until now she had often wished they would hold balls again at the Hong Kong factory, if only so she had something to do with her time. She had never hosted a ball in her life, but she suspected they required a great deal of organising.

'Have I done something to offend you?' Peri asked in a low voice, so that none of the others would hear.

'To upset me?' Killigrew was genuinely astonished. 'No. What makes you think that?'

'I cannot help thinking you have been avoiding me over the past month. Turning down my father's invitations. Turning down *my* invitations.'

'Please don't take it personally. My duties on board the *Tisiphone* have kept me busy.'

'Lord Hartcliffe has had plenty of time for social occasions.'

He smiled. 'Ah, well, that's seniority for you.'

She was not convinced. It was obvious something was troubling him, but he did not elaborate, pretending to concentrate on turning the mutton chops on the barbecue he and Hartcliffe had built.

It had been Prince Tan's idea to hold a picnic on the south coast of Hong Kong, on the rocky beach at Chek-py-wan where the off-shore island of Ap-li-chau provided shelter from the sea breezes. The gathering was mixed, but predominantly young: Prince Tan and Framjee were the oldest ones present, sitting some way off and talking confidentially. Peri's father had told her he wanted Prince Tan's help in setting up a school for the children of destitute Chinese families on Hong Kong, and he was obviously making the most of this opportunity. Mr Strachan had already erected the tent he used as a darkroom and was setting up his camera on a tripod to take some photographic pictures. Elsewhere young clerks and military officers flirted with the daughters of traders and senior officers and diplomats. Only Hartcliffe seemed aloof from such flirtations, sitting with Mr Cavan, one of the young midshipmen from the *Tisiphone*.

Peri glanced at Killigrew again, but his attention had strayed to where the Reverend Ultzmann was talking with a conspiratorial air to a young Eurasian beauty. Peri instantly felt jealous. 'You think she is attractive?' she asked Killigrew challengingly.

'The Eurasian girl? Don't you? Who is she?'

'I do not know, I am sure. She came with Prince Tan.'

He nodded. 'I saw her on his houseboat when I dined with him last month.'

'Your chops are burning.'

'Hm? Oh, Lor'!' He quickly lifted one of the chops from the griddle with a toasting fork and she held out a plate from one of the picnic hampers for him to drop it on. A moment later the second chop had joined it, and she handed the plate to Lieutenant Dwyer, the young officer of the Ceylon Rifles who had helped Cargill take Zhai Jing-mu into custody.

'Thank you, Miss Dadabhoy,' said Dwyer. 'Has anyone told you how ravishing you look today?'

'No.' She gave Killigrew a hard look, but he was oblivious, staring after Ultzmann and the Eurasian girl as they wandered out of sight behind a rocky outcrop further down the beach. 'They haven't.'

'You've been invited to this ball at the Bannatynes' next week?'

She nodded. 'Who has not?' The forthcoming ball was the talk of all Hong Kong. Balls were common enough, but this one was different: this was the first ball at the Grafton, Bannatyne & Co. factory in over a decade.

'I was wondering if I might be so bold as to ask for the honour of a dance with you?' asked Dwyer.

'But of course,' she said, giving Killigrew a sidelong glance to see how he would react. He was not even listening, curse him. 'Which one? You're the first man to ask me, so you may have your pick.'

'You astonish me, Miss Dadabhoy. I would have thought that young beaux would be queuing up to partner you.'

'Apparently not.'

'Then, since etiquette demands I dance with you no more than three times in one evening, I should like the first waltz, the last waltz, and any polka you care to choose.'

'I fear a polka might prove to be a little too strenuous for me, but you may have one of the waltzes.'

'I shall look forward to it.' Dwyer took one of her hands and kissed it gallantly. As he leaned forward, his chops slid off his carelessly tilted plate. They plummeted towards the hem of Peri's sari and she jumped back instinctively, tripping over. She felt herself falling backwards, and then a strong pair of arms had caught her.

'Are you all right?' asked Killigrew.

'Yes. Thank you,' she said breathlessly.

'My pleasure.'

'Oh, gosh, I'm sorry,' said Dwyer. 'That was clumsy of me.'

'Yes,' Peri agreed a little impatiently. 'Thank you, Mr Killigrew, but you don't need to hold me now.'

'Sorry.' He set her back on her feet.

Dwyer looked mournfully at the chops on the ground at his feet. 'Oh, rot it! I say, Killigrew. Any

159

chance of some fresh chops?'

Killigrew sighed. 'By all means...' He made as if to fetch some more from the food hamper, but Peri caught him firmly by the arm and pulled him away.

'Help yourself,' she told Dwyer, linking her arm through Killigrew's and leading him away.

'Where are we going?' asked Killigrew.

'For a walk.' She led him down the beach, in the opposite direction from which Ultzmann and the Eurasian girl had headed. 'Lieutenant Dwyer has asked me to dance with him at the Bannatynes' ball.'

'Good for him.'

'He is rather handsome, do you not think?'

'He's not my type,' Killigrew responded, deadpan.

She released his arm with a gesture of frustration. She had been planning what she was going to say to him today ever since she had learned he would be attending the picnic, and he was ruining it all, confusing her with his flippancy and apparent indifference. She took a deep breath and told herself to start again. 'Mr Killigrew, it may have escaped your attention, but I have a great deal of regard for you.'

'And I for you, Miss Dadabhoy.'

'You do not show it.'

'What would you have me do?'

She glanced back down the beach to where the others sat laughing and joking amongst themselves. No one was watching them. 'You might kiss me.'

He opened his mouth as if to respond, and for

a moment it looked as though he might do exactly as she wished, but he just set his jaw, shook his head sadly and strode on.

She lifted the hem of her sari with one hand and hurried after him. 'Mr Killigrew, I had hoped that you held me in higher regard than to be completely indifferent to my feelings...'

'Your feelings are irrelevant to me, Miss Dadabhoy.'

It felt like she had been kicked in the stomach. She stared after him for a moment, feeling humiliated, and was tempted to let him stride away. But she was not going to let him get away so easily. 'Do you really think so little of me?'

'Miss Dadabhoy...'

'Peri, please.'

'Peri. Please believe me, I hold you in the highest regard. But it can lead nowhere. If I cared nothing for you, it would be the easiest thing in the world for me to seduce you. But I respect you, very much, and I can see no benefit to either of us if we pursue this. We'll only end up hurting each other.'

'So proper! So formal! So cold!' she sneered. 'You have never been in love, have you, Mr Killigrew? You have no idea of what it feels like to be ... to be overwhelmed by such a consuming passion, to have it rob you of all your senses ...' She was hurrying after him so that when he stopped and turned abruptly she tumbled into his arms. He held her close and kissed her with a flood of pent-up passion. She did not know whether to be delighted or terrified, but delight won out and she responded. Then he broke off the kiss and stepped back, staring at her as if he were just as astonished at himself as she were.

'Mr Killigrew!'

'I'm sorry–'

'Do not apologise!'

'Miss Dadabhoy – Peri – don't imagine that it's any easier for me than it is for you. Don't imagine that ever since I first saw you on Zhai Jing-mu's junk you haven't been in my thoughts day and night, that I haven't wanted to sweep you into my arms and kiss you as I did just then, that I haven't spent every minute away from you longing for the next time I saw you...'

'Then why did you turn down all my invitations?'

'Because you know as well as I that it is impossible for there to be anything between us.'

She sighed and turned her head away. 'You could never marry an Indian girl, could you, Kit?' she said disdainfully. 'Whatever would your colleagues say?'

'The devil take my colleagues. It's *you* I'm concerned about. If you married me, you'd have to renounce your religion, your people, everything you believe in.'

'I believe in you.'

'I'm sorry.'

'For what?'

'For putting you in such a position. Forcing you to choose between me and your religion was the last thing I ever wanted.'

'I am not blaming you, Kit. It is not your fault I am a Zarathustrian. If anyone is to blame, it should be me.'

162

'For being born into a particular culture? No one can be blamed for that.'

'What about your religion, Kit? *Are* you religious?'

'Not really. I'm an Anglican.'

'But you go to church?'

'Regularly. Once a year, for the Christmas carol service.' He could hardly count divine service on deck every Sunday: attendance was compulsory. 'If I could become a Parsi I would, Peri. I've been reading up on Zarathustrianism. All that stuff about an eternal conflict between good and evil. It makes as much sense as any religion I've encountered.'

'There is not much comfort in a religion which forbids me to marry whom I please. Perhaps I could become a Christian, start a new life in England...'

He shook his head. 'And then what? Settle down in a country cottage as the wife of a naval officer? Have you any idea of what that's like? Being left on your own for years at a time? It just wouldn't work, Peri. It wouldn't be fair to you.'

'Do you not think I have the right to make that decision for myself?'

'Certainly. If you could be certain you were thinking straight.'

'You think I am making no sense?'

'All I know is that when *I* look at *you*, common sense goes by the board.'

'Why not go with it?' she suggested, taking a step towards him.

He moved away, shaking his head with a sad smile. 'Have you ever noticed that man is an inveterate categoriser?'

'What do you mean?'

'It's like Strachan with his notebooks, looking for new species so he can decide which phylum, order, and class they belong to. Everything has to be battened down and pigeonholed. Every*one*, too. I'm a British naval officer, you're a Parsi lady, and never the twain shall meet. And we all go along with it because we're terrified of not fitting in.'

'You do not strike me as the kind of man who worries about fitting in.'

'Don't be fooled. I'm as susceptible as the next man. When I was on board the *Dreadful* the oldsters used to sneer that I have "a touch of the tar brush". My mother was Greek; and, what's more unforgivable, it shows in my colouring.'

'I think it makes you look very handsome.' He accepted the compliment with an inclination of his head. 'Nevertheless, the gulf between two different European countries is hardly the same as that between Britain and India, Kit.'

He shrugged. 'There've always been those who've treated me as ... I don't know, somehow inferior. Even when they meant well. When they say things like, "Good work, Killigrew," I can't help wondering if what they're really thinking is: "Not bad, for a dago." '

'Are you sure it is not simply your imagination?'

'No, I'm not,' he admitted. 'But the uncertainty only makes it worse. A true English gentleman never doubts himself. So I think I have some idea of what it must be like for your father, trying to be something he can never really be, losing touch with his heritage and ending up being neither one thing nor the other.'

'You do not strike me as the kind of man who is troubled by self-doubt, either.'

He smiled. 'I've learned to conceal it.'

She moved closer to him and this time he did not move away. She encircled his neck with her arms and felt his arms around her waist. This time the kiss was more relaxed, but nonetheless passionate, as they both allowed it to last. Finally she broke off. 'Kit! I had no idea Englishmen could be so passionate.'

'That's the Greek half of me.'

'And that is the half you wish to deny?' she asked incredulously.

'We'd better get back to the others,' he said. 'If we're gone too long, someone will notice, and you know how tongues wag.'

'I do not care.'

'You should. What will happen to you when the *Tisiphone* is ordered away from here?'

She looked grave. 'I would prefer not to think of that.'

'So would I. But we can't afford not to think about it, either.'

They strolled back to where the others were still chatting merrily amongst themselves. No one remarked upon their return, except for Strachan, who gave Killigrew a quizzical look, which was ignored. Peri was about to walk away from the lieutenant to talk to her father, for form's sake, when the Eurasian girl Killigrew had been so fascinated by earlier reappeared around the headland at a run. A moment later Ultzmann appeared behind her, breathlessly trying to keep up.

'Ai-ling! Wait!'

One of Prince Tan's attendants intercepted her. He took her firmly by the arm and led her back to where Tan stood watching expressionlessly. Ultzmann tried to follow them, but Killigrew blocked his path.

'You should be ashamed of yourself, Reverend,' Peri heard him hiss under his breath.

Ultzmann glared at him. 'I advise you to keep your nose out of affairs which do not concern yourself, young man.' He pushed brusquely past Killigrew. The lieutenant turned as if to follow as Ultzmann continued after the girl. 'Ai-ling!'

Prince Tan was already helping her into a palanquin, but at the sound of Ultzmann's voice she paused and glanced over her shoulder at the reverend with tears glistening on her cheeks. Another of Tan's attendants stood firmly in Ultzmann's path and this time the reverend stopped. Tan pushed the girl into the palanquin and it was lifted on to the shoulders of two coolies and carried back up the bridle path to Victoria. Ultzmann turned away with his shoulders slumped.

Everyone had stopped talking to watch this tableau. 'Well I never!' huffed a dowager in a stage whisper that could have been heard on mainland China. 'And him a man of the cloth!'

Strachan stood up and nudged Killigrew in the ribs. 'The dirty scoundrel, eh? She's young enough to be his daughter!' The assistant

166

surgeon's voice was amused and envious.

The picnic started to break up shortly after that. As everyone climbed into the waiting calashes and landaus, Peri sought out Killigrew one last time as he was about to climb into the hackney the officers of the *Tisiphone* had clubbed together to rent for the afternoon. 'Shall I tell Lieutenant Dwyer that my last dance at the Bannatynes' is bespoken?'

He clasped her hand in such a way that no one else would notice. 'That would be ungallant.'

'But you will be there?'

He nodded.

'Peri!' called her father, standing at the door to his victoria. She hurried to obey, but she could not stop herself from glancing over her shoulder at Killigrew as she climbed into the carriage. He was still staring after her with a smile on his face, oblivious to the impatient calls of his fellow officers.

VI:

Tai-Pan

There were already a dozen carriages parked outside the gates of the Grafton, Bannatyne & Co. trading factory at East Point when Killigrew arrived on foot with Robertson, Hartcliffe, Strachan, and the other senior officers of the *Tisiphone*. The naval officers were in their full-dress uniforms: epauletted navy-blue tail-coats, cocked hats and white kid gloves. In place of the two sentries who usually stood at the factory gate there were two turbaned footmen in high-collared coats of salmon and gold brocade. Glancing up, Killigrew saw the usual guards patrolling the wall above, thrown into shadow by the bright lights which illuminated the compound. Presumably the last thing Bannatyne wanted was for his ball to be disrupted by Triads.

The footmen ushered the officers through. The compound had been brushed clean and paper lanterns had been hung all the way around the perimeter; a seven-piece band was tuning up in one corner. This would be where the company spent the evening dancing, but first they were escorted to the reception room where another footman relieved them of their hats. They were greeted by a handsome woman in a ball gown of rich green velvet which set off her emerald eyes and auburn hair to perfection: their hostess for the evening. Killigrew saw at once what Verran had been talking about, and could no longer blame his friend for risking dismissal – and perhaps worse – by seeking to seduce his employer's wife. As he waited his turn to be presented to Mrs Bannatyne, he wondered how his friend was getting along on that score, and felt unaccountably envious at the possibility that Verran might have succeeded by now.

Rear-Admiral Collier did the honours. 'Mrs Bannatyne, permit me to introduce the officers of Her Majesty's sloop *Tisiphone*: Mr Robertson, Lord Hartcliffe and ... uh...'

'My second lieutenant, Mr Killigrew,' Robertson continued on his superior's behalf.

'Ah, yes,' Collier said heavily. *'Killigrew.'*

Killigrew smiled wryly. He had never met the admiral before tonight; evidently a reputation of some sort had preceded him.

'Mr Westlake and Mr Strachan, my surgeon and assistant surgeon respectively,' said Robertson. 'Mr Vellacott, my purser and paymaster; and Mr Muir, my chief engineer.'

Collier nodded. 'Gentlemen, I give you: Mrs Epiphany Bannatyne.'

Robertson bowed stiffly. 'A pleasure to meet you, ma'am.'

'You are the gentlemen we have to thank for preserving Miss Dadabhoy's life?' asked Mrs Bannatyne.

'I don't believe she was in any real danger, ma'am,' said Killigrew. 'For all their villainy, the pilongs have a kind of twisted code. When they

169

take hostages at all, they generally treat them well.' Of course, if a certain pilong held a grudge towards someone, as Zhai Jing-mu's little speech when Killigrew had handed him over to Dwyer and Cargill seemed to indicate, then that was another matter entirely. But Zhai Jing-mu was safely locked behind bars, soon to be executed, and Killigrew saw no need to alarm the ladies with such thoughts.

'I didn't catch your name earlier, Mr...?'

'Killigrew, ma'am. At your service.' She gave him a brief, cold, appraising gaze, and nodded. He glanced about pointedly. 'Is Mr Bannatyne not joining us?'

She smiled thinly. 'My husband will be with us presently. He's just finishing off some paperwork in the study.'

'Probably planning a dramatic entrance,' muttered Strachan.

Drinks were handed out by footmen, and the gathering stood around and made polite small talk while they waited for the other guests to turn up. Strachan turned his attention to one of the paintings on the wall, a view across Victoria Harbour from Kowloon.

'Any good?' Killigrew knew enough about art to know how little he knew, and happily deferred to Strachan – an amateur artist before he had taken up photographic portraiture – in such matters.

'Very. By Mr Chinnery, a local artist. Not as good as Mr Turner, of course, but then who is?'

They both turned away from the wall, and Strachan nodded to where Commander Robertson was talking to General Staveley, the commander of the Hong Kong garrison. 'I didn't think the Old Man would come tonight,' murmured Strachan. 'I thought he loathed social functions?'

'Did you think he would turn down a chance to meet the great Mr Blase Bannatyne himself?' asked Killigrew, smiling. He nodded to where a white marble bust of Genghis Khan stood on a pedestal in a niche. 'Take that fellow there, for example. He may not have been everyone's cup of char, but if you had a chance to meet him, would you turn it down?'

'Rubbing shoulders with barba–' started Strachan, but he was interrupted by a new voice.

'Is that how you see me? A Genghis Khan of commerce?'

Killigrew turned and saw a man dressed soberly in a black neckcloth, frock coat and trousers, more like a clergyman than a China trader. His lank hair, still untouched by grey, was parted down the centre and slicked tightly against his skull with Macassar oil. If he was a day over forty, he looked good on it. His face was plain enough, almost boyish except for the blue-tinged jowls of a permanent five o'clock shadow, the features too regular to be handsome; a little lacking in character, but perhaps women might consider him attractive.

'Mr Bannatyne, I presume?' said Killigrew.

The *tai-pan* of Grafton, Bannatyne & Co. inclined the head which launched a thousand cargoes of opium. 'I have that honour. And you are...?'

171

'Lieutenant Killigrew, HMS *Tisiphone*. And this is Mr Strachan, our assistant surgeon.'

Bannatyne nodded to the bust of Genghis Khan. 'Mrs Bannatyne's handiwork. A woman should have a hobby, don't you think?'

'Keeps them out of trouble,' agreed Strachan.

'I've always found women more interesting when they're *in* trouble,' said Killigrew, and turned back to the bust. 'Your wife has a rare talent, sir.'

Mrs Bannatyne came across to join them. 'Is everything all right?' she asked her husband.

'We were just admiring your handiwork, ma'am,' said Killigrew. 'It's a magnificent piece. Have you had any formal training?'

She blushed. 'No. I don't know how I got into it. I needed some way to spend my time. I tried my hand at watercolours, but I wasn't very good. Then one day I found a block of marble in the potting shed left over from when the house was built, and some sculpting tools, and thought I'd try my hand. My early efforts were horrendous, but Mr Chinnery had a look at them and encouraged me to persevere.'

'Good for him,' said Killigrew. 'I should like to see the rest of your body of work, if I may.'

'It's really not all that good.'

'Perhaps later,' Bannatyne said gruffly, in a tone which said: *Over my rotting corpse.*

'If they're all as good as this one, you really ought to hold an exhibition, see if you can't sell some of your work,' said Strachan. 'It really would be a shame to hide such a talent under a bushel.'

172

'Mrs Bannatyne merely sculpts as a hobby,' Bannatyne said firmly. 'It would be unseemly for the wife of the *tai-pan* of Grafton, Bannatyne and Co. to be a professional artist.'

'Nonsense,' said Killigrew. 'Why, one only has to look at this piece here to see what a talent your wife has. Look at those beady eyes, that sneering, supercilious expression. It's easy to imagine this rapacious swine riding roughshod over all who stand in his way, with scant regard for human life. Where did you find such inspiration, ma'am?'

She looked bewildered. 'I really couldn't say. It just ... came to me.'

'I keep it there to remind me of whom I am dealing with whenever I have contact with the Chinese,' Bannatyne said in a calm, unruffled voice which was belied by the glare he gave Killigrew. 'Genghis Khan was a Tartar, just like the Manchu rulers of present-day China. "Know thy enemy and know thyself," Sun Tzu says in his *Art of War*, "and thou shalt be victorious a hundred times out of a hundred."'

'Doesn't he also say: "Those who win every battle are not truly skilled; those who render the armies of others helpless without fighting are the best of all"?'

'You are familiar with the Chinese classics, Mr Killigrew?'

'Only the ones I can obtain in translation. I'm afraid I haven't mastered Chinese script yet.'

'Yes, I found it rather difficult at first,' Bannatyne said airily. As Robertson and Hartcliffe approached, he turned to greet them, and behind his back Strachan mouthed: *Touché*.

173

Killigrew did not smile. 'You must be Commander Robertson?'

Robertson nodded. 'And you are Mr Bannatyne, I presume? I've heard a great deal about you, sir.'

Bannatyne smiled, almost bashfully. 'Don't believe above half of it, sir. And this gentleman is?'

'Lord Hartcliffe, my first lieutenant. I see you've already met Mr Killigrew and Mr Strachan. I'll introduce you to Mr Westlake, Mr Vellacott and Mr Muir later if the opportunity arises. My other officers send their apologies, but we could not leave the *Tisiphone* without someone on duty.'

'Very wise, sir. You heard about the salt boat that was cut out of the harbour by pilongs the other day? It must be very embarrassing for you gentlemen of the Royal Navy to have a boat with such a valuable cargo stolen right from under your noses.' Bannatyne watched Killigrew as he spoke, as if trying to gauge his response to this provocation. The lieutenant met his gaze and kept his face expressionless.

'I don't see what's so valuable about a cargo of salt,' snorted Strachan. 'I can only assume that the pirates must have been greatly disappointed.'

'You're new to China, aren't you, Mr Strachan?' said Bannatyne, without taking his eyes off Killigrew. 'If you had been here for any length of time, you would be aware that the Manchus maintain a monopoly on salt, which makes it a highly valuable commodity on the mainland.'

'Shouldn't we go through to the compound

174

now?' Mrs Bannatyne asked her husband.

He smiled tightly. 'You know it would be rude of us to proceed before the rest of our guests have arrived, madam. We're still waiting for Admiral Huang.'

For all his years in the Far East, the governor had not yet learned the Chinese art of masking astonishment. 'You invited Admiral Huang? And he *accepted*?'

Bannatyne nodded.

'He hasn't accepted any of my invitations to meet face to face,' spluttered Bonham. He was in his mid-forties, a dark-haired, thick-set man with a stiffly waxed moustache. 'Damn me, Bannatyne, how on earth did you winkle him out of that junk?'

The *tai-pan* smiled faintly. 'You have your ways of influencing people, Governor. I have mine.'

Killigrew did not doubt that Bannatyne's methods included bribery, corruption and even threats, but he was not convinced those were the methods that had induced the Chinese admiral to attend the ball. Huang might well be as corruptible as any government officer anywhere in the world, but no Chinese mandarin would ever have allowed himself to fall into the pocket of a Westerner, not even one as powerful and influential as Bannatyne.

'If we're waiting for a Chinaman to arrive, we'll be here long after the food's gone cold,' said General Staveley. 'Their mandarins always make a point of turning up late, and the more important they consider themselves the later they arrive.'

175

'Indeed,' said Bannatyne. 'Which is why I took the precaution of inviting the admiral to arrive two hours earlier than everyone else. Ah, and here he is now...'

A footman's voice boomed across the ballroom: 'His excellency Admiral Huang Hai-kwang of the Imperial Chinese Navy.'

Killigrew glanced up as Admiral Huang entered, wearing the traditional silk robes, thick-soled satin boots and conical hat of a mandarin. One could tell a great deal about a mandarin if you knew what to look for: Huang wore the red coral button, the yellow girdle, and the coveted double-eyed peacock's feather in his cap, while the image on his *buzi* – the 'mandarin square' embroidered on the front of his gown – was that of a highly stylised lion. In Chinese military official's insignia, the lion was the second rank, inferior only to the mythical *qilin*. All in all, Huang's robes proclaimed him to be a person of some substance.

He was a man of substance in terms of his build as well. His face had the characteristic Mongoloid features of the Tartar Manchus, the rolls of flesh emphasising the narrowness of the eyes which twinkled with mischief above cheeks so podgy they made it impossible to determine his age with any degree of certainty. He greeted everyone in turn in the Oriental manner, bowing with his hands clasped before him.

At a signal, two more footmen opened a pair of double doors leading back out to the compound. As the band struck up a quadrille the governor and Mrs Bannatyne started off the figures. Killigrew preferred waltzes, so he helped himself to a glass of champagne from the tray of a passing flunkey and sat the first dance out.

The quadrille ended and the first waltz began. Once again Killigrew stood on the sidelines, feeling envious as he watched Lieutenant Dwyer, resplendent in his bottle-green full-dress uniform with a crimson sash, lead Peri Dadabhoy around the floor. When the waltz ended, the men promenaded halfway round the floor with their partners, and Killigrew was about to go to where he guessed Peri and Dwyer would end up, but Bannatyne intercepted him, leading Admiral Huang.

'Not dancing, Mr Killigrew?' asked Bannatyne.

'Why? Are you offering?' Something about the *tai-pan*'s staid, dour manner brought out the lieutenant's flippant side.

Bannatyne frowned. 'Ah. I was warned you were something of a humorist. Perhaps I can introduce you to a fellow naval officer: Admiral Huang Hai-kwang. Admiral, this is Lieutenant Killigrew, one of the officers of Her Majesty's paddle-sloop *Tisiphone*.'

'Ah, yes,' said Huang. 'The young officer who was first over the wall at Chingkiang-fu.' His English, though thickly accented, was excellent.

'The first one who lived to tell the tale, at any rate,' admitted Killigrew. 'I'm surprised you've heard about that.'

'Your exploits in the late war are much spoken of by officers of the Imperial Navy.' Something about Huang's tone suggested that those officers would dearly love to avenge those exploits.

'As is your feat in getting the better of one of our gun-brigs.'

'The goddess T'ien Hou saw fit to smile on my endeavours.'

'In the Royal Navy we put our faith in steam engines and shell guns as much as in divine intervention.'

'Steam engines and shell guns are no match for karma.'

'Well, the proof of the pudding is in the eating.'

'Indeed, Lieutenant. But one pudding remains half baked.'

'Beware of what you wish for, Admiral. You might just burn your mouth.'

Huang smiled thinly. 'I understand you were one of the officers who captured the notorious pirate Zhai Jing-mu. You are to be congratulated. Many have tried to bring him to justice before.'

'Yourself included? You haven't had much luck there, either. Presumably T'ien Hou didn't see fit to smile on your endeavours?'

'Another pudding which is yet uneaten. While Zhai Jing-mu still breathes he remains a threat. It is more than a month since you captured him, and still we await his execution.'

'You'll have to accept our apologies. In Britain we believe in giving a man a fair trial before we hang him.'

'In China we also have proper legal procedures.'

'Judicial torture, you mean?'

Huang inclined his head. 'You are a clever man, Lieutenant Killigrew. I hope for your sake you are clever enough not to fall foul of it.' Huang turned to Bannatyne. 'Perhaps now you should introduce me to Mr Bonham, Bannatyne-qua?'

'Of course. If you'll excuse us, Mr Killigrew?' The *tai-pan* led Huang across to where the governor stood talking to Mrs Staveley.

Killigrew was still pondering his encounter with Huang when Peri appeared at his side. 'You promised me the second waltz, Kit.'

He turned with a smile. 'Have I missed it already, Peri? I'm sorry. Perhaps the next?'

'I have already promised that to Captain Verran.'

Killigrew glanced across to where Verran had cornered an uncomfortable-looking Mrs Bannatyne. 'From where I'm standing, I'd say Jago's got his hands full as it is.'

'You are a fine one to talk, Kit. I saw you fawning to our hostess in the reception room earlier.'

'I was merely admiring her bust.'

'So I noticed,' Peri said coolly. She gazed around at the gathering. 'It is strange. The last time I attended a ball at the Grafton, Bannatyne and Co. factory here I was only a child. That was when Sir George was *tai-pan*, of course, when we were based in Canton. Tell me, is Sir George as renowned for his balls in London as he was here in Hong Kong?'

'Only the ones he talks in the House of Commons,' Killigrew murmured absent-mindedly.

'What were you discussing with Admiral Huang?'

'Talking shop, I'm afraid. I wouldn't want to bore you.'

She smiled. 'I would rather be bored by you than fascinated by any other man.'

They danced the next waltz together, and when they had finished promenading the band struck up a lively polka. 'Shall we?' suggested Killigrew.

'Oh, no, I could not!'

'You don't know until you've tried. Come on ... just follow me ... and *one* two, *one* two...'

She struggled at first in her sari, but he supported her. Eventually she fell into the rhythm of the lively step and relaxed enough to enjoy it, laughing with delight as he whirled her round and round. When the polka ended, it was too soon for both of them, although both were breathing hard.

'Oh, Kit! That was wonderful!'

'Aren't you glad I persuaded you to change your mind? You see? You should never close your mind to new experiences.'

'You dance superbly.'

'Better than Dwyer?'

'Why? Are you jealous?'

'Should I be?'

She shook her head, making her curls dance prettily. 'No,' she said, and lowered her voice to a whisper. 'He kept treading on my toes.' She wafted her face with her fan.

'Warm?' he asked her. She nodded. 'Come on.'

He took her by the hand and they slipped through a door. He was unfamiliar with the layout of the factory but he had a good sense of direction and it did not take him long to find the verandah overlooking the landing stage at the back.

It was a warm night for February, even in Hong Kong, and the clear sky above was peppered with stars. The rainy season would not start for a few weeks yet. Across the harbour, the lights of the fishing station at Kowloon glittered in the shimmering waters. A long, low shape glided into the harbour from the direction of the Cap-sing-mun Passage.

'There's a smug boat over there without any lights on,' remarked Killigrew. 'Can't be smugglers...'

Peri took him gently by the lapels of his tail-coat and turned him to face her. 'Are you a customs and excise man now?'

He slipped his hands around her waist and drew her closer. 'Why? Are you carrying any contraband?'

'You will have to search me to find out,' she teased archly.

He drew her closer to him and at the touch of their bodies felt desire well up within him. She pushed back against him so forcefully he had to brace himself against the balustrade. He felt the thrill of mutually recognised need and was about to suggest that they find a more secluded nook where he could carry out his search more fully when he became aware of someone standing in the doorway.

'I came out to tell you that dinner is served,' said Mrs Bannatyne. 'I can see that you're both hungry,' she added drily.

'Pardon me.' Blushing furiously, Peri squeezed past Mrs Bannatyne and went back into the ballroom where the other guests were already

181

filing through to the dining room.

'Your timing *could* be more perfect, ma'am.' Killigrew was about to follow Peri inside when Mrs Bannatyne moved to block his path.

'From whose point of view, Mr Killigrew? Yours? Or Miss Dadabhoy's?'

'I'd rather got the impression that in this instance they were one and the same thing. Or are you concerned that my intentions towards Miss Dadabhoy might not be strictly honourable?'

'It's difficult to see where a romance between a naval officer and the daughter of one of the richest Parsi merchants in the world can go.'

'It's early days yet, but a short walk down the aisle hasn't been ruled out.'

'You think her father would approve of you?'

Killigrew smiled. 'Why? Do you think he'd object to the colour of my skin?'

'I think it's the colour of your money he'd be more concerned about.'

'You do both myself and Miss Dadabhoy an injustice if you think I'd marry her for her money.'

'Then perhaps you should think about how Society back in England would view a naval officer who married an Indian girl.'

'If you knew the first thing about me, Mrs Bannatyne, you'd know I'm not the kind of man who gives a damn what other people think.'

'I'll try to bear that in mind.'

'Hadn't we better go in ourselves, ma'am? The turtle soup will be getting cold. Besides, if we stay out here unchaperoned much longer, it will be *us* people start to talk about.'

'You needn't concern yourself on that account, Mr Killigrew. If they do, I shall be the very first to correct any misapprehensions they may entertain on the subject.'

With a thin smile, Killigrew gestured for her to precede him into the banqueting hall.

Bannatyne might not do much entertaining at the factory, but that had not stopped his architects from building an impressive dining hall, which probably doubled as a boardroom during the day. The grandiose proportions of the pillars which lead up to the vaulted ceiling were clearly designed to awe.

Most of the other guests had already found their places at the immense, damask-covered dining table. A massive silver candelabra dominated as the centrepiece. Footmen were lined up on either side of the hall, as precisely arrayed as guardsmen on parade. Footmen the world over tended to be chosen for their imposing size rather than their competence, but there was something about these which suggested the muscles beneath their uniforms were very real indeed. A broken nose here, a scarred face there, their ramrod-straight backs all hinted that these were veteran sepoys of the Honourable East India Company's army.

Killigrew easily found his place with the other officers of the *Tisiphone*, near the bottom of the table, a long way away from the Framjees who sat with Governor Bonham, General Staveley and Prince Tan near the head of the table, where Bannatyne himself sat. Peri avoided Killigrew's gaze.

The small talk was stilted, as it tended to be at such functions. 'So, you were at Chingkiang-fu, Mr Killigrew?' Bannatyne remarked as the main course – stewed beef *à la jardinière* – was served. He spoke loudly to make himself heard at such a great distance, and the lieutenant had to respond with equal volume, conscious that the conversation was being listened to by everyone at the table, from the governor of Hong Kong down to ... well, probably himself and Strachan, in order of social rank.

'Yes.' The monosyllable was intended to deter further enquiries.

'You should be more proud of having done military service for your country.'

'You've never done military service, have you, sir?'

Bannatyne smiled. 'My goodness, no. I'm a man of peace. Why do you ask?'

Killigrew shook his head. 'If you had, you would know that military service is nothing to be proud of.'

'A strange thing to say for a young man who has chosen service in Her Majesty's navy as a career.'

'There's more to active service than waging war, sir. Think of all the good work the navy does against slavers and pirates.'

'Making the seas safe for trade,' said Rear-Admiral Collier. 'You should be grateful for that, Bannatyne,' he added, trying to keep his tone jovial.

'When the pilongs cease to be a threat to my shipping, I'll be grateful.'

184

'That's something we intend to take care of in the very near future, sir, I can assure you,' said Collier.

'I'm glad to hear it,' said Bannatyne. 'But tell me, Mr Killigrew: do you not feel that war can also be an honourable enterprise?'

'It's conceivable, I suppose, though I cannot think of any recent examples in history.'

'What about the war against China? After all, that too was in defence of British trade.'

'Perhaps you should ask Admiral Huang here how *he* feels about having opium smuggled into his country.'

'Are you not a believer in free trade, Mr Killigrew?'

'Oh, I'm a staunch defender of free trade. What I don't approve of is extraterritoriality.'

Bannatyne arched his eyebrows at that and a few of the other European men present looked shocked. 'British law for British subjects? Surely you can have no quarrel with that, Mr Killigrew?'

'British law in British *jurisdiction* would be a more reasonable policy. If a Chinaman were to murder an Englishman in London, would you think it reasonable if the Chinese insisted he were tried by a court of law in Peking?'

'Of course not!' spluttered General Staveley.

'Yet that is exactly the principle we insist on applying when British sailors cause trouble in Canton,' Killigrew pointed out.

'We make sure that justice is done,' asserted a justice of the peace. 'There's no favouritism in my court on account of nationality.'

'Yet we do not trust the Chinese courts, when

185

anyone who has taken the trouble to study the Manchu penal system knows it is much less harsh than our own.'

'To their own people, I dare say...' snorted Staveley.

'Interesting that you should express righteous dissatisfaction with the terms insisted upon by your own people in the Unfair Treaties,' said Huang, speaking for the first time during the course of the meal. 'However, I trust that we will all get a fairer picture of British justice when Zhai Jing-mu is put on trial in your admiralty court tomorrow.'

'You may be assured of that,' said Bonham. 'Is it your intention to attend?'

'Regrettably, my own work will keep me in Canton. But I shall follow the law reports in the *Hong Kong Register* most closely. So too, I suspect, will the unrighteous Brotherhood of Heaven, Earth and Man.'

'Who's that?' asked Strachan.

'Triads,' growled Staveley. 'Chinese thugs.'

Bannatyne shook his head. 'The Triads are more than mere criminals, general. You must remember that to many Chinese the Daoguang Emperor, as a member of the Ch'ing Dynasty, is still seen as a foreign invader. The Triads are a political movement, a ruthless, sinister organisation whose tentacles reach into every quarter of society, intent on overturning the social order with no regard for the anarchy into which their own country might subsequently fall.'

'Rather like the Whigs,' elucidated Killigrew, well aware that Bannatyne was the president of the Hong Kong Chapter of the Reform Club.

The *tai-pan* was unamused. 'A good deal more dangerous than the Whigs, Mr Killigrew.'

'Oh, I don't know. Why don't you ask the victims of Lord Palmerston's foreign policy what they think?'

Bannatyne smiled thinly. 'Laugh if you will, Mr Killigrew. But I tell you this: if you intend to testify against Zhai Jing-mu you should watch your step very carefully. The Triads are dangerous and vengeful enemies, and their reach is long.'

'If they try anything here on Hong Kong they'll soon have cause to regret it,' asserted the justice of the peace.

'You seem to be singularly well-informed about these Triads, Mr Bannatyne,' remarked Killigrew.

'Information is power, Mr Killigrew. In my business it pays to be well informed.'

'I regret to have to contradict what you say,' Huang told the justice of the peace. 'But my information is that since Hong Kong was stolen from the direct control of the Imperial Government by the Unfair Treaties, the island has become a refuge for the worst dregs of the Brotherhood of Heaven, Earth and Man.'

'There was nothing unfair about those treaties!' snapped Staveley. 'If the Chinese weren't so damned arrogant and had accepted the not unreasonable demands of Western trade, then there would have been no need for the war in the first place.'

'There would have been no need for war if the rebellious high-nosed barbarians had not persisted in defying the edicts of the Occupant of the Dragon Throne by perfidiously smuggling their foreign mud into the Celestial Kingdom.'

'Rebellious!' Staveley ignored Bonham's attempts to calm the situation. 'Damn your eyes! Great Britain is a sovereign nation, and not part of your heathen, degenerate, so-called Celestial Empire!'

Huang was on his feet in an instant. 'It is your barbarians who are the degenerates, profaning the Celestial Kingdom with your opium, your war and your missionaries!'

'All right, William,' Bonham told Staveley. 'That will do.'

'Damn it, George, they make me sick!'

'For heaven's sake, General! There are ladies present.'

'I can't help that! Yellow-belly scum, calling us high-nosed barbarians! They're the arrogant ones...'

Killigrew glanced at Bannatyne. The *tai-pan* sat back in his seat with a faint smile playing on his lips, as if he was enjoying it all immensely.

'Oh!' Mrs Bannatyne threw a faint, doubtless with the specific intention of trying to claw back some semblance of decorum from the shambles of the evening. Verran caught her before she fell from her chair – her cry gave him plenty of warning – and was all gallantry as he wafted a napkin in her face to give her air. The sight of a woman in a sorry plight was enough to make even the general realise he had gone too far, and he sat down, his face as scarlet as his tunic with anger and embarrassment.

Admiral Huang had risen to his feet. 'I humbly apologise, but I fear this assault on my dignity tonight is beyond harmonious toleration.'

The *tai-pan* stood up and bowed. 'Please accept my sincerest apologies on behalf of the general—'

'You'll do no such thing!' snarled Staveley.

'For God's sake, William!' hissed Bonham. 'Haven't you done enough damage for one night?'

'I do sincerely regret that this most unpleasant scene should have occurred under my roof,' Bannatyne told Huang gravely. 'I must humbly accept all responsibility for what has happened here tonight, and offer my apologies.' He made a half-hearted attempt to persuade Huang to stay and, when he saw the Chinese admiral was implacable, escorted him to the door.

'Well done, William,' Bonham muttered while Bannatyne was out of the room, mopping his brow with his napkin. 'Another startling diplomatic coup.'

The general was all contrition, but it was too late. Bonham was going to have to spend weeks repairing the damage that had been done in a few short minutes.

The ladies had withdrawn to leave the men to their port and cigars by the time Bannatyne returned. 'I think I managed to calm him down a little,' he told Bonham. 'You know what the Chinese are like. So worried about losing face. No need to be concerned. I'm certain this will all blow over.'

'I wish I shared your optimism,' said Bonham. 'I suppose I shall have to send his excellency some particularly generous gift to smooth it over.'

'You know, sometimes I wonder if we don't bend over backwards a little too far when it comes to handling Chinese sensibilities,' Bannatyne said airily. 'It's not as if we have anything to fear from another war with them. We beat them easily before, we can beat them easily again.'

'Do you think so?' said Killigrew, lighting a cheroot. 'It didn't seem so easy from the battlements of Chingkiang-fu.'

'You're missing the point, Mr Killigrew,' said Bannatyne. 'The fact is that the Chinese have no grasp of reality. Do you know their philosophy of the world? They believe that Heaven is circular, and the world is square. China is that part of the square which benefits from the celestial influences of being directly beneath that circle. All the rest of the world – the corners – are uncivilised in their eyes. To them we're no more than barbarian states which should bow down before them. We'll never be able to trade with them on equal terms until they realise that China isn't the centre of the world.'

'Neither is Great Britain. If we wish to trade with them on equal terms, perhaps we should find something they actually want to buy.'

'There's no question that the Chinese wish to buy opium, Mr Killigrew. The profits of Grafton, Bannatyne and Co. prove that beyond a shadow of a doubt.'

'I was thinking of something more beneficial than opium, Mr Bannatyne. If opium is the best merchandise our culture can offer the Chinese,

190

then perhaps we should accept their view of us as barbarians.'

'You do not consider opium to be beneficial, Mr Killigrew? You would do well to consider that it is the wealth made by men such as myself which makes Britain great. And it is that wealth which pays for the Royal Navy.'

'As it should, since the Royal Navy keeps the seas safe for your opium clippers.'

'I haven't seen much evidence of that recently, Mr Killigrew. Nine opium clippers disappeared between Singapore and Hong Kong last year, three are missing already this year, not counting the one you found attacked by Zhai Jing-mu.'

The carriage clock on the mantelpiece chimed ten. 'Time to rejoin the ladies for coffee, I think,' said Rear-Admiral Collier, shooting Killigrew a warning look. Junior officers were not supposed to bandy words with respected citizens like Blase Bannatyne.

An upper-storey verandah facing across the harbour had been chosen to stand in for a drawing room. Killigrew found himself seated on the opposite side of the verandah from Peri and exchanged private smiles with her as one of the older ladies lectured on the uselessness of Chinese as servants. Peri was looking lovelier than ever tonight and as he gazed at her Killigrew reached a decision: there was no doubt in his mind that he wanted to spend the rest of his life with her. To hell with the navy, with Society, with the whole damned bigoted bunch of snobs: he would propose to her. Not tonight – he wanted to do it properly; Hartcliffe would lend him the

191

money for an engagement ring. He would get a civil licence from the superintendent-registrar: he could not see Peri wanting to get married in a Christian church, and he had never had his heart set on a church wedding.

Assuming, of course, she accepted his proposal. Whatever she thought or said, it was a hard life for the wife of a naval officer, being left alone for years at a time. If he loved her, could he do that to her?

But the solution, he knew, was obvious.

He broke off his reverie when he realised that Bannatyne had risen to his feet and was making an announcement. 'Ladies and gentlemen, I hope you won't take exception, but in order to make tonight a particularly memorable occasion I've laid on an unusual entertainment which I hope you'll all find diverting...'

'Doesn't he think it's been memorable enough already?' Killigrew murmured to Strachan.

'If you'll please follow me through...' said Bannatyne.

Killigrew noticed that Mrs Bannatyne looked distinctly uncomfortable – he wondered if she was going to be asked to entertain them at the pianoforte – but when they all trooped back to the compound he saw at once that Bannatyne had something else in mind. Row upon row of chairs had been set up facing the stage where the orchestra had played earlier in a quarter-circle, with an aisle running through them at an angle. On the stage itself there was a scene which suggested some kind of building repairs were in progress: and there were curious arrangements of

192

bricks, trestles and thick wooden planks.

Once everyone was seated, the biggest Chinese Killigrew had ever seen entered, dressed in some kind of white pyjama suit, his buttonless jacket fastened only with a black girdle tied around his waist, the gap above revealing a triangle of a smooth, glistening chest with well-defined muscles. It was hardly the kind of sight Killigrew expected to be offered after a meal. Instead of wearing his hair in the Manchu queue like every other Chinaman Killigrew had ever seen, this one wore a thick, black mop in the Western-style, parted to one side.

'Ladies and gentlemen, allow me to introduce my comprador, Shen Meng-fu,' said Bannatyne. 'Mr Shen has generously agreed to give us a demonstration of the ancient Chinese martial art of *wu-yi*. When you are ready, Mr Shen?'

Shen picked up three thick planks of wood and handed one each to Bonham, General Staveley, and Killigrew.

'If you would examine the planks, gentlemen, to confirm for yourselves that they are indeed ordinary pieces of timber, uninterfered with, and that there is no kind of trickery involved in what you are about to see,' said Bannatyne.

So that's it, thought Killigrew. *A magic show.* He stifled a yawn and examined his plank, although he did not expect to find anything. If there was anything to see, he would not have been allowed to handle it.

Shen gathered in the planks and laid the three of them one atop another across the trestles. Then he stood behind the trestle, took three deep breaths, and suddenly brought the edge of his hand down against the planks with a primeval yell which made some of the ladies present – and a few of the men – squeal in fright.

All three planks had been broken in the middle.

'Good God!' exclaimed Staveley.

'It must be some kind of trick,' said Strachan. 'There's something up his sleeve ...'

'No trickery, I assure you, ladies and gentlemen,' said Bannatyne. 'Mr Shen, roll up your sleeves and show your arms to these people.'

Mr Shen did just that. His forearms were like hocks of ham. He crossed to where a small block of masonry rested across another trestle. He gave another cry and brought his forehead down against it sharply. There was a loud crack, and the block crashed to the floor in two pieces.

'*Wu-yi*, ladies and gentlemen,' said Bannatyne, as the audience applauded uncertainly. 'The power of mind over matter.'

The demonstration lasted about five minutes, and even Killigrew could not help but be impressed as Shen smashed thick boards, bricks and masonry blocks with no more than his bare hands and feet, apparently without injury to himself.

'For the next part of our demonstration, Mr Shen requires the assistance of someone from our audience,' said Bannatyne. As a showman, he could have given Mr P. T. Barnum a run for his money. 'Mr Killigrew, perhaps you would care to step up?'

'That depends.' Killigrew rose to his feet. 'He's not going to put *me* across one of those trestles, is he?'

194

Smiling, Bannatyne shook his head. 'A demonstration of the "iron shirt", ladies and gentlemen. *Wu-yi* experts must learn the technique of receiving blows as well as giving them. Are you a practitioner of the noble art of pugilism, Mr Killigrew?'

'Not if I can help it. Fencing's more my cup of char.'

'But a young man with your widespread military experience must have some knowledge of hand-to-hand combat. I dare say you think you can deliver a powerful blow with your bare hands?'

'I have been known to, when the necessity arose.'

Bannatyne indicated Shen. 'Please demonstrate.'

'And have him chop me up like so much lumber?'

'Mr Shen will not retaliate. He will stand perfectly still and allow you to strike him wherever you will. Perhaps I can offer you a set of brass knuckles?'

'Not the sort of assistance a gentleman requires, I assure you.' Killigrew unbuttoned his tail-coat and handed it to Strachan.

'So be it.' Bannatyne gestured to Shen once more. The Chinese stood with every muscle in his body tensed, his feet braced squarely on the ground.

'And he won't hit me back?'

'You have my word on it, Mr Killigrew.'

The lieutenant squared up to Shen. Killigrew was tall, even for a European, but Shen met him eye to eye, and was nearly half as broad again across the shoulders. Killigrew half turned back to Bannatyne. 'There's just one thing I don't understand...' he said, and in the same breath turned back to Shen and drove his fist into his solar plexus with all his might.

As Bannatyne had surmised, Killigrew had picked up a few pugilistic tricks, and he kept himself in good shape. He knew a blow like that should have brought even a fit young man to his knees. But it was like punching a block of rubber. Shen did not even flinch, except to crack his smooth face into a smile.

Killigrew stepped back and shook his hand before flexing his fingers. He suspected the blow had hurt himself more than it had hurt the Chinese. 'Of course, in a real fight I would be more inclined to go for the face,' he said, knowing he was just making excuses now.

'Please try it,' said Mr Bannatyne. 'Once again, I assure you Mr Shen will not retaliate.'

Killigrew drove his fist at Shen's face and put all his strength behind the blow. One of Shen's hands whipped up as fast as a cobra, caught Killigrew's fist and stopped it dead in its tracks.

As a final demonstration, Shen turned and drove a hand through a wooden board: not a fist, but his *outstretched fingertips*. The board splintered effortlessly. He turned back to Killigrew with a smile which seemed to say: *I could do the same to your ribcage.*

Killigrew returned his smile. 'Very impressive,' he said, reaching into his pocket for a guinea. 'What does he do for an encore? Sing a couple of choruses from "Oh Rest Thee, My Darling"?' He tossed the coin on the stage at Shen's feet. 'There's a shiner for your trouble.'

Shen merely folded his arms across his brawny chest with a look of disdain.

'Don't think that Mr Shen can be bought, Mr Killigrew,' Bannatyne said coldly. 'I pay him extraordinarily well.'

'If he's so strong, let him prove it by picking up the coin.'

For the first time a look of helplessness entered Shen's eyes.

Killigrew smiled. 'He can't, can he? His *wu-yi* has so toughened the skin on his hands he's lost all sensitivity in them. Such a skill is not won without great cost. One thing I have learned in the navy, Mr Bannatyne. Brute strength is no match for subtlety and intelligence.'

Shen left the coin on the ground and stomped inside.

'I don't need to employ anyone to be subtle or intelligent on my behalf, Mr Killigrew,' Bannatyne said tightly.

Killigrew took back his tail-coat from Strachan and shrugged it on. He was still buttoning it up with a sense of satisfaction when Shen returned from the banqueting hall with a dab of gravy on the tip of his finger. He bent down and pressed it against the coin. When he lifted the finger, the coin had stuck to his fingertip long enough for him to be able to pinch it between thumb and forefinger.

Some of the spectators applauded. 'Oh, I say!' exclaimed Framjee. 'That's jolly clever!'

Jago Verran grinned. 'What were you saying about subtlety and intelligence, Kit?'

Glaring at Killigrew, Shen exerted pressure on the coin between his fingers until his whole arm trembled and the veins stood out in his forehead. Just when Killigrew thought the Chinese was going to have a seizure, the coin snapped with a sound like a musket-shot. The impressive effect was marred by the way one half of the coin shot across the room, narrowly missing Mrs Staveley's head and bringing down one of the Chinese lanterns which promptly burst into flames. Two footmen hurriedly ran across to stamp it out.

'Damn it, man!' General Staveley snarled at Bannatyne. 'Your trained monkey almost had my wife's eye out! Enough of this damned tom-foolery!'

'All right, Shen, you can go,' snapped Bannatyne, his face flushed.

'I think we can all go,' said Bonham. 'We've seen enough.'

Bannatyne remained in the compound as everyone filed in to the reception room. His wife escorted them and a footman handed out hats. No one congratulated her on the ball, except Killigrew, who hung back long enough to make sure he was the last to leave. 'Capital ball, ma'am,' he said as he set his cocked hat on his head at a rakish angle. 'Are all your parties this much of a lark?'

She smiled thinly and gestured to the door. Grinning, he touched the prow of his hat in salute to her, and then strolled out after the others.

He tripped lightly down the steps into the compound. Most of the carriages had already gone. He caught up with Strachan. 'The others have gone ahead,' said the assistant surgeon.

Killigrew nodded. The two of them were about to walk through the gate when the last carriage rattled up behind them. Killigrew pulled Strachan back out of harm's way, but the Sikh coachman had seen them and reined in. Sir Dadabhoy Framjee leaned out of the window.

'Can I give you and your friend a ride, Mr Killigrew? Perhaps you would care to join Peri and I for a drink before we part? It is still quite early.'

Killigrew and Strachan exchanged glances; there was no need for anything to be said. 'We'd be delighted,' Killigrew told Framjee as he and his friend sat down opposite Framjee and his daughter. The Parsi rapped the ferrule of his cane on the floor of the victoria and they rattled off. 'Well, I don't know about the rest of you, but I've certainly enjoyed this evening,' said Killigrew.

'Indeed!' beamed Framjee. 'It is wrong of me, I know, but I certainly enjoyed watching Bannatyne's first attempt at a ball end in disaster. I wonder if tonight's events will have put him off hosting any more?'

'Only time will tell, sir. But somehow I think he'll get over tonight's humiliation.'

At length the coachman reined in the horses in front of Framjee's villa. As they climbed down from the carriage, the butler emerged from the house to greet them.

'We'll take coffee in the drawing room,

Gobinda,' Framjee told him as they passed inside, and turned to Strachan. 'I understand you are an artist, Mr Strachan.'

'Well, I wouldn't go that far, sir. I used to dabble a little; sketches and that sort of stuff. These days photography's more my game, though I still do the occasional aquatint.'

'Do you think it is true that photography will replace painting altogether?'

'I don't know. I think art will have to become more innovative to stay ahead if it's going to survive. The camera can only show what it sees, but the artist can see so much more, tell the story behind the picture.' When it came to art, Strachan displayed the same enthusiasm he had towards fossils. 'In fact, I think there's a chance photography could be the saving of art. It's been getting awfully stale of late.'

'We have some of Mr Chinnery's landscapes in the upper gallery, if you would care to see them?'

'I'd be delighted.'

Framjee turned to his daughter. 'Peri, perhaps you'd care to show Mr Strachan while I have a word with Mr Killigrew here?'

Killigrew nodded to himself. He had been wondering what Framjee's motive in inviting him back here so late had been. Now he had a pretty good idea. So did Peri, if the concerned glance she gave him over her shoulder as she led Strachan upstairs was any indication.

Framjee had opened the door to his library and gestured for Killigrew to precede him. Inside, the Parsi sat down behind his desk with his fingers steepled. He did not invite Killigrew to sit. 'I wish to speak to you about Peri. And your intentions towards her.'

'Strictly honourable, sir, I assure you.'

'I do not doubt it. But I am wondering if your concept of what is and what is not honourable is the same as those accepted by most other people. You are aware, I take it, that her religion forbids her from marrying anyone other than another Parsi?'

Killigrew smiled. 'I could convert.'

'You could become a Zarathustrian. But you could never become a Parsi. Unless both your parents were Parsis, which I must confess I very much doubt.'

'She could convert.'

'She could. If she wished so. But my Peri is very proud of her heritage.' Framjee opened a drawer in his desk and took out a cheque. He dipped his pen in an inkwell and started to write.

'Don't you think that's for your daughter to decide?' Killigrew asked coldly.

'What kind of father would I be if I did not concern myself about what is best for my daughter?' Framjee dried the cheque with blotting paper and handed it to Killigrew. It was made out for five thousand pounds.

The lieutenant resisted the urge to let out a low whistle. 'A princely sum. I'm not sure whether to be flattered or insulted.'

'I am not asking you never to see her again. But I would be happier if you faced the fact that there can be no future for you and my daughter. No more unchaperoned walks together, eh, Mr Killigrew?'

The lieutenant slowly and deliberately tore up the cheque, scattering the pieces across the top of Framjee's desk. 'I can't be bought.'

The Parsi reached for another cheque. 'Every man has his price,' he said, dipping his pen into the inkwell once more.

'Don't bother. Mine isn't money.'

Framjee sighed and drained the ink from his nib before replacing the pen in its holder. 'You are a man of principle, Mr Killigrew. I respect you for that. To tell the truth, I think I would have been disappointed if you *had* accepted my cheque. Then let me conclude by asking you, as a man of honour, to bear in mind all the consequences for my daughter if you persist in your attentions towards her.'

'I don't need to be told to do that. Harming her is the last thing on my mind.'

'I appreciate that. But it is often the case that common sense does not get a fair hearing when passions rule the day.'

'The one must be balanced against the other,' allowed Killigrew. 'Now if you'll excuse me, sir, I think it's time I returned to the *Tisiphone*.'

Framjee inclined his head. The two of them went upstairs to the gallery where they found Peri and Strachan admiring a watercolour of Victoria Harbour.

'Come on, Strachan,' said Killigrew. 'We've outstayed our welcome.'

Peri looked at him with concern. 'Is everything all right?'

'Everything is fine, my child,' said Framjee. 'Mr Killigrew and I had some business to attend to.

Now it is concluded, he feels it is appropriate he leaves. I am in agreement.'

'I thought we were staying for a dram?' protested Strachan.

'Come on.' Killigrew took his friend by the arm and all but dragged him back downstairs. The butler showed them out.

'Take care, gentlemen,' Framjee called after them. 'Victoria is a dangerous place at night.'

'Don't worry about us, sir,' said Strachan. 'It's only five minutes' walk to the waterfront from here. What can possibly go wrong in that time?'

'What did you say to him?' Peri demanded as her father returned inside and Gobinda closed the door behind him.

Framjee said nothing, but walked softly to the drawing room. Peri followed him. 'Father, what did you say to upset him like that?'

Her father sat down on the divan and rubbed his temples wearily.

'You tried to buy him off, didn't you?' persisted Peri. 'That is it, is it not? You offered him money.'

Framjee nodded.

She turned away, not even trusting herself to look at her father. 'Oh, how could you? You always said I could marry whom I chose, just as Mother defied her parents to marry you!'

'I never thought you would choose a penniless British naval officer!'

'Am I a chattel, to be bought and sold like a slave girl?'

'I only want what is best for you, my child. That is all I have ever wanted for you.'

'Do you not think I am able to judge what is best for me?'

'Are you not curious to know what he said?'

She turned back to face him.

'He tore the cheque up and threw it back at me.'

She stared at him, not sure if she had heard him right. 'He did that?'

Framjee nodded. 'A cheque for five thousand pounds, and he tore it up without hesitation. When I offered to write him another, made out to any amount he cared to name, he still refused. He must love you very much, my child.'

She sat down beside him and clasped his hands. 'And I love him, Father.'

'If you married him, you would be an outcast from your own people.'

'And from you, Father?'

'No, my child. You will always be my daughter. But I cannot have my daughter married to a penniless naval officer, so ... I fear your dowry will have to be very generous indeed.'

She hugged him. 'Oh, Father!'

'Be still, my child! He has not yet asked for your hand!'

'Oh, but he will if I tell him we have your blessing.'

'I think if Mr Killigrew has it in his mind to marry you, he will do so with or without my blessing.' Framjee chuckled. 'Just as I married your mother. But I do not think it would be a good idea to tell him that I will pay any dowry. If he loves you he will need no encouragement, and he would not want people to think he had married you for money.'

'He'll ask, Father. I know he will!'

'What was all that about?' Strachan asked Killigrew as they ambled down Caine Road towards the top of Ladder Street. 'No, wait, let me guess: he was trying to buy you off, wasn't he?'

'If he was, that's between Sir Dadabhoy and myself.'

'I'll bet he was. How much did he offer you?'

'None of your damned business.'

'She's a braw lassie,' Strachan admitted. 'I hope you don't mind me asking, Killigrew, but what...?'

'If you're going to lecture me, please don't,' said Killigrew. 'I had enough of that tonight from Mrs Bannatyne and Sir Dadabhoy.'

'Ah. I noticed our hostess looked a little flushed when the two of you came in to dinner tonight. I wasn't sure if you'd been rowing or spooning with her.'

'I never get involved with married women.'

'More fool you. She deserves better than that smug bastard Bannatyne... Do you think she really sculpted that bust of Genghis Khan?'

'Why not?'

'Because it's damned good, that's why. As good as any modern sculpture I've ever seen, and better than most. You know, I rather liked her.'

'You want to bed her, you mean.'

'Please, Killigrew. Just this once could you credit me with having finer feelings?'

They walked down Ladder Street in silence.

'I'm thinking of resigning my commission,' Killigrew suddenly announced.

Strachan stopped and turned to stare at him. 'I beg your pardon?'

'I said: I'm thinking of resigning my commission.'

'You? Leave the navy? That'll be the day!'

'Why not? My Uncle William's always pressing me to work for his company in the City. I'd get paid six times what I'm earning at the moment.'

'And you'd die of boredom within a week. How long have I known you, Killigrew? Two years? The navy's your life. You're never happier than when you're chasing slavers or crossing swords with pirates. You think you'd get the same kind of satisfaction from some sinecure in the City?'

'A City job would leave me more time for other pursuits. Charitable works. Politics, perhaps. I'm always mocking politicians for being corrupt; perhaps it's time I stood for office myself, introduced a bit of decency into the House of Commons.'

'You wouldn't last five minutes in Parliament. What, do you want to become everything you despise? Someone like Blase Bannatyne and Sir George Grafton?'

'I'm more worried I'll become everything I despise if I stay in the service much longer, Strachan. I tell myself I fight the slavers and the pirates because it's the right thing to do; but is it? I kill them as ruthlessly as they kill their victims. Am I really any better than them?'

'Yes, you are, and you damned well know it.' Strachan narrowed his eyes shrewdly. 'This isn't about pirates and slavers, is it? This is about Miss Dadabhoy.'

'I don't know what you mean, I'm sure.'

'You're going to ask her to marry you, aren't you? That's why you want to leave the service: you don't want her to live the life of a naval officer's wife.'

Killigrew sighed and thrust his hands into his pockets. 'If she marries me, she'll no longer be accepted as a Parsi. If she's prepared to make that kind of sacrifice, isn't it fair that I make a sacrifice in turn?'

'She's a lovely girl, Killigrew. Damn me, I'm envious. But have you really considered what you'd be giving up? I mean, *really* considered?'

Before Killigrew could reply, a shot sounded nearby. 'That was a firecracker, wasn't it?' Strachan said nervously. 'It's the Chinese New Year about now, isn't it? Please tell me that was a firecracker.'

'There was no firecracker.'

'I was afraid you were going to say that. Maybe it would be best if we didn't get involved...'

'It sounded as if it came from the direction of the gaol. You run to the barracks and raise the alarm.'

'Good idea,' Strachan said with relief. He took a few hurried steps down Hollywood Road, and then stopped and turned back. 'Killigrew? You're not going to do anything ... *rash* ... are you?'

'You know me, Strachan.'

'In other words, "yes".' The assistant surgeon sighed and set off for the barracks at a sprint.

Killigrew strode towards the gaol. He was halfway there when another muffled shot sounded somewhere up ahead. He broke into a run and a moment later there came a third shot.

He rounded the next corner and saw the gaol immediately ahead of him, its barred windows a blaze of light, the door wide open. The smell of gunsmoke was heavy on the air, and he could smell something else: something sulphurous.

Conscious that the only weapon he had was his dress-sword, he drew it from its scabbard and dashed across the street to press himself up against the wall by the door. He listened for a moment. Inside, all was silent. He peered through the door and jerked his head back quickly, but in that split second he had seen enough to reassure him that no one had a gun lined up on the door. He took a deep breath and dashed through, turning as soon as he was inside to make sure that no one was lurking in wait just inside.

There was no one in sight. He took a step closer to the counter and felt something crunch under his foot. Glancing down he saw that the floor was covered in pottery shards: stink-pots.

It was a favourite trick of the pilongs to make grenades by filling small earthenware pots with a combustible mixture of brimstone, gunpowder, nitre, bitumen, rosin and other noxious substances. A fuse was inserted in the neck and lit before the stink-pot was thrown on to the deck of another vessel. The explosion was usually sufficient to daze and choke everyone within ten yards for a few seconds, and if enough stink-pots were thrown it gave the pilongs time to board the vessel unopposed. Whoever had attacked the gaol had simply used the same tactic on land.

Killigrew leaned over the counter and craned his head to look through the doorway behind. There was no one in the next room, but he spotted a puddle of blood on the floor beneath him.

Sword in hand, he vaulted over the counter. The Sikh constable whose body had been shoved under the counter had been all but decapitated by a sword-stroke.

His heart pounding, Killigrew slipped into the next room and found two more constables, as savagely murdered as the first had been. He was about to go back and wait outside for Strachan to return with reinforcements when he heard a muffled sound from the door leading to the back of the building. Still gripping his sword, he took another deep breath and dived through.

The Triad waited for him with a crossbow lined up on the doorway from the far end of the corridor. Killigrew froze, knowing he could not hope to kill the man with a sword at that distance. He braced himself for the shot – at that range there was a good chance the pilong might miss.

A moment later something connected with the back of his neck. He dropped the sword and sank to his knees. Another blow struck him on the back of the head, and the last thing he saw before the cobwebs of oblivion wrapped him in their coils was the floor rushing up to meet him.

VII:

Wu-Yi

The gig bumped against the *Tisiphone*'s side, and Robertson, Hartcliffe, Westlake, Vellacott and Muir climbed up the side-ladder to the entry port. At the top, Robertson turned to address the coxswain. 'You'd better row back to the wharf and wait for Killigrew and Strachan, Ågård.'

'Aye, aye, sir. All right, lads, you heard him. Shove off and give way together.'

There were three men in the gig in addition to Ågård: Molineaux, Dando and O'Connor. They pulled for the wharf and Molineaux jumped on to the stone steps cut in the quayside to tie the gig's painter to an iron ring.

O'Connor produced his pipe and lit it. 'All right then, Wes, what's all this I hear about you going to the rescue of some yellow-belly lass?'

'You know me, Joe. Never could resist going to the aid of a damsel in distress.'

'Is it true what they'm be saying?' asked Dando. 'About what?'

'About Chinese girls being ... different ... to English lasses.'

'In what way?'

'Well, you know how English lasses be ... rigged fore and aft ... down below? Be it true that Chinese girls be rigged athwartships?'

'Rigged athwartships ... Jem, where the hell do you come up with this hogwash?'

'Well? Be it true? Or didn't you find out?'

'That ain't the kind of question a gentleman answers.'

'Arr, but you bain't be no gentleman.'

'What the hell's going on over there?' asked Ågård suddenly. He was narrowing his eyes to where a group of figures had just emerged from a side-street and were dashing through the darkness to where a smug boat was tied up at the next wharf. Molineaux heard voices calling out in Cantonese.

'Trouble,' he said, well aware that the Chinese were not allowed to wander the streets of Victoria after curfew without a light and a pass from their employer.

'I reckon we'd best stay here and wait for Tom Tidley and the assistant sawbones,' O'Connor said nervously.

'You can wait here,' said Molineaux. 'I'm going to investigate.' He hurried across the waterfront followed by Ågård, Dando and a reluctant O'Connor. 'Hey!' he called out as they drew near. 'Anyone here speakee English?'

The dozen or so shadowy figures on the wharf froze. Out of the corner of his eye, Molineaux saw something fizzle on the gunwale of the smug boat. 'Swivel!' he yelled.

The four seamen threw themselves to the ground a moment before the swivel gun boomed. Molineaux felt something sting his left buttock, but he was on his feet a moment later. The Chinese on the dock made a dash for the

211

gangplank leading down to the smug boat's deck, but Molineaux caught one around the waist in a flying tackle and brought him down. The two of them rolled over and over, until Molineaux knocked his opponent unconscious with a punch to the jaw.

He looked up. The other three seamen were getting stuck in. Molineaux recognised Zhai Jing-mu amongst the men hurrying for the boat as the mooring ropes were cast off. He went after him and got halfway down the gangplank before one of the Triads came up to meet him: a young, rather effeminate-looking Chinese. Like most of his race, he was not tall, and he was less muscular than many of his compatriots. This one looked as though a slight breeze might be enough to blow him down.

Molineaux reached behind him and pulled his Bowie knife from a sheath he wore in the small of his back. 'Out of my way!'

'You go to hell!' the Chinese snapped back. He jumped into the air. One foot connected with Molineaux's wrist, dashing the Bowie knife from his grip, while the other smashed into his jaw. He staggered and had to seize the hand-rope to stop himself from falling in the water.

The Chinese seized his advantage and charged forwards, delivering a succession of rib-jarring blows to his chest. Molineaux managed to land a lucky punch on the Chinese's jaw. The pilong staggered back and stepped off the gangplank. Molineaux glanced down and saw the Chinese catch hold of the side of the gangplank, swinging underneath it as nimbly as an acrobat. As

Molineaux bent over to try to see where he had gone, the Chinese's feet connected with his buttocks. The seaman was knocked forwards and plunged headfirst into the water.

When he surfaced he saw the gangplank being taken on board while the oars were lowered from the smug boat's sides. One of them nearly brained him. He grabbed hold of it in a futile attempt to impede the boat's progress. A figure appeared at the gunwale above him and a moment later a pistol cracked with a flash and a bullet kicked up a spurt of water only inches from where Molineaux trod water. He relinquished his hold on the oar and ducked beneath the waves.

By the time he had surfaced the smug boat was already fifty yards away, the oarsmen pulling strongly for the harbour mouth. Molineaux punched the water in frustration and swam back to the dock where Ågård helped him out. 'You all right, Wes?'

'I got shot in the bum, kicked in the nut and knocked in the drink,' snarled Molineaux. 'Do I look oh-kay to you?'

Ågård grinned. 'You'll survive.'

Molineaux reached inside his trousers to explore his stinging buttock gingerly. There was no blood: the pellet which had hit him must have ricocheted off the quayside first. He glanced about the waterfront. Dando was nursing a cut on his arm while O'Connor tied up the pilong Molineaux had knocked out. 'Well, at least we got one of them,' said Ågård.

Molineaux bent to retrieve his Bowie knife,

which had fallen on the quayside. 'But we let Zhai Jing-mu get away.'

The first indication Killigrew had that he was still alive was the pain. It coursed through the very fibre of his being, through every limb and nerve-ending, but it was concentrated in a pounding ache in the back of his skull.

He lay still for a moment, listening, but heard nothing. Opening an eye fractionally, he saw only the floor of the corridor. His sword lay a foot away. He snatched it up and jumped to his feet, but there was no one else in sight. Then the intensified throbbing in his skull forced him to slump to the floor once more, his back to the wall. Feeling sick and woozy, he checked his fob watch: a quarter past midnight. He could not have been unconscious for more than a couple of minutes, but it had been enough time for the Triads to make good their escape.

He reached inside his coat, produced a cheroot and lit it. The rich taste of the tobacco helped to stimulate him enough to find the strength to rise to his feet.

'Who's there?' a voice called from one of the offices leading off the corridor.

'Lieutenant Killigrew, HMS *Tisiphone*.'

'You! What the deuce are you doing here?'

Killigrew recognised Cargill's voice. He staggered into the office and found the assistant superintendent braced behind a cabinet with a single-shot percussion pistol held in both hands.

'I was on my way back from the ball at Bannatyne's when I heard shooting. Thought I'd better come and investigate.'

'I'm glad you did. You must've frightened them off.'

'Zhai Jing-mu?'

'Let's check, shall we?' Cargill produced a bunch of keys and led the way downstairs to the cells. Killigrew noticed that the policeman was limping, bleeding from a wound in his leg.

'What happened to you?'

'Hmm?' Cargill glanced down at his leg. 'Oh, that's nothing. Just a scratch.'

Still feeling groggy, Killigrew rubbed the back of his head. 'They knocked me out. Why the devil didn't they kill me when they had the chance?'

They stepped into the lock-up. The cells were all empty. 'Because they got what they came for?' Cargill suggested bitterly.

'The man I saw wore the same clothes as those Triads who attacked me in the joss house,' said Killigrew.

Cargill nodded. 'Looks like you were right, Killigrew. The Triads and the pilongs are working hand in glove. I should have listened to you.'

'Would it have made any difference?'

'Probably not,' Cargill admitted ruefully, and then slammed his fist against the stone wall. 'Damn it to blazes! How could I have let this happen?'

Killigrew remembered the smug boat he had seen from the terrace of Bannatyne's house. 'Maybe he hasn't got away yet. I saw a smug boat in the harbour. That must be how they're planning to get away from Hong Kong, while we're still too stunned to do anything about it.'

'You're right, by George!' Cargill led the way back upstairs. They dashed out of the gaol and a moment later a musket-shot sounded. Killigrew felt the ball whip-crack through the air close to his head and flung himself down on the ground.

'Hold your fire, damn your eyes!' shouted someone. 'They're English!'

Killigrew raised his head and saw a squad of a dozen sepoys with Lieutenant Dwyer and Strachan. He pushed himself to his feet and helped Cargill up after him.

'What happened?' asked Dwyer.

'Gaolbreak,' said Killigrew. 'We think they're heading for the harbour.'

'Come on, then.'

By the time they reached the waterfront the smug boat had long gone. The only figure on the quayside was Molineaux, seated on a low shape. The seaman stood up and put one foot on the shape. Killigrew recognised it as a Triad.

'Good evening, Molineaux.' He indicated the seaman's prisoner. 'Seen any more like that?'

''Bout a dozen of 'em, sir. Our old sparring partner Zhai Jing-mu was with 'em. They jumped on to a smug boat and cut and ran. Olly, Jem and Joe went back aboard the *Tisiphone* in the gig to alert the cap'n.'

Killigrew glanced across the harbour to see that the *Tisiphone* was under sail, moving out from her anchorage. But the wind was light, the sails sagging limply from the yards, and there was no sign of the smug boat. Such vessels were also known as 'fast boats' with good reason. The *Tisiphone* would have had her fires banked, and it would be

216

some time before she could get steam up.

'Damn it!' Killigrew rammed his dress-sword back in its scabbard with a gesture of frustration.

'But apart from that, sir, how did you enjoy the ball?' asked Molineaux.

With the *Tisiphone* off on its futile pursuit of Zhai Jing-mu, there was nothing for it but for Killigrew and Strachan to spend the night at the Hong Kong Club, where Lieutenant Dwyer signed them in as guests.

Killigrew was so tired he fell fast asleep at once, but he was troubled by nightmares. He slept fitfully until the creeping light of dawn slipped through the louvres on the window to tickle him awake long before one of the club stewards came to rouse him. He shaved, washed and dressed – back in his dress uniform – and made his way downstairs to take breakfast on the verandah. Presently Strachan joined him, yawning, blinking owlishly, his hair every which way but flat. The assistant surgeon was not a morning person.

'Is the *Tisiphone* back yet?'

Killigrew had already surveyed the ships in the harbour and he did not bother to look up from his newspaper. 'Not yet.' He was nursing a pounding headache and his neck felt as though it had been put through a wringer. Whoever had hit him the previous night had a punch like a steam-hammer.

Strachan slumped into a chair in time to order devilled kidneys for breakfast, while Killigrew preferred scrambled eggs on toast. They were reading the morning papers over a pot of tea when Lieutenant Dwyer entered.

'Good morning, gentlemen. I trust you slept well?'

'As well as can be expected,' said Killigrew. 'Will you join us for a cup of tea?'

'I do believe I shall.' He signalled for a flunkey to bring a third cup and saucer. While the tea was being poured out, one of the white-coated club porters approached the table with three envelopes on a silver salver. He placed the salver on the table. 'Hullo,' said Dwyer, shuffling the envelopes. 'One for you here, Killigrew.'

Killigrew tore open his letter. 'Ah. From Rear-Admiral Collier. He wants me to report to him on board the *Hastings* at nine.'

'You too, eh?' Dwyer held up one of his letters, an almost exact replica of the one Killigrew held, before opening the other.

'How come I don't get invited?' asked Strachan.

'Be grateful,' Killigrew told him. 'After last night's fiasco, I don't think anything the admiral's going to have to say to us is likely to be complimentary.' He glanced across and saw Dwyer frown as he perused his other letter. 'Bad news?'

Dwyer glanced up, quickly folded the envelope and tucked it inside his jacket. 'No. Possibly good news, actually. What time do you make it?'

'Nearly eight o'clock. We'd better get underway if we're to report to the admiral on time.' Killigrew dabbed his lips with a napkin and rose to his feet, leading the way outside. Under the portico in front of the club, Dwyer seemed to hesitate.

'Not coming with us, Lieutenant?' asked Killigrew.

'Erm ... no. Give the admiral my apologies, would you? I'm afraid I've got another appointment.'

Army officers were not at the beck and call of the navy; nevertheless, it was not done for a mere lieutenant to snub a rear-admiral. But if that was what Dwyer intended to do, that was his business, no matter how curious Killigrew might find it. 'All right. We'll see you later, perhaps.'

Killigrew and Strachan found Molineaux waiting for them outside the gates to the club grounds. 'Good God, Molineaux!' exclaimed Killigrew. 'You haven't been out here all night, have you? I do apologise for my thoughtlessness, if I'd known... You really should have said something...'

'Not me, sir. I spent the night on a *yolo*.'

'This wouldn't be the same *yolo* on which you had your little altercation with Captain Ingersoll, would it?'

Molineaux grinned. 'That'd be telling, sir.'

As the three of them made their way down to the wharf they saw the *Tisiphone* returning to harbour under steam. 'Think you can persuade your Tanka girl to take us back?'

'A dollar could do it better than me, sir.'

As Mei-rong sculled Killigrew, Strachan and Molineaux back to the steam-sloop, the signals flew thick and fast between the *Tisiphone* and the *Hastings*. Commander Robertson was likewise being summoned into the presence of the rear-admiral; it was reassuring for Killigrew that he would not have to face Collier's wrath alone.

The *yolo* bumped against the *Tisiphone*'s side and Killigrew paid Mei-rong a dollar before following Strachan and Molineaux up the side-ladder. Hartcliffe awaited them on deck.

'I'm damnably sorry, Killigrew. I'm afraid that devil gave us the slip. We spent all night looking for him, but he just vanished into thin air.'

Killigrew shook his head. 'There must be a thousand creeks and inlets within ten miles of here that haven't been charted, and I'll lay odds Zhai Jing-mu knows them all like the back of his hand.'

Robertson came up on deck and the gig was lowered from its davits to carry him and Killigrew across to the *Hastings*. The gig reached the flag-ship's accommodation ladder first and Robertson and Killigrew climbed up to the quarterdeck where they found the *Hastings'* commander, Captain Francis Morgan, awaiting them.

'You're a couple of minutes early, gentlemen.'

'We didn't want to keep the admiral waiting, sir.'

A dour, strait-laced, humourless man, the very antithesis of the Captain Morgan of buccaneering fame, Morgan sniffed and escorted the two of them down to the admiral's quarters. He knocked on the door.

'Who is it?'

'Morgan, sir, with Commander Robertson and Lieutenant Killigrew to see you, sir.'

'Show them in.' Collier's voice sounded deceptively mild. *The calm before the storm*, thought Killigrew.

Morgan ushered them inside. Collier sat at the table in his day room, going over some paperwork. He did not look up as the three men stood to attention before him. Collier made another note in the margin of the report he was reading before he spoke, still without looking up. 'Where's Lieutenant Dwyer?'

'Had another appointment, sir,' said Killigrew.

Collier glanced up at him. He was a choleric man and he did not look pleased. 'Oh, did he?' he said heavily. 'Well, Commander? Did you catch Zhai Jing-mu?'

'No, sir,' Robertson replied flatly.

Collier drained the excess ink from the nib of his pen and leaned back in his chair. 'There have been some great days in the annals of the Royal Navy, gentlemen. Days like the Nile, Trafalgar, the Glorious First of June. On the other hand, there have been some downright disastrous days. Days like the fall of Minorca, the sinking of the *Royal George*, and Admiral Sir Cloudesley Shovell's attempt to take a short cut through the Scilly Isles. I put it to you, gentlemen, that last night's fiasco was on a par with those.'

'An exaggeration, I think, sir,' ventured Killigrew. 'Besides, it was not the responsibility of the Royal Navy to keep Zhai Jing-mu under lock and key.'

Collier looked up at the lieutenant and glared. 'It may not have been our responsibility, Mr Killigrew, but the fact remains that you had Zhai Jing-mu in your hands, and you let him slip away! Three navy ships in the harbour, God knows how many men in Staveley's garrison, not to mention the Hong Kong Police, and against all that a handful of Triads were able to sail straight into the harbour unchallenged, break Zhai Jing-mu out of the gaol, and then escape again without let or hindrance.'

'According to one of my hands who confronted the Triads on the wharf as they made their escape, there were at least a dozen men involved in the breakout,' Robertson said mildly. 'Not counting the crew of the smug boat. It's difficult to see what Killigrew could have done against them on his own.'

'Perhaps *not* charging in through the front door – while Zhai Jing-mu was charging out of the back, leaving only a rearguard to take care of foolhardy naval lieutenants – would have been a good start,' snorted Collier. 'Assistant Super-intendent Cargill tells me you allowed yourself to be knocked unconscious, Killigrew. Might I ask how?'

'I suspect one of the Triads used *wu-yi* on me, sir. You know, like Bannatyne's comprador did at the ball last night.'

'If one more clipper is lost because you let Zhai Jing-mu slip through your fingers, Lieutenant, I'll do a damned sight worse than use *wu-yi* on you. You made a laughing stock of the navy last night. Fortunately today's papers went to press before news of last night's débâcle came out, but I'm not looking forward to reading tomorrow's. There are elements in the House of Commons – you know who I'm talking about – who'd like to see swingeing cuts in the naval estimates. The mess you made of things last night is nothing more than grist to their mill. Go on, get out of my sight, the pair of you. And don't let me see you again until you've brought me Zhai Jing-mu's head on a platter.'

Robertson and Killigrew saluted and made their way back to the gig tied up alongside. 'Thank you, sir,' Killigrew said as they were rowed back to the *Tisiphone*.

'For what?'

'Coming to my defence.'

'Hmph. Don't know why I bothered. Collier's absolutely right, Second. We made utter fools of ourselves last night.'

'There is a solution, sir.'

'Oh, please enlighten me, Lieutenant, do!'

'We find Zhai Jing-mu and his fleet and sink it.'

'Capital notion. And how do you propose we go about that?'

'Zhai Jing-mu is supposed to have a fleet of over fifty junks, sir. You can't hide that many junks easily. He must have a base of operations somewhere, a place where he can careen them, grave their hulls, ship supplies, ammunition, unload his plunder.'

'The thought had occurred to me, Second,' said Robertson. 'Just how do you propose we find this base? There are over two thousand miles of coastline between Saigon and Shanghai; not counting every island, creek, river, lagoon and inlet large enough to conceal a fleet of fifty junks. At present Collier has seven vessels under his command. Do you have any idea how long it would take to search it all?'

'We faced a similar problem on the Guinea

223

Coast, sir. We still managed to find the Owodunni Barracoon.'

'Yes, Mr Killigrew, thanks to Admiral Napier I'm well aware of your exploits at Owodunni the year before last. I hope you're not seriously proposing to try to join the crew of a pilong junk? Somehow I can't see you passing yourself off as a Chinaman.'

'No, sir, but there are easier ways of finding something than an exhaustive search. *Someone* knows where that pilong base is. We just have to ask the right man.'

'Take your pick, Mr Killigrew. The population of China is said to number in hundreds of millions.'

'With your permission, sir, I'd like to start with the Triad Able Seaman Molineaux captured last night. If the Triads have such close links with the pilongs–'

'I hardly think he'll blurt out the location of Zhai Jing-mu's base to you.'

'That all depends on how I ask him, sir.'

'If you weren't an officer and a gentleman, Killigrew – and I confess I sometimes have my doubts – I'd say that sounded like a proposal to inflict torture on the fellow.'

'Wouldn't dream of it, sir.'

'I should hope not. All right, Second, take the rest of the day off. What you choose to do with it is your own affair. If you can find out where Zhai Jing-mu's base is, all well and good. If I hear you've been torturing prisoners awaiting trial, I'll disown you. Do I make myself clear?'

'As crystal, sir.'

Captain d'Acosta of the Royal Engineers reined in his horse on the bridle path leading south from Happy Valley, high up in the central mountains of the island. 'Dwyer!'

Lieutenant Dwyer wheeled back to where he had halted. 'Sir?'

'Show me the letter again.'

Dwyer reached inside his tunic and passed the letter he had received at the Hong Kong Club that morning to his friend.

D'Acosta scanned the single page. 'It says to come alone. Why alone, Dwyer? And why in the middle of nowhere, on the south side of the island? It's got to be a trap.'

'Of course. Why do you think I'm not going alone?'

'But why d'you have to drag me into this?'

'Because I know I can trust you. Look, maybe it isn't a trap. Shen is Bannatyne's comprador, for God's sake. He's not going to try anything against two of Her Majesty's officers. Maybe he does know where we can find Zhai Jing-mu. If he does, there are plenty of reasons why he wouldn't want to meet us in Victoria.'

'Such as?'

'Maybe he's frightened that the Triads will see him talking to us and guess he's betraying them. And even if it is a trap; well, if there's more than two of them we'll just turn tail and get the deuce out of there. Discretion's the better part of valour, after all. And if there's only a couple of them we'll take them into custody and hand them over to Cargill.'

'If you ask me we should hand this letter over to Cargill and be done with it, let the police deal with it.'

'And let them get all the glory of capturing Zhai Jing-mu for themselves? I told you what a hash they made of things last night, ably abetted by Her Majesty's navy. Well, here's a chance for the army to succeed where everyone else has failed, and I'm not going to let it pass.' Without waiting to see if d'Acosta followed, Dwyer dug his spurs into his horse's flanks and rode down the slope towards Tai Tam Bay on the south side of the island.

The fishing station was where Shen's letter had said the rendezvous would be, on the peninsula which formed the right-hand side of the bay. The mat-shed building looked ramshackle and deserted. Dwyer reined his horse about fifty yards down the beach and swung himself down from the saddle, checking his percussion pistol while he waited for d'Acosta to catch up.

The captain of Engineers rode up and reined in. He nodded to the fishing station. 'In there?' he exclaimed incredulously.

Dwyer nodded. 'Come on, man. Show some spunk. Got your pistol?'

'And my sword.'

They tied their horses to a wooden post which might once have formed part of a breakwater, and then crunched across the shingle to the fishing station. Dwyer stepped on to the boardwalk outside and pushed the door open. It creaked eerily to reveal Shen seated in the gloom within, dressed in a white linen suit. The comprador struck a brimstone match and opened an oil lamp to apply it to the wick within, before shaking out the match. 'Come in, Lieutenant Dwyer.'

Dwyer glanced about cautiously, but it was obvious the comprador was alone in the place. Reassured, he entered. 'You said in your letter you might know where I could find Zhai Jing-mu.'

'You have brought the letter?'

Dwyer nodded. 'Captain d'Acosta's got it.'

'Call him in. He is too conspicuous standing out there.'

'Sir!'

The engineer captain entered. Seeing only Shen, he too relaxed, although not so far as to return his pistol to its holster.

Shen got up and crossed to the door, glancing out before closing it behind them. 'You made sure you were not followed?'

'Yes, yes!' Dwyer said impatiently. 'Are you going to tell us where Zhai Jing-mu is, or not?'

'I asked you to come alone.'

'I wasn't sure if this was a trap.'

'A wise precaution. What I have to tell you is for your ears only, however.'

'Anything you've got to say to me you can say to Captain d'Acosta as well.'

'I think not.' Shen brought the edge of his open hand down against the side of d'Acosta's neck. Dwyer heard the bone snap audibly. He whirled with the pistol in his hand. Shen's leg shot out and smashed Dwyer's wrist against the wall. The lieutenant dropped the pistol with an agonised

227

sob. He sank to the floor and pulled his sword from its scabbard, trying to ward off the comprador.

Shen snatched the sword effortlessly from his grip. Sneering, he bent it into a U-shape before tossing it into one corner of the room. Then he picked up a rough sack.

'What's in there?' Dwyer whispered fearfully.

'Nothing. Yet. Soon it will be full of heads.'

'Heads...?'

'Lieutenant Killigrew's; Miss Dadabhoy's; and yours, Lieutenant. I have a message from Zhai Jing-mu.' Shen grabbed Dwyer by the front of his tunic and hoisted him to his feet. 'He asked me to tell you he always keeps his promises.'

The last thing Dwyer saw before one of his own ribs stabbed his heart was Shen's fingertips effortlessly piercing his chest.

VIII:

The *Akhandata*

Back on board the *Tisiphone* Killigrew made his way to his cabin, changed into his pea jacket and pilot cap, packed some things in a holdall, and got some of the hands to row him to the wharf. He made his way first to the police office and was presently ushered into Assistant Superintendent Cargill's presence.

'Killigrew!' Cargill leaped to his feet and came around the desk to pump his hand. 'Good to see you back on your feet so soon!' He clapped him on the back. 'How are you feeling?'

'Fine. How's that leg of yours?'

'Not too bad. It only needed a couple of stitches. I said it was just a scratch, didn't I? Well, what can I do for you?'

'I'd like to question the Triad who was arrested last night, see if we can get him to tell us where Zhai Jing-mu's base is.'

'Forget it. I've been questioning him all morning. He's not saying anything. Some damned fool told him his rights.'

'Perhaps you haven't been asking him nicely enough.'

'You think you might be able to get something out of him?'

'I have my methods, Mr Cargill.'

229

The police officer looked shocked. 'Mr Killigrew, I hope you're not proposing to torture him?'

Killigrew opened his holdall so that Cargill could see inside. 'I think this should do the trick.'

Cargill blanched. 'Good God, man! You're not serious, are you?'

'I'm in deadly earnest, Mr Cargill. You know the Chinese say that if you save a man's life, you're responsible for his actions thereafter?' Cargill nodded. 'By letting Zhai Jing-mu get away last night, I saved his life. If he attacks one more clipper before we can get to him, it will be on my head.'

'*Our* heads, Mr Killigrew. I was there too, remember? All right, we'll have a stab at it.'

They made their way to the gaol. A coolie was still washing the blood off the floor. Cargill showed Killigrew down to the cells where the sole prisoner glared at them sullenly. The assistant superintendent turned to two of his men. 'All right, let's be having him. Clap a pair of darbies on him, Constable. Knowing our luck, he'll probably turn out to be another *wu-yi* expert.'

The prisoner was dragged up to one of the offices and seated in a chair behind the desk. Cargill told the two constables to stand on guard outside, and then closed the door. 'Let's get it over with. I can't say I relish doing this to a prisoner, Triad or otherwise.'

'Ruthless men require ruthless methods,' Killigrew said firmly, and sat down opposite the Triad. 'Speakee English?'

230

'My no makee-tellee nothing, *fan-kwae*!' spat the prisoner.

'Oh, but I think you will,' Killigrew said with soft menace. The Triad's eyes widened in apprehension when the lieutenant opened his holdall. Then Killigrew placed a bottle of whiskey and a tumbler on the table between them. 'Care for a drink?'

'You my number-one frien',' slurred the Triad. 'What you wantchee savvy? I tellee you alla.'

'You might start by letting me know where I can find Zhai Jing-mu,' said Killigrew.

'Whiskey finishee, Missee Killigrew.' The prisoner held out his tumbler in his shackled hands.

Killigrew sighed and reached for the bottle.

'Are you sure that's a good idea?' asked Cargill. 'He looks like he's had enough to me.'

'I think we're getting close.' Killigrew topped up the prisoner's tumbler. 'Chin-chin.'

'Chin-chin.' The prisoner knocked it back in one and gasped with pleasure. 'How-how-ah!'

Cargill looked at his watch.

'My b'long Triad no longer. They makee-tellee barbarian bad, but you no bad, Missee Killigrew, you my number-one frien'.'

'Friends shouldn't have secrets from one another, should they, Chan?'

The prisoner shook his head woozily. Cargill had to move quickly to stop him from falling out of his chair. When he had propped up Chan, he glanced at his watch again.

'So, where can I find Zhai Jing-mu?'

231

'So sorry, Missee Killigrew. No can tellee. My tellee you where catchee Zhai Jing-mu, Triad spilum Chan.' He was clearly terrified the Triads would murder him if he betrayed them.

'Yes, but if you don't tell us, you see, you'll be put on trial, found guilty and be hanged. If you help us, on the other hand, we can protect you.'

Chan held out the tumbler once more. 'Whiskey finishee, Missee Killigrew.'

There was a knock at the door. Cargill opened it and stepped outside to take a message.

'Now look, Chan, you're not such a bad fellow,' persevered Killigrew. 'All right, so you've been a Triad. But the way I understand it, some Triads are traitors, others are no worse than Chartists. You were led astray, that's all.'

'What Chartist?'

'Never mind. You don't want to be executed because of Zhai Jing-mu, do you?'

'Zhai Jing-mu number-one hero to Han people. Him givee Manchu plenty trub.'

'He's a pirate, Chan, a common thief and a murderer. However much the Triads may try to make a hero out of him, he's only interested in himself. I've even heard that he's offered to become an imperial admiral, and to sweep all the other pilongs from the seas, in return for amnesty for all his past crimes. Is that true, Chan?'

'*Hai*. Is true. Zhai Jing-mu scarum Manchu so muchee, they wantchee makee agree.'

'And where will that leave the rest of you?'

Chan gazed into his tumbler and said nothing.

'You see, Chan? Zhai Jing-mu doesn't care about the Han people. He'd make a covenant

232

with the Devil as quickly as with the Manchus, if it was to his profit. And if that means selling you and your friends down the river, he doesn't care one jot. Are you really willing to die to protect such a man?'

'What river?' asked Chan.

The door opened and Cargill stuck his head through, his face grim. 'Can I have a word?'

Killigrew nodded and stepped outside, leaving a delighted Chan to help himself to more whiskey. In the corridor, Killigrew closed the door behind him. 'What's wrong?'

Cargill jerked his head at the door. 'Has he told you anything yet?'

'Not yet, but I think he's ready to talk...'

A crash sounded on the other side of the door. The two of them burst through to find that Chan had fallen from the chair and was fast asleep on the floor, snoring.

Killigrew sighed.

'Never mind,' said Cargill. 'It was a nice idea.'

'When he wakes up, he's going to have a number-one headache. Don't let him have anything to drink – not even a sip of water – until he talks.'

'By George, Killigrew! You really are a ruthless bastard, aren't you?' Cargill said admiringly.

'You were going to tell me something?'

The assistant superintendent's face became grim. 'It's bad news, Killigrew. Lieutenant Dwyer. He's been murdered.'

Killigrew stared at him. 'Murdered? By whom?'

'We don't know. His body was found alongside that of Captain d'Acosta at a place called Wong-ma-kok on the south side of the island.' Cargill

233

gripped his upper arm. 'They cut off their heads, Killigrew. Those swines butchered them. They were only identified by their uniforms and the papers they were carrying on them.'

Killigrew shook his head in disbelief. It had only been that very morning that he had breakfasted with Dwyer. Then he remembered something. 'Did Dwyer have a letter on him?'

'A letter? What sort of letter?'

'I was with Dwyer at the Hong Kong Club this morning when he received a letter. He seemed fairly excited by it. Then he left suddenly, saying something about an appointment. If you can find that letter, there's a chance it will lead you to his murderer.'

'It's a slim chance,' said Cargill. 'But it's worth looking into.'

Another, grimmer thought struck Killigrew, and he suddenly felt chilled. 'What's the date today?'

'The twenty-fifth of February. What's that got to do with anything?'

'No, I mean, in the Chinese calendar?'

'Let me see ... the year of the Rooster, the rabbit moon...' He counted on his fingers: 'One, two, three ... the sixth day of the rabbit moon.' He looked up at Killigrew in horror. 'Oh Christ!'

The Sikh butler who opened the door of the Framjee residence peered at Killigrew disdainfully. 'Yes, *sahib*? May I help you?'

'I need to see Miss Dadabhoy.'

'If you'll give me your card, *sahib*, I'll see if she is in.'

Killigrew pushed him aside. 'This isn't a social call, damn your eyes, this is an emergency. Her life's in danger.' He strode across the marble-floored hall. 'Peri? Peri!' He checked the parlour and the drawing room, but both were deserted. The butler tried to grab him, but he pulled free and ran for the stairs. 'Peri!'

Framjee emerged from a door on the landing and leaned on the banister. 'Mr Killigrew! What in the world is going on?'

'I am sorry, sir,' said the butler. 'I tried to stop him, but he pushed past me and–'

Framjee made a calming gesture. 'That is all right, Gobinda.' He met Killigrew at the top of the stairs. 'Mr Killigrew, what is the meaning of this?'

'Where's your daughter, sir?'

'In the garden, I should imagine. Why? What-ever can the matter be?'

Killigrew ran halfway back down the stairs before taking a shortcut by vaulting over the banisters. He ran into the ballroom and out through the French windows on to the terrace where he found Peri relaxing on a swing-seat with Tennyson's *The Lady of Shallot*.

'Kit! You are early.'

'Are you all right?'

'Yes, of course...'

He pulled her off the seat and into his arms. He kissed her and held her close. 'Thank God! Thank God!'

Framjee emerged on to the terrace followed by the butler. 'Mr Killigrew! I demand an explana-tion.'

The lieutenant released Peri and turned to her father. 'Your daughter must leave Hong Kong, sir. Now. Do you have any ships bound for Bombay in the harbour?'

'The *Akhandata* is in the Cap-sing-mun anchorage ... but I cannot just send my daughter away at a moment's notice.'

Killigrew gripped him by the shoulders. 'Sir, please believe me, your daughter is in deadly danger.'

'Mr Killigrew, please!'

'When the *Tisiphone* first moored in the harbour and I handed Zhai Jing-mu over to Assistant Superintendent Cargill and Lieutenant Dwyer, he said something about him being free and the rest of us being dead before the end of the first week in the rabbit moon. Well, today is the sixth day in the rabbit moon. And Zhai Jing-mu escaped last night.'

Framjee nodded impatiently. 'I heard all about the gaolbreak. But if Zhai Jing-mu escaped only last night, surely he will be lying low? The last thing he will want to do is risk recapture by seeking to fulfil some threat he made.'

'That's what I thought. Until I learned Lieutenant Dwyer was murdered this morning.'

Framjee's face turned ashen.

'Zhai Jing-mu may be in hiding now, but he has plenty of friends,' continued Killigrew. 'The Triads, for one. Sir, your daughter was included in his threat. If it hadn't been for her, he might still have escaped that day he attacked the clipper. They've already got one of us, they'll be coming after the rest. They've got less than thirty hours to make good his threat, but I'm convinced they'll try.'

Framjee nodded. 'Peri, go up to your room and pack for a voyage back to Bombay.'

'Yes, Father.'

'Go with her, Gobinda,' Killigrew told the butler. Gobinda nodded and followed Peri inside. 'Can you trust the crew of the *Akhandata*?' Killigrew asked Framjee.

'Implicitly, Mr Killigrew. Once she is on board, she will be safe.'

'What if the pilongs try to stop her before she gets to Bombay?'

'They can try. But at this time of year the monsoon winds will be behind the clipper all the way to Singapore. There is not a ship in the world which can catch the *Akhandata* when she has a following wind, Mr Killigrew, not even one of your steamers.'

'All right. I'll escort your daughter to the anchorage and see her safely on board. Have you got any guns? I'm afraid I came out unarmed.'

'I keep my shotguns in a cabinet in the billiards room.'

'I'll fetch them. Tell your coachman to prepare your carriage. As soon as Peri's ready, we'll leave. If we can stay one step ahead of the pilongs, there's every chance we can beat them.'

Killigrew made his way to the billiards room. The gun cabinet was locked, but under the circumstances he had no qualms about breaking it open with a billiards cue. Ammunition was in a drawer below. He loaded and primed two double-barrelled sporting guns and stuffed his pockets with cartridges.

When he emerged into the hallway, Peri was already coming down the stairs while behind her two footmen carried a trunk between them. 'Put that on the carriage,' Framjee told them. 'Do not worry, my dear,' he added to his daughter. 'Gobinda will go with you to Bombay, to protect you.'

'Know how to use one of these things?' Killigrew asked the butler, holding up one of the shotguns.

Gobinda stood erect. 'I was a havildar in the Twenty-First Bengal Native Infantry.'

Killigrew tossed him one of the shotguns. Gobinda caught it by the barrel in one hand and checked that it was loaded. They went outside and the butler climbed on to the roof of the carriage to sit beside the coachman while Killigrew, Framjee and Peri rode inside.

'Are all these guns really necessary?' asked Peri.

'Just a precaution,' said Killigrew. He sat facing forwards, peering out of the side window in the hope of spotting any trouble ahead before it was too late. The trip to the harbour was the most dangerous time; once they were on board the *Akhandata* they would be safe.

They reached Framjee's trading factory without incident and the carriage drove unchallenged past the guards into the compound. 'Close the gates!' ordered Framjee. There was no sign of the genial, humble Parsi now: here was a man who could think and act in the same breath, the man who had built up a business empire worth hundreds of thousands of rupees. The guards stood aside as he led the way. The back of the factory overhung the waterfront, and a thirty-four foot side-wheel steam-pinnace was tied up there. A white sailor with a silk neckerchief was polishing the engine. As Framjee stepped out on to the stage, the sailor stood to attention.

'How soon can you get steam up, Mr Endicott?'

'Fifteen minutes, sir.' Endicott was a Liverpudlian by his accent, with lank, straw-coloured hair slicked to his head with a centre parting.

'Get on with it, then.'

'Aye, aye, sir.'

'Put the trunk in the pinnace,' Framjee ordered the flunkeys, and marched back into the factory. 'I shall write a letter for the captain of the *Akhandata*,' he explained to Killigrew. 'He will know what to do.'

The Parsi disappeared into an office and left Peri seated on a bench in the corridor with Killigrew. 'You're going to be all right,' he told her. 'Don't worry, Peri, it won't be for long. By the time you reach Bombay, I expect your father will be writing to tell you we've got the whole thing cleared up and it's safe for you to come home.'

'You will not be coming with me?'

He shook his head. 'I can't go absent without leave. I have my duties to attend to. And those include dealing with Zhai Jing-mu.'

As she looked up at him, her round eyes moist with tears, he was tempted to ask her to marry him there and then. But that would not have been fair: she had too much on her mind; the last

239

thing she needed to worry about now was a marriage proposal. He kissed her instead and she held him close.

'I'm frightened, Kit.'

'Don't worry, everything's going to be just fine.'

He heard a cough behind him and broke off the embrace to find Framjee standing over him. Killigrew rose to his feet but made no attempt to apologise.

'Give this to the captain of the *Akhandata*,' ordered Framjee, holding out an envelope. Killigrew nodded and slipped the letter inside his jacket.

'Are you sure you will not come, Father?' asked Peri, as they made their way out on to the landing stage. 'I shall miss you.'

Framjee shook his head. 'I have to stay here and run the company. Do not worry, my dear, I shall be perfectly safe. The pilongs would never assassinate me. That would be killing the goose that lays the golden eggs. Is that not so, Mr Killigrew?'

'That's more or less the long and the short of it, sir.'

Peri nodded and dabbed at her eyes with a handkerchief. 'All right, Kit. I am ready now.'

Killigrew handed her down into the steam-pinnace where Gobinda already waited with the trunk. Then he untied the painter and jumped down after them. She waved her handkerchief at her father – already a forlorn figure without the company of his daughter – while Endicott opened the valve which engaged the steam engine, a miniature version of the kind on the

Tisiphone. It hissed and rattled into life, and the paddle-wheels drove the pinnace westwards across the harbour.

'Give those other vessels a wide berth,' Killigrew told Endicott, indicating Admiral Huang's junk and a couple of sampans moored in mid-harbour. If there were Triads on board either vessel, they might try to take a pot shot at himself or Peri with a *gingall*. Endicott nodded and adjusted the tiller with a wink at Peri. She did not notice.

'Have you been working for Framjee and Co. long?' asked Killigrew.

Endicott glanced up. 'Me, sir? Nah. Only a few months. I used to work for Grafton, Bannatyne and Co., until I got my walking papers.'

They chugged past Stonecutters Island at the mouth of the harbour. Five miles away, the jagged spine of Lan-tao Island rose up through the haze which hung above the sea. Endicott adjusted the tiller and the pinnace headed for the Cap-sing-mun Passage between Lan-tao Island and the mainland. It was a pleasantly mild day, and as Killigrew sat beside Endicott in the stern he lit a cheroot, but he could not relax. It was dangerous to underestimate the Triads, and he knew Peri would not be safe until the *Akhandata* was underway. Even this close to Hong Kong, the Triads and pilongs would not hesitate to try something. The question was, what? He kept his eyes on the shore and on the other vessels that passed him: smug boats, sampans, and lorchas bustling between Cap-sing-mun and Hong Kong.

It took them the best part of an hour to reach the passage. Lan-tao was about eleven miles long, the north-eastern tip about a mile from the mainland, but the passage was divided in two by the islet of Ma Wan. As they passed through on the south side of the islet, the steep shore seemed to loom over them menacingly. But it was just Killigrew's imagination, and a few moments later they rounded the northern tip of Lan-tao and entered the Cap-sing-mun anchorage.

If Hong Kong was the head of the opium trade, then Cap-sing-mun was its heart. Here were moored the receiving ships of the trading companies, the opium hulks: ancient merchantmen with their masts taken down and their deck houses roofed over so that they looked like the prison hulks at Woolwich and Portsmouth. The holds of the hulks acted as stores for the opium brought by clipper from Bengal and Turkey to be exchanged for green tea brought down the Pearl River Estuary by smug boat. The smug boats would off-load their cargoes on to the waiting clippers and then take on cargoes of opium from the hulks to be touted along the southern coast of China.

Theoretically, importing opium into the Celestial Kingdom was forbidden, but there were plenty of buyers and, since the Manchus paid their mandarins poorly, expecting them to supplement their incomes with *cumshaw* – or 'squeeze', as bribery was known – it was easy to find a prefect who could be persuaded to look the other way when opium was smuggled through his district. Occasionally the authorities in Canton would receive an order from Peking to step up their suppression of the barbarian opium smugglers. When that happened, Imperial war-junks would be sent down the Pearl River estuary, but only after the barbarians had been given plenty of warning, and only opening fire once the barbarian clippers were out of range. The authorities in Canton had borne the brunt of the war, while the Imperial Grand Council in Peking had been relatively unscathed, so the Cantonese knew better than the Dragon-Emperor's advisers that the Celestial Kingdom could not afford to risk another war by offending the barbarians. And the China Traders made it worth the Cantonese authorities' while to turn a blind eye when necessary.

The opium hulks were moored in the lee of Lan-tao Island and another island off Lan-tao's north-shore, Chek-lap-kok. Smoke curled from beneath the conical hats of chimneys, and laundry hung to dry from washing lines, a reminder that many men not only worked on board the hulks but also lived, ate and slept there. Some of the hulks were decorated with flower pots on their roofs, an indication that there were few, if any, seamen in their crew: sailors were superstitious about having flowers on ships – they considered them too reminiscent of funeral wreaths – and would not tolerate them. All hulks bore the flag of their respective trading houses, and the golden dragon of Grafton, Bannatyne & Co. fluttered from the mast of the *Buchan Prayer.*

'There's the *Akhandata.*' Endicott pointed to

where the clipper was moored a short distance away from the Framjee opium hulk, and adjusted the pinnace's tiller accordingly. The clipper rode at anchor with all sails furled and looked curiously peaceful.

Peri smiled sadly. 'I would feel a good deal happier if you were coming with me, Kit.'

'I wish I could come, too. But someone's got to stay here and find Zhai Jing-mu. Once he's been taken care of, you'll be safe enough.'

She shook her head. 'How did we get into this predicament, Kit? What did we ever do to deserve this?'

'It isn't a question of deserving, Peri. Your father worked hard all his life to get himself where he is today. Some people envy that. That's your only crime.'

At last the pinnace bumped against the *Akhandata*'s hull. The side ladder was already down and Killigrew climbed up to the entry port.

The deck was deserted.

Killigrew could feel the hairs prickle on the back of his neck. He turned back to the pinnace. 'Wait there. Something's wrong. Pass me one of those shotguns, Gobinda. I'm going to look for the captain. Have you got a watch?'

The butler nodded.

'If I'm not back in two minutes, get out of here. Go back to Hong Kong, go to the *Tisiphone*, got that? You'll be safe there.'

'Be careful!' called Peri.

Killigrew nodded as he took the shotgun Gobinda passed up to him. 'Two minutes,' he reminded the butler, and then crossed the deck to the after-hatch.

All was eerily silent on board the *Akhandata*, except for the creaking of the ship's timbers. His finger on the shotgun's trigger, Killigrew descended the companion way to the lower deck. There was no sign of anyone. As he tiptoed along the corridor to the captain's quarters, something shot out of a cabin and ran over his feet. He almost jumped out of his skin.

The cat ran up the companionway and disappeared through the hatch. Killigrew continued to the end of the corridor and laid his left hand on the doorknob. He eased back the hammers on the shotgun, wincing at each click. Then he kicked the door open and went through, moving quickly to one side, sweeping the day room with the shotgun's twin muzzles.

The captain, a European, sat at his table.

Killigrew felt the tension flood out of him. 'For Christ's sake, Captain! What kind of a ship are you running–' He broke off. When a stranger with a shotgun burst into a room, some kind of reaction was to be expected, but the captain just sat there, staring. Killigrew crossed the deck with two long strides and pulled the captain forwards. The man slumped across the table. There was a bloody slit in his back. He had bled, but not much: the blade must have gone straight to his heart.

Killigrew swore and dashed back out of the cabin. He reached the foot of the companionway and was about to ascend when a shadow fell across him. He looked up, raising the shotgun along with his eyes, but it was only Gobinda.

'I thought I told you to stay with Miss Dadabhoy?' Killigrew demanded angrily.

Gobinda took two steps down the companionway. Then his legs crumpled beneath him and he toppled forwards. Killigrew side-stepped as the butler sprawled at his feet, a dagger planted firmly between his shoulder blades.

The lieutenant was about to launch himself up the ladder when Peri appeared at the hatch above him. And Zhai Jing-mu was beside her, holding a flintlock pistol to her head. Her face was pale and streaked with tears.

'Lieutenant Killigrew,' observed the *lao-pan*. 'I hear you've been looking for me.' He gave Peri a push, and followed her down.

'It's all right, Peri,' said Killigrew, struggling to keep the tremor out of his voice. 'Everything's going to be all right. It looks like you won't have to go to Bombay after all. I think we can settle this whole thing right here and now.'

'That remains to be seen,' said the *lao-pan*. 'Put the shotgun down, Mr Killigrew.'

The lieutenant was filled with loathing for Zhai Jing-mu, for using someone he cared about to get at him. He would kill the pilong without hesitation, if only he had not been terrified of hurting Peri. He had to get her safely out of the way; then he could deal with Zhai Jing-mu once and for all. 'The girl's done nothing to harm you. Let her go.'

'I intend to. Once you've put the gun down.'

Killigrew did not believe that for a moment. 'So you can shoot her and then kill me? No can do, Zhai. Put the girl back in the pinnace and then

246

we'll settle this between us, just you and me.'

The *lao-pan* thumbed back the hammer of his pistol. 'Put the gun down. Or I will shoot her.'

Killigrew shook his head. 'I don't think so, Zhai. Right now she's the only thing between you and me. If you kill her, so help me, I'll tear your heart out.'

'Last chance, Lieutenant. I mean what I say.'

'Go ahead,' bluffed Killigrew. He knew that Zhai Jing-mu would not waste his only bullet on his hostage and leave himself defenceless. 'Shoot her. She means nothing to me.'

Zhai Jing-mu shrugged. 'As you will.' He pulled the trigger.

IX:

Pipe Dreams

The sound of the shot was deafening in the confined space below decks. Peri Dadabhoy's face exploded outwards, her blood spattering the bulkheads. Her lifeless body toppled down the companionway.

The horror hit Killigrew like a physical blow. He stared down at her corpse, not believing the evidence of his own eyes. He had killed her.

'That is what you wanted, is it not?' Zhai Jing-mu asked with a smirk.

Killigrew raised his brown eyes to meet the pilong's blue ones. His guts seethed with hatred. He brought up the barrels of the shotgun, determined to wipe the smile off the pilong's face for ever. As his finger tightened on the first trigger, however, a hand shot out from his left and grabbed the barrels. The gun was tugged aside and the shot blew a hole in the bulkhead beside the *lao-pan*.

A moment later something smashed into Killigrew's jaw. He had been concentrating on Zhai Jing-mu and it had never occurred to him that the *lao-pan* might have an accomplice creeping up behind him. He staggered to his right and felt the shotgun pulled from his grip. As the accomplice tried to reverse the weapon,

Killigrew kicked him in the stomach. The man doubled up and the second barrel discharged itself into the deck.

Killigrew turned and ran, determined to stay alive long enough to avenge Peri.

'Don't let him escape!' shouted Zhai Jing-mu.

The lieutenant reached the door to the captain's quarters. A bullet spanged over his head and smashed a hole in the glass of the stern window. He slammed the door behind him and looked about the day room. He dragged the chair from beneath the dead captain, letting the corpse sprawl on the floor, and positioned it with the back rest wedged under the doorknob. A moment later the door shuddered as someone on the other side threw his shoulder against it.

Killigrew grabbed the table and pushed it into the middle of the room, beneath the skylight. By standing on top of the table he was able to reach the catch. He threw the skylight open and hauled himself up on deck. He crossed to the after-hatch, slammed it shut, and quickly battened it down so that no one could get up from below. He hoped it would hold long enough for what he had to do.

He crossed to the entry port and glanced down. There was another pilong in the boat, holding a shotgun at Endicott's throat. As Killigrew's shadow fell across him, he glanced up and took the gun off the sailor to aim it at him. Killigrew ducked back and a moment later shot peppered the bulwark. Then he heard a groan.

'Lieutenant!' called Endicott.

He glanced cautiously over the bulwark. The

pilong was dead, a dagger thrust between his ribs. Endicott threw the shotgun up to him.

He caught it in both hands. 'Good work! Now get the hell out of here!'

'What about you?'

'I've got someone to take care of first. Go on, go!'

As Endicott got the pinnace's steam engine going again, someone hammered on the underside of the after-hatch. Killigrew ran across to the forecastle. He could see Framjee's opium hulk less than three cables away. He waved his head above his arms, trying to get someone's attention. Surely they had heard the shooting?

He heard a sound behind him and saw two pilongs come up through the after-hatch. He emptied the shotgun's other barrel at them – next to useless, at that range – jumped down the fore-hatch and found himself in a charnel house.

There were bodies everywhere: the crew of the *Akhandata*, slaughtered to a man. The deck was awash with blood.

Choking back the bile, Killigrew fumbled in his pockets for a couple of fresh cartridges. He had just snapped the breech shut when a figure appeared at the hatchway above him. He thumbed back one hammer and let the pilong have it in the chest.

Killigrew ejected the spent cartridge, reloaded that barrel and thumbed back both hammers. How many pilongs were there on board the clipper? Enough to slaughter the entire crew. More than enough to slaughter him.

Gasping for breath, he made his way down to

the lower deck. He found what he was looking for amidships: the magazine. Even clippers needed a powder room, to supply the guns they carried as protection against pilongs. There were only three barrels of gunpowder in there: Killigrew hoped it would be enough. A kind of Viking funeral for Peri, one that Zhai Jing-mu would not live to forget. He hoped Framjee would understand.

There were no fuses, so he had to do it the old-fashioned way, breaking open one of the barrels of powder and tipping it on its side. He could hear footsteps on the deck above him, the pilongs searching the ship for him. They had not got to the lower deck yet, but they would. He found a small pail and scooped it full of gunpowder, using it to lay a long, winding trail out of the powder room, glancing fearfully over his shoulder every few seconds.

A footfall sounded on the deck behind him. He whirled and brought up the barrels of the shotgun. There was a pilong behind him with a crossbow.

Killigrew fired first. The pilong fell to the deck. Then he heard a pistol being cocked behind him.

He turned. Twenty feet away, Zhai Jing-mu crouched halfway down the companion ladder leading up to the next deck. He had a pistol in each hand, both levelled at Killigrew.

'Drop the shotgun, Mr Killigrew. It is useless at this range.'

'Those peashooters of yours aren't going to be much better, unless you're a damned fine shot.'

'Is that a chance you are willing to take?'

251

Killigrew lowered the muzzles of the shotgun to the deck, and shrugged. 'You're going to kill me anyway.'

'Precisely so.' Zhai Jing-mu fired.

A searing pain lashed through the side of Killigrew's head. He pulled the trigger of the shotgun. The muzzle flash sparked the trail of gunpowder. The powder flared and the flame raced back along the trail towards the magazine. He had the satisfaction of seeing Zhai Jing-mu's eyes widen in horror as he realised what he had done.

Then the pilong fired the other pistol, but in his panic the shot went wide. Zhai Jing-mu dropped both pistols and scrambled back up the companion ladder. He was halfway through the forward hatch when Killigrew caught him by the sash and pulled him back down.

'Oh no you don't, you sonuvabitch! You're going down with the ship. Or rather, up.'

The two of them grappled at the foot of the companionway. Killigrew grabbed hold of one of the rungs and pulled himself up to kick the pilong in the face with both feet. 'When you get to Davy Jones' locker, you can pay your respects to Peri!'

Zhai Jing-mu staggered back and tripped over the coaming of the hatch leading down to the lower deck. As he fell out of sight, Killigrew ascended the last few rungs to the upper deck. He ran across the forecastle and dived over the bulwark. A moment later the *Akhandata* blew up.

'Here it comes.' As the men of the *Tisiphone*'s

252

starboard watch took on board barrels of water from a harbour lighter, Ågård nudged Molineaux and nodded to where Captain Morgan was being rowed out to the sloop in a gig from HMS *Hastings*. Rear-Admiral Collier had been laid low by an apoplectic stroke two weeks earlier and Morgan was now the senior naval officer in Hong Kong. 'From the look on his face, someone's going to catch it now.'

'Yeah,' said Molineaux. 'And I think I can guess who.'

'Boat ahoy!' challenged the marine sentry at the gangway.

'*Hastings!*' returned the gig's coxswain.

'Molineaux!' called the boatswain's mate. 'Run below like one o'clock and inform Commander Robertson that Captain Morgan is coming on board.'

'Aye, aye, Mr Fanning.' Molineaux went down the after-hatch and approached the marine on duty outside Robertson's door. 'Message for the cap'n. Cap'n Morgan coming on board.'

The sentry crashed the stock of his musket against the deck. 'Message for the captain! Captain Morgan coming on board.'

'Tell him I'll be up directly,' Robertson's voice called out.

'Tell him he'll be–' began the sentry.

'Yeah, all right, Barnes, I think I got that,' Molineaux replied sarcastically. He went up on deck and relayed the message to the boatswain's mate.

'All right, Molineaux, back to work.'

Fanning piped Morgan on board and Com-

253

mander Robertson met him on the quarterdeck. Neither of them smiled. 'An unexpected pleasure, Captain,' said Robertson.

'Hardly unexpected,' Morgan said coldly. 'And unlikely to be a pleasure. For either of us.'

Robertson nodded. 'Shall we go down to my day room?' he suggested, and shot a glance at where Molineaux was pretending to check a cask for leaks. 'Fewer prying ears.'

Morgan nodded and the two of them descended through the after-hatch.

'I wouldn't mind being a fly on the wall in Tommy Pipes's day room right now,' said O'Connor.

'Looks like you're not the only one.' Molineaux nodded to where two of the *Tisiphone*'s landsmen scrubbed the quarterdeck. The skylight over the captain's day room was ajar and the two landsmen were taking an inordinately long time to scrub the adjacent deck.

The boatswain's mate saw them. 'If you scrub that patch of deck any longer, gentlemen, you'll fall through it!' he snarled. 'All right, you can leave that for now. Go and clean the head.' He watched the two landsmen until they had reached the forecastle, and then got down on his hands and knees by the skylight. A moment later Ågård, Molineaux and O'Connor had joined him. The boatswain's mate scowled at them, but could not tell them to leave without the captain hearing him and spoiling the game for all of them.

'...don't mind if I have one, do you, sir?' Robertson was saying.

'No, go ahead,' replied Morgan, and crystal clinked as Robertson poured himself a drink from a decanter.

'This is a very painful duty for me,' said Morgan, when Robertson had settled down. 'Now I know that Lieutenant Killigrew has done good work on behalf of the navy in the past, but ... well, to be frank, his methods have increasingly begun to raise eyebrows in certain quarters, if you know what I mean.'

'*Who* you mean, more like.'

'And his latest escapade only seems to confirm what they've been saying. Frankly, Robertson, to me it looks like the proverbial last straw. The question is, what are we going to do about it?'

'*Do* about it, sir? I'm not sure that we need to *do* anything about it. I've read Killigrew's report, questioned him closely and found that he behaved perfectly satisfactorily.'

'Perfectly satisfactorily! For pity's sake, Robertson! He blew up a clipper! Right in the middle of Cap-sing mun anchorage!'

'I'm sure Sir Dadabhoy is fully insured.'

'Against acts of God, Commander. I believe that acts of Lieutenant Killigrew are something of a grey area as far as insurance companies are concerned.'

Robertson chuckled. 'Yes, I'd been warned that he had a callous disregard for the safety of property. I'm amazed that no enterprising marine insurance company has yet offered a policy with our indomitable lieutenant in mind.'

'This is no time for levity, Robertson. Aside from the destruction of the *Akhandata*, there's also the question of loss of life to be taken into account.'

'I'm fully aware of that, sir. My people spent most of last Sunday afternoon pulling bodies out of the anchorage. We can hardly blame Killigrew for the slaughter of the crew of the *Akhandata*; and as for the pilongs, he was only doing his job.'

'And Miss Dadabhoy? The daughter of Sir Dadabhoy Framjee, an extremely influential man in these parts?'

'How much influence Sir Dadabhoy has is hardly the point, a fact which I'm sure – if he was here to speak for himself – he would be the first to point out.'

'*Au contraire*, Commander Robertson, that is *precisely* the point. How am I to explain to the other traders that the daughter of one of their associates was killed because Lieutenant Killigrew thought he could play games with the girl's life?'

Molineaux, Ågård, O'Connor and the boatswain's mate jumped as something slammed in the cabin below: Robertson's glass against the table, by the sound of it. 'With all due respect, sir, bearing in mind the particular regard in which Killigrew held Miss Dadabhoy, I would imagine he did everything in his power to save that poor girl.'

'And I put it to you, Commander, that he allowed his personal feelings to cloud his judgement.'

'We've all made mistakes in our youth, sir. Killigrew's a damned fine officer and I believe he did everything he could. The sad fact of the matter is that sometimes everything simply isn't enough. It's a tragedy, but there it is. You didn't see him after Mr Endicott pulled him out of the harbour. I did. I know that young man, and believe me, if he could turn the clock back and exchange his life for hers, I truly think he would do just that.'

'Hmph. Well, he *can't* turn the clock back. Where is he? I think it's high time I had a word with him myself. I'm sure he's had plenty of time to recover from his injuries.'

'Ah. I'm afraid he isn't on board at the moment, sir. I told him to take a fortnight off to rest and make sure he was fully recovered.'

'Is that so, Commander? I was informed you'd given him a week. That was twelve days ago.'

'Who told you that, sir? No, don't tell me, let me guess: that priggish little squit Norris.'

Norris was one of the *Tisiphone*'s mates, a devout, self-righteous Christian, and thoroughly disliked by the hands. It was news to Molineaux that Robertson shared their dislike.

'Well, it hardly matters, does it?' continued Robertson. 'Lieutenant Killigrew is my officer. If I choose to extend his leave indefinitely, that's between him and me.'

'Her Majesty's government does not pay its officers to keep their feet up in Hong Kong, Commander. I expect to see Lieutenant Killigrew back on duty by Monday morning, is that understood?' Chair legs scraped against the deck.

'You have to make allowances. Killigrew was deeply upset by what happened to Miss Dadabhoy. I may not blame him for what happened to

257

her. That does not mean he doesn't blame himself. I think under the circumstances–'

'Monday morning, Commander. I shall expect to see him in my cabin in *Hastings* at nine a.m. on Monday. If he does not appear, I shall have no option but to recommend that Lieutenant Killigrew be court-martialled for gross dereliction of duty and desertion. Do I make myself clear?'

'Abundantly so, sir.'

The door slammed. Molineaux and the others stood up and quickly tiptoed away from the skylight so that when Morgan emerged on deck they were back at their duties. The boatswain's mate piped the captain over the side.

As soon as Morgan's gig was on its way back to the *Hastings*, O'Connor turned to Molineaux and Ågård. 'Hear that, lads? Tom Tidley's gone adrift!'

'Don't you believe it!' snorted Ågård. 'If I know him, he's probably off doing secret work somewhere, tracking down the rest of them yellow-belly pilongs. You mark my words, lads, he'll turn up just as the ship's bell's chiming the end of the middle watch on Monday morning, ready to present his compliments to Cap'n Morgan, along with the exact whereabouts of a pirate lair!'

One of the marines emerged from the after-hatch and faced the boatswain's mate.

'Mr Fanning? The Cap'n wants to see you in his day room. Along with Ågård, Molineaux and O'Connor?'

The four seamen presented themselves in

Robertson's day room and stood to attention in a line. The commander paced up and down in front of them. 'I'm sure I don't have to remind you four that eavesdropping at skylights is an extremely nasty habit, and I won't tolerate it on board this vessel. I hope I don't ever catch any of you at it.'

The boatswain's mate exchanged glances with the others. 'No, sir.'

'Glad to hear it. Dismissed, gentlemen.'

As soon as the afternoon watch was over, Molineaux made his way forward to the sick berth and knocked on the door.

'Come in,' called Mr Strachan.

Molineaux entered and closed the door behind him. The surgeon, Westlake, avoided the sick berth if at all possible as a consequence of which it had become the domain of Mr Strachan. The young assistant surgeon kept everything in neat and pristine condition, if only so he could use the place as a developing room for his photographic plates. He had stretched lines across the deck head and pictures of the local flora and fauna hung side by side with surgical appliances.

'Drop your breeks,' said Strachan, his nose buried in Knox's *Anatomy*.

'Sir?'

'You want me to inspect you for social diseases, don't you?' Strachan turned a page with a sigh. 'It's always the same with you fellows. When are you going to learn that prevention is far better than cure? Wash your parts with coal-tar soap and I'll put you down for a course of mercury treatment—'

'This isn't about my parts, sir,' interrupted Molineaux. 'It's about Mr Killigrew.'

Strachan looked up. 'Killigrew's contracted a social disease? I'd've thought he'd know better.'

This was a possibility which had not occurred to Molineaux. 'I don't know about that, sir. He's gone missing.'

'Well? What do you want me to do about it?'

'You're his friend, aren't you?'

'I'd like to think so. Not that it's any of your business, Molineaux.'

'Aren't you worried about him, sir?'

'Damn your impertinence! Killigrew can look after himself.'

'What if he can't?'

'You think he might be in trouble?'

'He already is. He's gone adrift, hasn't he?'

'Killigrew wouldn't go absent without the captain's permission unless he had a good reason.'

'Wouldn't he, sir?'

'What are you suggesting?'

'He was sticking it away prettily heavily the other Sunday evening, wasn't he?'

'Damn your eyes, Molineaux! How much Mr Killigrew chooses to drink is no concern of yours!'

'Sir, I'd like to think that Mr Killigrew is a friend of mine, too. Now if he *has* got a good reason for being adrift, then it probably means he's in danger and needs our help, if he isn't already dead. If he hasn't got a reason, then don't you think it would be better if his friends found him drunk in a tavern before his superiors did?'

Strachan stared at him for a moment. 'Be so

good as to have the dingy lowered, Molineaux,' he said, closing his book. 'I'm going ashore.'

'It would be more discreet if we got one of the *yolos* to take us ashore.'

'Us?'

'A gentry cove like yourself can't be seen frequenting the waterfront gatherings, any more than I could get into the saloon of the Hong Kong Club or the Victoria Hotel.'

'All right.' Strachan reached for his hat and coat.

On deck, Molineaux crossed to the entry port and looked about. He recognised Mei-rong's *yolo* amongst the bumboats and waved her across. She started to scull towards the foot of the side ladder.

A voice in Molineaux's ear almost made him jump out of his skin. 'Going somewhere?' asked the boatswain.

Strachan intervened. 'Ah, Bosun. I'm just going ashore to pick up some medical supplies from the naval stores. I've asked Able Seaman Molineaux to assist me.'

'Very good, sir,' the boatswain said obsequiously, and turned to Molineaux with a snarl. 'Now you behave yourself ashore, Molineaux. I don't want to hear from Mr Strachan here you've been giving him any trouble.' He turned back to Strachan. 'If he gives you any jaw, sir, you just let me know. I'll sort him out.'

Strachan smiled nervously. Molineaux had noticed that the assistant surgeon was as frightened of the boatswain as any of the ratings. 'I shall, Bosun. Don't worry, I'm sure Molineaux

261

will be on his best behaviour.'

'That ain't saying much,' sniffed the boatswain. 'Er ... would you like me to have the dinghy lowered, sir?'

'That's all right, Bosun. We'll take a *yolo*.'

'As you will, sir.'

Molineaux and Strachan climbed into the *yolo* and Mei-rong sculled them across to the wharf. 'Give her a dollar, sir,' Molineaux told Strachan when they reached the quayside.

'A dollar!' protested Strachan, horrified. 'Just for rowing us across the harbour?'

'Got to keep the natives friendly,' said Molineaux, deadpan. Strachan sighed and reached into his pocket while Molineaux kissed Mei-rong goodbye and told her not to wait for them.

'Won't we need a boat to take us back?' asked Strachan as they watched her row back out to the *Tisiphone*.

'No shortage of boats round here, sir,' he said, gesturing at the sampans and *yolos* which crowded the waterfront. He cast his eyes over the town: it was still not that large, but there were plenty of nooks and crannies into which a drunken sailor might crawl, and the setting sun was spinning a web of darkness over the rooftops. 'Hadn't we better start searching?'

Strachan nodded. 'You try the waterfront taverns, I'll check the Hong Kong Club and places like that.' He checked his watch. 'We'll meet outside the post office on Queen's Road in three hours, at half-past nine.'

While Strachan glanced under newspapers draped over sleeping gentlemen in the rooms of the Hong Kong Club, Molineaux lifted sailor's faces out of puddles of their own vomit in the gutters of alleys behind taverns. When the seaman reached the post office shortly before nine, Strachan already awaited him. 'Any luck, sir?'

Strachan shook his head. 'You?'

'I spoke to a Portuguese sailor who things he saw someone answering Killigrew's description heading off towards Tai-ping-shan.'

They both glanced down Queen's Street to westward. 'Why would he go down there?'

Molineaux shrugged. 'You tell me, sir.'

'Maybe he picked up a trail that might lead him to the pirates,' said Strachan. 'How long ago did this fellow see Killigrew going towards Tai-ping-shan?'

'Sunday evening, sir.'

'Five days ago?' spluttered Strachan.

Molineaux coughed. 'A week ago on Sunday evening, I mean.'

'*Twelve* days! And no one's seen him since?'

'Doesn't sound too good, does it? You want me to go in after him?'

'On your own? By jings, no! Naturally I'll come with you.'

Molineaux gave him a funny look. 'You ever been into Tai-ping-shan, sir?'

'Have you?' countered Strachan.

'No, sir. But from what I hear, it's not all that different from a rookery. You ever been in a rookery?'

Strachan looked bewildered. 'What, you mean like, where rooks live?'

Molineaux took a deep breath. Strachan might know all there was to know about scurvy and yellowjack – although sometimes Molineaux had his doubts – but when it came to the flash world Strachan was greener than an Irish pasture in spring. 'Not rooks, sir. Crooks. The kind of places where the crushers daren't go because they know what the locals will do to them.'

'Oh! I see. Well, I can't very well let you go into a place like that alone,' Strachan said staunchly.

Molineaux was not convinced that Strachan would be more of a help than a hindrance, but he decided to say nothing. His main objection was that Strachan would stick out in a rookery anywhere in the world like a man wearing a sandwich board with the slogan: 'prime plant'; but Molineaux had to acknowledge that he himself was not likely to pass unnoticed through the streets of a Chinese shantytown.

'Stick close to me, sir. And try to look as though you've got every right to go where you're going.'

'Well, haven't I?'

Molineaux sighed. 'Yes, that's right, sir. You just remember that.'

Tai-ping-shan was less than a mile down Queen's Road, but it was a thousand leagues from the broad, elegant streets of Victoria. It was every bit as filthy and poverty-stricken as the back streets of Seven Dials parish in London, but while the tumbledown shacks were even more precarious than the ancient tenements of the slums back home, at least here one could see one's hand in front of one's face in a town where there were no factory chimneys to enhance the fog. An Oriental band played music somewhere in the distance, while Chinese voices jabbered excitedly inside a gaming den the two Britons passed. Children peered out of the gloom at them, eyes a thousand years old set in faces that were barely past puberty.

'You wantchee suckee-fuckee?' asked one girl who looked young enough to be Strachan's daughter. 'My givee good suckee-fuckee, only twenty cash!'

'What's suckee-fuckee?' Strachan asked Molineaux.

'It's a local delicacy. Come on, sir, let's keep moving. And for God's sake keep your watch chain covered and one hand on your pocket book.'

It was too late: three shadows moved out of the gloom to block their path. Molineaux glanced instinctively over his shoulder and saw two more men behind him. He was glad he had brought his 'persuader' – a brass belaying pin – tucked up his sleeve.

'You givee money!' hissed one.

'What's the cause?' asked Molineaux, allowing his persuader to slide down into his hand.

The first robber looked puzzled. 'Cause?'

'Sure. I can't give away money unless it's in a good cause.'

The robbers looked bewildered, and Molineaux took advantage of it to strike the first across the face with the belaying pin. Even as the first went down, he whirled and struck one of the men behind him across the cheek. The second man whirled with blood on his face, and the remaining two in front of them hesitated uncertainly.

Molineaux reached behind him, pulled his Bowie knife from its sheath and showed it to the ruffians. 'You want some of this? Come on and get it, you sons of bitches!'

They shook their heads, still hesitating. The first man Molineaux had hit groaned, but made no attempt to get up.

Molineaux glanced sideways at Strachan. The assistant surgeon had adopted the traditional boxing stance, his guard high. Molineaux suppressed another sigh. 'Come on, sir.' He led the way forward, and Strachan followed him. One of the robbers tried to block their path, but Molineaux brandished the Bowie knife and the robber melted aside. The two Britons hurried on down the street.

Thirty yards further on, Strachan glanced over his shoulder. 'Are they coming after us?' asked Molineaux. His heart was pounding in his chest.

'Doesn't look like it.'

'Don't worry. They will.'

As soon as they were around the next corner they both broke into a run. Molineaux took care to make sure Strachan did not get away from him; the assistant surgeon would not last five minutes on his own in Tai-ping-shan. Molineaux was not even convinced that he himself could last ten.

Around another corner they paused to catch their breath. 'Oh-kay, I think we lost them.'

'It's a damnable disgrace!' said Strachan. 'Someone ought to call a constable.'

'Whatever you say, sir.' Molineaux looked

around. There was no one in sight, but that did not reassure him. 'This was a chuckle-headed idea. We're wasting our time. If Mr Killigrew is around here – and if he ain't already dead – we're never going to find him.'

'All right.' Strachan hesitated. 'Which way is back?'

Molineaux looked around him again. He was not sure.

'Are we lost?' asked Strachan.

'Of course not. All we have to do is go downhill until we get to the shore, and then turn right and keep going.'

'What's that reek? I can't quite place it...'

Molineaux recognised the odour, like rotting vegetables and yet somehow sickly sweet at the same time. 'Opium, sir.' He nodded to the door of a mat-shed. 'Seems to be coming from in there. Must be an opium den. No point looking for Killigrew in there. Even he's not that much of a booby...'

The two of them stared at one another.

'I suppose it's worth taking a look,' said Strachan.

Molineaux nodded.

The interior of the mat-shed was a noisome, poky place, the scent of opium almost over-powering. A few paper lanterns which hung from overhead beams provided enough light for Molineaux to be able to make out the trestle tables arranged all around the walls. On some of them men reclined in a state of unconsciousness, so still they might have been dead. Perhaps they were.

An old man pottered up to Molineaux and Strachan and with a toothy grin he offered them a pipe: a reed about an inch in diameter with a bowl at one end. 'Smokee?'

'No smokee,' Molineaux told him.

'We're looking for an Englishman...' began Strachan.

'Blissful dreamy. Plenty blissful dreamy.'

It was obvious the attendant did not understand English and had learned only a few words by rote, just those pertaining to his job.

'No, thanks,' said Molineaux. 'Come on, sir. Let's work our way around until we find him.'

A small lamp stood at the head of each couch, and by the light of those they could make out the faces of the dreamers. They appeared old and wizened, their faces drawn, pallid, haggard and skull-like. They were oblivious to the two Britons who moved amongst them.

'Molineaux!' Strachan called from the other side of the room. The seaman crossed to stand beside the assistant surgeon, and gazed down at where Killigrew lay on his back, an imbecilic grin on his ashen, unshaven face. He was dead to the world.

Molineaux swore. 'How the hell are we going to explain *this* to Commander Robertson?'

Killigrew lay on a tropical beach in Peri Dadabhoy's arms and enjoyed the warmth of the sun on his body. There was not a cloud to be seen in the azure sky, and the junks bobbing on the waves out to sea had a calm, peaceful look. On the beach all was silent but for the gentle lapping of the waves. He turned to Peri. She smiled up at him, and he kissed her.

Some instinct made him glance over his shoulder, and he gaped. A great Chinese dragon flew through the sky, twisting and turning, looping its long, slender body back and forth on itself like a crepe streamer. Its scaly body was golden, and it cracked with lightning.

He wondered if he were imagining it and turned to Peri. She saw it too, and she smiled. The next thing he knew she had risen to her feet and was walking naked across the sand towards the water, waving her arms over her head at the dragon in the sky.

But he sensed the dragon was dangerous. He called out after her, but she did not seem to hear him. She waded out into the water until she was waist deep in the surf, and then dived forward and swam out towards the fishing junks to get closer to the dragon.

The dragon stopped, beating its leathery wings as it hovered high above them in the sky. Then it swooped and dived like a hawk, plunging towards its prey.

Killigrew was on his feet in an instant. He started to run down the beach, but before he had gone a dozen paces the fine white grains beneath his feet turned to quicksand and he sank up to his waist.

As the dragon swooped low over the junks it spread its jaws wide and a jet of flame poured forth. The junks were instantly charred to a crisp and the air filled with black, sickly sweet smoke. But Peri had not seen the attack on the junks and she still swam out towards the dragon. Killigrew tried to climb out of the quicksand, but the harder he struggled the more it held him back and sucked him under.

The dragon swooped on Peri, skimming the water and rising with her caught in its talons. Killigrew tried to scream but the quicksand filled his mouth and he choked.

As the dragon flew overhead Peri's body dropped to the sand only a few feet from where Killigrew struggled in the quicksand. It landed with a thud. She too had been charred to a crisp.

The quicksand evaporated and he ran to where she lay on the deck of a tea clipper, but by the time he had climbed over the bulwark her body had vanished. He glanced across to the poop deck and saw Jago Verran at the helm. The captain laughed. 'She's not for you, jobbernowl!'

Furious, he ran across the deck and climbed the companionway to the poop after Verran, but as he reached the top of the ladder Zhai Jing-mu appeared above him and kicked him in the face. He felt no pain, but was conscious that he was falling backwards, down and down, taking for ever to hit the deck below. When he finally landed it was in something soft and sticky which broke his fall, like molasses.

He tried to swim back to the island but it was far away, and when he finally reached the sandy shore the palm trees which had fringed the beach had vanished, as had the sea behind him, and he was in an endless desert beneath a suffocating sun which blistered his skin. Then he looked up and realised it was not the sun which burned him, but the dragon. It hovered above his head and breathed black smoke over him. He watched in horror as his own skin blistered and burned.

He looked up at the dragon, pleading, but saw no mercy in its reptilian eyes...

His own eyes.

'Bring her back!' he roared at the dragon.

But now the dragon had his own face. It laughed at him.

He looked down at his skin. The blisters had formed into scabs, and the scabs grew four pairs of legs each and turned into spiders which ran all over his body, tearing at his flesh with their massive, venom-filled mandibles. He screamed and tried to brush them off, but at that moment the dragon swooped on him and enfolded him in its leathery wings. He fought his way out of the wings and found himself lying on a bed in a room that was ten feet wide and a thousand miles long.

At the far end of the room he could just make out three figures, a European man and woman, and a black man wearing pusser's slops and holding a sennit hat before him. They looked vaguely familiar, as if he had known them in a dream, except that each of them had a nose that was a mile long. They swung those hideous noses in his direction as they turned to look at him.

Is he all right? Asked the woman.

He's having a nightmare, said the white man. *I've heard it's not uncommon when a man's been deprived of the drug he's come to depend on.*

He's awake, said the black man.

Killigrew nodded. They spoke as if they cared about him, but he knew they were lying. They

271

were plotting against him. Plotting to keep him away from Peri. They were going to murder him!

The white man came towards him. His elongated nose seemed to fly at Killigrew like a lance. Killigrew tried to crawl away with a yelp of terror. He was going to be skewered on that elongated proboscis. 'No! Stay away from me! You're going to kill me!'

It's all right, said the white man. *I've brought you some medicine.* He showed Killigrew a small brown bottle.

'No! It's poison! Stay away from me! You're trying to poison me! Where's my pipe? Give me another pipe, damn your eyes!'

It's laudanum, said the white man. *It will help wean you off the opium...*

Killigrew glanced at the bottle in the man's hand, but it had changed into Peri, and she was the size of a doll. 'Kit!' she called. 'Kit!'

He sobbed. 'Peri! You bastards, what have you done with her? Give her back to me!'

Be sure you drink it all, said the man, and handed Peri to him. She seemed to grow back to full size in his arms. He kissed her greedily and at once a warmth seemed to spread through him. The strange room faded and he was back on the beach with Peri in his arms. He settled back in the hammock with a smile of blissful ecstasy.

X:

Happy Valley

Killigrew woke up in bed and turned to where Peri lay, but she was not there. Panic seized him at once and he cried out for her.

The door opened and Molineaux burst into the room. He took one look at Killigrew and swore irritably. 'Another nightmare, I suppose?'

'I hope so,' Killigrew said hoarsely, hoping he would wake up next to Peri and it would be all over. 'Where's my pipe? Bring me another pipe, damn your eyes!'

Molineaux rolled his eyes. 'Here we go again. No more pipes, sir. How many times do I have to tell you? You want me to ask the sawbones for some more laudanum?'

'Where's the necessary?' Killigrew's voice sounded harsh and unfamiliar to his own ears.

'Right here.' Molineaux reached under the bed and pulled out a chamber pot decorated with Napoleon Bonaparte's face on the inside. 'You mean to say you're actually going to *use* that thing for once, instead of having a jerry-go-nimble in the bed?'

'A gentleman does not excrete in his bed, Molineaux.' Killigrew was trying to get up, but his emaciated limbs responded clumsily.

'Oh, right. I suppose you're going to tell me the

Triads have been sneaking in here and doing dockyard jobs on your mattress – and worse – while you slept?' Molineaux helped him up.

Killigrew felt weak and shaky all over as he relieved himself into the chamber pot. As soon as he had finished he sat down once more, exhausted. 'Where am I?' he croaked.

'The Bannatyne house.'

'The Bannatynes'...!' Killigrew sat up sharply, and immediately regretted it. 'How long have I been here?'

'Four weeks, give or take.'

'Four weeks!' Killigrew pushed himself up and lunged for the door. 'I have to get out of here. I have to get back on duty...' He only made it halfway before his legs crumpled beneath him and he sprawled on the rug before Molineaux could catch him.

'Calm down, sir.' Molineaux tried to pick him up.

Killigrew cried out. 'Don't touch me!' he snapped irritably.

'Oh-kay, oh-kay! I was only trying to help! You don't have to worry about getting back on duty just yet,' Molineaux continued as Killigrew sat back on the bed. 'It's all taken care of, thanks to your pals Wes Molineaux and Mr Strachan. Not to mention Mr and Mrs Bannatyne, who've kindly put you up until you recover from your illness.'

That worried Killigrew, but his brain was still too addled to work out why. 'What about the *Tisiphone*?' he said weakly, sniffing.

'Don't worry about that. That Strachan ain't as

green as I first thought. He came up with a downy fakement and no mistake. He told Commander Robertson that you'd contracted some rare, highly infectious tropical disease with a long Latin name I can't remember. Probably made it up there and then, but even that daft old bugger Westlake didn't dare gainsay him. So instead of being kept in the naval hospital Strachan told them you'd have to be kept up here in quarantine, where the higher altitude would do you good.'

Killigrew sniffed. 'Have I contracted a rare disease?'

'Lumme, sir, try to keep up, will you? Mr Strachan says you've got a dependency on opium.'

'Opium...?' Killigrew had known there was something he wanted. 'Where's my pipe?'

'Oh, Lor'! Don't let's go through that again. Mr Strachan's gone down to Victoria with Mrs Bannatyne to fetch you some laudanum.'

'Who else knows I'm here?'

'Everyone. But only me, Strachan, and the Bannatynes know the real reason why. Even their servants have been kept at arm's length; though it wasn't difficult, once they heard you had an infectious disease.' He took out a clean handkerchief and held it out when Killigrew sniffed again.

The lieutenant took it from him and blew his runny nose. 'Thank you,' he said grudgingly. Suddenly feeling cold, he dragged the blankets off the bed and wrapped them around his shoulders, shivering.

He heard a door open in the next room, and Strachan's voice: 'By jings, that hill takes it out of me every time.'

'Mr Strachan?' called Molineaux. 'In here. He's awake. And making sense. Sort of.'

The door opened, but it was Mrs Bannatyne who entered, looking especially fetching in a white muslin morning gown. 'How are you feeling?'

'Damnable.'

'You look much improved.'

'Have you got a looking-glass?'

'I'll go fetch one,' said Molineaux, and went out.

A moment later Strachan entered with a small phial and a crystal sherry glass. 'And how's the patient this morning?'

'Spare me your bedside manner, Mr Strachan.'

'I'd say he's on the road to a full recovery,' Mrs Bannatyne said drily.

Strachan emptied the contents of the phial into the glass and handed it to Killigrew. 'Get that down you.'

'What is it?'

'Laudanum. We've been giving it to you twice a day, a smaller and smaller dosage each time. Do you not remember?'

Killigrew ached to toss the contents of the glass down his throat so desperately he suddenly found himself wanting not to, just to be bloody-minded and prove to himself he could do it. 'Am I sick, Strachan? I feel like I've got a chill.'

'You're suffering from the same symptoms as a lot of patients I've know coming off an opium-based medication.'

'So what am I supposed to do? Keep on taking laudanum for the rest of my life?'

'Not a wise notion,' said Strachan. 'An old friend of mine from Edinburgh works as an apothecary in Manchester now. He's often told me how a lot of his customers from the labouring classes buy opium lozenges. They keep on coming back for larger and larger doses. He thinks that the more opium one takes, the more the body becomes used to it, and the more it craves it. It's an awful nasty vicious circle, and we've got to break you out of it. So we're weaning you off it.'

Molineaux returned with a looking-glass and held it up so Killigrew could see his own reflection. It took Killigrew a few seconds before he realised that the pallid, haggard face which stared back at him was his own. He reached up tentatively to touch his cheek, and then stroked his smooth jaw. 'I thought you said I'd been here for four weeks? Someone's shaved me.'

'Someone's shaved you, bathed you, changed your soiled sheets and fed you,' said Mrs Bannatyne.

'You?'

'Joint effort,' she said. 'Mr Molineaux's been helping cook with the food.'

'Was it any good?'

'Not according to you,' Molineaux said surlily. 'One time you hurled your plate at my head and swore blue murder at me.' He indicated a stain on the wall beside the door.

Killigrew felt ashamed. 'Sorry. That would have

been the opium talking.'

'That's what Mr Strachan said, sir.'

The lieutenant glanced at the glass of laudanum in his hand, and with slow deliberation tipped it into the chamber pot. He glanced up at them and grinned sheepishly. 'I've made rather an ass of myself, haven't I?'

All three of them folded their arms and nodded firmly.

'Well, I'm glad to see your condition seems to be much improved,' said Strachan. 'There's nothing like enjoying the occasional success to renew a man's faith in his own abilities. I'd better go now. I have to get back to the *Tisiphone*.'

'What about you, Molineaux?' asked Killigrew. 'Haven't you got duties to attend to?'

The seaman grinned. 'Mr Strachan was kind enough to get me appointed to full-time nursing duties until you're fit enough to join polite society once more, sir. So take your time getting better.'

'But you could walk back down to Victoria with cook to help her with the shopping, Mr Molineaux,' said Mrs Bannatyne.

'Couldn't you have got it just now, when you were in town, Mrs B?'

She glared at him. 'I hope you're not suggesting I should go *shopping*, as if I were some common housekeeper?'

'What do *I* look like?' demanded Molineaux. 'The chambermaid?'

'That reminds me,' said Killigrew, and handed him the chamber pot. 'You can empty that on your way out.'

278

Molineaux sighed. 'It's a man's life in the navy.'

As soon as Strachan and Molineaux had gone, Killigrew eased himself out of bed. Mrs Bannatyne tried to stop him, but Killigrew managed to turn an attempt to push him back into an act of supporting him.

'You should be resting,' she chided.

'I've been resting for four weeks,' he told her. 'Now I have to build up my strength. Help me across to the window.'

They pushed the shutters open and saw the rooftops of Victoria laid out far below them.

'Nice view,' said Killigrew. 'So tell me, since when did you and your husband become so concerned about my welfare?'

'Ever since Mr Strachan came to tell us you were sick and needed a place to rest until you could be cured.'

'Well, at least now you've had a chance to see the pernicious effects of the drug your husband imports into China.'

'I'd heard you were in favour of the drug.'

'It's freedom of choice I'm in favour of. Instead of worrying about the fact that people smoke opium we should concern ourselves with what drives them to seek oblivion in such vices.'

'That was going to be my next question.'

He sighed and made for a chair. She tried to help him, but he shook his head. 'I need to do it for myself.'

'As you wish.'

It was touch and go, but he made it to the chair. She sat down on the bed facing him. 'You cared for her very much, didn't you, Mr Killigrew?'

'Who?'

'You know perfectly well whom I mean. Miss Dadabhoy.'

'I can't have cared that much for her,' he replied bitterly. 'I was the one who got her killed.'

'You did everything you could to save her.'

'Oh, I did everything I could, all right. I led her straight into a trap on board the *Akhandata*, and then goaded Zhai Jing-mu into shooting her. How's Sir Dadabhoy?'

'Putting a brave face on it. But her death has hit him hard. He's a broken man. All his wealth ... I think he'd give up everything to have her back.'

'Two lives broken. I'm a veritable Jonah, aren't I?'

'You mustn't blame yourself, Mr Killigrew. You were not the one who pulled the trigger. And at least Zhai Jing-mu got his comeuppance.'

'That won't bring her back, though, will it?' Talking about Peri had brought back the craving which seemed to permeate every fibre of his being. 'Molineaux didn't ... ah ... empty the necessary, did he?'

'The one with the laudanum and your ... you know what ... in it? Oh, Mr Killigrew! Surely you cannot be that desperate? How low can a man sink?'

'Pretty low, I can assure you. Where does Strachan keep the laudanum?'

'I thought you'd decided that you didn't need it any more?'

'I don't. I just want a sip...'

'There's none in the house. Mr Strachan made sure there was never any more laudanum in the house than was necessary for your next dosage. He knew there would be moments like this.'

'That son of a bitch!'

'That's no way to talk about a friend who's nursed you, put up with weeks of abuse from you and made sure your superiors never discovered what a disgrace you'd become.'

Killigrew took a deep breath. 'I'm sorry. I just want a little sip, that's all...'

'Mr Killigrew, I would have thought that even you would have worked it out by now. It's not opium you want, it's Miss Dadabhoy. The opium's just a substitute. You have to accept that she's gone, and get on with your life.'

'My life's over. What have I got to live for, now that she's dead?'

'There are other women in the world, you know, in case you hadn't noticed?'

'Not like Peri. Couldn't you send one of the servants down to Victoria to get some laudanum? I don't need much, just a sip. You must know which apothecary Strachan buys it from.'

'No! You must find something to take your mind off it, that's all.' There was a firm rap on the door, and she stood up sharply. 'Come in.'

Bannatyne entered and regarded his wife with surprise. 'I did not expect to find you in here, madam,' he said with cold formality.

'I was just keeping Mr Killigrew company.'

Bannatyne turned his gaze on the lieutenant. 'Good to see you up and about, Mr Killigrew. How are you feeling?'

'Much improved, thank you. And I want to thank both you and your wife for your kindness in taking me in.'

'Not at all, Mr Killigrew. It's the least we could do. It would be a terrible shame if the navy lost such a promising young officer all because of one momentary and entirely understandable indiscretion.' Bannatyne turned to his wife. 'I wonder if I might have a word with Mr Killigrew in private, madam?'

She nodded and left the room without arguing. Bannatyne crossed to the window. 'I trust everything is to your satisfaction, Mr Killigrew?'

'You've been more than hospitable, Mr Bannatyne. So much so that I can't help wondering–'

'Why?' Bannatyne finished for him.

Killigrew nodded.

'You do not care for me, Mr Killigrew. I can see that. No, don't deny it. I understand from the Reverend Mr Ultzmann that you blame Grafton, Bannatyne and Co. for the war with China. Well, I can see that we are not going to be able to agree on whether or not the war was justified. But that was seven years ago. Both Britain and China need to put the war behind them, to forge a new relationship based on trust and mutual respect.'

'You make it sound so easy.'

Bannatyne turned back from the window with a faint smile. 'I did not intend to. I have enough experience of the Chinese – and, yes, of the Foreign Office – to know it will not be that straightforward. It may also be as difficult for you and I to forge a new relationship, Mr Killigrew. But I can assure you that just as Britain and China will be best served by recognising their mutual interests, so it is with you and I. We must put the past behind us and work together.'

'And what mutual interests do we share?'

'Zhai Jing-mu may be dead thanks to your efforts, Mr Killigrew, but there are plenty of other pirates out there. Traders like myself need men like you to keep the pilongs suppressed. I scratch your back, Mr Killigrew; I expect you to scratch mine.'

In other words, thought Killigrew, *if I don't do what you want, Captain Morgan is going to find out the real cause of my 'illness'*. 'I'm afraid my naval training hasn't equipped me with back-scratching skills, Mr Bannatyne.'

'Oh, I certainly wouldn't ask you to do anything contrary to your sense of duty, Mr Killigrew. All I ask is that you make a speedy recovery, and then you can get back where you belong, out hunting pirates.'

Killigrew did not believe a word of it, except perhaps the implication that the sooner he was out of the house, the happier Bannatyne would be. He shivered, and not just because he still felt a little feverish.

'Good God, man!' Captain Morgan exclaimed on seeing Killigrew. 'You look dreadful!'

'Thank you, sir. Very good of you to say so.'

Irony was wasted on Morgan. 'You know, Killigrew, I thought maybe you were malingering, feeling sorry for yourself. I must apologise. You've clearly been very ill indeed. Still, Mr Strachan assures me you're past the infectious stage. Think you'll be ready to come back on duty soon?'

283

'Yes, sir.' Killigrew felt embarrassed by Morgan's solicitation, especially since he was now well aware that, in effect, feeling sorry for himself was exactly what he had been doing. 'I'm feeling much stronger now.'

Bannatyne's butler entered the room. 'Dinner is served.'

They went through: Mr and Mrs Bannatyne, Jago Verran, Captain Morgan, Commander Robertson and Killigrew. Verran was a regular guest at the Bannatynes' dining table, but Killigrew did not know why the reclusive Bannatyne had taken it into his head to invite Morgan and Robertson for dinner.

Table talk at the Bannatynes' had invariably been stilted since Killigrew had been a guest there – although he suspected that it had always been like that, and his presence was not to be blamed – but with Morgan and Robertson there the atmosphere seemed even more uncomfortable than usual. The only compensation was the food, which was up to its usual standards. Whatever Bannatyne's faults, he certainly knew how to live.

'I understand another clipper has been reported missing on the voyage to Singapore,' Bannatyne remarked over the *escalopes d'agneau à la Clamart*.

'Damn it, the Royal Navy can't be everywhere,' muttered Morgan. 'We only have limited resources...'

'Oh, it was not my intention to imply anything to the contrary,' said Bannatyne. 'Please don't think that we China traders don't appreciate your

284

sterling efforts against the pilongs. As it happens, I've been thinking about what was said at my ball in February, and I think I may have come up with a possible solution.'

'Oh?' Morgan asked cautiously.

'It seems to me we are on the same side, after all. That helping you to bring the pilongs to justice is in my interests as much as anyone's. So I have decided to put the *Golden Dragon* and her crew at your disposal.'

Killigrew glanced at Verran, who grinned. The *tai-pan* had obviously already discussed this with him.

'That's damned generous of you, sir,' said Morgan. Killigrew had the feeling that if Bannatyne had suggested that the captain strip naked and paint himself with woad while singing 'Buffalo Gals, Won't You Come Out Tonight?' accompanied by Ethiopian serenaders, Morgan would have agreed with alacrity.

'She's a steamer, and shallow-draughted,' continued Bannatyne. 'Just the thing for chasing pirate junks in and out of the creeks and bays on this coast. And Captain Verran here knows these waters better than any other European. I'll put him and his crew entirely at your disposal.'

'Naturally we accept,' said Morgan.

'There is one condition, however,' said Bannatyne.

Somehow Killigrew had expected as much. He reached for his wine glass and took a sip, desperately wishing it were a glass of laudanum.

'Under such circumstances you would want a naval officer on board, in command?' Bannatyne asked Morgan.

'Well, naturally.'

'Then I must insist that Mr Killigrew be given the honour.'

Killigrew almost choked on his wine. 'Me?'

'Out of the question,' Morgan said quickly. 'Do you want the *Golden Dragon* to go the way of the *Akhandata*?'

Bannatyne smiled. 'I know all about what happened on board the *Akhandata*, Captain Morgan. As far as I understand it, Killigrew acted with remarkable presence of mind and followed the only course of action open to him, other than to permit Zhai Jing-mu to escape. I've also spoken to Sir Dadabhoy and several of the other traders. We all agreed that the loss of a clipper was a price worth paying to rid the seas of Zhai Jing-mu.'

Killigrew had not seen Framjee since the day Peri had been killed. 'And what about the loss of his daughter?' he asked Bannatyne bitterly. 'Was that a price worth paying?'

'You mustn't blame yourself, Mr Killigrew,' said Mrs Bannatyne, with concern in her eyes.

Her husband reached across and took her hand. She seemed surprised by the gesture. 'Unfortunately the union of Mrs Bannatyne and I has not yet been blessed with issue, so never having had a daughter I cannot presume to imagine what it must be like to lose one. Our hearts are all with Sir Dadabhoy at this difficult time. But I think we should also bear in mind that it was Zhai Jing-mu who murdered Miss Dadabhoy, not Mr Killigrew here. The lieutenant did everything he could to save that girl's life, and I think we are indebted to him for that. And while Zhai Jing-mu is dead – thanks solely to Killigrew's efforts – I also think we should bear in mind that there are plenty of other pilongs in the South China Sea, and we all have loved ones who might one day fall prey to their depredations. If I loan the *Golden Dragon* to the Royal Navy, I do not want it to be wasted through over-cautiousness.'

'There are no officers under my command who can be accused of overcautiousness,' said Morgan.

'I also have Captain Verran's sensibilities to take into account,' said Bannatyne, and Verran winked mischievously at Killigrew. Bannatyne smiled. 'I'm sure you gentlemen must know how possessive captains are about vessels which, strictly speaking, do not belong to them. Since Verran is my best captain, it is not my desire to go against his wishes in this matter. He served with Lieutenant Killigrew when he was in the navy, and he knows the two of them can work together.'

'That's as maybe,' snorted Morgan. 'But I have plenty of other officers who can do the job just as well, if not better.'

Bannatyne sat back in his chair. 'Then my offer must be withdrawn.'

Morgan smiled uneasily. 'Come now, sir. You said it yourself: we are fighting on the same side here. What does it matter which naval officer is put in command of the *Golden Dragon*?'

'To you, perhaps, nothing. But to myself and

Captain Verran it matters a great deal. I gather from speaking to Mr Killigrew that he holds me responsible for the China War. While our opinions are divided on the necessity of that war, there is nothing I would like better than to put those days behind us. The colony of Hong Kong has a glorious future ahead of it, and we must look to that future. It will doubtless surprise Mr Killigrew, but his disapproval does upset me. I just want him to see that while we may not see eye-to-eye on everything, we are fighting on the same side.'

Morgan caved in. 'Killigrew is Commander Robertson's second lieutenant...'

'I have no objections, sir,' said Robertson. 'If Mr Killigrew accepts, of course,' he added quickly.

'Well, Mr Killigrew?'

Killigrew stared at Bannatyne while trying to make up his mind. In all his days he had never heard so much hypocrisy and cant as Bannatyne had uttered in the past few minutes and he did not trust the *tai-pan* an inch. Bannatyne was plotting something, but what, the lieutenant could not imagine. But accepting his offer seemed to be the only way out, and at least with Verran to watch his back Killigrew knew he would be safe.

'Very well,' he said at last. 'I accept.'

'Can I buy you fellers a wet?' the sailor asked in a Liverpudlian accent.

'That depends,' said Molineaux. 'What's in it for you?'

288

The monsoon season had arrived with a vengeance, and outside the rain hammered against the shutters of Labtat's Tavern. The wind forced it under the shingles and the landlord had put pails at strategic points about the room to catch the unending succession of drips. But the fire in the hearth was warm and Molineaux and Ågård were cosy and dry as they stood at the bar and listened to the drops plopping into the overflowing buckets.

The Liverpudlian grinned. 'Well, if your cap'n's looking to take on hands, you might mention my tally. Endicott's the name: Seth Endicott.'

'Olly Ågård and Wes Molineaux,' said Ågård. 'You haven't run from one of the clippers in the Cap-sing-mun anchorage, have you? Our cap'n don't hold with deserters.'

'Wait a moment, Olly,' said Molineaux. 'I know this feller. Weren't you the cove who pulled Tom Tidley out of the drink after the *Akhandata* blew up?'

'Tom Tidley?' said Endicott, bewildered.

'That's what we calls our second lieutenant,' explained Ågård. 'On account of how he always keeps his rig tidley...'

'...Even when he's got a bit tidley himself,' finished Molineaux.

'Your second lieutenant? You mean Mr Killigrew. Oh aye, I took him out to Cap-sing-mun, and I brought him back.' Endicott looked grim. 'Only problem is, there were three passengers on my pinnace when we left and only one when I returned.'

'If you work for Framjee, how come you're

looking for a new berth?' asked Molineaux.

'Got the sack, didn't I?' Endicott said bitterly. 'Youse fellers must know 'tweren't my fault Miss Dadabhoy got herself killed. But Sir Dadabhoy didn't see it that way.'

'The poor bloke's upset,' Molineaux pointed out. 'He's just lost his daughter, for Chrissakes. Maybe when he's had a chance to recover from his loss...'

'Nah.' Endicott shook his head. 'I need blunt now, if I ain't going to go hungry. Besides, I'm sick of working for these jumped-up *tai-pans*: Framjee, Bannatyne, the whole bloody lot of 'em. They can all go to hell in a handcart as far as I'm concerned. No, give me a job in the Andrew Miller any day. At least you know where you stand, then.'

'Aye,' said Ågård. 'Up to your neck in it at the bottom of the heap.'

'Did you used to work for Bannatyne?' Molineaux asked Endicott.

'Oh aye. I was on board the *Arachne* until I got my walking papers.'

'What did you get the sack for?'

''Tweren't my fault–'

'No, it never is, is it?' muttered Molineaux.

'No, really. They never told us. If you ask me it was to keep crew costs down. The next time she went out she was precious short-handed. Hardly surprising she went down.'

'Typhoon?'

'Pilongs. At least, that's what they say. No survivors ... and if you believe that, you'll believe anything.'

'What do you mean?'

'When I was on the *Arachne*, the *ghaut serang* – that's what we call bosuns on the clippers, *ghaut serangs* – name of Kneebone, Jake Kneebone. Well, the day before the *Arachne* sailed, half of us was sacked and replaced with a few yellow-bellies. The *tai-pan* trying to save himself some blunt; leastways, that's what I thought at the time. A few weeks later word comes back from Singapore: the *Arachne* never arrived. Well, I thought nothing more of it until a few months after, when who should I see walking around as large as life but Jake Kneebone? He pretended like he didn't know me, but it were him all right.'

Molineaux reached into his pocket. 'Let *me* buy *you* that drink.'

Molineaux made his way round to the back of the Bannatynes' house and knocked on the kitchen door. The Chinese parlour maid opened it and he at once seized her in his arms and gave her a kiss.

'Let go!' she protested. 'You all wet!'

'A little water never hurt anyone,' he told her, peeling off his rain-cape and tarpaulin hat and hanging them from a peg close to the cooking range. 'Is Mr Killigrew in?'

'Yes, but you no go up there,' said the parlour maid.

'Who's going to stop me?' Molineaux pointed out. He gave her another peck on the cheek and slipped upstairs.

He was wandering about in search of the lieutenant when a footman emerged from one of the rooms. 'May I help you?' he demanded disdainfully.

'Yes, I'm looking for Mr Killigrew.'

'How did you get in? I did not hear you ring the bell.'

'I can't help that. Where can I find Mr Killigrew?'

'I must ask you to wait outside until I can ascertain if the lieutenant–'

A door opened further down the corridor and Mrs Bannatyne emerged. 'What is it, Ranjit?'

'This negro is looking for Mr Killigrew, ma'am.'

'That's all right, Ranjit. Be about your duties. Come and join us in the games room, Mr Molineaux. Mr Killigrew is teaching me to play All-Fours.'

Dressed in white trousers and a linen shirt, Killigrew sat at a card table topped with green baize. He looked a good deal better than he had done of late, but not as healthy as he usually was, his eyes still sunken in his head and his complexion pallid.

'What is it you want, Molineaux? Has the captain sent you with a message?'

'Yes, sir. For your ears only.'

Mrs Bannatyne smiled thinly. 'I'll be in the drawing room,' she told Killigrew, and went out.

'Bad timing, sir?' asked Molineaux.

'I'll say. I was just teaching her to beg in All-Fours.'

'It's all right for some. How are you feeling, sir?'

'Much improved, thank you for asking. And thank you for helping Strachan and Mrs

Bannatyne look after me. I'm sorry I was so unappreciative at the time.'

'That's oh-kay, sir. Still think opium should be freely available?'

'It's no good banning it: you might as well ban carving knives for fear that people will cut their fingers off.'

'Carving knives have uses other than cutting off fingers, sir.'

'And opium's a powerful medicine. But people need to be educated about the dangers before they make up their own minds whether or not to use it. I only went into that opium den for one night. If I'd known I'd become so ... so...'

'Mr Strachan calls it an "addiction", sir.'

Killigrew nodded. 'My God, it's the perfect commodity – from the supplier's point of view. The more of it you sell, the more the customer needs to buy. I wonder if Sir Dadabhoy knows that?'

'I don't know, sir. But I'll wager Bannatyne does.'

The lieutenant looked thoughtful for a moment, and then glanced up at Molineaux. 'What's the message that's for my ears only? Or was that merely a ruse to get rid of Mrs Bannatyne?'

'Merely a ruse.' Molineaux lowered his voice and told Killigrew what he had learned from Endicott.

'If this fellow was dismissed from the crew of one of Bannatyne's ships, he probably held a grudge,' Killigrew said when the seaman had finished. 'He might have made the whole story up.'

'Yur, that's what I reckoned at first. So I went to the offices of the *Hong Kong Register* and did some checking up in their library. The *Arachne* was rated A1 at Lloyd's, but from what Seth told me she would've struggled to be rated C3. She was a floating coffin, sir, fit only to be broken up or used for target practice. If the pilongs hadn't sunk her, the next big wave would have done the job twice as easily. If it *was* pilongs that sunk her.'

Killigrew took out his linen handkerchief to blow his nose. 'You think it might have been an insurance swindle?' he asked, tucking it up his sleeve.

'More than that, sir. I also did some cross-checking. Every big company that trades with China has lost at least half a dozen clippers to pilongs in the past four years. Every company except for Grafton, Bannatyne and Co. They've only lost the one ship, sir. The *Arachne*.'

'That doesn't prove anything, Molineaux,' Killigrew said carefully.

'Maybe not, sir; but it makes you wonder, doesn't it? And there's something else you should know about. I've been doing some thinking, and it doesn't make sense.'

'What doesn't make sense?'

'This whole Zhai Jing-mu bobbery. You know that Triad you were questioning on the morning that ... you know, when the *Akhandata* went down?'

'Chan? What about him?'

'Did you know he died?'

Killigrew regarded the seaman in shock. 'Died? Good God, I never intended to—'

294

'Oh, don't you worry about that, sir. 'Tweren't your fault.'

'But ... the whiskey I gave him ... wasn't it alcohol poisoning?'

'Mr Strachan had a look-see at the stiff 'un, sir. He reckons arsenic did for him. And that only takes a quarter of an hour to take effect, he says. And it was four days after you gave the Triad whiskey that he cocked his toes. Mr Cargill traced the poison to the bakery which provides the coop with its bread, but the trail goes cold there. Apparently one of the baker's boys mizzled that night.'

'Mizzled?'

'Cut and run, sir. Disappeared.'

'Strachan never said anything about this to me.'

'He didn't want to, sir. Thought it best not to worry you while you was on the mend. I agreed, until I got to thinking: why would anyone want to burke the Triad?'

'To stop him from talking, I suppose.'

'Talking about what, sir? Everyone knew that Zhai Jing-mu was dead by the time that poison must've gone into the toke; so who was the prisoner trying to protect?'

'His fellow Triads, perhaps?'

'Maybe. Or maybe Zhai Jing-mu ain't dead.'

'Don't be ridiculous, Molineaux. He was on board the *Akhandata* when it blew up.'

'I helped pull the bodies out of the water. But I didn't see Zhai Jing-mu's body.'

Killigrew looked thoughtful. 'Did you recover *all* the bodies from the *Akhandata*?'

'Difficult to say, sir, since we don't know how

many were on the clipper to start with. But all the members of the crew were found, along with...' Molineaux's words trailed off when he saw the haggard look on Killigrew's face. The lieutenant might be at pains to conceal it, but there was no hiding the fact that Miss Dadabhoy's death had hit him hard. 'Well, you take my point, sir. We also found the bodies of half a dozen unidentified Chinamen, most of 'em with shotgun pellets in them. But one thing's for sure: none of 'em belonged to Zhai Jing-mu. Dead or alive, I'd know that blue-eyed bastard anywhere.'

'There could be a dozen reasonable explanations as to why his body was never recovered. It might have gone down with the ship, or else been carried out to sea with the tide.'

'You willing to stake your life on that, sir?'

Killigrew ruminated for a moment. 'Have you shared this theory with anyone on board the *Tisiphone* yet?'

'Mr Strachan and me put it to Commander Robertson, sir.'

'And what did he say?'

'The same as you: he thought it was all gammon. Only difference was, when he said it, I could tell he believed it *was* gammon.'

Killigrew found Sir Dadabhoy Framjee at Peri's sepulchre in the cemetery in Happy Valley. The Parsi looked as if he had lost a great deal of weight in the past two months, his sorrowful eyes shrunk deep into his skull, his once rubicund cheeks now hanging slack from his face. Unlike Killigrew, he carried no umbrella against the slashing rain, yet he was heedless of the fact that he was getting soaked through.

This was the first time the two of them had spoken since Peri had been murdered. Killigrew had been in two minds as to whether he should speak to Framjee at all and he braced himself for an outburst of bitterness and recrimination, but at the sound of his footsteps on the gravel path the Parsi merely looked up and smiled wanly.

'Mr Killigrew.'

'Sir Dadabhoy.' Killigrew held his umbrella to give the Parsi some shelter from the rain.

'Every morning I go into the parlour for breakfast and expect to see her, waiting to read the papers to me as she always used to. Then I come down here, in the hope it will help me to understand she is never coming back.' Framjee kneeled and laid the wreath he had brought before the sepulchre.

Killigrew laid his own wreath next to it. 'I understood the coffin was sent back to Bombay?'

Framjee nodded. 'For a traditional Zarathustrian funeral. She was always proud of her religious heritage, so much so that sometimes she made me feel ashamed...'

'I suspect you're a better Zarathustrian than I am a Christian, sir.'

'You are very kind to say so.' Framjee gestured to the sepulchre. 'I wanted a memorial to her here on Hong Kong, to remind people at what cost this colony is maintained. Does that seem foolish to you, Mr Killigrew?'

Killigrew shook his head.

'Walk with me, sir.' Framjee gestured to the

entrance gate, and the two of them wandered side by side down the path with their hands clasped behind their backs. 'I am given to understand that you blame yourself for what happened to my daughter.'

Killigrew smiled sadly. 'Wouldn't you, sir? I led her right into that trap, I goaded Zhai Jing-mu into shooting her...'

'You tried to bluff him, just as you did when you first saved her from him back in January. You did what you thought was right; you must not blame yourself. It was not your finger on the trigger.'

'It might as well have been.'

'No, Mr Killigrew. I have heard a great deal about you: the work you did against the pirates in Borneo, and against the slavers on the Guinea Coast. If anyone is to blame, it should be me. You advised me to send Peri back to Bombay back in January, and we pooh-poohed your advice. If we had listened to you, Peri would still be alive today.'

'Or her ship might have been attacked by pilongs on the way, or it might have foundered and sunk in a typhoon.'

Framjee nodded. 'So many ifs. Only one man had his finger on the trigger, and that was Zhai Jing-mu himself. Blaming ourselves will not bring her back.' He looked at Killigrew speculatively. 'I have also heard people say that you are something of a pirate yourself; is it not true? But there is one difference between you and the pilongs. They are motivated by greed and avarice: you are motivated by a strong sense of justice.'

Killigrew grinned cynically. 'Ah, yes. Good old British fair play.'

'You do yourself an injustice, Mr Killigrew. We both know that the British Empire has hardly brought the happiness to the lives of all the people it has touched in the way that some back in London might like to think. But we must never lose sight of the fact that the Pax Britannica has done *some* good. At least Zhai Jing-mu will never trouble any more innocent people.'

'I wish I could be sure of that.'

Framjee looked at Killigrew in surprise. 'You think he might still be alive?'

'I'm almost certain of it, sir.'

The Parsi shook his head sorrowfully. The two of them walked on in silence to the entrance of the cemetery. Killigrew felt uneasy, as if by allowing Zhai Jing-mu to escape yet again, he had somehow let the Parsi down; and let Peri down, as well.

Framjee seemed to have reached a similar conclusion. 'Perhaps it is wrong of me to think it, but I do not believe the spirit of my daughter will ever be at rest while her murderer is at large,' he said when they reached the gate. He looked up at Killigrew. 'You are going after him, are you not?'

'That's my intention.'

'I shall pay you one thousand pounds if you see to it that his reign of terror is finally brought to an end.'

Killigrew did not know which shocked him most: the implication that he act as a hired assassin, or the high price that Framjee put on such an act; at his current salary, it would take him over five years to earn that much money. But there could only be one answer to the Parsi's offer.

'I'm sorry, sir. It's a generous offer, but I couldn't possibly accept. I have my duty to do.'

Framjee looked despondent. 'So you will catch him again, God willing, and bring him back to Hong Kong, and he will escape again before he can be brought to trial, and then we shall be back where we started.'

Killigrew shook his head. 'You misunderstand me, sir. I may have only one reason to want Zhai Jing-mu dead, but it far outweighs the thousand you're offering me.'

XI:

The Spider and the Fly

Li Cheng hurried through the muddy streets of Tai-ping-shan to get out of the pelting downpour as quickly as possible. He hated the monsoon; but also recognised that if there were no rainy season, no one would appreciate the dry season. That was *yin-yang*: no shadow without illumination, no light without darkness. He sometimes wondered if the barbarians were the *yang* to the Chinese *yin*. That would account for why the gods had seen fit to create such loathsome, uncivilised beings.

The streets were deserted except for those few people who had no choice other than to be outside in such relentless rain. Here a few wizened faces peered from windows with mournful expressions; there a coolie squatted beneath the eaves of a shack with the rain streaming off his broad conical hat.

At the eating stall opposite the joss house on Hollywood Road two men sat at one of the tables, heedless of the rain. Li Cheng did not spare them a glance, but entered the adjoining tea house. He purchased a pot of tea with a couple of copper cash from the money-string on his belt and went upstairs. At a table in one corner four old men were playing mah-jongg,

301

shouting the calls noisily each time they slammed one of the elaborately carved bone tiles. The place was busy, but Li had no difficulty finding a table. It was perfectly positioned, beside a window overlooking the street outside. While he was waiting for an attendant to bring his tea, he took a leather pouch from his belt and emptied the pieces of a tangram on to the table.

The tangram was an ebony tile perhaps four inches square, cut into seven pieces of different shapes: a square, a lozenge-shape, different-sized triangles. The trick was to jumble the pieces up and then see how quickly one could form them back into the square. It was trickier than it looked, but Li could do it in seconds with his eyes closed. A skilled tangram player could also arrange the pieces to form pictures: a coolie, a farmhouse, whatever the imagination could conceive; the number of permutations was infinite.

Li arranged the pieces to form a representation of a barbarian devil-ship. Playing with his tangram helped him to think, to visualise problems from alternative directions.

'You are a little old to be playing with a child's toy,' snorted a familiar voice. Li glanced up and saw a bulky figure, dressed as a coolie, standing over the table.

Li Cheng concealed his irritation. Admiral Huang was a Manchu, what the barbarians called a Tartar. Not being Han Chinese, he was unable to appreciate fully the subtleties and complexities of Chinese culture. But even the Manchus could have their uses sometimes, when one needed a blunt instrument.

'Admiral,' murmured Li. 'Please accept my humble apologies for failing to kowtow as befits one of your exalted station, but I am discreetly reluctant to betray your identity.'

'Spare me the pig shit, Li.' Huang took out a silver cigarette case and lit a Russian cigarette. 'Tell me what you have managed to learn so far.'

'Did you see the two men sitting at the eating stall next door when you arrived?'

'Yes. What of them?'

'They are constables of the Hong Kong Police, disguised to look like civilians. They are watching the temple.'

'Why do they not raid it, if they know it is a Triad lair?'

'They think that watching who comes and goes will lead them to bigger fish.'

'Will it?'

'No.'

'Good. The last thing we need is for the barbarians to go clumsily blundering in and spoil everything. What about Framjee?'

'He knows nothing.'

'Pah! Then the trouble we took to infiltrate you into his employment was wasted.'

Li rearranged the pieces of the tangram and then tapped a finger on the table to indicate them to the admiral. 'What do you see?'

'A tangram.'

'A rabbit,' said Li. With one finger deftly pushing the pieces around the table top, he rearranged them. 'And yet with a different rearrangement of pieces, we see a dragon.'

'All I see is a tangram,' insisted Huang. Li knew

the admiral was not stupid, but sometimes he could be deliberately, frustratingly obtuse.

'The mystery we now face is like the tangram. We have all the pieces before us, but until we can put them together the right way round we will not see what is right under our noses. We arranged them badly to start with, and that led us to see a connection with Framjee where no connection existed.'

'Very philosophical. Confucius would be proud of you,' sneered Huang, and gazed out of the window. Something seemed to catch his attention. 'Interesting...'

Li followed his gaze and saw a barbarian in a greatcoat and pilot cap striding through the muddy puddles with a grim expression on his pale face. 'Killigrew.'

'Ah, so you know the barbarian naval officer?'

'We have encountered one another on several occasions,' Li admitted with a faint smile. 'He followed me into that very temple four months ago. The Triads tried to kill him. I had to jump out of a window and steal a constable's turban to make him and his friend follow me, so they would intervene without the necessity of my revealing my purpose.' He watched as Killigrew entered the joss house a second time.

'It would have been easier to let the Triads kill him,' snorted Huang.

'Easier, but less expedient. If a barbarian is attacked by Triads in a temple, then the barbarian police watch the temple.' By leaning out of the window and craning his neck, Li could just see the two plainclothes policemen arguing about whether or not to follow Killigrew into the temple. He ducked back inside and sat down again. 'But if a barbarian is killed there, then the police will tear everything apart in their search for the killers. I did not think I could afford to let that happen.'

A crash sounded across the street from inside the temple. 'It sounds like everything is being torn apart anyway,' said Huang.

'It is too late now. He will learn nothing. What are the two policemen doing?'

'One of them is running up the road to Victoria. The other remains in his seat.'

Li nodded. 'They have been given strict instructions to observe, but not to reveal their presence.' He chuckled softly. 'As if every man who walks down this street does not recognise them at once as lackeys of the barbarians.'

Another splintering crash echoed from inside the temple, followed by shouts of protest, a scream and another crash.

Huang toyed with the pieces of the tangram on the table before him. 'You said you had encountered Killigrew more than once?'

Li nodded. 'When we rescued Zhai Jing-mu from the gaol. Zhai left Yeh and I to watch the front while he and the others escaped from the back. Yeh would have shot Killigrew if I had not knocked the barbarian out with a blow from behind.'

Yet another crash sounded across the street. Both Huang and Li turned their heads with mild curiosity as a young priest came flying headfirst through the splintered shutters of the temple to fall in the mud outside. A moment later Killigrew appeared in the doorway and marched across to where the priest was trying to crawl away. He grabbed the priest by the throat and hoisted him to his feet.

'Where can I find him?' the barbarian demanded in his execrable Cantonese.

The priest tried to kick Killigrew in the crotch, but the barbarian twisted aside and caught the blow on his thigh. He punched the priest on the jaw and threw him into the mud once again.

'Where?'

Huang sighed and turned his attention back to the tangram. 'These barbarians are crude and unsubtle in their methods. His blundering will spoil everything.'

'Do you want me to kill him?' offered Li, rising to his feet.

Before Huang could reply, something outside caught his attention again. Two Triad hatchet men had appeared and stood in the rain facing Killigrew. The barbarian grinned. 'Ah, at last. Just the gentlemen I'm looking for.'

'Wait,' Huang told Li. 'I want to see this.'

Li nodded and sat down again.

The Triads each drew their hatchets and circled around until they were standing on either side of the barbarian. Killigrew reached under his coat and drew his cutlass. One of the hatchet men charged with a wild shout. Killigrew dodged him and danced to one side so that he could keep an eye on both of them at once. The second attacked. Killigrew parried the Triad's hatchet and ducked, turning away, as the first came at him again. Their weapons clashed, and the head was sliced from the haft of the hatchet. As the hatchet man staggered forwards, Killigrew struck him on the back of the head with the hilt of his cutlass. Dazed, the Triad stumbled into the wall of the temple and sank into the mud.

The second hatchet man struck at Killigrew from behind but the barbarian seemed to sense it coming. He whirled away, the skirts of his greatcoat flying, and parried the Triad's next blow. A swipe from the Triad's hatchet caught the hilt of the cutlass and tore it from his grip. Then the first was back on his feet again and seized Killigrew from behind in an arm lock.

Grinning victoriously, the second advanced on Killigrew and raised his hatchet to bury it in his skull. The barbarian kicked him in the crotch. As the Triad doubled up with a howl, Killigrew flicked a boot into his face and the hatchet man sank into the mud.

'He is a meritorious fighter,' observed Huang.

'For one who knows nothing of *wu-yi*,' Li sniffed contemptuously.

Still caught in the first Triad's arm lock, Killigrew threw himself backwards across the street. The Triad's feet slipped in the mud and he was thrown across one of the tables at the eating stall. The plainclothes policeman jumped up and ran clear to stand under the eaves of the next shop along. He watched, reluctant to get involved and looking as forlorn as the last *dim-sum* at a banquet.

The Triad recovered and pushed the barbarian off, still holding one of his arms in the small of his back. He pushed Killigrew's face towards the glowing cinders of the eating stall's cove. The barbarian pushed back, but the Triad was stronger. Killigrew reached up until his fingers closed around the handle of a wok hanging from an overhead rack. A resounding clang sounded across the street and the Triad staggered back with blood gushing from his nose.

'Resourceful, too,' said Huang.

The Triad shook his head muzzily, noticed the barbarian's cutlass at his feet and snatched it up. He circled Killigrew once more, grinning wolfishly. The barbarian parried a sword-stroke with the wok and then threw it at the Triad's head, but the hatchet man ducked and the wok splashed into the mud.

The Triad charged. Killigrew fumbled on the table behind him and snatched up an implement. Holding it before him, he revealed it to be a single chopstick.

Li almost laughed out loud, but Huang was watching the fight intently.

The Triad charged, swinging the cutlass at Killigrew's neck. The barbarian side-stepped, slipped in the mud and thus by accident rather than design avoided a blow which would otherwise have decapitated him.

'He possesses that quality which even the best of us cannot survive without,' said Huang. 'Good fortune.'

'But fortune is a fickle mistress,' pointed out Li, wafting his hand half-heartedly at a fly which had buzzed in out of the rain. 'See, now he is finished.'

The Triad stood over Killigrew and tried to stab him in the chest with the cutlass. The barbarian caught him by the wrist and pulled him down. The two of them rolled over and over until Killigrew was on top. He banged a fist into the Triad's throat, and when he took his hand away Li saw a chopstick embedded there. Ironic, when one remembered that Confucius had said that chopsticks were preferable to knives because knives could be used as deadly weapons.

Staggering with exhaustion, Killigrew pushed himself to his feet. He looked around, the rain cutting rivulets through the mud which caked his face. He saw the second Triad recovering consciousness and splashed over to where he lay. Realising his peril, the Triad tried to crawl away but Killigrew caught him by one ankle and dragged him back through the mud to the eating stall. He dropped the Triad's leg, grabbed him by the tunic, and pulled him up out of the mud to throw him across one of the tables. Still holding him by the shirt front, he snarled in his face.

'Where's Zhai Jing-mu?'

Before the Triad could reply, a single shot rang out across the street and the top of his head was blown off. Killigrew looked around sharply. So did Li and Huang. Assistant Superintendent Cargill was sprinting through the mud with a pistol in one hand, the other plainclothes officer hard on his heels.

'You damned idiot!' Killigrew snarled furiously. 'He was about to tell me where Zhai Jing-mu is!'

Cargill reached down, seized the dead Triad's right arm and lifted it so that Killigrew could see the dagger in his hand. 'The only thing he was about to do was stick this between your ribs. What the deuce are you trying to do? Tackle the Brotherhood of Heaven, Earth and Man single-handed?'

'If that's what it takes.'

'I told you before. You worry about the pilongs and let me worry about the Triads.'

'And I told you: they're working together. The Triads could be the only link to Zhai Jing-mu.'

'If he's still alive.'

'Oh, he's alive, all right.'

'Then I dare say you won't have to go looking for him. He'll make his presence felt soon enough.'

Li and Huang watched the two barbarians walk away through the rain while the constables ordered a coolie to fetch a barrow to bear away the two dead Triads. The priest had crawled off shortly after the arrival of the two hatchet men.

'Do you still want me to kill him?' Li asked Huang.

'Do you think you can?'

The fly was buzzing about their heads again. Li watched it for a moment while taking out his chopsticks. A lightning-like movement, and he had seized the fly between the sticks. 'Catching that fly was difficult. Exterminating the *fan kwae* will be easy.' He released the fly and it buzzed away.

'You did not kill the fly, Li.'

'I saw no reason to.'

The admiral chuckled. 'The time you spent learning *wu-yi* at that Shaolin Temple has left you with Buddhist tendencies, Li Cheng.'

Li did not smile. 'When the propitious moment arrives, I shall do what needs to be done.'

'The barbarian is no more dangerous than that fly.'

'But he has a potentially fatal tendency to turn up in the wrong place at the wrong time,' pointed out Li.

'You were right earlier when you said that killing a barbarian naval officer would draw too much attention. If Killigrew carries on the way he has done these past few months, it is likely he will get himself killed and save you the trouble. But if he gets too close, if he becomes a threat ... I leave it to your discretion.'

Li nodded his head. 'Zhai tells me he has set up a rendezvous with Admiral Nie to arrange for him to be granted full pardon in return for helping to suppress the other pilongs on this coast.'

The admiral's brow became clouded. 'Curse Nie's interference! He must be stopped.'

Li stared down at the pieces of the tangram. There was something not right about the way they were arranged.

Huang opened a fist to show one of the pieces nestling there. He must have palmed it while Li was gazing out of the window. 'Is this what you are looking for? Make sure you have all the pieces of the puzzle before you try to see the picture. Remember, there is too much at stake for any errors. The destiny of the Celestial Kingdom depends on us.'

'Rumour has it that the *Golden Dragon* sails

311

next week with a fortune in silver bullion stowed in her hold. And Killigrew on board.'

'It is obviously a trap,' snorted Huang.

'Yes,' agreed Li. 'But who is the spider, and who is the fly?'

'Are you certain you're fit for duty, Second?' Commander Robertson peered from beneath his bushy eyebrows as Killigrew stood to attention before the table in his day room.

'Never felt better, sir.' Even four weeks after moving out of the Bannatyne residence, the lieutenant still felt dreadful, his craving for laudanum as strong as his craving for opium had ever been, but at least he had strength enough to conceal the shakiness he felt. 'I've been taking plenty of exercise, trying to get myself back in shape.'

'Yes, Mr Cargill told me about your jaunt into Tai-ping-shan last week,' Morgan said drily. 'I can't say I approve of this plan you've drawn up with Captain Verran,' he snorted. 'Why not put more guns on the *Golden Dragon*? Or take more men? You'll be helpless if the pilongs attack.'

'No, sir. The pilongs must have plenty of spies here in Victoria. If they see us cramming men and guns on to the *Golden Dragon*, they'll know it's a trap. The only reason the pilongs have never attacked her before is because they've never had incentive enough to do so.' Verran had put word out that the steamer was carrying a fortune in silver bullion, although if an attack on the *Golden Dragon* was successful, the pilongs were going to be sorely disappointed: her cargo consisted of nothing more valuable than several strongboxes packed with bars of iron ballast.

'At least let me follow in the *Tisiphone*,' urged Robertson. 'That way, if the pilongs do attack, we'll be there almost at once, to even the odds...'

'No, sir. The pilongs will see the *Tisiphone* leave in our wake and again know it's a trap.'

'I suppose it makes sense,' said Morgan. 'I'm just worried that in your eagerness to make the *Golden Dragon* look like a temptingly helpless target, you might make her too helpless in reality.'

'Captain Verran's confident that the *Golden Dragon* can hold her own against a pilong attack, sir, and I trust him to pick a crew he can rely on utterly.'

'On your own head be it, Lieutenant,' said Morgan. 'But bear in mind that if things go wrong this time, it won't be a question of what I'll do to you: the pilongs will make any punishment I can cook up for you a purely academic question.'

They stood up and left Robertson's quarters. 'You still haven't told me which four men you want to take,' the commander remarked to Killigrew as they headed for the companionway.

'I thought I'd take O'Connor, Dando, Firebrace and Gadsby.'

'Firebrace and Gadsby!' exclaimed Morgan. 'Aren't those the two you recently had flogged for desertion, Commander?'

Robertson nodded.

'They've been punished for their crime, sir,' said Killigrew. He had been the one who had

313

dragged the two absconders from their hiding place in a brothel in Tai-ping-shan back in January, only to see them subjected to the barbarity of the lash. It had not made him feel proud.

'That's debatable,' snorted Morgan. 'If it were up to me, I'd've hanged the swine.'

'I thought it would help restore their self-esteem if we showed we had some trust in them. A sailor without self-esteem is no good to anyone.'

'I understand your thinking, Killigrew,' Robertson said as they ascended the companionway. 'But are you sure that on a voyage as perilous as this one, you wouldn't prefer to have someone more experienced at your back? I understand that Molineaux has already volunteered, and I'm sure I could spare Ågård.'

'I wouldn't want to be accused of favouritism, sir,' Killigrew replied as they emerged from the after-hatch on to the quarterdeck. Heavy raindrops pattered noisily against the awning spread over the deck and churned the waters of Victoria Harbour into an unending dance of bouncing droplets. 'Besides, Firebrace and Gadsby will never get any experience if we keep relying on the experienced men. Dando and O'Connor are both stout hands; and I'm gambling that Firebrace and Gadsby will be seeking to redeem themselves.'

'I suppose you know what you're doing,' Robertson sighed in a tone of voice which suggested he did not believe a word of it. He turned to the boatswain. 'Have Able Seamen

314

Dando and O'Connor, and Landsmen Firebrace and Gadsby, report to me at once.'

'Aye, aye, sir.'

Killigrew pulled the brim of his cap down over his eyes against the rain and buttoned his greatcoat, tying the belt in a casual knot. 'Go to my cabin and fetch my dunnage,' he told Dando when the four sailors reported on the quarterdeck. 'Then fetch your kit bag. Same goes for the rest of you. We'll be spending a few weeks on detached service on board the *Golden Dragon*.'

The four seamen exchanged puzzled glances. Of all the ratings on board the *Tisiphone*, only Ågård and Molineaux knew about the proposed plan to use the *Golden Dragon* to trap the pilongs, and Killigrew knew they could both be trusted to keep their mouths shut. Scuttlebutt being what it was, what became known amongst the hands would soon be common knowledge ashore, and that would ruin everything. He hoped that Verran had shown a similar discretion with the hands aboard the *Golden Dragon*.

They went down into Morgan's waiting gig with the captain and were rowed through the driving rain to where the *Golden Dragon* was anchored, loading supplies for the coming voyage from a harbour lighter.

Morgan cast his gaze across the harbour to where some Chinese were laying the keels of some large canoes on the stocks. 'What are they building over there?' he wondered out loud. 'Fishing boats?'

Killigrew took out his pocket telescope and levelled it briefly. 'Dragon boats, sir.'

'Dragon boats?'

'Yes, sir. For the festival next month. The Chinese hold the dragon boat festival every year around the fifth day of the fifth month of their lunar calendar. It's supposed to commemorate an ancient Chinese poet and statesman who drowned himself in a river. The people set out to find his body, but to no avail, so they made offerings to the gods of the river. The dragon boat race commemorates it. The different Chinese trade guilds each build their own dragon boat and race against one another. It's quite a spectacle to see.'

They were drawing closer to the *Golden Dragon* now. A hundred feet from stem to stern, the steamer was even smaller than the *Tisiphone*. Like the *Tisiphone*, she was a 'flapper' – a paddle-steamer; what the Chinese referred to as an 'outside-walkee' – with two masts straddling the single funnel.

By the time they climbed up the accommodation ladder, Captain Verran awaited them at the entry port with Assistant Superintendent Cargill. For once Verran's characteristic insouciant grin was in abeyance. 'Welcome aboard, Kit.' He ignored Captain Morgan for the moment, clearly enjoying the chance to snub a man he would have to have shown deference to in his navy days. 'These your lads?' He indicated Dando, Firebrace, Gadsby and O'Connor.

Killigrew nodded, dusting rainwater from his cap with the back of his hand.

'Hassan!' Verran waved across one of his petty officers, a brown-limbed Malay. 'This is Abdul

316

Hassan, my *ghaut serang*,' he added to Killigrew. Verran turned back to Hassan. 'This is Lieutenant Killigrew; he's going to be in command of the *Golden Dragon* for our next voyage. As long as he's on board, you'll obey one of his own orders as if it were my own.'

Hassan bowed before Killigrew. *'Tuan.'*

'Have Mr Killigrew's dunnage taken below to his cabin and see his men to their berths in the fo'c'sle.'

'Aye, aye, sir.' Hassan snapped his fingers at a couple of Filipino sea-cunnies and issued orders to them in rapid Malay.

Studying the upper deck, Killigrew saw that the *Golden Dragon* was well run, the decks not unnecessarily cluttered, all ropes ends squared off, the rigging taut and in good condition. He also noticed that she had her own cannon: a thirty-six-pound bow-chaser and an eight-inch pivot gun in the stern, which made her armament only slightly inferior to that of the *Tisiphone*. He hoped it would be enough to defend the steamer against any ambush that Zhai Jing-mu might be planning for them.

Morgan cast a disdainful eye over Verran's crew, a mixture of Lascars, Malays and Filipinos, most of them carrying daggers, swords and wavy-bladed krises in their sashes. One or two even carried ancient flintlock pistols which looked as if they might be as hazardous to the firer as to the target. They scuttled about the rigging with all the agility of spiders negotiating their own webs. 'Are all your crew natives, Mr Verran?' asked Morgan.

317

'All except my two *tindals* ... mates, I mean.'

'I know what *tindals* are, Mr Verran.'

'They're both Yankees. I'll introduce you to them later, Kit.'

'They're a piratical-looking bunch,' said Morgan.

Verran grinned. 'I suppose so. I dare say some of them have been pirates, at some point in their lives. But there isn't a man on board who isn't one hundred per cent loyal to me. And these sea-cunnies are some of the best sailors in the world, Cap'n Morgan.'

'Except the British sailor,' sniffed Morgan.

'And the Krumen,' added Killigrew.

Verran bowed mockingly in deference to Morgan's superior wisdom.

'Before I can send you off on this voyage there are certain formalities to be attended to,' said Morgan, and indicated his clerk. 'Taylor has the paperwork with him. May we use your day room?'

'But of course, Cap'n.' Verran ushered Morgan and his clerk down the after-hatch, winked at Killigrew, and followed them below.

Killigrew was about to go after them, but Cargill stopped him. 'Wondered if I might have a word?' he asked, stroking his whiskers.

'By all means.' Killigrew guided the assistant superintendent over to one corner of the quarterdeck where they could talk with some degree of privacy.

'I'm sorry about what happened to Miss Dadabhoy. I know you were fond of her. Her murder shocked us all. I think you should know

318

that no one blames you for what happened.'

'Except myself,' Killigrew said tightly. He did not like to talk about what had happened, but every night he lay awake, wondering if she might still be alive if he had played things differently.

'It was Zhai Jing-mu who killed her. Now you know what kind of men you're up against, Killigrew. It's all very well the lawyers talking about due process and prisoners' rights; that's what allowed Zhai Jing-mu to escape in the first place. But I'm sure I don't have to tell you that what answers in the Admiralty Court doesn't necessarily answer on the South China Sea.'

'I hear that someone poisoned the prisoner we had in the gaol.'

Cargill nodded grimly. 'My fault. I should have known that someone would try to hush him. But it only shows what ruthless villains we're dealing with. You can't afford to take half-measures. This is war, and the only good pilong is a dead pilong.' Cargill clapped Killigrew on the shoulder as Verran, Morgan and his clerk re-emerged from the after-hatch. 'I'm going ashore with Captain Morgan. Good luck, Killigrew. I only wish I were coming with you. Next time, perhaps, eh?'

As Verran stood at the entry port to see Morgan off, Cargill had a word with him before he descended the accommodation ladder. Something he said made Verran glance back at Killigrew. When he saw the lieutenant watching them, Verran smiled and waved before turning back to Cargill.

'Loo-tenant Killigrew?'

Killigrew turned and saw a young man of about

319

twenty. He was snub-nosed, and although he had obviously grown a beard to make him look older, it actually had the opposite effect. 'Hayes is the name, sir. Billy Hayes. I'm the number-one *tindal*.' He grinned. 'What you'd be calling the first mate. Welcome aboard, sir. The cap'n asked me to show you to your cabin.'

'Much obliged.' Killigrew allowed the *tindal* to show him below decks. 'So tell me, Mr Hayes, how does a son of Columbia come to be serving on a British steamer in Chinese waters crewed by sea-cunnies?'

Hayes grinned. 'When I was a kid I used to work on my pa's barquentine on Lake Erie, running furs down from Canada. Then I got a job on the brig *Pilgrim*, out of Boston, sailing around the Horn to fetch bullocks' hides from California. I met Cap'n Verran in San Diego and he offered to pay me twice what I was getting on the *Pilgrim*.'

'What was Verran doing in San Diego?'

Hayes turned away to open the door to one of the cabins for him. 'Running mails across to the States for Mr Bannatyne. This here's your cabin, sir. Hope it suits.'

Killigrew took in the accommodation. The cabin was marginally smaller than the one he enjoyed on the *Tisiphone*, which was small enough. But what this one lacked in space it certainly made up for in comfort and style, with polished teak fittings and plush velvet furnishings. 'Don't worry,' he told Hayes with a faint smile. 'It won't be the first time I've had to rough it.'

Hayes grinned. 'Yeah, the cap'n's told me all about you, sir. Syria, Borneo, China, the Guinea Coast... Reckon if your navy had had a few more boys like you back in 1812, things might have been real different. Good to have you aboard, sir. We'll soon bring them pilongs to heel. Cap'n says to let you unpack and then you can join him on the quarterdeck. We'll be setting sail on the afternoon tide.'

'Thank you, Mr Hayes.'

'Call me Bully.'

Killigrew waited until the *tindal* had gone out before opening his sea chest. Then he took out his pepperbox, checked it was loaded and slipped it into one of the capacious pockets of his greatcoat. He was unpacking his shirts into a drawer when he found a full bottle of laudanum. He took it out and stared at it for a moment.

'Thanks, Jago, but no thanks.'

He crossed to the porthole and was about to throw the bottle out when instead he pulled out the stopper, took a sip, and smiled. He had forgotten how good the taste was. He took a longer pull, and at once a warm feeling of contentment spread outwards from his stomach. He replaced the stopper and put the bottle back in the drawer.

XII:

Wheel of Death

Killigrew and his opponent circled one another on the quarterdeck of the *Golden Dragon*, where the awning stretched overhead protected them from the heavy rain. Both of them were out of breath from wielding their heavy cutlasses. Killigrew aimed a slash at his opponent's head and the man brought his own blade up to parry, but the blow was a feint and Killigrew tried to slide in under his guard. His opponent was as fast as lightning, though, and managed to knock the thrust aside before it went home. He took a step back, drawing the lieutenant on. Killigrew lunged but his opponent side-stepped, caught him off balance and slashed at him as he staggered past. His razor-sharp blade sliced through the fabric of Killigrew's sleeve and drew blood from his upper arm.

'*Touché!*'

'*Pax!*' responded Killigrew.

Verran grinned. 'You're slowing up in your old age, Kit.'

'And you've learned a few tricks since we were in the *Dreadful.*' Killigrew parted the rent in his sleeve to study the cut below.

'Gosh, did I do that?' Verran exclaimed as they both slotted their cutlasses into their scabbards.

'Sorry. I just got carried away...'

'Lack of control, Jago. Didn't I always tell you control was paramount?'

'Yes, but that was in another context, I seem to recall.'

'Never mind. It's just a scratch,' Killigrew said truthfully enough. 'I think you won that bout.'

'And the match. Well! I never thought the day would come when I could get the better of Kit Killigrew with a cutlass! This deserves an entry all of its own in my journal.' Verran turned to his steward. 'Fetchee two-piecey char, Muda.'

The Malay grinned. *'Hai,* Missee Verran.' He scurried below.

The *Golden Dragon* was two days out of Victoria, having touched at Macao before turning south for Cape Padaran on the coast of Cochin China. The rain continued ceaselessly, falling from a leaden sky which stretched from horizon to horizon, so dark there was little to choose between day and night. The steamer's engineer, a cheerful Scot named MacGillivray, had kept steam up in the boilers in case they needed to manoeuvre quickly if and when the pilongs attacked, but so far they had been able to run before a soldier's wind from abaft and they had made an average of seven knots under sail alone. The steamer pitched roughly over the steep, foam-veined waves, but two seasoned sailors like Killigrew and Verran had little difficulty maintaining their balance. They had been overhauled by a couple of clippers and passed a Peninsula and Oriental steamer bound for Hong Kong, but had yet to sight any pirates.

'The wind's freshening,' remarked Verran. 'Better take in the t'gallants, Mr Boggs.'

'Aye, aye, sir!' Verran's number-two *tindal*, a handsome youth with a girlish face and delicate hands, turned away to issue orders to the hands. Killigrew watched as Dando, Firebrace, Gadsby and O'Connor ascended the rigging with the sea-cunnies to furl the topgallant sails.

'What do you think of my crew, Kit?' asked Verran.

'Morgan was right about one thing: they *are* a villainous-looking bunch of pirates. But they know what they're about, I'll say that much for them. What about my lads? I trust they're pulling their weight?'

'I've had no complaints.'

Killigrew watched as Boggs played a rope's end against the backs of some sea-cunnies who were not hauling on the clew lines fast enough for his taste. 'Your number-two *tindal*'s a little on the young side, isn't he?'

'Boggs? Perhaps. But this is a young man's game; you know that, Kit. Besides, he's got a sharp mind, a firm hand and the ambition to go places. You mark my words, one day Mr Boggs is going to make a name for himself in these waters.'

'Light off the port bow!' called the look-out at the masthead.

Killigrew and Verran exchanged glances. 'Want to go and see what it is?' suggested Verran.

Killigrew nodded and took the telescope from the binnacle. He climbed a short way up the ratlines, hooking one elbow around a shroud to secure himself, and pointed the telescope with one hand over the lens to try to keep the rain off it. It was almost impossible to make anything out through the sheeting downpour, yet he could see not one but two blazing fires about a mile away.

He closed the telescope and climbed back down to the deck. 'Looks like a couple of junks on fire.' He remembered that they were approaching the reefs and islands of the Paracels, where he had first encountered Zhai Jing-mu.

'Looks like there's mischief afoot,' said Verran. 'Must be the work of pilongs. Two points to starboard, Suleiman. Better bring in the flying jib and have the leadsman in the chains, Hassan.'

'*Tuan*, Missee Verran. All hand to quarter!'

'There could be men dying on those junks, Jago,' Killigrew murmured as the *Golden Dragon* nosed her way forward, the leadsman calling the soundings from the chains.

'I know, Kit, but there are dangers in these waters other than pilongs. I don't want to go steaming in only for us to tear our bottom out on a reef. Mr Boggs, go below and tell Mr MacGillivray to have the engines ready to turn full astern when I give the word. If this turns out to be a trap, I want us to be ready to pull back in a hurry.'

'Aye, aye, sir.' Boggs went below to the engine room.

At length the *Golden Dragon* crested another steep wave and suddenly the junks – there were three of them – leaped into clear view through the sheeting rain, less than two cables away. All three were on fire, but only one was fully ablaze.

Another had sunk with only its topmasts showing above the waves, but the fire had never really caught hold of the largest and now the spume and the rain had conspired all but to extinguish its charred timbers.

'Imperial men-o'-war,' said Verran.

Killigrew nodded. He had already seen the three tigers' heads painted on the stern of the largest. He knew it could not be Admiral Huang's junk; that had still been moored in Victoria Harbour when the *Golden Dragon* had sailed, and while junks were deceptively swift there was no way Huang could have got here ahead of them.

There was a regular booming crash, the sound of breakers on a reef, and the next time a wave lifted the *Golden Dragon* out of a trough they could see the white horses pounding over the rocks about half a mile away beyond the junks. Hassan, the *ghaut serang*, ordered the sails boxed, and the steamer hove to.

Killigrew studied the flagship through the telescope. It was massive, as big as Huang's. There was no sign of life on deck, but even at that distance the high-sided junk seemed to tower over the steamer.

'I'm going on board the flagship,' Killigrew said in a firm voice. He half expected Verran to argue – they both knew it would be madness to try in these conditions – but the captain merely nodded.

'Mr Hayes! Prepare the jolly boat. We're sending a search party on board the big junk.'

The jolly boat was swung out in its davits.

Killigrew and the boat's crew went below to put on their oilskins before they emerged from beneath the *Golden Dragon*'s awning. 'Watch yourself, Kit,' Verran warned Killigrew as he prepared to join Hayes and the others in the boat. 'It could be a trap.'

'I don't think we'll find any pilongs lying in wait. They're bold fellows, but not bold enough to linger on board a junk which is being carried towards a reef while they're waiting on the chance that we might turn up.'

'Perhaps. But don't you linger too long, either. I reckon you've got less than an hour before she strikes. And leave one man on deck, watching this ship. If I see any other vessels put in an appearance, I'll send up a blue light. When that happens you come straight back, all right? I don't care if you find the Crown Jewels on board, you leave them.'

'I just want to take a look-see, to try to find out what happened here.'

Killigrew climbed down the side ladder to where the jolly boat bobbed up and down in the *Golden Dragon*'s lee quarter with Hayes and half a dozen seamen in it. He waited until the boat neared the zenith of its next rise, and then jumped down, when the drop was shortest. Then the wave slipped away from beneath them and the boat dropped sickeningly away from the steamer's side.

'All right, pull!' roared Hayes. 'Every mother's son of you! Pull, damn you!'

The rain lashed them as the boat was tossed up and down by the heavy seas. In less than a minute every man in the boat was drenched through in spite of their oilskins. Killigrew knew that even if he had been able to get at the pepperbox he wore beneath his rain-cape, it would be useless, the powder soaked through.

The brightly painted junk towered over them, its open gun ports dark and forbidding. A rope ladder hung down its side from the entry port in the lee waist, twenty feet above them. Killigrew stood up in the boat's prow and prepared to jump.

'I sure hope you know what you're doing, mister!' Hayes had to yell to make himself heard above the noise of the wind and the rain.

Killigrew took a deep breath, waited for the next wave to bring the ladder closer, and jumped. He hooked both hands over the second-from-bottom rung, but his fingers slipped on the wet board and left him dangling from one arm. He gripped the rope and hauled himself up until he could get one foot on the lowermost rung.

Gasping for breath, he tilted his head back and felt the heavy rain sting his face. There was no point in hanging around. Wondering what would be waiting for him on deck, he began to climb. Once he was immediately below the entry port, he hooked one arm around a rung and reached under his rain-cape to draw his cutlass. He took a deep breath and scrambled up the last couple of feet.

Whenever he remembered Chingkiang-fu, he was always at a loss to decide which was the greatest horror: the terrible hand-to-hand conflict on the battlements of the walled city, or the sights which had greeted him within the walls once the city had fallen. After one last desperate defence at the centre of the city, the Tartar soldiers had gone back to their homes, slaughtered their wives and daughters rather than let them be raped by the barbarian invaders, and then committed suicide. Killigrew would never forget wandering through those streets, where every house concealed the bodies of women hanged from the roof-beams with silken scarves in nooses about their necks, and children of all ages – even tiny babies – with their throats slit, their bodies tumbled into wells and fishponds. The stench of death in his nostrils, the blood of innocents wherever he turned, innumerable flies buzzing around the fast-rotting corpses on that stiflingly hot day. The memory was as fresh in 1849 as it had been seven years earlier.

As soon as he pulled himself through the entry port and crouched in the lee of the bulwark, sweeping the deck with his eyes for danger, Killigrew knew he had a new memory to add to the album. As horrific as the aftermath of Chingkiang-fu had been, it had been meant – in the eyes of the perpetrators, at least – as an act of kindness.

There was no evidence of any kindness on the junk. The lucky ones had died swiftly from sword-slashes. Each time the deck rolled, half a dozen decapitated heads tumbled from one side to the other. Even the slicing rain could not wash away all the blood. Others had died harder, tortured by men who took pleasure in suffering, then roasted alive. One man had been pinned to the door leading into the poop, skewered on a bamboo spear, his curved sword still hanging from his wrist by a leather thong. Another – a mandarin, from what Killigrew could see of his charred robes – had been hung by a long rope tied about his ankles from a crossbeam slung from the truck of the mainmast, high above. A fire had been lit below him, so that each roll of the junk's deck had swung his head through the flames.

Killigrew bit back the bile which rose to his gorge.

'Sweet Jesus!' gasped Hayes, appearing at the entry port beside him. Both of them were too stunned to say anything for a few moments. They gazed at the grisly scene with horror and revulsion as four of the sea-cunnies climbed up the side ladder behind them, leaving two in the boat.

Hayes was the first to find his tongue again. 'Goddamned heathens! Zhai Jing-mu's work?'

'Who else would do such a thing?' Killigrew's hoarse voice cracked. 'Come on. Let's see what we can find.'

'What are we supposed to be looking for?'

'I don't know,' Killigrew said irritably. It was not the slaughter he found so offensive. He himself had had recourse to killing enough times in his career not to condemn it out of hand, and these poor devils had been sailors of the Imperial Chinese Navy who, like the men on board the *Tisiphone*, had known what they were signing up for when they had joined. What was so sickening was the relish that had obviously gone into this atrocity. Killigrew bottled up his anger; he swore to himself he would uncork it at a later date, and let Zhai Jing-mu have a taste of the vintage. 'There may be survivors.'

''Vast heaving, Killigrew! Seems to me the pilongs have done a goddamn thorough job.'

'Nevertheless, Mr Hayes, we must be certain.' Killigrew picked his way between the corpses and headed aft to the cabin beneath the poop. Much of the raised stern had been burned away, the charred timbers steaming slightly in the incessant rain. There was more blood here, another body, huddled in a shapeless mass at the foot of a bulkhead.

He found a hatch and descended. The rainwater which gathered on deck trickled steadily from the corners of the hatch and made crazy patterns on this lower deck. The paper lanterns which illuminated the 'tween decks still burned, and as they swung with the rolling of the junk they cast eerie shadows back and forth. The rain hammered down above, and the timbers creaked, but even so it was quiet enough for Killigrew to be aware of his own breath rasping raggedly through his teeth.

Below decks, the junk's hull was divided up into a series of watertight compartments which could be sealed off in the event of the hull being breached; another ingenious Chinese innovation. Killigrew stepped up to one of the doors and listened. Was it his imagination, or could he hear sobbing on the other side of the door? He flexed his fingers around the grip of his cutlass, balanced on one foot, and kicked the door. It

331

swung open, stopped short before it reached the bulkhead as it struck something with a thud, and then swung back. In the same instant he heard a yelp of pain.

He pushed the door open once more and barged through, whirling to face the young Chinese who had been hiding behind the door. The man looked dazed – a massive bruise already swelled on his forehead – but his eyes widened when he saw Killigrew and he snatched up the curved sword he had dropped. He was dressed in the sky-blue uniform of an Imperial soldier, a black silk cap with an upturned brim and two squirrels' tails hanging down behind, and a yellow patch on his chest embroidered with the Chinese character for 'brave'. He was clearly terrified as he pointed his sword at Killigrew with trembling fingers. Killigrew could hardly blame him. The brave must have hidden down here when the pilongs had attacked the junk. He must have heard the screams of his comrades as they had been tortured to death, knowing that a similar fate must await him if his hiding place was discovered. And now, after being stranded on this drifting junk with no company but corpses, the vessel which had come to rescue him was crewed by 'ocean ghosts'.

Killigrew backed away from the terrified brave. 'Do not be alarmed,' he said in Cantonese. 'I mean you no harm. I will try to help you, if I can. See, I am going to put my sword away.' He slotted his cutlass into its scabbard. The brave regarded him with suspicion, but lowered his sword after a moment.

'What have you got?' demanded Hayes, coming through the door behind him.

The brave immediately brought up his sword once more. His grimy face was streaked with tears, but his expression was grimly determined.

'Tartar brave,' Killigrew said in English, and switched back to Cantonese for the soldier's benefit. 'It is all right, he is a friend. We are not going to harm you. What is your name?'

The brave cuffed the tears from his cheeks. 'Yan.'

'All right, Yan. My name is Kit Killigrew; I'm an officer of the British navy. You understand British navy?'

Yan nodded. 'High-nose barbarians enemies of Celestial Kingdom.'

Killigrew shook his head. 'Not enemies. Friends. Britain and China are at peace now. We're going to help you. But you must come with us. This junk is adrift and being carried towards a reef. In a few minutes, the rocks will tear out her keel. Then she will either sink or be pounded on the reef. Understand?'

Yan nodded, and sheathed his sword.

The boarding party made a cursory search of the rest of the junk but found no one else. They put Yan in the boat and rowed back to where Verran awaited them on the deck of the *Golden Dragon*. Yan had never been on a barbarian devil-ship before and was apprehensive, but Killigrew managed to reassure him. He took Yan down to the saloon, gave him a towel to dry himself and a shot of brandy to steady his nerves. He poured himself a generous measure, too. He felt he needed it after the sights he had seen on the deck of the junk. There was still some laudanum in the bottle Verran had left in his cabin; he would need it to help him sleep tonight.

Yan gasped as he swallowed the fiery liquor. 'How-how-ah!'

'Good?'

'Very good!'

Killigrew smiled and sat down facing the brave. 'Yan, I need you to tell me what happened. Most importantly, I need you to tell me how much time passed between the pilongs leaving the junk and our arrival. Do you have any idea?'

Yan shook his head. 'I know they attacked at the Hour of the Snake. After that I lost track of the time.'

Killigrew knew that the Hour of the Snake could mean any time between nine and eleven o'clock in the morning. He glanced at the chronometer on the sideboard. It was twenty-three minutes past one. 'So there was not much time between the pilongs leaving and our arrival?'

Yan grimaced. He seemed much more relaxed now. 'It felt like much time.'

'I know, Yan, I'm sure it did.' Killigrew's mind was racing. Even if the pilongs had attacked the junks at nine, they could not be more than a couple of hours away. 'Did you see which direction they sailed in?'

Yan shook his head. 'No. I was hiding below decks. I stayed there until all was quiet, and then I waited longer. I thought it might be a trick, to make me come out of hiding.' He hung his head. 'I was very afraid.'

334

'That's only natural. Amongst my people I am considered very brave, but I am frightened sometimes too. I know if I had been through what you have endured today, I would have gone out of my mind with terror.'

Yan looked morose. 'I am a coward. I hid and left my comrades to die.'

'Listen, Yan. You followed the only sensible course of action. If you had come out of hiding, you too would have been killed, and there would have been no benefit. But now you can help us catch the pilongs who attacked your junk, and avenge the deaths of your comrades.'

Yan did not look much cheered by this prospect. Before Killigrew could urge him to try to remember some clue which might give them an indication as to which direction the pilongs had sailed in, there was a knock at the door. Still jumpy, Yan looked up in alarm.

'It's all right, Yan. You stay there.' Killigrew stood up and opened the door a crack.

It was Muda, the *Golden Dragon*'s Malay steward, with a tray of food for the prisoner. 'Captainee wantchee savvy if Chinee man tellee alla yet?'

'Not yet, Muda.' Killigrew took the tray from the steward and closed the door behind him with his heel. He put the tray down in front of Yan. 'Are you hungry?'

Yan nodded. 'Very.'

'The ship's cook prepared this for you.' The tray bore a bowl of stewed pork, another of fried rice, and a pair of chopsticks: a reassuringly Oriental meal for their Chinese guest. Yan thanked Killigrew and tucked in eagerly.

The lieutenant sat back in his chair and lit a cheroot. He was impatient to get in pursuit of the pilongs, but he knew that pressing the brave would only make him panic, and a man who was panicking could not think clearly.

Yan was almost halfway through the meal when he looked up suddenly. 'I heard! I heard the pilongs talking. They said something about "the brothers".'

For a moment Killigrew wondered if he was talking about the Brotherhood of Heaven, Earth and Man, and then it clicked. There were two islets off the coast of Lan-tao Island known as 'the Brothers'. But that was in Cap-sing-mun anchorage, right beneath the noses of the barbarians, and seemed an unlikely rendezvous for pilongs. Dredging his memory he remembered there were two more islets, also named 'the brothers', off the coast of Hainan Island.

'Did they mean the ones off the south coast of Hainan?' he asked.

'I do not know. I suppose that might be what they meant.'

'All right, Yan. You stay here and finish your dinner. I'll tell Captain Verran.'

Even as Killigrew made his way from the saloon to Verran's quarters, his initial elation was overhauled by suspicion. He did not doubt Yan was telling the truth, but it was all too easy. Could it be the pilongs had known that the *Golden Dragon* was coming, and they had deliberately let Yan overhear them talking about the Brothers as the bait to an elaborate trap?

He knocked on the door to Verran's day room.

'Who is it?'

'Killigrew.'

'Come in, Kit.' Verran's day room was decorated like any English parlour, with chintz antimacassars over the easy chairs and lace curtains as delicate as cobwebs stretched over the stern window. Verran was sitting down to dinner. 'Close the door behind you. Has your new pal told you anything yet?'

'He overheard the pilongs say something about the Brothers.'

'Off Hainan?' Verran was on his feet in an instant. He crossed to the door and called up. 'Mr Boggs!'

'Sir?'

'Set a course north by north-west for the Brothers, off Hainan Island. Tell Mr MacGillivray full speed ahead.'

'Aye, aye, sir.'

Verran closed the door and sat down again. 'We can reach the Brothers in a day's steaming,' he told Killigrew enthusiastically. 'If we're only a few hours behind the pilongs there's every chance we'll overhaul them on the way.'

'Perhaps that's what they want.'

'What do you mean?'

'It's all too convenient, Yan having overheard a vital clue like that.'

'You think your new pal might be a plant?'

'Even William Macready isn't that good an actor. But it could be they deliberately let him escape detection, and then let him overhear their intentions.'

Verran stared at him, and then laughed. 'By God, Kit, you're a suspicious son of a gun, aren't you?'

'Doctor's orders. He says I'll increase my life expectancy so long as I don't accept anything at face value.'

Verran chuckled. 'I'm surprised your doctor didn't recommend you swallow the anchor and take a job in the City, if he's so worried about your life expectancy.'

Killigrew grinned. 'He did. I told him it was out of the question.'

'He's probably worried about whether or not you'll live long enough to pay his bills. Don't worry, Kit. If it *is* a trap, the pilongs are going to discover that this dragon has sharp claws.'

Killigrew almost choked when Yan told him that the three Imperial junks had sailed to the Paracels not to catch Zhai Jing-mu, but to parley with him. 'Admiral Nie wanted to offer him an amnesty for all his crimes and a post in the Imperial Navy, in return for his helping to sweep the other pilongs from the seas,' explained Yan.

'Was Admiral Nie acting on Imperial authority? I mean, did the Imperial Grand Council *know* what Nie was doing?'

'I do not know. I am only small fry; humble soldiers like me are told nothing. But I got the impression that negotiations had been going on between Admiral Nie and Zhai Jing-mu for many months. That is why the admiral thought it would be safe to meet Zhai at the rendezvous, why we let him and his men on board the flagship. We

338

only allowed a few to board. We did not know that Zhai had other agents amongst our crew.'

'What happened? Did the negotiations fall apart?'

'I do not think so, Killigrew-qua. As soon as the pilongs had a foothold on board the flagship, the shooting began.'

'So either something changed Zhai's mind about accepting the amnesty, or he had been planning this for months, stringing Admiral Nie along with the attack in mind.'

'I suppose so.'

Killigrew wondered what Zhai Jing-mu hoped to achieve by attacking three Imperial men-o'-war, apart from annoying the Imperial authorities even further. 'Was there any treasure on board any of the junks in the flotilla?' he asked Yan.

'I do not think so, but after the slaughter, I heard the pilongs taking armaments and ammunition from the junk: cannon, gunpowder, shot, *gingalls*, swords.'

'A valuable haul to a man like Zhai Jing-mu, but at a devilish price: I can't imagine anyone being foolish enough to offer him another chance at amnesty after this. He made the Imperial authorities lose 'face'. They'll go all out to catch him now. As long as the Ch'ing Dynasty rules in Peking, he'll never be safe.'

It was the morning of the day after they had found the three junks stricken off the Paracels. The monsoon was over, the rain had stopped abruptly and the heavy swells of the sea had given way to a light chop. The *Golden Dragon* steamed along the coast of Hainan Island, off the south coast of China, the sails close-hauled to give the steamer an extra few knots.

Killigrew had taken Yan on a tour of the steamer, explaining to him as simply as possible how the steam from the boilers powered the pistons which drove the paddle-wheels, and showing him the thirty-six pounder in the forecastle and the eight-inch shell-gun in the stern to reassure him they had nothing to fear from the pilongs they were sailing to meet. 'One hit from a shell can sometimes be enough to blow a junk clean out of the water,' he had told Yan. 'I know: I've seen it happen.' Sensible to the fact that if these barbarians meant him harm they had already had every opportunity to kill him, Yan was much more calm than he had been the day before.

'On deck there!' cried the look-out at the masthead. 'Sail ho!'

'Where away?' demanded Hayes.

'Dead ahead!'

Killigrew took the telescope from the binnacle and ascended to the top of the starboard paddle-box. Bracing his legs on the flat keel of the upturned paddle-box boat there, he extended the telescope and peered through the rain. Almost at once he picked out the mat-and-rattan sails of two three-masted junks sailing abreast before the wind. He descended to the quarterdeck once more.

'What's their heading?' asked Verran.

'West by north.'

'Coming straight towards us, you mean.'

Killigrew nodded. 'Or sailing along the coast in the opposite direction to us, depending on which way you look at it. You think it could be Zhai Jing-mu?'

'I doubt it. He's supposed to be sailing away from us, not towards us, remember?' He took the telescope from Killigrew and lifted it to his eye. 'It's probably just a pair of fishing junks.'

'All the same, if he was only a couple of hours ahead of us we should have caught him by now. You don't suppose we passed them in the night, do you?'

'It's possible. My people would have kept a pretty sharp look-out for them, but we could have passed them as they tacked miles to one side of our course.' He snapped the telescope shut and handed it to Hassan to replace in the binnacle. 'Still, at least we know where they're going. And if it's a trap, I'm sure they'll make certain we find them.'

'I still don't like it.' Killigrew lowered his voice. 'The most powerful shell-gun in the world can only shoot one junk at a time, and you know how these pilongs rely on force of numbers. If we find ourselves heavily outnumbered...'

Verran stared at him in astonishment. 'Kit! Surely you're not suggesting we turn tail and run back to Hong Kong?'

'Christ, no! But I want to make sure we give ourselves every possible advantage. If it *is* a trap, the pilongs will be expecting us to sail for the Brothers, correct?' Verran nodded. 'Why make it easy for them? The Brothers could be where their ambush is laid. I say we heave-to in Galong Bay,

341

a couple of miles to westward. We'll stop the engines so the smoke from our funnel doesn't give them advance warning of our approach, anchor in the bay and send a boat ashore. A landing party can approach the Brothers from landward, and see what the pilongs have got in store for us.'

'Sounds like a first-rate plan to me. Let's go below and work out the details.'

'Later.' Killigrew nodded to where they were fast coming up on the two junks. 'These may not be Zhai Jing-mu's junks, but there's no reason why we should limit ourselves to him. There are plenty of other pilongs in these waters. We'll stop these two and search them. If they're not pilongs, they may be able to give us some information about where the pilongs are.'

'All right,' Verran said cautiously. 'We'll hail them as they pass us, then come about and overhaul them from astern. Hassan, call all hands to quarters.'

As the *Golden Dragon*'s crew scuttled to their action stations, Killigrew took out his pepperbox and checked each of the barrels was primed and loaded. He had cleaned it out after the soaking it had got the previous day; as long as he stayed under the awning which kept the worst of the rain off the steamer's deck, it should be all right.

He glanced up at the two junks again, so close now that all but their masts and sails were hidden beneath the *Golden Dragon*'s prow from where Killigrew stood on the quarterdeck. Both junks were less than half the size of Admiral Nie's flagship and if they were not careful they were going to be run-down by the steamer.

'Hadn't you better put the helm over?' asked Killigrew.

Verran grinned. 'The hell with them. They can move for us.'

For a moment it looked as though the two junks would sail under the steamer's prow, but when they were less than two cables away they suddenly parted so that they would pass on either side of the *Golden Dragon*. Killigrew relaxed.

When the two junks were a hundred feet apart, a cable suddenly rose up out of the water between them, running between the sterns of the two junks.

It came to Killigrew in a flash: this was how they were able to catch and board faster vessels, meeting them head on; the cable would catch across the *Golden Dragon*'s prow, and the two junks would be swung in towards the steamer's sides, coming against her bulwarks fifty feet abaft of the prow. The pilongs would be perfectly placed to throw grappling irons over the steamer's bulwarks.

They meant to board the *Golden Dragon*!

Killigrew crossed the deck to where Dando, Firebrace, Gadsby and O'Connor stood on the forecastle with the rest of the bow-chaser's gun crew. 'Push her over to the aftermost port-side gun port! We'll knock out the one to port first as she comes under our prow; then we'll have only one left to worry about...'

Dando and O'Connor put their shoulders to the thirty-six-pounder and tried to slide it on its brass racers, but it was too heavy for just the two of them.

Killigrew rounded furiously on the two landsmen, Firebrace and Gadsby. 'Don't just stand there, you horse-marines! Bear a hand!' Swearing, Killigrew joined Dando and O'Connor at trying to move the bow-chaser.

A couple of pistol shots sounded and O'Connor gasped. Next to him, Dando slumped over the gun. Killigrew stared at them both in astonishment. O'Connor slid to the deck, dead, and Killigrew saw a bloody wound in Dando's back. He realised the shots had come not from the junks, but from behind him. As the two junks sailed past the prow on either side, he glanced over his shoulder and saw Firebrace with a pair of smoking pistols in his hands.

'Are you insane?' he spluttered.

Gadsby also had a pistol in one hand and he levelled it at Killigrew. 'Never saner, you sonuvabitch. Hand over the pepperbox.'

Killigrew stared at him for a moment. The two junks bumped against the steamer on either side, just ahead of the paddle-boxes. The rest of the *Golden Dragon*'s crew, far from preparing to repel boarders, were making fast the ropes which the pilongs threw up to them. A moment later the paddle-wheels stopped turning and Hassan ordered the sails boxed.

Realising that he had been betrayed on all sides, Killigrew put his hand on the grip of his pepperbox.

'Uh-hunh!' growled Gadsby. 'Handsomely does it, Mr Killigrew. Cap'n Verran says he wants

344

you taken alive, but I'll put a bullet in your skull before I risk my own skin.'

Pinching the pistol between forefinger and thumb, Killigrew slowly unhooked his pepperbox from his belt. Gadsby grinned victoriously.

Killigrew tossed the pistol at him. 'Catch!'

Caught off guard, Gadsby dropped his own gun instinctively to clutch at the pepperbox. Killigrew kicked him in the crotch, and threw a left cross at Firebrace's jaw.

Hayes appeared behind them with a pistol in either hand. 'Not smart, Loo-tenant. You don't know when you're whupped, do you?'

Killigrew backed away. 'I'm a fast learner.'

Hayes smiled. 'Glad to hear it. Clasp your hands behind your head. Get his sword, Boggs.'

The number-two *tindal* dragged Killigrew's cutlass from its scabbard and backed away as the pilongs swarmed over the *Golden Dragon*'s sides. Somehow Killigrew was less than surprised to see Li Cheng amongst them, along with the Triad who had almost shot him the night of the gaolbreak. Li met his eyes with a penetrating glance, but it was impossible to tell what he was thinking. There was no sign of Zhai Jing-mu himself.

'Turn around.' Hayes gestured with one of his pistols. Killigrew had no choice but to obey. A moment later Boggs had thrown him against the thirty-six-pounder – for such a slight-looking youth, he was surprisingly strong – and Killigrew's wrists were bound behind his back.

Then a new voice cut across the words of command being given on the *Golden Dragon*'s deck. 'Everyone throw down their weapons!' a voice commanded in Cantonese. 'Or Captain Verran is the next to die!'

All eyes turned to the quarterdeck, where Yan stood behind Verran with a sword at the captain's throat. Verran did not look particularly troubled by this new development.

'He did his job well,' the *lao-pan* of one of the junks said in Cantonese. Killigrew recognised him as the Triad who had menaced him with a crossbow at Victoria gaol. 'Unwitting fool!'

'Yes,' Verran agreed in the same language. 'But we no longer have any purpose for him.'

Killigrew saw what was coming next. He looked about to see if there was some way he could forestall the inevitable, but with his hands tied behind his back he was helpless.

'Muda!' snapped Verran. Seated astride the main yard, the *Golden Dragon*'s steward raised an eight-foot-long bamboo blowpipe – Killigrew recognised the Malay sumpitan – to his lips.

'Look out, Yan!' yelled Killigrew.

It was too late: one puff from Muda, and a moment later Yan had released Verran to stagger back with his throat skewered by a long dart; tipped with deadly *radjun* venom, Killigrew had no doubt.

As Yan dropped to the deck, Verran nonchalantly flicked a piece of fluff from his shoulder, raised a hand in acknowledgement to Muda, and then exchanged bows of greeting with the *lao-pan*. Then he beckoned for Hayes to approach.

Hayes turned to Firebrace and Gadsby. 'Bring

him,' he ordered curtly, indicating Killigrew.

The lieutenant was dragged across the quarter-deck. 'Running with the hare and hiding with the hounds?' he asked his one-time friend bitterly.

Verran grinned. 'I find life so much more exhilarating this way.'

'How much is Bannatyne paying you, Jago?'

'You think I'm in it for the money? Kit! I thought you knew me better than that.'

'Then why? Surely you don't find common cause with Zhai Jing-mu and the Triads?'

'Sheer devilment, old boy. Who'd've thought that pimply little Jago Verran would one day help to make history? I'd've asked you to join us if I'd thought you'd say yes, but you always were an utter prig, weren't you?'

'Better a prig than a murderous fiend. How can you work with a man like Zhai Jing-mu, damn you? He killed Peri in cold blood!'

Verran tutted. 'You were the one who took her to the *Akhandata* that day, Kit, not me.' Killigrew lunged for him furiously, but Firebrace and Gadsby held him back. After a moment he stopped struggling. 'As hot-blooded as ever, eh?' Verran continued. 'Perhaps if you hadn't been so fired up about avenging her death, Zhai Jing-mu wouldn't want your head on a plate for blowing him up.'

'You're going to burn in hell for this, Jago.'

'Oh, I dare say. But not for a very long time.'

Killigrew turned to Firebrace and Gadsby. 'I might have known this humbug would turn traitor, but what about you two?'

'Cap'n Verran here made us a better offer,'

347

sneered Gadsby. 'Did you think that by showing you still had faith in us in spite of everything, you'd win our eternal loyalty?'

'That was the general idea,' Killigrew admitted ruefully.

Gadsby laughed. 'Your faith in human nature is touching, Killigrew, but sorely misplaced.'

'Jago and I were friends once,' Killigrew told them. He glared bitterly at Verran, who shrugged indifferently. 'Not too long ago, I might add. It didn't take long before he sold me down the river. If he can throw so many years of friendship away in a brace of shakes, how long do you two expect to last?'

'You'd say anything to save your own neck,' spat Firebrace.

Boggs handed Killigrew's pepperbox to Verran. The captain turned the revolving pistol over in his hands. 'Actually, Mr Firebrace, I'm afraid Mr Killigrew is absolutely right.'

Firebrace and Gadsby turned to stare at him with uneasy smiles. 'You wouldn't, would you?' pleaded Gadsby. 'We did everything you told us to. We had a deal...'

Verran rubbed his cheek with the muzzles of the pepperbox. 'What was it you said to Mr Killigrew just now? Ah, yes, that was it...' Verran levelled the pepperbox at Gadsby's head. ' "Your faith in human nature is touching, but sorely misplaced." '

He blew Gadsby's brains out. Firebrace turned and ran for the side. Verran's second shot took him between the shoulder blades before he got halfway across the deck. He sprawled on his face

348

and lay motionless.

Verran turned to Li Cheng. 'Weigh the bodies down with chains and send them to Davey Jones' locker.'

Killigrew felt sick as he watched the bodies of Dando, Firebrace, Gadsby, O'Connor and Yan being tipped unceremoniously over the side. Perhaps Firebrace and Gadsby had got no more than they deserved, but Killigrew had served with Dando and O'Connor for nearly four years now and they had been loyal, while Yan had been an innocent pawn in all this, and had proved himself worthy of the title 'brave' in the final analysis, even if it had achieved nothing.

'I suppose a similar fate awaits me?' he asked Verran.

'Nothing so quick and painless, I assure you. It's nothing personal, you understand, but I have my orders.'

'So you take your orders from Zhai Jing-mu now?'

'For as long as it serves my purpose,' admitted Verran. 'He's very keen to renew his acquaintance with you, Kit. He said something about "an eye for an eye". I'm sure he'll explain it better than I can when we get where we're going.'

'And that would be...?'

'His lair, of course. What, did you think I would blurt out the location, so you could escape and then lead a flotilla of navy ships there? What is it my namesake says in the play? "Demand me nothing: what you know, you know." ' Verran shook his head and tutted. 'You never do give up, do you, Kit?'

'Not while there's breath in my body.'

'A circumstance which Zhai Jing-mu will not hesitate to rectify, I assure you.' Verran turned to the second *tindal*. 'Put him in irons in the lazarette, Mr Boggs. And watch him – he's a tricky devil.'

Boggs nodded and started to drag the lieutenant towards the forward hatch. Killigrew went willingly at first, then stopped abruptly. He pulled Boggs off balance, and then tripped him up with a sweep of one leg. Boggs hit the deck before anyone had a chance to realise what was happening. Killigrew ran on to the forecastle, got one foot on the carriage of the thirty-six-pounder and the other on the gun itself. A bullet whistled past his head. Balancing with difficulty because of his hands tied behind his back, he ran down the barrel towards the muzzle and then launched himself head-first over the side.

He plunged straight under, then jack-knifed his body under the prow and allowed the air trapped inside his clothes to buoy him up against the hull until he felt the keel between his shoulder blades. The keel was hardly sharp, but it was encrusted with barnacles which provided a rough, abrasive surface. He sawed the rope binding his hands against it, while the air in his lungs rapidly ran out.

A dark shape loomed through the water towards him: a shark. It zoomed straight at him, then seemed to change its mind and darted off in another direction. Another shark drifted past, further away. The blood from the bodies of the men tossed overboard would bring every shark for miles around: the sooner he got out of the water, the better.

The tightness in his chest was almost unbearable and for a moment he thought he was going to drown. The water had seeped through his clothes and he was losing his buoyancy, drifting down from the hull of the *Golden Dragon*. He pulled on his bonds in desperation and they snapped. Feeling a dark mist sweep over him, he kicked and clawed his way to the surface. He came up beneath the square-cut prow of the junk grappled to the starboard side of the steamer and whooped a great gulp of air into his lungs as he trod water.

He could hear footsteps pound the decks above him, and voices cried out confused orders in English, Malay and Cantonese. 'Find him, and kill him! Do whatever you have to do, but don't let him get away!'

'Over here!' shouted a voice immediately above Killigrew's head. 'I think I heard him surface!'

'Lower the jolly boat, chop chop!' shouted Verran. 'A hundred dollars to the man who brings me his head!'

A couple of bodies splashed into the water in quick succession and two pilongs surfaced, grinning savagely as they gripped daggers between their teeth. Killigrew ducked back under the water and swam beneath the *Golden Dragon*'s keel. No sooner had he surfaced in the lee of the other junk than a shot sounded from the deck of the steamer and a *gingall*-ball kicked up a spout of water close by. He swam in towards the *Golden*

Dragon's side, sheltering beneath the rear overhang of the paddle-box where the wheel itself gave him some cover from the deck of the second junk.

Something grabbed his ankle. He kicked instinctively with his other leg, hoping it was a pilong rather than a shark, and felt the sole of his foot connect with something. The other pilong had surfaced a short distance away.

Killigrew duck-tailed beneath the waves once more. Dazed, the first pilong was striking for the surface. Above Killigrew, the lower-most boards of the paddle-wheel hung motionless in the water. He pulled himself up between two of them. They were six feet across but only two and a half feet apart: a tight fit, but not too tight. He climbed up until he was inside the paddle-wheel. If the engines were started now, the barnacle-encrusted boards would slice him up like a Chinese cook preparing Peking duck.

As he stood on the inner-edge of the lower-most board, the axle was two feet above his head, but stanchions running across the wheel from side to side connected the spokes at chest height. The stanchions were slippery with marine slime, but by gripping on to one of the spokes he was able to balance enough to haul himself up until he could get both his feet on to the stanchion while wrapping his arms about the greasy axle.

Both the pilongs climbed into the wheel below him. 'We have him trapped!' once of them shouted in Cantonese. 'He's in the port-side paddle-wheel!'

'We could get at him if we lifted the paddle-box

352

boat,' offered Hayes, somewhere above Killigrew's head.

'Why bother?' Verran called back. 'Have Mr MacGillivray start the engines: full ahead. I've always wondered what would happen if a man was inside the wheel when the engines were started,' he added sadistically.

XIII:

Give a Dog a Bad Name...

The two pilongs in the paddle-wheel must have understood English, for they exchanged shocked glances when they realised that they were expendable in Verran's eyes – and about to be expended. Killigrew was less shocked – it no longer came as any surprise to him that Verran wanted him dead – and he recovered first, kicking one pilong in the mouth in which he gripped his dagger. The pilong screamed as blood spurted. Moaning, he gave up trying to catch Killigrew and instead began to ease himself through the boards to get out of the wheel before it started to turn.

Killigrew was already climbing. It would take only a few seconds for the order to be relayed to MacGillivray in the engine room. The other pilong tucked his dagger in his sash and climbed nimbly up after him. He got his arms over the axle and grabbed one of Killigrew's ankles. The lieutenant kicked him in the wrist and continued climbing until he was able to reach up through the upper boards and pull himself up. There was not much space above the wheel, where the paddle-box boat formed the ceiling, but he squeezed through. He tried to climb through the thwarts of the upturned boat and still had his feet on the boards when the wheel started to rotate.

The pilong was climbing up and had his feet on the axle and his arms on one of the stanchions. He cried out. Killigrew stepped on to the next board, and then the next, struggling to keep from falling as the boards moved beneath his feet with increasing speed.

The wounded pilong was only halfway between two of the boards when the top half of his body was smashed against the edge of the paddle-box. One of the boards snapped against his torso, and his body flopped free. It got caught on the paddles below and was swept up on the outside edges of the boards.

Killigrew kicked off with one final effort and pushed himself through the thwarts, lifting his feet clear before he missed his footing on the broken board. A moment later the sodden corpse of the first pilong was carried past inches from his face.

The second pilong still had his feet on the axle and gripped the stanchion, but now the stanchion was below the axle rather than above it and the pilong was upside down. His screams of terror were almost drowned out by the churning of the waters as the boards thrashed down against the waves. The first pilong was deposited in the water which churned in the wheel's wake.

The second pilong was brought upright again, and as Killigrew glimpsed his horror-stricken face through the speeding boards he felt only pity. As a pilong he deserved to die, but not like that. No one deserved to die like that. As the water churned and dripped the spokes and stanchions became even more slippery until the pilong lost his grip. He bounced off one of the stanchions below. Another stanchion came up to meet him and Killigrew heard a bone snap sickeningly. Then the pilong landed on the boards at the bottom of the wheel. They quickly dragged him to the top and dropped him down through the whirling stanchions once more. Killigrew could only squeeze his eyes shut. After what seemed like forever, the throb of the engine faded and he opened his eyes once more. There was nothing left of the pilong, nothing that was too large to slip between the boards at least, and as the wheel's rotation slowed he saw that the water which dripped down from the boards was tinged vermilion with blood. Abaft, the sharks snapped at chunks of meat which floated in the water.

Outside the wheel, he glimpsed the prow of the jolly boat. 'Bring me his body!' Verran ordered from the steamer's deck.

But the men in the boat were going nowhere near that feeding frenzy. 'Sorry, Cap'n!' Killigrew heard Boggs call. 'Looks like the sharks beat you to it!'

'I wonder...' Verran did not sound convinced. Killigrew knew what was coming next. 'Let's have the port-side paddle-box boat up, Mr Hayes, just to make sure.'

Feet sounded on the deck as the hands attached the cradle supporting the paddle-box boat to the inboard davits. Ropes creaked and a moment later light flooded through the gap beneath the boat as it was hoisted up an inch at a time. Unarmed, pinned above the thwarts of the upturned boat, there was nothing Killigrew could do to defend himself. Six inches, seven inches, eight inches... The boat was lifted inexorably higher. Sooner or later someone was going to look underneath and his hiding place would be revealed.

Twelve inches, thirteen inches, fourteen inches... A shadow appeared, and a moment later a head was thrust through the gap between boat and paddle-box. Killigrew saw a Manchu queue. Then the head rotated as the man craned his neck to glance into the boat above him.

Killigrew looked around for something he could use as a weapon, but there was nothing.

His eyes met those of the man with the queue, and he recognised Li Cheng. The two of them stared at one another for what seemed like an eternity. All Li had to do was call out 'He's here!' and Killigrew would be a dead man.

Instead, the Chinese merely winked and withdrew his head.

Killigrew blinked. He had never seen a Chinese wink before.

'It is clear, Captain Verran,' he heard Li Cheng say. 'The sharks must have got him.'

'All right. Lower the boat back in place and let's get underway again.'

Killigrew wondered why the Chinese had helped him. What did he have to gain? It was impossible to guess. Perhaps this was someone's idea of a joke: as soon as Li was out of earshot he would tell Verran exactly where Killigrew was hiding, and they could both have a good laugh about it, safe in the knowledge that the lieutenant was right where they wanted him and in great discomfort to boot.

But he did not have to stay there. Indeed, if they were going to use steam to get underway, he had only a few seconds to climb back down into the water or else be trapped until the next time they stopped the engines.

The men in the jolly boat were rowing back around the stern, but they would have their faces turned towards the paddle-wheel. This was going to have to be timed to a nicety, if it could be timed at all. Killigrew could not wait until the jolly boat was out of sight: he eased his legs between the boards and lowered himself until he dangled at the fullest extent of his arms from one of the thwarts. He moved his grip from the thwart to one of the boards, one hand after the other, until he was able to get his feet on one of the stanchions. He just glimpsed the stern of the jolly boat as it disappeared from view.

He dropped to the axle. His feet slipped and he fell face-down across one of the stanchions. The wind was pounded from him and tears came to his eyes as he choked back a gasp of agony which would have given the game away. The sharks still fought for the last few shreds of pilong, but Killigrew knew he would be safer in the water with them than he would up on deck with Verran and his murderous crew.

He pushed himself back off the stanchion and eased himself feet first into the water. The broken board was immediately below him and he slipped into the water with barely a ripple. The sharks were too busy fighting amongst themselves to pay him any heed. He swam under the hull of the junk grappled to the *Golden Dragon*'s port side, out of sight of anyone on deck. He was too far away to be able to hear what was going on on the steamer's deck, but all seemed quiet enough on the junk. He trod water for a minute or two, using shallow, controlled breaths until he had got his wind back.

The shore was visible about half a mile away. As soon as his breathing was more even, Killigrew ducked under the water and swam for the stony beach until the tightness in his aching lungs forced him to surface once more. He flipped on to his back and allowed himself to float to the surface until his face kissed the air. He could see the two junks casting off from the *Golden Dragon* now, hoisting their sails. Everyone on board was too busy to spy him in the water, perhaps a cable's length from the nearest junk. He took a couple of deep breaths and submerged once more. When he next surfaced, he was too exhausted to swim underwater any longer. He was closer to the shore than to the three vessels now, and besides, the *Golden Dragon* was getting steam up. Killigrew rolled on to his front and struck out for the shore with a gentle breast-stroke. A few minutes later he crawled up through the surf on to the stony beach, and reflected that there had to be easier ways of earning a hundred and eighty pounds a year. Suddenly the prospect of a tedious sinecure in the City of London did not seem so awful after all.

Verran watched the shore astern through his telescope. After a moment, he chuckled softly to himself and snapped it shut.

'Something amusing, Captain Verran?' asked Li Cheng.

'He made it. The sly son of a gun actually made it ashore.'

'Who made it?' asked Hayes.

'Killigrew. Here– ' Verran handed the *tindal* his telescope– 'see for yourself.'

Hayes peered through the telescope. 'I see a figure, but you must have the eyes of a hawk if you can tell who it is from here.'

'It's Killigrew, all right. Who else would it be?'

'How the hell could he have escaped?' demanded Boggs. 'The paddle-wheel, the sharks...'

'You should never underestimate a man like Kit Killigrew, Mr Boggs.'

'We got to turn back and go after him.'

'Do you want me to kill him?' offered Li Cheng. Not betraying the barbarian's hiding place underneath the paddle-box boat had been an unnecessary risk; Li's mission was of far greater importance than the life of a barbarian. But he was starting to wonder if the lieutenant might not prove useful. Nonetheless, if Verran suspected Killigrew had escaped with Li's help, he would be as good as dead.

Verran gestured dismissively. 'What's the point? By the time we've put about, steamed back and put a boat over the side, and the boat's rowed to shore, he'll be long gone.'

'If he makes it back to Hong Kong and tells

everyone we've been working with the pilongs, then we'll all be up the creek,' warned Hayes.

'Then we'll have to see to it he isn't believed, shan't we?'

'And how the hell do you intend to do that? Who's going to take the word of a merchant captain over that of a naval officer?'

Verran checked his watch. 'The Hoi-how fleet should reach the fishing grounds off Saddle Island in a couple of hours, shouldn't it?' he asked Yeh, the *lao-pan* of the pilong junk which had brought Li Cheng to this rendezvous. Yeh nodded. 'Set sail for Saddle Island,' Verran ordered Hayes. 'Full ahead.'

'Aye, aye, Cap'n.'

Verran turned to Li Cheng and Yeh. 'You two come with me.'

They followed him down to his day room. He reached for a bottle of rum. 'Drink?'

Both Yeh and Li Cheng shook their heads. Verran poured himself a generous measure. 'I know Zhai Jing-mu had his heart set on dealing with Killigrew personally, but I'm afraid that's not going to be possible now.'

'Because you let him get away,' Yeh said coldly.

Verran shook a warning finger. '*We* let him get away, remember?'

'If he gets back to Hong Kong and warns the authorities...'

Verran laughed. 'Warns them about what? He knows nothing.'

'He knows you are in league with Zhai Jing-mu.'

'You let me worry about that. In a few hours he

361

can tell them the sky is blue and no one's going to believe him. He's already got a reputation with his superiors for being reckless and unstable. I'm going to make sure that reputation is trebly confirmed.'

'What do you intend to do?'

'Give my men some target practice.'

It took them seven hours to sail around the south-east coast of Hainan Island to where Saddle Island rose up four and a half miles off shore. The small junks of the Hoi-how fishing fleet were there, their lights coming on as the sun set over the shore. Li Cheng counted about two dozen of them. Seeing the junks reminded him of his own childhood at Canton, where his father had worked as a fisherman amongst the islands of the Pearl River estuary; until he had been killed by the barbarians.

'Well, there's the fishing fleet,' Hayes remarked when Verran came up on deck. 'What do you want us to do now?'

'Sink it,' Verran said simply.

'What, sink them all?'

'No, no! Leave one. We want a witness to return to Hoi-how and report what was done.'

'Have you got a screw lose? The yellow-bellies may be crazy, but they ain't stupid. They'll have no problems identifying the *Golden Dragon*...'

'A ship which is under the command of Lieutenant Kit Killigrew of Her Majesty's navy, as far as the authorities in Hong Kong are aware.'

'Until this morning.'

'After this evening's work I expect tensions in Hoi-how will be running too high for anyone to worry about a discrepancy of a few hours. It will take Killigrew days to travel overland from the south coast of the island to Hoi-how. By then all anyone in the city will remember is that the fishing fleet was attacked by a barbarian devil-ship, and Killigrew will be a barbarian from that same ship. When he realises the magnitude of his crime, what more natural than he should lie about the time he swam to the coast of the island?'

Boggs grinned. 'I get it,' he said, and ran to the bow-chaser on the forecastle calling for the gun crew.

'You ain't making a heap of sense, Cap'n,' protested Hayes.

'Do try to keep up, Hayes. It's perfectly simple. Killigrew went insane and ordered his men to start shooting at the fishing junks. He insisted they were pirates, though Heaven knows we tried to tell him otherwise. He was crazy for opium – the *tai-pan* and his wife will confirm that he was recovering from being an opium user, and I've got an empty laudanum bottle below which he polished off – and thirsting for revenge against the yellow-bellies after the murder of his lady love.'

Hayes stared at Verran and a smile spread slowly across his face. 'Sweet Jesus, Cap'n. It's perfect!'

' "We tried to stop him, Captain Morgan." ' Li realised that Verran was already rehearsing what he would tell the barbarian authorities when they got back to Hong Kong. ' "But his men wouldn't listen to us. They just kept blasting away, while Killigrew kept us covered with a pepperbox, frothing at the mouth and calling us mutineers while urging his men on to greater slaughter. God knows what they thought they were doing: maybe they really believed they were firing at pilong junks, maybe they were just trained to obey orders, or maybe they just didn't give a damn ... in the end, I could bear it no longer. I tackled Killigrew, tried to wrest the gun from him ... there was a scuffle ... his men came to his aid, they were killed ... Killigrew jumped overboard and swam for the coast of Hainan. There was nothing we could do but pull a couple of survivors from the water and head home to report this sorry tale.'"

'Survivors?' asked Hayes.

Verran indicated Yeh and Li Cheng. 'I'm sure these gentlemen will have no hesitation in playing the part of fishermen from Hoi-how when they testify in Victoria to Killigrew's moment of madness.'

Li Cheng shook his head. 'I cannot go. I am known in Hong Kong. If I am recognised the whole calumny falls apart.'

Verran turned to Yeh. 'What about you?'

'I will do it. If we stop off at Liu-chu on the way back, I can pick up some friends who can testify also.'

'Excellent! So you see, I don't think we need to worry about Mr Killigrew any more.'

Hayes nodded. 'As you say, he'll head for Hoi-how: it's the shortest route to the mainland, and the likeliest place he'll get passage back to Hong Kong. If the crowd doesn't tear him to shreds, the authorities will execute him for piracy. And even if they don't – even if they choose to abide by the Treaty of Nanking and hand him over to the British in Hong Kong – we'll have arrived days ahead of him to spread the bad word. Cap'n, you're a goddamned genius.'

Verran beamed. 'I know.'

The bow-chaser boomed, startling Li Cheng, and a moment later a fishing junk was lifted out of the water by a direct hit from a shell. Boggs and his gun crew worked quickly to reload the thirty-two-pounder. Within a couple of minutes, the gun boomed again and another junk was destroyed. Some of the fishermen on the deck were hurled screaming through the air. Verran laughed to see them.

The third shot and the explosion of the third junk finally snapped Li Cheng out of his awed reverie. Until then he had stood as a helpless spectator, knowing he could not betray himself by revealing the slightest weakness, and there was nothing he could do against so many men. It was nothing to him if the barbarian Killigrew was lynched by the people of Hoi-how, but he could not stand back and allow these fishermen to be slaughtered.

Perhaps there was something he could do after all.

He made his way down to the orlop deck where he found a storeroom. There were kegs, ropes, boxes, sacks. He ran his finger over the writing on one of the canisters. He spoke English fluently, but struggled with the barbarian method of spelling, using a small number of characters to represent different sounds, and using those sounds to spell out words.

'P ... en ... jellee's p ... pa ... te ... patent la ... lamp oh-ill. Penjelly's patent lamp oil.' He took the canister down from the shelf, unscrewed the lid and took a sniff. This was what he was looking for.

The thirty-two-pounder two decks above boomed again, reminding him he had no time to waste. He picked up a box of matches and carried them aft with the canister of lamp oil. A constant succession of crewmen ascended and descended the companionway between the upper deck and the magazine, but everyone was too busy to pay any attention to Li. The rest of the ship seemed deserted. To avoid MacGillivray and the stokers in the engine room he ascended to the lower deck and headed aft to Verran's day room. He closed the door, took the cap off the canister and splashed lamp oil everywhere: over the deck, the bulkheads, the furniture. He had almost finished when the door burst open. It was Yeh.

'Li Cheng, what are you doing in here? Every hand is needed on deck–' He broke off when he saw the empty canister of lamp oil in Li's hands.

Li threw the canister at his head. Yeh swatted it aside and drew his sword. Li leaped on to the table. The *lao-pan* slashed at his ankles, but Li jumped over the arcing blade and caught hold of the rim of the skylight above his head. He kicked the *lao-pan* in the chest with both feet, and then dropped to the floor. As Yeh came at him again, he kicked the sword from his hand.

Yeh stared at him. 'So, you know *wu-yi*, eh?' He adopted the classic martial arts fighting stance.

366

'Well, I am a master of the black belt!'

As the two of them circled, Li shook his head. 'You are mistaken. Once you were a master of the black belt. Now you are dead.' He took out the matches, and as the *lao-pan* stared at him in horror, Li struck one and dropped it to the floor.

Yeh cried out as the flames spread quickly through every part of the room. Li snatched up a chair and threw it at the stern window. The panes of glass between the leading shattered. The flames blazed all around Li now and his left sleeve was on fire. He smashed the chair against the leading until it fell out, then used the legs to sweep away the last jagged shards of glass around the frame. Then he dived out.

The water extinguished his burning clothes. He surfaced in the wake of the *Golden Dragon* and looked around, treading water. The nearest junk was a hundred yards away, but it was in flames. He struck out for one further off while the steamer's bow-chaser continued to sink the fishing boats remorselessly.

After he had swum a few hundred yards Li found himself surrounded by men and women from junks which had already been sunk, some of them horribly injured. He heard a woman scream and twisted in the water to see a shark's fin angling towards her. He grabbed her and pulled her out of the way.

'Don't struggle!' he hissed.

The shock of being seized paralysed her with fear, and it saved her life. The shark swam past only inches away and another man struggling in the water was abruptly dragged under.

A piece of wreckage drifted past. Li grabbed it and helped the woman cling on to it beside him. 'Rest now. Kicking in the water only attracts the sharks.'

She nodded. The mass of struggling bodies in the water became the focus of a feeding frenzy about twenty yards from Li Cheng and the woman.

He turned to where the *Golden Dragon* steamed on, glowing sparks flying from the funnel in the gathering dusk. Her bow-chaser had fallen silent: the men on deck were too busy fighting the fire in the day room to have any thought for pressing home their attack on the fishing fleet.

A junk altered course to pick up the men in the water. Li waved a hand above his head to attract the attention of her crew. She hove to close by and Li and the woman risked a few kicks to bring them close to her hull. Fishing nets were thrown over the gunwales to help the men and women in the water climb aboard. Li Cheng helped the woman on board and then climbed up after her. He stayed at the gunwale to help everyone else climb out of the water – after the sharks had finished with them, there were few survivors – but even so the deck of the small junk was crowded. Out of a fleet of about two dozen, only eight still floated.

Exhausted, Li collapsed in the lee of the bulwark in the junk's waist. He looked at the faces of the men and women on deck: tired, bedraggled, stunned and shocked. How many loved ones had they lost?

One of the fishermen shook a fist at the

departing steamer. 'Cursed barbarian devil-ship! May the goddess T'ien Hou condemn you to an eternity in the Hell of Ten Thousand Knives!'

'What I don't understand is, why?' sobbed the woman Li Cheng had rescued from the water. 'Why did they attack us? What did we do to harm them?'

'The barbarians need no excuses. They are cruel savages who kill for the pleasure of it.'

Li Cheng was starting to think that the fisherman was right. So many people killed, just to destroy the reputation of one barbarian naval officer. Captain Verran was deranged; and so were the men who had gone along with it.

One youth had been pulled out of the water with his legs bitten off above the knees by a shark. The fishermen did what they could for him, but his life poured out on to the deck with his blood. The woman Li had pulled out of the water cradled the youth's head and shoulders in her arms. 'It is all right, Bao. Everything is going to be all right. Do not die, please do not die...'

She was the only one who could not see what was obvious to everyone else: the youth was already dead. Finally one of the men pried her away from the corpse.

'The men who did this will be made to pay dearly,' snarled Li.

The fishermen all turned to stare at him. 'Who are you?' demanded one. 'I do not recognise you.'

'Yes. Where did you come from? You're not one of us.'

'He must have come from the barbarian devil-ship!'

'What is your name?' demanded the skipper of the junk.

'My name is Li Cheng and I am an Imperial spy. And it is of vital importance that you take me to Hong Kong at once. I have to report to Admiral Huang.'

'No ... no ... no...' With a growing sense of weariness, Strachan sorted through the bones Mei-rong had brought him in her *yolo*. There were dog bones, cat bones, pig bones, cattle bones, even – rather disturbingly – human bones; but none of them was what he was looking for.

'What for you no likee bones?' asked Mei-rong.

'They're bonny bones, but I wanted dinosaur bones.'

'What is dinosaur?'

'Dragon. Dragon bones.' The dragon was such a prominent motif in Chinese art and culture, he was sure that at some point in Chinese history an entire dinosaur skeleton had been found by some imaginative peasant, sparking off the whole dragon culture. Perhaps more than a skeleton. An iguanodon, maybe, or a megalosaurus, or even a species of dinosaur as yet undiscovered by man.

Strachanosaurus.

But if strachanosaurus were out there, there were no traces of it amongst the bones in Mei-rong's boat.

She said something to her sister, and the two of them fell about laughing hysterically. 'That's the way to do it, Mr Strachan,' Molineaux called from the entry port of the *Tisiphone*. 'Get 'em laughing. Works for me every time.'

Strachan scowled up at him. 'Now really, Molineaux! For your information I'll have you know I'm engaged in serious scientific research.'

Before Molineaux could reply, a hubbub arose from the bumboats crowded round the far side of the stern, which quickly spread through all the boats there. 'What is it?' Strachan asked Mei-rong. 'What's going on?'

'My go now. You wantchee bones or no?'

'No ... er ... look, here's a shilling for your trouble...'

'Ahem!' said Molineaux.

'Half a crown, I mean.'

'Ahem!'

'All right, a crown.' Strachan paid up and Mei-rong hurried up out of the boat and back up the side ladder. 'I don't mind you driving a hard bargain, Molineaux, but do you have to do it on behalf of others? At my expense?'

'Have a heart, sir. I'll bet she spent hours collecting all those bones.'

'She probably just rifled through a rubbish heap outside a butcher's shop.'

'And how much would I have to pay you to get *you* to rifle through a rubbish heap outside a butcher's shop, sir?'

'When you put it like that...'

From the deck of the *Tisiphone*, Strachan could see what had excited so much interest amongst the bumboats: the *Golden Dragon* had rounded Belcher Point and was entering Victoria Harbour. She anchored a short distance away and the bumboats swarmed round her like beaux

371

abandoning the prettiest belle at the ball when an even prettier one arrived. 'Looks like Mr Killigrew's back,' said Molineaux, and grinned. 'What do you think, sir? Reckon he's got Zhai Jing-mu chained up in the hold?'

'News of that hempie's death will be more than sufficient for me,' said Strachan. He gazed across at the steamer and had the unaccountable feeling that something was not right. Perhaps it was the sails and rigging: he did not know about such things to be able to say when they were not shipshape and Bristol-fashioned. Perhaps there was something else. If he had not been a scientific man, he might have said he was feeling fey.

The *Golden Dragon* lowered its jolly boat and the crew rowed it across to the *Tisiphone*. As it approached, Strachan saw Killigrew's friend Captain Verran in the stern, but there was no sign of Killigrew himself, or of Dando, Firebrace, Gadsby, or O'Connor.

Molineaux had noticed that too. 'Maybe he's asleep in his cabin,' he said dubiously. There was no need for him to say who 'he' was. 'Tiring work, fighting pilongs all day long.'

'Maybe,' allowed Strachan.

By the time the *Golden Dragon*'s jolly boat bumped against the *Tisiphone*'s side, Robertson had come up on deck. 'Permission to come on board, Commander?' Verran, grim-faced, called up from the jolly boat.

'Permission granted, Mr Verran. Where's Killigrew?'

'We need to talk, sir. In private.' Verran climbed

up the side ladder and went below with Robert-son without another word.

'Something's wrong,' Molineaux said with certainty.

Verran and Robertson were closeted in the commander's day room for an hour, during which speculation ran rife on the decks of the *Tisiphone*. Voices were raised in the day room, but this time Robertson had made sure that the skylight was closed, in spite of the heat of the day, and it was impossible for anyone on deck to make out what was said. After a while, Robertson and Verran emerged on deck. 'Prepare my gig, Bosun,' ordered the commander. 'We're going across to the *Hastings*.'

'Aye, aye, sir.'

While the gig was being lowered, Verran climbed down the side ladder to where his men waited in the *Golden Dragon*'s jolly boat and had a quiet word with the coxswain. The coxswain nodded, and as Verran climbed back on the *Tisiphone*'s deck the jolly boat rowed for the wharf. When the gig was lowered, Robertson and Verran descended the side ladder and were rowed across to the *Hastings*.

All this only intensified the speculation. 'What the deuce is going on, do you think, Mr Strachan?' asked Hartcliffe.

'I don't know, my lord. But I don't like this one little bit. Why hasn't Killigrew shown himself yet?'

'Maybe he's not on the *Golden Dragon*,' said Molineaux. 'Maybe he's in trouble.'

'Then why hasn't the cap'n given orders for us

to get under way?' asked Ågård.

'Maybe Tom Tidley's dead,' said Fanning.

'Killigrew dead?' scoffed Molineaux. 'He'll out-live us all, that one. What about the others? That's what I want to know. Dando and O'Connor, and those two fat-heads Gadsby and Firebrace?'

Robertson and Verran had been on board the *Hastings* for nearly half an hour when Strachan saw one of the petty officers on deck call instructions down to the coxswain of the gig. It rowed back to the *Tisiphone*. 'Captain Morgan presents his compliments and requests that Mr Strachan attend him on board the *Hastings*,' the coxswain called up.

Strachan crossed to the entry port. 'Me?' he asked in astonishment. 'What does he want with me?'

'He didn't say, sir, but if I'm any judge it wouldn't do to keep him waiting.'

It did not do to keep Morgan waiting at the best of times, and Strachan had the feeling that this was not the best of times. He climbed down the side ladder and was rowed across to the *Hastings*, where a marine showed him below decks and knocked on the door of Morgan's day room. 'Mr Strachan to see you, sir.'

'Then send him in at once!' snapped Morgan.

The marine opened the door for Strachan and closed it behind him.

Morgan, Robertson and Verran all sat around the table in the middle of the room, their faces bleak. The assistant surgeon was not invited to sit.

'Mr Strachan, when Mr Killigrew was ill and

374

you attended him at Mr Bannatyne's home, what was it you said he was suffering from?' asked Robertson. He checked some notes he had made at the time. '"Temporomandibular amenorrhoea"?'

'That was it, sir.'

'Are you sure you wouldn't like to revise that statement, Mr Strachan?'

'May I ask what all this is about, sir?'

'Answer the question, damn your eyes!' snapped Morgan.

Robertson, maintaining a tight grip on himself, held up a hand for calm. 'According to Captain Verran here, Mr Killigrew went insane and ordered his men to open fire on a fleet of fishing junks. When Verran and his crew tried to stop him, there was a scuffle in which Seamen Dando and O'Connor, and Landsmen Firebrace and Gadsby, were killed. Mr Killigrew then jumped overboard and swam ashore, where he evaded the attempts of Captain Verran and his men to recapture him.'

Stunned, Strachan stared at Verran. 'I don't believe it, sir.'

'I'm afraid it's true,' said the merchant captain. 'Any member of my crew will confirm it. As will the three men I have on board the *Golden Dragon* whom I pulled out of the water after their junk had been sunk. They were amongst the lucky ones. I think some of the junks got away; I expect we'll be hearing from the Chinese authorities soon enough. They'll confirm everything I've said.'

'What's your man Killigrew trying to do,

375

Robertson?' snarled Morgan. 'Start another war with the Celestials?'

'But why would he do such a thing?'

'We thought you might be able to enlighten us on that score, Mr Strachan,' said Robertson. 'Perhaps he had not fully recovered from his bout of...' he checked the log again, '...temporo-mandibular amenorrhoea.' He said the term in a tone of voice which implied that at some point he had gone ashore, consulted a medical dictionary in a bookseller's and discovered that amenorr-hoea – temporomandibular or otherwise – was an ailment which troubled only the fair sex. 'Per-haps it had affected his state of mind in some way?'

'Mr Killigrew was as sane as you or I when he boarded the *Golden Dragon*, sir,' Strachan said stoutly.

'I'm afraid that's not entirely true, sir.'

Strachan turned to see Blase Bannatyne enter behind him.

Everyone rose to their feet as the *tai-pan* doffed his top hat. 'I came as soon as I heard, gentlemen. No, please, don't stand.'

Morgan pulled out a chair for Bannatyne. 'Please be seated, sir. Can I get you a drink?'

'No, thank you.'

'You were saying, Mr Bannatyne?' Robertson demanded impatiently.

'I'm afraid I'm partly to blame for this. You see, it was my idea to try to conceal the truth of Killigrew's illness. Mr Strachan here wanted to report it to you, but I was the one who pointed out that by doing so he would be in danger of

376

ruining Mr Killigrew's career. Gentlemen, it grieves me to have to inform you that Lieutenant Killigrew had become an opium user.'

Morgan rounded on Strachan. 'Well, sir? What do you have to say for yourself?'

Strachan knew when he was beaten. 'All right, it's true up to a point. He started smoking opium after Miss Dadabhoy was killed. But we'd weaned him off before he went aboard the *Golden Dragon*. I would never have permitted him to return to active duty if I hadn't thought he was fit enough.'

'I'm afraid he must have had a relapse, Dr Strachan,' said Verran.

'*Mr* Strachan, actually,' the assistant surgeon corrected him tersely.

Bannatyne regarded him in surprise. 'Oh, so you're not a fully qualified doctor, then?' he said, as if this were the first he had heard of it.

Strachan blushed. 'I'm a Licentiate of the Society of Apothecaries.'

'But not an MD.'

'Neither is Mr Westlake, my surgeon,' pointed out Robertson. 'Calm down, Mr Strachan. No one is calling your medical competence into question.'

'To the contrary, Robertson,' said Morgan. 'I think Strachan's medical competence is exactly the question here. He certified Killigrew as fit for duty when clearly the lieutenant was not.'

'He had a relapse,' said Verran. 'It wasn't until we'd gone to sea that I noticed he was swilling back the laudanum pretty heavily. I didn't like to say anything. I suppose I should have realised; in some ways it was my fault...'

Strachan could not believe any of this. 'Oh, but this is utter gammon! Opiates calm people down, they don't overstimulate them. The behaviour which Mr Verran here has described is hardly symptomatic of a man taking laudanum.'

'How about a man undergoing withdrawal symptoms after his laudanum ran out?' suggested Verran. 'He was fine for the first couple of days, but after that he grew increasingly irritable.'

'Irritable perhaps,' said Strachan. 'I get irritable if I have too many cups of coffee in the morning. But I don't go murdering dozens of innocent Chinese fishermen!'

'But if he mistook them for pilongs,' said Verran. 'If he was thirsting for vengeance after the murder of the woman he loved...'

'I always said that Killigrew's buccaneering ways would lead him to a bad end,' said Morgan. 'I'm afraid none of this comes as a surprise to me. Knowing Killigrew, I think something like this was bound to happen sooner or later. Forgive me, Mr Bannatyne, but you cannot say I did not warn you.'

Bannatyne shook his head sorrowfully. 'I know, Captain. You're perfectly right, I fear. I should have listened to you.'

'I think we should hear what Killigrew has to say for himself before we condemn him,' Robertson said mildly.

'*If* we see him again,' said Morgan. 'Oh, he'll be given a chance to explain himself, all right. At his court martial. And as for this scoundrel,' he indicated Strachan, 'it's my recommendation that you dismiss him at once. And I shall be writing a very strongly worded letter to the medical director-general regarding his conduct. As far as I can see there is nothing further to be said. Commander Robertson, Mr Strachan, you may consider yourselves dismissed.'

Robertson and Strachan took their leave and made their way up on deck. They were followed a moment later by Bannatyne and Verran.

The *tai-pan* gestured helplessly. 'I cannot tell you how much I deeply regret all this, Commander Robertson. I blame myself...'

'I'm sure you did what you thought was right, sir.'

Bannatyne and Verran climbed into the flory boat that had brought the *tai-pan* out from the quayside, as soon as they were heading out of earshot, Strachan turned to Robertson. 'If you want my letter of resignation from the service, sir...'

'...I shall ask for it,' Robertson concluded for him gruffly, and gestured for him to follow him down to the gig. 'What do you make of all that, Mr Strachan?' he asked as they were being rowed back to the *Tisiphone*.

'I don't know, sir. It seems awful suspicious to me. But I do know one thing: Killigrew wouldn't have attacked an innocent fishing fleet, not without good reason.'

'I'm inclined to agree with you there. I must say, I'd feel a good deal happier if Dando or O'Connor were alive to confirm or deny these accusations. Deuced rum that all four of the sailors we put on board the *Golden Dragon* with

379

Killigrew should have died in that scuffle. You'd think that Verran and his men would have been able to subdue at least one of them without killing the poor devil.'

'Yes, sir.'

'And another thing. You as good as accused Verran of lying.'

'I did?'

'Yes indeed, Mr Strachan. And a man like that would not normally allow his honour to be impugned. He'd've called you out.'

'Perhaps he was frightened I might be a better pistol shot than he, sir?' Strachan had never fired a pistol in his life, but Verran did not know that.

'As the injured party he'd've had choice of weapons. He'd've chosen swords. And from what I've heard of Verran, he's got nothing to fear from anyone in that field. No, Mr Strachan. Verran *was* lying. What I don't understand is: why?'

'I've a feeling only Killigrew will be able to tell us that, sir.'

'Then we'd better hope that Morgan gets to him before the Celestials do. Because at least that way he'll get a chance to defend himself.'

It took Killigrew the best part of a week to cross the south side of Hainan Island to Hoi-how, the main settlement of the island, on the north. From there he hoped to cross to the mainland and continue his journey overland, or better still to get passage on a ship to Hong Kong, nearly three hundred miles away.

Food was no problem. Killigrew always carried a couple of gold sovereigns on him in case of situations like this. Queen Victoria's head might not be known in a humble tavern on the south side of Hainan – one of the few places where it was not – but gold was recognised everywhere. Unable to provide Killigrew with enough copper cash to cover the change for a bed for a night, a hot meal of fish stew and rice, and several cups of rice wine, the innkeeper had gone through the rigmarole of refusing to accept a bargain so profitable to himself, like a priest refusing a bishopric three times before accepting. Killigrew reckoned that he paid the equivalent of ten shillings for that warm but hard, louse-infected bed, but when he woke up his clothes had been dried over a smoky fire and he had enough copper cash in change to take him to Hoi-how. The next day he was offered a ride on an ox cart to the next village on the road, but climbed down and walked when he realised he would make better time on foot.

Wherever he went, the people were a little afraid of him. They had heard of barbarians, but he suspected that most had never seen one in these remote parts, and he was aware – not of stares, the Chinese thought it rude to stare – but of a distinct *absence* of stares, as everyone pointedly averted their gazes. But they were hospitable enough, and polite, and grateful when he paid them. When they saw that for all that he was a barbarian, he was still a human being like them, they were warm and friendly.

The journey reminded him how much he loved China. Nothing was ever too much trouble for the people. Most of the time they seemed to be able to anticipate everything he wanted, and when they could not provide it their apologies were excruciating. When he thought of the treatment a shipwrecked Chinese would have received in Europe, he cringed inwardly with shame for his own race, and he cringed even more when he thought of the ghastly war he had taken part in against these people, when he had been young enough to believe the nonsense he had been fed about the Chinese being an evil race with no sense of morality. The years had taught Killigrew that a different system of values was not necessarily a worse one; he only wished he could make other people see that.

He did not blame the ignorant people of Great Britain, who clamoured for war against the Chinese when they heard of the atrocities which had been committed against the China traders. They could only believe what they heard, and all that they heard was told to them by men who should have known better, but found it in their own interests to whip up such hatred against an alien race. Men like Sir George Grafton and Blase Bannatyne, who manipulated public opinion for their own ends.

Chinese hospitality came to an abrupt end when Killigrew reached Hoi-how, however. He could not blame the people, of course; they seemed to have enough problems of their own. Everyone was dressed in white – the funereal colour in China – and in the harbour he saw dozens of coffins being brought ashore. Some terrible disaster at sea, it seemed.

'What happened?' he asked one mourner,

amidst the wailing and sobbing that was going on all around them.

The man merely turned, scowled, and spat in his face. 'Barbarian devil! Go back to your own country!'

A Chinese constable, dressed in blue robes and a red cap, and armed with a rattan cane and a whip, stood nearby. He also scowled when he saw Killigrew, who bowed in the Chinese manner to mollify him. 'Can you direct me to the *yamen*, please?' The *yamen* was the centre of local administration, where Killigrew hoped to find a mandarin who would arrange to ship him back to Hong Kong in return for a generous promise of *cumshaw*.

'The *yamen*?' The constable looked Killigrew up and down. 'I'll escort you there myself.'

'That is very kind of you, but it isn't necessary–'

The constable ignored him and signalled for three of his colleagues to assist him by holding up a hand, palm-down, and beckoning with his fingers. From the grim looks on their faces, Killigrew had the feeling that a rejection of their assistance might create trouble, and that was the last thing he needed. 'Since you insist...'

They escorted him to the imposing gate of the *yamen* where half a dozen guards were on duty. 'A barbarian!' exclaimed one of them. 'Where did you find him?'

'He approached me in the street,' said the first constable. 'He wanted directions to the *yamen*.'

'Did he, indeed!'

'Yes,' said Killigrew, and bowed again. 'I would

be humbly grateful if the magistrate showed the generosity of spirit to grant a barbarian such as myself the honour of an interview. I am a British naval officer who has been marooned on this island, and I only wish to return to Hong Kong. Naturally anyone who helps me will be generously rewarded.'

'Marooned, you say?' asked the chief guard.

'Yes.' Killigrew bowed again, buying himself more time while he tried to make up his mind about how much of his story he wanted to explain to these minions, when he knew he would only have to repeat himself when he was taken before the magistrate. 'I was on the devil-ship *Golden Dragon* when it was seized by pilongs and...'

Killigrew's words trailed off as he found his neck surrounded by a ring of razor-edged swords. 'So sorry, is my pronunciation at fault?' he asked nervously.

384

XIV:

Tuen Ng

'Do you honestly expect me to believe that?'

Hearing her husband's voice in the hall, Mrs Bannatyne rose from the writing desk in her boudoir and went out to greet him. She was curious to know why he had been called away so suddenly. She emerged on to the landing, and as the two of them crossed the hall below she heard Jago Verran reply.

'It's the truth, sir. He jumped overboard and swam under the keel–'

'With his hands tied behind his back.'

'He must've got them undone, somehow.'

'Perhaps he persuaded one of those sharks to gnaw through his bonds,' said Bannatyne. What her husband did not know about sarcasm was not worth knowing. She paused on the landing without showing herself, curious to know what they were discussing.

'He's a downy fellow, sir. You can't overestimate a man like Kit Killigrew.'

'*I* don't intend to. *You* were the one who let him escape.'

'I've seen to that...' The two of them went into the parlour and their voices became muffled. Mrs Bannatyne tiptoed downstairs and stood close enough to the door to listen.

'Verran, you're a damned fool!' Bannatyne's tone, imperturbable as ever, was a good deal more temperate than his words.

'You wanted the Royal Navy and the Chinese at each other's throats, didn't you?'

'Leave that part of it to me. Your job was to deliver Killigrew to Zhai Jing-mu...'

Mrs Bannatyne felt as shocked as if she had been punched in the stomach. She reached for the doorknob to enter and protest, then caught herself and continued to listen instead.

'The *Golden Dragon* is well known as a vessel of the house of Grafton, Bannatyne and Co.,' her husband was saying. 'It will be my throat the Chinese will be at, not the Royal Navy's. And what am I to say to Zhai Jing-mu? He'll think I've humbugged him. And men like Zhai Jing-mu do not care to be humbugged.'

'Yeh was there. He saw what happened. He'll explain everything to Zhai.'

'And if Killigrew somehow eludes the Chinese and makes it back to Hong Kong? If he tells Captain Morgan that you're working with the pilongs? That will immediately point the finger of suspicion at me.'

'He won't be believed. You saw Morgan just now. He was only too willing to believe Killigrew ran amok and attacked a fishing fleet. So if the yellow-bellies don't kill him, his own navy will. Rather clever of me, I thought.'

'Leave the thinking to me in future, Verran. Have you any idea what kind of hornets' nest your antics have stirred up? If his navy *does* get hold of Killigrew, they'll court martial him. He'll be able to tell them everything he knows. He may not be believed, but a great deal of mud will get thrown around and some of it may stick to me. I can't afford that, not with the *Tuen Ng* so close. So you get back on board the *Golden Dragon*, return to Hainan, find Killigrew, and kill him.'

'We haven't finished repairing the fire damage in my day room yet,' protested Verran.

'Get it done *en route*. I don't care what it takes: I want Killigrew dead.'

The door opened abruptly and Mrs Bannatyne found herself face to face with her husband. It was difficult to say which of them was more surprised, but she recovered quickly.

'Oh, hello, Blase. I didn't hear you come in. Did I leave my parasol in there?'

'Your parasol?'

'Yes, I'm going to take tea with Mrs Dent this afternoon. Unless you have any objection?'

Bannatyne smiled. 'But of course, madam. You do as you please. I'll have Amrish prepare the carriage.'

She went back upstairs and changed quickly into her afternoon dress in time to meet the carriage as the coachman drew up outside the front door. 'Harbour Master's Wharf, please, Amrish.'

The coachman opened the door for her and she was astonished to find her husband already seated there with Verran. Bannatyne had a calfskin holdall at his feet. 'Get in,' he snapped at her.

She stared at him.

Verran reached inside his coat, pulled out a

pistol and levelled it at her. 'Do as your husband says, ma'am. Didn't you once promise to love, honour and obey him?'

'This is ridiculous!' she protested. 'Blase, how dare you let him sit there and wave that thing at me?'

'Get in,' Bannatyne repeated tersely. 'We have a lot to discuss.'

She climbed into the carriage and the coachman closed the door behind her. Faced with a choice of sharing a seat with her husband or Verran it was a difficult decision, but in the end she plumped for her husband.

Bannatyne rapped his cane on the ceiling of the carriage. 'The factory, Amrish.'

'Yes, *sahib.*' The coachman whipped up the horses and the carriage started down the drive.

Bannatyne turned to his wife. 'How much of my conversation with Verran did you overhear earlier?'

'Conversation? What conversation? I don't understand–'

'Oh, come now, madam. You know as well as I do that the Dents' house is not on Harbour Master's Wharf. Who were you going to see? Captain Morgan? Commander Robertson? Since when did your social activities include taking tea with naval officers?'

'For Heaven's sake, Blase! I'm sure I don't know what you're talking about.'

'Really, madam. Do you really take me for a fool, after all these years?'

'Why not? It's now patently clear that you've always taken me for a fool–'

Bannatyne slapped her viciously. 'What were you going to tell Robertson? Come along, speak up. I haven't got all day.'

Stunned with shock as much as pain, she shrank into the corner of the carriage and stared at her husband in disbelief. 'I'm sure I don't know what any of this is about,' she said dully.

'Give her to me for half an hour, sir,' leered Verran. 'I'll make her talk.'

'Yes, you'd like that, wouldn't you?' she spat.

The carriage passed through the gates of the Grafton, Bannatyne & Co. trading factory at East Point and the coachman reined in in the compound. 'Put her in my cabin on board the *Golden Dragon*, and take her to the Cap-sing-mun anchorage,' Bannatyne ordered Verran. 'I'll deal with her in the fullness of time.'

'But if she knows too much about our plans...' warned Verran.

'She knows nothing of our plans. We did not discuss them this morning. And ... Verran?'

'Sir?'

'If Mr Shen tells me you've harmed Mrs Bannatyne in my absence, I'll kill you myself. She is still my wife. Do you understand me?'

'Yes, sir,' Verran said surlily.

'What are you going to do with me?' Mrs Bannatyne demanded fearfully.

'Just put you out of the way for a while. There won't be any visits to officers of Her Majesty's ships, not until it's too late. By then the Royal Navy will have enough problems of its own, without having to concern itself with any far-fetched rumours about the *tai-pan* of Grafton,

Bannatyne and Co.' Bannatyne reached down and took a bottle and a gauze pad from the holdall at his feet. He tipped some of the clear liquid in the bottle on to the pad.

'What's that?' asked Mrs Bannatyne.

'A new discovery from Europe, my dear. It's called chloroform. Doctors use it as an anaesthetic in operations, so their patients don't feel any pain.'

Mrs Bannatyne did not feel reassured. She struggled as he clamped the pad over her nose and mouth.

'...Just breathe normally, my dear...'

Killigrew was woken by the tramp of marching feet and the jingle of arms. He stood up and crossed to the door of his cell in the *yamen*. Peering out through the bars, he saw a troop of Imperial bannermen crossing the courtyard to his cell.

He knew they were coming to drag him to his place of execution. If he was going to think of a way to escape, now would be a good time to do it.

He had been kept in the cell for over a fortnight before the trial. He had been bedraggled and lousy enough after his trek across Hainan Island. Now what was left of his uniform was filthy and ragged, the kerseymere trousers and linen shirt now nearer black than their original white, his hair long and matted, three weeks' growth of beard on his chin, his underclothes crawling with lice.

The trial had been conducted in Mandarin

Chinese, too swift for his understanding of the Cantonese dialect to be able to keep up with. Only the occasional phrase had filtered through: 'piracy', 'mass murder', and 'death by strangulation' had been common themes. There had been no jury: the magistrate had weighed up the evidence and assigned the punishment according to the Manchu Code. All Killigrew knew was that he had been set up somehow by Verran and his crew.

His craving for laudanum was gone, thanks to enforced deprivation, but it had been a hard two weeks: a fortnight of nightmares both sleeping and waking, almost driving him to the verge of insanity. But now the craving was gone, and he was starting to feel himself once more. In fact, he felt better than he had done since Peri had been killed.

And the men who were responsible for her murder were going to get away with it, while he was executed for a crime he had not committed.

He looked desperately about his bare, filthy cell for something he could use to defend himself, but there was nothing. With the heavy wooden cangue locked about his neck and wrists, like a portable set of stocks, he was hardly in much of a position to defend himself anyway.

One of the bannermen unlocked the cell, flanked by men who kept Killigrew covered with drawn bows. The bannerman entered, unfastened the chain which shackled the cangue to the rear wall of the cell, and then led Killigrew outside like a dog on a leash. He indicated the wooden bamboo cage they had brought with them.

'Get in,' he growled.

'You know that if you execute a barbarian, China will be breaching the Treaty of Nanking. It will mean war between your people and the barbarians, and China will be humiliated again.' For all that Killigrew did not approve of the treaty and the principle of extraterritoriality enshrined in it, he could not allow an innocent man to be put to death. Especially not when the innocent man was himself.

The bannerman tugged on the chain, pulling Killigrew off balance so that he fell painfully on his knees. 'In!'

Killigrew was manhandled into the cage. It was so cramped, he had to sit with his thighs against his stomach and the edge of the cangue hooked over his knees. It was excruciatingly uncomfortable. The door was closed and locked, and then four coolies hefted the cage on to their shoulders. Then they proceeded to the main gate of the *yamen*, with six bannermen before the cage and six more behind it.

There was a crowd outside the *yamen*, a hundred faces twisted in scowls of hatred and rage, spitting, throwing rotten fruit and eggs, chanting: 'Death to the *fan kwae*! Death to the *fan kwae*!' The guards struggled to clear a passage, and for a while Killigrew feared he might be lynched before he reached the place of execution, wherever that might be.

The uncomfortable journey took him down to the docks, where a massive war-junk seemed to tower over the small, single-storey hovels and godowns which lined the waterfront. At the foot of the gangplank, the senior bannerman read out a proclamation.

'By the order of his Imperial Excellency Governor-General Xu Guang-jin, it has been decreed that the high-nose barbarian will be taken to Canton to be executed before the barbarian merchants in Canton, as a warning to their people.'

There was a roar from the crowd – part approval that the barbarians would be made to lose face, part disappointment that the crowd would not get to see a malefactor executed for their edification and entertainment (just like any crowd outside Newgate, Killigrew could not help thinking) – and for a few seconds the rain of rotten fruit and eggs being pelted at him seemed to intensify. Then the bannerman signalled the deck of the junk, where the Chinese sailors were already making preparations to get under way. The cage was manhandled below decks, through a series of ill-lit compartments like a rabbit warren. Eventually it was put down in a pitch-black chamber.

'Leave him here,' ordered the senior bannerman. Footsteps sounded on the deck as the coolies withdrew from the chamber, and Killigrew heard the door being locked and closed. Everything was silent but for the creak of the timbers and the slop of water close by.

In the pitch-darkness, Killigrew had no concept of how long he was kept there. His limbs were already numb from being cooped up at such an awkward angle, and if he were kept like this all the way to Canton, he would be unable to walk once they arrived. Not that he would need to be able to walk to be executed.

After a while the creak of the junk's timbers changed, and the motion of the rolling deck seemed to increase. They were sailing out to sea. It was over three hundred miles to Canton; with fair winds, the junk would arrive within a few days.

He heard the door open and saw a glimmer of light in the darkness, a taper jogging along unsteadily as if carried in someone's hand. He heard footsteps: two people, but lighter of foot than bannermen or coolies. The door was closed behind them, and he heard a wooden bar slide into place from outside. The taper circled the compartment, lighting a number of lanterns, until there was enough light for Killigrew to see that, far from being in a fetid orlop deck, he was in a chamber luxuriously hung with crimson silk and furnished with soft cushions. Beside the cage was a large tub of steaming, soapy water.

The two people in the room were a couple of pretty *amah* girls. The one holding the taper blew it out, and then they both bowed to him. The other had a set of keys which she promptly demonstrated fitted the lock on the cage, and the cangue about his neck. Having set him free, they stepped back and bowed again, apparently unaware they were locked in a chamber with a barbarian convicted of piracy and mass murder. There was a shaving razor and a pair of scissors on a tray close by, but there seemed little point in using them as weapons to hold these girls hostage so he could bargain for his freedom: they would be slaves, expendable, otherwise they would not have been put in this situation.

Killigrew rubbed his chafed wrists, stretched aching limbs, scratched his louse-bites as discreetly as possible in the presence of ladies, and eyed them warily. 'Perhaps I'm looking a gift horse in the mouth,' he remarked in Cantonese, 'but to what do I owe the special treatment? I'm sure not all convicted criminals are treated like this.'

The two girls giggled. 'You are to refresh yourself before you take dinner with Admiral Huang.'

'Refresh myself?'

'We have been ordered to fulfil your every desire,' said the girl, and the two of them giggled again.

He eyed them appraisingly. 'Well, let's start with a bath and a shave, shall we?'

One bath, shave, haircut, massage, manicure and change of clothes later, Killigrew found himself dressed in a black silk tunic, pyjamy trousers and silk boots. He was ushered on to the poop deck, where Admiral Huang sat at a table beneath a silk awning to protect him from the heat of the sun. He rose to his feet and bowed. Dazed by all this fine treatment, Killigrew bowed back.

Huang indicated a chair. 'Please be seated, Lieutenant,' he said in English.

They sat down facing one another. A servant brought a tureen of soup on to the poop deck and started to ladle it into their bowls. 'Shark's fin?' Killigrew asked his host.

Huang nodded. 'You must be hungry. I do not

imagine that gaol food is particularly sustaining.'

'No worse than you'd get in a British gaol, I'm sure.'

'I am sorry we are unable to provide you with barbarian food. My cook has prepared the finest banquet he could, under such circumstances.'

'Oh, I like Chinese food.'

His host nodded approvingly and tucked in. After a few moments, Huang looked up. 'You are not eating, Lieutenant Killigrew. I trust you do not fear the food is poisoned?'

'No. I'm just curious to know why I'm getting the mandarin treatment. Two hours ago I was being conveyed to my execution. Or is this the hearty meal for the condemned man?'

'Please forgive the subterfuge, Lieutenant. I hope the manner of your being brought aboard this vessel did not incommode you unnecessarily. Feelings are running high in Hoi-how. There are few families who did not lose a loved one in the perfidious attack on the fishing fleet. If we had announced that you were to be handed back to your people in Hong Kong, then there would have been severe disturbances.'

'So you intend to abide by the treaty?'

'May demons wipe their backsides on your unfair barbarian treaties!' snarled Huang. 'If I thought you were the man who had master-minded the attack on the fishing fleet, then I would kill you myself, with my bare hands!'

Killigrew refused to be flustered by the admiral's sudden rage. 'Since you haven't, I can only suppose that you believe in my innocence.'

'We Chinese are not fools, Lieutenant. Why

would a man on board a ship attack a fishing fleet, and then jump overboard and swim to an island where he could expect to encounter only hostility for his crime? The ways of you barbarians are curious, but not suicidal. I learned from an informant that you jumped off the *Golden Dragon* seven hours before it attacked the fishing fleet.'

'An informant?' Killigrew thought for a moment. 'Li Cheng?'

Huang nodded. 'I had the matter looked into. One of my men found the inn where you had dinner on the afternoon that you landed.' He tossed a gold sovereign on the table. 'Yours, I believe. At the hour of the rooster – when the *Golden Dragon* attacked the fishing fleet – you were eating fish stew and rice, and doing your best to drink up the innkeeper's entire stock of rice wine.'

'If you'd been through what I'd been through that day, you'd've needed a drink, too.'

Huang lit a Russian cigarette and took a long drag. He breathed smoke out through his nostrils and fixed Killigrew with his gimlet eyes. 'What do you know of a plot to overthrow the Ch'ing Dynasty, Lieutenant?'

'I didn't know there was one. Who's behind it?'

Huang smiled, the corners of his eyes crinkling into crow's feet. 'Ah. You think perhaps it is me, working to overthrow the dynasty from within?'

'The thought had occurred to me,' Killigrew replied sardonically. 'But I dismissed it.'

'Oh? May I ask why?'

'You're a Tartar – a Manchu. What would you

397

have to gain by allying yourself with the pilongs and Triads?'

Huang chuckled. 'Well done, Lieutenant. I am pleased to see you are not as ignorant of civilised politics as many of your compatriots. You are absolutely right. I am loyal to my emperor. But I am also loyal to my country, and that country is China. As an admiral in the Imperial Navy I must serve both my emperor and my people as I think fit, and as long as the Ch'ing Dynasty rules in the Forbidden City then the people I am responsible to include both the Manchus and the Han.'

'All right. So if not you, then who?'

'That is what I am trying to find out. A barbarian, perhaps?'

'What would a barbarian have to gain?'

'Plenty, if he were the *tai-pan* of one of your trading companies. I am well aware that these merchants complain of what they consider to be the restrictive trade practices of my country.'

'Can you blame them? The West has a great deal to offer China, just as China has a great deal to offer the West. But if your people insist on sneering at the industrial produce of the West and refuse to buy it, can you blame the China traders if they're forced to sell opium to purchase tea?'

'It is not for me to criticise Imperial policy. But if there is a threat against the state then it is my job to expose it and crush it. Zhai Jing-mu has grown as powerful as any pirate chief can, but he wants more. He wants legitimacy.'

'You're thinking of the deal he tried to cut with Admiral Nie? No, Zhai must have changed his mind. You'll find what's left of Nie's flotilla floating amongst the Paracels.'

'So I have been informed. I tried to stop Nie from going to that rendezvous, but he would not listen. He paid the ultimate price for his foolishness. What I must now ask myself is, what made Zhai Jing-mu change his mind? The terms proposed by Nie were generous.'

'Zhai must have got a better offer.'

Huang nodded. 'He believes that the Triads must be close to their aim of overthrowing the Ch'ing Dynasty, otherwise he would not ally himself to them. But the Triads have been trying to overthrow the Manchus ever since my ancestors invaded China over two hundred years ago. What makes Zhai think that now they may finally succeed?'

'The Triads must be getting help from a new source,' deduced Killigrew. 'Someone outside China.'

'Very good, Lieutenant. Keep going.'

'A foreign power?' Killigrew tried to think of all the nations who envied Britain's position at the forefront of trade with China. 'France? The United States? Russia?'

Huang shook his head. 'You disappoint me, Lieutenant. Think of someone closer to home.'

'Sir Dadabhoy Framjee?'

'My first thought. But an agent I infiltrated into Framjee's company managed to eliminate the Parsi from his enquiries.'

'Mr Li has been a busy little bee, hasn't he?'

Beaming, Huang inclined his head.

'All right, not Sir Dadabhoy. Zhai's murder of

his daughter ruled him out anyway. Who does that leave? There are dozens of China traders to choose from.'

'You are not thinking, Lieutenant. Which of the companies is large enough to provide the Triads with the resources to overthrow the Ch'ing Dynasty? Which *tai-pan* held a ball at his factory on the night that Zhai Jing-mu was freed from his gaol, thus ensuring all the senior officers of Hong Kong were elsewhere at the time? Who had Sir John Davis – a man renowned for his conciliatory attitude towards China – dismissed as Governor of Hong Kong, and replaced by the more aggressive Mr George Bonham? Who do you think gave the order for you to be handed over to Zhai Jing-mu?'

Killigrew nodded. He felt as if he were finally awakening from a dream. When the admiral laid all the pieces on the table, it fitted perfectly. 'Bannatyne.'

'Yes. Blase Bannatyne.'

'Have you thought of explaining this to the British authorities?'

'Which British authorities? Mr Bonham? I am not suggesting the plenipotentiary is in Bannatyne's pocket, but you have seen how he acts in Bannatyne's presence. Bonham cannot govern Hong Kong without the support of the China traders, and Bannatyne is their leader. Besides, what would I tell Bonham? That I suspect that Bannatyne is behind some plot to overthrow the Ch'ing Dynasty, but I do not know what the plot is and I have no proof of Bannatyne's involvement? That is where you come in, Lieutenant.'

'You want me to spy on Bannatyne?'

'You are the only barbarian I can trust. Perhaps the only man I can trust.'

'What makes you think you can trust me?'

'Zhai wants you dead. So does Bannatyne. Whichever side you are on, it is not theirs. Besides, your persistent bumbling has damaged Bannatyne's plans as much as it damaged my own.'

Killigrew almost choked on his soup. 'My bumbling...?'

'I successfully infiltrated one of my spies into the Tai-ping-shan chapter of the Triads. He was on a junk which would eventually have led him to Zhai Jing-mu's lair and perhaps provide proof of a link between Bannatyne and the Triads. Your escape from the *Golden Dragon* scotched that plan and forced him to compromise himself in order to mitigate the severity of the attack on the fishing fleet.'

'Well, of course if I'd known Li was one of your spies, I'd happily have let Verran take me to Zhai Jing-mu to be tortured to death,' Killigrew said sardonically.

'Li Cheng is a good agent, but sometimes he lets his heart rule his head.'

'I still don't understand. You talk of a plot to overthrow the Ch'ing Dynasty. But you don't know what it is and you're not sure who's behind it. Forgive me for saying so, but what makes you think there's a plot at all?'

'Li's predecessor. His instructions were much simpler: infiltrate the Triads in Tai-ping-shan as a stepping stone to locating Zhai Jing-mu's lair.

That was a year ago. Six months ago he stumbled into the *yamen* at Canton, mortally wounded. Fortunately he managed to get past the guards and gain entry to the private chamber of Xu Guang-jin. He knew he could not trust the information he had discovered to anyone of a lesser rank than the governor-general. With his dying breath he warned his excellency of a plot to overthrow the Ch'ing Dynasty that would take place in Hong Kong at the time of the *Tuen Ng.*'

'The *Tuen Ng*?' Killigrew had heard that phrase before somewhere, although it took him a moment to remember what it signified. 'The dragon boat festival.'

Huang nodded. 'Four days from now.'

'Oi! And where do you think you're going, slanty-eyes?'

As Killigrew climbed the side ladder to the deck of the *Tisiphone*, he tilted his head back so that his face was no longer hidden from the boatswain by the conical hat he wore. 'I may be out of uniform, Bosun,' he said tightly, 'but nonetheless I must insist you address me as either "sir" or "lieutenant".'

The boatswain's eyes bulged out of his head. 'Lieutenant Killigrew! Sir! Sorry, sir, didn't recognise you in them chinky-chonk clothes.'

All the hands on deck crowded round to stare. 'That you, sir? We heard you was dead!' said Molineaux.

'Or captured by the yellow-bellies,' said Ågård.

'I was.' Killigrew gestured to where Huang had moored his junk a short distance away. 'Fortunately, Admiral Huang was kind enough to bring me back to Hong Kong.'

'You may not want to stay put, sir,' warned Ågård. 'They're saying you went nuts and attacked a fishing fleet. Not,' he added loyally, 'that any of us believed it for a moment.'

'I'm glad to hear that, Mr Ågård.'

'All right, all right, get back to work, you lot!' growled the boatswain. 'Begging your pardon, Mr Killigrew, sir, but Commander Robertson left instructions that if you was brung back on board you was to be taken to him at once.'

Killigrew gestured to his Chinese clothes. 'Don't I get a chance to change into my spare uniform first?'

'He was very specific about the "at once" part of the order, sir.'

Killigrew allowed the boatswain to escort him down to Robertson's day room, where the commander was in conference with Lord Hartcliffe. Both of them leaped to their feet when the marine sentry ushered Killigrew in, and Hartcliffe pumped his hand vigorously.

'Kit! By all that's wonderful! I was starting to fear the worst!'

'All right, First, that will do,' snapped Robertson. 'You can try to dislocate his arm later. Killigrew, you do realise that Captain Morgan has had a warrant put out for your arrest, don't you?'

'No, sir. But if I can convince Admiral Huang of my innocence, sir, I'm sure I can do the same for Morgan.'

'Huang?' Robertson glanced out of the window

403

to where the admiral's junk rode at anchor. 'So, he brought you back, eh? And I suppose he provided you with those ridiculous clothes as well?'

'After a fortnight in a gaol cell, sir, I'm afraid the uniform I was wearing was only fit to be burned.'

'All right. You can change later. Word of your return has probably reached the shore already. I dare say we haven't much time before Morgan arrives with Mr Cargill and demands that you be clapped in irons, so make your explanation short, and don't leave out anything pertinent.'

'I'll start at the beginning, sir, and you'll have to bear with me. I'm still trying to get all this straightened out in my mind. A lot of what I have to say is supposition, but if you'll bear with me you'll see it fits. Bannatyne is in league with the pilongs.'

'Capital idea, Killigrew,' Robertson said sarcastically. 'Get the supposition over and done with. Do you have any proof of that?'

'No, sir. But Grafton, Bannatyne and Co. have lost fewer ships to pilongs than any other company trading with China. One, to be precise, and it looks like even that may have been an insurance swindle. Bannatyne provides Zhai Jing-mu with all the information he needs about shipping movements to and from Hong Kong: not just which ships are sailing when – Zhai could pick up that kind of information from the *Hong Kong Register* – but what cargoes they're carrying. He's a sharp one, I'll lay odds he has had at least one spy in each of his rivals' factories.

So Zhai Jing-mu gets information and in return Bannatyne has his ships left alone; at the same time as his rivals lose millions from Zhai's depredations.'

'It's a little far-fetched, but it does make a kind of sense,' Robertson admitted grudgingly. 'Go on.'

'All right. Let's suppose that Zhai Jing-mu wasn't killed when the *Akhandata* went down. Even if he wasn't badly injured, he must have been upset. He laid a trap for Peri and me, but he only got half of what he was after. I escaped and killed several of his men into the bargain. Zhai Jing-mu lost face that day. He's only a man, surrounded by other men just as ambitious as he is. Each time one of his schemes goes awry he loses a little of the mystique which gives him such a powerful hold over his followers. The only way he can remedy that is to correct his earlier mistake, make it clear to all that anyone who stands in his way will die horribly. So he lays another trap, this time with the help of his friend Bannatyne.'

'So that was why Bannatyne lent us the *Golden Dragon*? As a ruse to capture you?'

'Verran knew it was the perfect bait. Every man has his weakness. With some it's women, with others gaming.' Killigrew grinned ruefully. 'With me I'm afraid it might be the chance of an independent command and an opportunity to take a crack at the pilongs.'

'All right, what exactly happened?'

Killigrew told him quickly about the 'attack' on the *Golden Dragon*. 'They tried to take me

405

prisoner, but I managed to jump overboard and swim ashore,' he concluded briefly. 'It took me the best part of a week to walk across Hainan to Hoi-how. When I got there I reported to the magistrate at the *yamen* and was promptly arrested for the attack on the fishing fleet. That seems to have been genuine enough. Verran must have opened fire on those junks just to make it look as if I'd run amok, so that no one would believe me if I came back here to tell you he was in league with the pilongs.'

'Frankly, Second, I'm still not sure that I *do* believe you. But I believe Verran even less. Yet even if what you've told me is true, that hardly proves your wild allegations about Bannatyne. Solid proof is what we need.'

'We'll get it,' said Killigrew. It might have been Zhai Jing-mu who had pulled the trigger when Peri had been murdered, but it was obvious that Bannatyne had been behind it all, pulling the strings. 'When I catch up with Verran, he'll tell us all. His only chance now is to turn Queen's evidence. He's just a pawn in this whole thing. Bannatyne's the spider lurking at the middle of this web, and it's him I want.'

There was a knock at the door. 'Begging your pardon, sir,' called the marine sentry. 'But apparently Assistant Superintendent Cargill of the Hong Kong Police wishes permission to come on board.'

'That's all right, Barnes. Have him shown down here at once.'

'Very good, sir.'

Robertson checked his watch. 'Ten minutes:

remarkably swift work for a policeman.'

'That Cargill's no fool,' allowed Killigrew.

While they were waiting, the sound of sawing and hammering from the waterfront drew his attention out of the stern window, open to let some air flow through the room on such a stifling day, and he saw some kind of scaffold being built on the open space in front of the barracks. Wherever he looked preparations were underway, strings of paper lanterns being hung from buildings and across streets, and temporary spectator stands being built wherever there was space on the waterfront. 'What's going on out there?'

'Preparations for the dragon boat festival on Tuesday night,' explained Robertson. 'They're making a big thing of it this year.'

Killigrew nodded. Westerners usually looked down their noses at Chinese festivals, but entertainment was so difficult to come by in the colony that anything which could be used as an excuse for a celebration was usually seized upon. He wondered if what Huang had told him about a possible plot taking place at the festival was true. It was now Sunday afternoon, which meant that if there was a plot he had just over two days to expose it. He hoped that if he could find proof to convict Bannatyne of aiding and abetting pirates that would scupper whatever scheme was being hatched.

Cargill was shown into the day room. 'Come in, come in, Mr Cargill,' said Robertson. 'I believe you already know Lord Hartcliffe and Mr Killigrew?'

Looking flushed, Cargill nodded. 'Yes, sir. I'm

sure you know why I'm here.' He took a piece of paper from inside his coat and unfolded it. 'I have a warrant for the arrest of Lieutenant Christopher I. Killigrew, suspected of having–'

'Yes, yes, yes!' Robertson said impatiently. 'We know all about that. Stow it, Cargill. That's fine, except you need to cross out Killigrew's name and write Captain Jago Verran's in its place.'

Cargill looked at them in surprise. 'Captain Verran!' He brushed his whiskers thoughtfully. 'That would explain it...'

'Explain what? Explain yourself, man!'

'I've got a missing person's report on Captain Verran. In fact, I've got a missing ship report. He's disappeared, along with the *Golden Dragon* and her crew. Mr Bannatyne only informed me this morning. The *Golden Dragon* left for Macao a couple of days ago with Mrs Bannatyne on board, but it never arrived. I'd assumed it must've been attacked by pilongs.'

'Damned inconvenient,' said Hartcliffe.

'Not from Bannatyne's point of view,' said Killigrew. 'All too convenient, if you ask me. I've a feeling Mrs Bannatyne is in deadly danger.'

'How so, Second?'

'I should have expected Verran to disappear with the *Golden Dragon*. Bannatyne knew his story wouldn't hold water if I made it back here. If Verran's gone adrift he can't be made to answer any awkward questions.'

'But what about Mrs Bannatyne?' asked Hartcliffe. 'Why should she disappear? Unless she was involved in some way...'

Killigrew shook his head grimly. 'No. That's

just it. She wasn't involved at all. She must've stumbled across something proving her husband's collusion with the pirates. She's not the first member of her family to disappear while sailing to Macao on a vessel captained by Verran.'

'You're referring to her father?' Cargill drew himself up to his full height. 'I conducted the inquiry into his death personally. The coroner's verdict was death by misadventure. Gentlemen, I'm afraid I'm a little behind you all here. Are you suggesting that Mr Bannatyne is in league with the pilongs?'

'Isn't it obvious?' asked Killigrew.

'That's an extremely serious accusation, sir. I know it's not my place to give you advice, but nevertheless I feel I must remind you that Mr Bannatyne is an extremely influential man. Both here and back in England.'

'We're well aware of that,' Robertson said tersely.

'I trust you have some proof of what you suggest?'

'If I had proof, Mr Cargill, we wouldn't be standing here jawing, we'd be on our way to Bannatyne's house to put that devil under arrest.'

'Are you absolutely sure you're not misconstruing this, sir? I mean, I know it's not my place to speculate, but from what Mr Bannatyne said to me this morning ... well, I rather got the impression he thought his wife might have run away with Captain Verran.'

'Perhaps,' Killigrew said dubiously. 'But it doesn't alter the fact that Verran's guilty of piracy and murder.'

'It's still a case of your word against his,' pointed out Cargill. 'And the word of his crew, and three Chinese fishermen Captain Verran pulled out of the water after you sank the fishing fleet.'

Killigrew was on his feet again in an instant. 'Jesus Christ! You don't honestly believe that, do you?'

'It's not a question of what I believe. It's a question of what the jury's going to believe. And I'm afraid the word of an opium smoker isn't going to count for much.'

'An opium smoker? Who told you that?'

'It wasn't Strachan, if that's what you're thinking,' said Robertson. 'Bannatyne told us.'

Killigrew grimaced. 'I should have seen that one coming.'

'Do you deny it?'

Killigrew sighed. 'No. But I'm off the filthy stuff now. And I certainly didn't order an attack on any damned fishing fleet.'

'I never believed *that* for a moment,' said Robertson. 'But you must take Mr Cargill's point. You're batting off a sticky wicket here.'

'I'm sorry, sir,' said Cargill. 'But until this whole matter has been cleared up, I'm going to have to take Mr Killigrew in for questioning at the very least.'

'Now hold on a moment, Assistant Super-intendent. I'm sure we can come to a mutually satisfactory arrangement here. I'm going to speak to Captain Morgan immediately to try to get him to see this business isn't as clear-cut as it first appears. While I'm doing that, would you have

410

any objections if Mr Killigrew were to stay on board the *Tisiphone*? I'm sure he'll give you his word of honour as an officer and a gentleman that he won't go anywhere.'

Killigrew stuck his hands in his pockets and nodded.

'I suppose that's all right,' mused Cargill.

'Very well, then,' said Robertson. 'That's settled. You and I shall go and see Captain Morgan while Killigrew remains here.'

Killigrew and Hartcliffe went up on deck to see Robertson and Cargill off.

As soon as the gig was out of earshot, Killigrew turned to Molineaux. 'Fancy a jaunt to the *Buchan Prayer*?'

Molineaux raised an eyebrow. 'I take it we don't have an invitation, sir?'

'That's why I'd like you to come with me. I need your skill at picking locks and breaking and entering.'

'I came to sea so I could get away from a life of crime,' Molineaux said huffily.

'Just one last time. Remember, you're on the side of justice now.'

'Tell it to the beak when he has me lagged for breaking and entering.'

'Actually, in law I don't think you can be transported to Australia for trespassing on a private vessel.'

'No?'

Killigrew shook his head. 'This will count as piracy. You know what penalty that carries, don't you?'

Molineaux sighed. 'I wish you'd kept your trap

411

shut, sir. I was just starting to think this might not be such a daft idea.'

'It would hardly be fair to ask you to do this without letting you know the risks involved. If you want to back out, I shan't think any the less of you.'

'In a pig's eye!'

'I can't order you to do this.'

'Oh-kay, oh-kay. I'll help.'

Hartcliffe was horrified. 'Killigrew, what are you talking about? I thought you were going to stay here?'

'While Cargill and Morgan prepare the case for the prosecution? No can do, my lord. We have to find the *Golden Dragon* before it's too late. Verran hasn't got the sand to disobey Bannatyne. Our friend the *tai-pan* knows exactly where his missing steamer is, and it's my guess we'll find the information we're looking for on board Bannatyne's receiving ship. We may even find proof of Bannatyne's involvement with the pilongs.'

'Please, Killigrew, I'm begging you. The Old Man's going to have me strung up from the yardarm if he gets back and finds I've let you cut and run. Besides, you promised Cargill on your word of honour. As an officer and a gentleman.'

Killigrew grinned boyishly. 'I had my fingers crossed.'

XV:

The *Buchan* Prayer

Killigrew was still dressed in his Chinese clothes – conical hat and all – when he climbed into Mei-rong's *yolo* with Molineaux. If one of Cargill's constables – or one of Bannatyne's spies, for that matter – saw a man in the uniform of a naval officer being sculled away in a *yolo*, that would give the game away; the black silk tunic and pyjamy trousers would also provide better camouflage than his white pantaloons and shirt when Killigrew climbed aboard the *Buchan Prayer* at night.

'I hope you know what you're doing, Killigrew,' Hartcliffe called down softly from the entry port.

'That makes two of us,' Killigrew heard Molineaux mutter under his breath. The seaman was dressed in his pusser's slops, just another sailor and hardly likely to arouse any suspicions on shore. Both Killigrew and Molineaux quickly sat down beneath the matting awning while Mei-rong sat cross-legged in the stern, sculling the boat towards Possession Point and beyond, swirling figures of eight in the water with well-practised motions.

'How long will it take us to reach Discovery Bay, Mei-rong?' asked Killigrew. They were headed for Lan-tao Island, and Discovery Bay would make a good place to land, on the far side from the Cap-sing-mun anchorage but at the narrowest part of the island.

'Four hour.'

Killigrew nodded. It would be twilight by then; they would have a bite to eat, and then walk across the island. Then it should be dark enough to swim out to the *Buchan Prayer* unobserved. 'Once we get out of the harbour, Molineaux can scull,' he said, and the Able Seaman nodded eagerly.

'No can do!' hissed Mei-rong. 'My boat, my rowum. My no trustee barbarian rowum.' She grinned. 'You no worry; my plenty strong, my gettee you there in plenty good hour.'

Killigrew shrugged and made himself comfortable amongst the rough cushions and bolsters. 'I'm going to get some sleep, Molineaux. Wake me in a couple of hours and then you can take a spell.'

'Aye, aye, sir.'

Killigrew tipped his conical hat over his eyes and went to sleep. The sea was no place for insomniacs; one soon learned to sleep when and where one could.

Twilight was descending when he awoke. Glancing out from beneath the awning, he could see the shore of Lan-tao only a couple of cables' lengths away. He heard a low murmur of voices behind him and twisted to see Molineaux seated at the rear of the awning, talking to Mei-rong as she continued to scull them as tirelessly as ever towards the island. 'I thought you were going to wake me when we got halfway?'

'Is that the time already, sir? I had no idea it was so late.'

'You need your sleep just as much as I do, Molineaux.'

The seaman grinned. 'You looked so peaceful, sir; seemed a shame to wake you.'

Killigrew joined them in the stern and indicated a cove to the east of Discovery Bay. 'Can you put us ashore there?' he asked Mei-rong.

She nodded and sculled the boat in through the surf. Killigrew and Molineaux jumped overboard and dragged the boat over the shingle into a place of concealment between two boulders. Mei-rong had cooking utensils and a stove on board and she prepared fish stew and fried rice for them.

'There's something I don't understand, Mei-rong,' said Molineaux. 'You Chinese are s'posed to be an ancient and wise people, right?'

She nodded. *'Hai.'*

'You invented paper, printing, gunpowder, the compass and all kinds of useful stuff like that, right?'

'Hai. What you wantchee savvy?'

'So how come you never invented bloody forks?'

She laughed. 'Chopstick plenty good for civilised Chinee. Missee Killigrew, him eatee with chopstick, can. Only barbarian needee fork.'

Molineaux produced his Bowie knife and used the blade to balance his food on as he scooped it into his mouth. 'Where did you get that?' asked Killigrew. 'I've seen cutlasses with smaller blades.'

'Took it off a slaver at the Owodunni Barracoon, sir. It's called a Bowie knife. Invented by some Yankee cove who got cramped at the Alamo.'

'If that's the kind of weaponry the Texans had at the Alamo, it's hardly surprising they held out for so long.'

'You got any weapons, sir?'

Killigrew shook his head. 'Remember, if we bump into any guards, they may just be innocent employees of Grafton, Bannatyne and Co.'

'Innocent!' scoffed Molineaux, who did not share Killigrew's free-trade principles. 'Don't see as how anyone who works smuggling opium can be called "innocent", sir.'

'All the same, they're not guilty of anything under British law.'

'Is it oh-kay to scrag them in self-defence?'

'If you must,' sighed Killigrew. 'But *only* if you must. If all goes well we won't need any weapons.'

'And if all *doesn't* go well?'

'I'd rather not think about that.'

'You needn't worry, sir. If the worst comes to the worst and they catch us, somehow I don't think it will ever come to a trial.'

They washed down their food with some rice wine and Killigrew glanced about at the gathering dusk. 'Time to go,' he decided.

'You be plenty careful!' Mei-rong warned them.

Molineaux nodded. 'Remember, if we're not back by sun up, you head back for Victoria Harbour and pretend you never even heard of us.'

416

Killigrew and Molineaux set off walking across the island. Complete darkness had fallen by the time they reached the far side, but paper lanterns lit up the decks of all the receiving ships. They could just make out the guards patrolling the decks. The opium-stuffed hulks were prime targets for pilongs, and they were well defended with cannons and swivel guns.

A strong sea ran through the Cap-sing-mun Passage and it was hard work just to swim out to the *Buchan Prayer*. They reached the hulk without anyone on deck raising the alarm, and swam round to the stern. Both stern ports were barred shut: somehow Killigrew had not expected getting aboard to be easy, but it had been worth a try.

They swam the length of the hull to the anchor chain, using a gentle breaststroke that caused hardly a ripple. On the deck above them there would be a watch on duty, but no one was gazing over the bulwarks. 'I'll go up first,' whispered Killigrew. 'When I signal the coast is clear, you follow.'

Molineaux shook his head. 'Better leave this to me, sir. I've done this kind of thing before. On land, at any rate.' Before Killigrew could protest, Molineaux was climbing nimbly up the taut anchor chain. He reached the hawse hole and from there he could get one foot on the cheeks of the port bow. He scrambled over the rails on to the beak over the prow and was gone from sight.

A moment later his head appeared at the rail, peering down to where Killigrew still trod water by the anchor chain. Molineaux pointed to some-

417

thing, and in the dim illumination of a paper lantern Killigrew could make out a sentry armed with a musket standing on the forecastle. The sentry faced forwards; the only reason he could not see Molineaux was because the seaman was in shadow. If Molineaux tried to climb on to the forecastle he would be spotted and the alarm would be raised. Killigrew saw Molineaux stick two fingers in his mouth, and for a moment he thought the seaman was going to whistle. Then he understood: Molineaux wanted a distraction, something to make the sentry turn away from the prow.

Killigrew had a better idea. He slapped the water beside him with the flat of his hand to make a splashing noise.

The sentry crossed to the starboard-side rail of the forecastle and glanced down. He carried a bull's-eye lantern and suddenly opened the shutter so that the beam fell on Killigrew. Still treading water, the lieutenant smiled and waved. A moment later the sentry crumpled as Molineaux stepped up behind him and hit him on the back of the neck with the haft of his Bowie knife. The seaman caught him before he could hit the deck with a noisy thump and then signalled that the coast was clear.

Killigrew shinned up the anchor chain and was about to climb over the rail to join Molineaux on the forecastle when he heard a voice as another sentry appeared from behind a deck house. 'You all right, Zeke?'

'He just collapsed,' Molineaux called softly. He was no fool: he must have known that all the second sentry could see was one figure crouched over another slumped on deck. He motioned for the other sentry to approach.

The second sentry hurried forward, reassured by Molineaux's distinctly non-Chinese accent. 'Is he all right?'

Molineaux stood up and punched the man in the throat. He gave a strangled gasp, and Molineaux hit him again. This time he went down. 'No worse than you,' he told the second sentry's unconscious body.

Killigrew climbed over the rail. 'Everything all right?' he whispered.

'Nothing I couldn't handle,' Molineaux assured him. 'Help me get this one trussed up and we'll lower them on to the head. They'll be out of sight there.'

Killigrew nodded. 'All the same, someone's bound to notice their absence. We may not have much time.'

'We'd best look lively then, sir.'

Molineaux had already gagged and bound the first sentry with his own belt, bootlaces and musket-sling. They did the same for the second, and gently lowered both to the grating of the head, more so as not to make any unnecessary noise than because they did not want to hurt the men.

'Now what?' asked Molineaux.

'We'll search the ship separately. You try the offices in the stern deck-house; see what papers you can find in the safe. I'll check the accommodation below decks, see if Mrs Bannatyne's being held on board.' Killigrew was hoping against all common sense that the *tai-pan* would not have it in his heart to murder his own wife in cold blood; but if Huang's theories were correct, Bannatyne was a ruthless man who would stop at nothing, and Mrs Bannatyne was probably at the bottom of the South China Sea. But until he knew that for certain, Killigrew had to do everything in his power to rescue her; after the way she had cared for him during his sickness, he owed her that much at least. 'If someone raises the alarm, it's every man for himself. If either of us doesn't make it back to where we left Mei-rong with the *yolo*, then he takes his own chances.'

Molineaux nodded. They both crept along the deck, leaving a trail of wet footprints that would lead anyone who stumbled across them straight after the two trespassers, but that could not be helped. Molineaux opened the door to the aftermost deck house and peered through for a moment before stepping inside and closing the door behind him.

As soon as the seaman was out of sight, Killigrew glanced about until he found the after-hatch. He descended a companionway to a narrow corridor with doors leading off on either side. He listened at the first, heard nothing, and gently rapped his knuckles against it. There was no reply, but he opened it anyway, to find an empty cabin with linen folded on the bare mattress of the bunk. He was about to try the door of the next cabin when he heard sounds coming from the door behind him. Creaking and moaning. He glanced at the sign on the door –

'Captain Ingersoll' – and smiled. He grasped the handle and slowly eased the door open.

Ingersoll lay on the bunk with his head thrown back on the pillows, his eyes closed in ecstasy. A Chinese girl sat astride his hips, her head thrown back, her back to the door. A percussion pistol lay on a chair next to the bed: Ingersoll was clearly not a man who liked to take chances.

Both were too focused on what they were doing to notice Killigrew enter the cabin and close the door behind him. He tiptoed across the deck, picked up the pistol, encircled the girl's neck in the crook of an elbow and clamped a hand over her mouth while he levelled the pistol at the man's head.

The girl writhed in panic and moaned. 'Oh, yes!' gasped the man. 'Yes! That's it! Yes!'

Killigrew tapped him on the chest with the cold muzzle of the pistol. Ingersoll's eyes opened and his hand shot out towards the chair, fumbling for the pistol which was no longer there. He stared at Killigrew in shock. 'What the...? Who the hell be you?'

'The questions you should be asking at this juncture are: what do I want, and what's going to happen to you if I don't get it? Speakee English?' he asked the girl.

She nodded as best she could.

'I'm going to take my hand from your mouth in a moment. If you scream, he dies. Then you. Savvy?'

She nodded again.

He took his hand away. 'Put on that robe.' He jerked his head to where a scarlet silk robe, the kind of thing Chinese prostitutes wore, was tossed on the deck.

She climbed off Ingersoll. 'You him spilum, my no care,' she said with defiant truculence, but she was trembling and did as she was told.

Killigrew kept the pistol levelled at Ingersoll. 'You be Killigrew!' the captain exclaimed in shock.

'I'm honoured that my reputation has preceded me. Get up.' Killigrew backed away and gestured to the girl with the pistol. 'Tie her up and gag her. No snowball hitches.'

Ingersoll scowled. 'All right, missy. On the bunk, face down. You won't be tied up for long.'

'Most time my makee payee plenty extra for this.'

Killigrew picked up a silk scarf with his left hand and passed it to Ingersoll. 'Gag her. I think we've both had enough from her for one night.'

'Speak for yourself,' scowled Ingersoll. 'What do you want?'

'Where's the *Golden Dragon*?'

Ingersoll grinned. 'You best be asking Cap'n Verran that, matey.'

'It's Verran I'm looking for. Go to the porthole and put your hands behind your back.'

He had to put the pistol down to tie Ingersoll's hands. The captain launched himself backwards off the bulkhead and cannoned into Killigrew's body. He was bigger and stronger than Killigrew, and when they crashed into the door it was the lieutenant who bore the brunt of it.

Then Ingersoll threw himself across the room and snatched the pistol from the chair. Killigrew caught him by the wrists before he could level it, but Ingersoll managed to squeeze a shot into the deck head. It was deafeningly loud in the confined space of the cabin. The lieutenant rammed a knee into Ingersoll's dangling scrotum and the captain dropped with a strangled scream. Killigrew prised the pistol from his grip and hit him with it.

While Ingersoll was still dazed, Killigrew gagged him and bound his hands behind his back. He could hear feet pounding the deck above his head. By the time he opened the door and pushed Ingersoll out before him, two guards were descending the companionway at the far end of the corridor.

Killigrew held the pistol to Ingersoll's head. 'Put down your muskets and back away, or I'll shoot your captain!'

Ingersoll made moaning sounds behind the sock Killigrew had gagged him with. The guards lowered their muskets to the floor and backed up the companionway. Killigrew pushed Ingersoll before him until he could pick up one musket in his left hand and hold the muzzle to Ingersoll's head. Then he dropped the pistol and picked up the other musket, slinging it across his shoulder. He goaded Ingersoll up the companion ladder and they joined the two guards on deck.

'Much obliged,' said Killigrew. 'I think your captain was trying to tell you the pistol was empty.'

'That's all right, matey,' said one of the guards, grinning. 'So were our muskets.'

Still holding the musket's muzzle to Ingersoll's

head, Killigrew pulled the trigger. The hammer fell with a hollow snap.

One of the guards punched him in the face. He felt his knees crumple beneath him and then the empty musket was snatched from his grasp. A moment later the butt was rammed into his stomach.

The other guard took out a clasp-knife and sliced through Ingersoll's bonds. The captain tore off the gag. 'That be right good work, lads,' he said as more guards arrived. 'Let's drag him in the office, afore I be freezing to death.'

Killigrew's arms were seized and he was hoisted to his feet. They manhandled him through a door into one of the deck houses: the same deck house Killigrew had seen Molineaux enter a few minutes earlier. There was no sign of the seaman now except for the last traces of some wet footprints which faded on the way to the safe. Ingersoll and his men did not seem to notice them.

The captain reached behind the door and produced a greatcoat which he quickly put on to cover his nakedness. Killigrew was thrown into a chair. 'Shall we tie him up, Cap'n?' asked one of the guards.

'Why bother?' Ingersoll took a musket off one of the guards. 'Be this primed and loaded?'

'Aye, aye, Cap'n.'

'Good.' Ingersoll raised the stock to his shoulder and levelled it at Killigrew's face from almost point-blank range. There was murder in his eyes. 'There be only one way to deal with scum like this...'

Molineaux slipped into the office on board the *Buchan Prayer* and closed the door behind him. Everything was dark. He squeezed his eyes shut and counted slowly to ten in his head. When he opened them again, he was able to see the safe which stood in one corner. He crossed for a closer examination. A Chubb safe with a combination lock: a cracksman's worst nightmare.

But, as his mother never tired of reminding him, he could do anything if he put his mind to it. He looked about the office, his eyes growing more and more accustomed with every passing moment to the faint light which filtered through the portholes. He found a pencil on the desk and some papers. Looking at the top sheet, he saw it was a receipt for an eight-inch shell gun. That meant nothing: all tea clippers carried cannon to defend themselves from pilongs, and a man like Bannatyne would want his ships to have the biggest and best guns money could buy. Searching in the drawers he found a bottle of rum and a tumbler. He took the tumbler and, on second thoughts, took a fortifying nip of Nelson's blood straight from the bottle. Then he sat down cross-legged beside the safe. Chubb offered a reward of a thousand pounds to any man who could crack one of these things. Molineaux wondered if he would ever be able to claim the prize if he succeeded tonight.

He pressed the tumbler to the door of the safe and his ear to the tumbler. Then he slowly turned the dial until he heard the first, faint click. Left six. He made a note on the back of the piece of paper and then turned the dial clockwise until he heard the next click. Right eleven. Click. Another note. Left nineteen. Click. Right sixty-nine.

He grasped the handle, took a deep breath, turned it, and...

The safe stayed locked.

'Bugger.'

He was about to start again when he heard what sounded like a pistol-shot. He thrust the paper inside his shirt and put the pencil and tumbler back where he had found them. Then he crossed to the door and opened it a crack. Two guards charged down the deck towards him. He quickly pushed the door to and reached for his Bowie knife, but the footsteps on the deck turned outside the deck house and clattered down a hatchway. He heard tense, muffled voices, and then the footsteps came back up the companionway, more slowly now.

'Much obliged.' Molineaux recognised Killigrew's voice immediately outside the door. 'I think your captain was trying to tell you the pistol was empty.'

Molineaux heaved a sigh of relief. It sounded as though the lieutenant had everything under control. He was about to go outside and help him when another voice spoke.

'That's all right, matey. So were our muskets.'

There was a pregnant pause, followed by a snap. Then there was a thump, a gasp, and another thump. Someone – Killigrew by the sound of it – groaned.

'That be right good work, lads,' a third voice declared a moment later. 'Let's drag him in the

426

office, afore I be freezing to death.'

Still clutching his Bowie knife, Molineaux pressed himself up against the bulkhead beside the door and a moment later it was thrown open, partially concealing him. A hairy hand came round the door and reached for a greatcoat which hung on a hook an inch from Molineaux's face. The hand was as likely to find his nose as the greatcoat. He took the coat off the peg and held it where the groping hand would find it. The coat was accepted and a moment later Captain Ingersoll, as naked as the day he was born, stepped into sight. He had his back to Molineaux as he shrugged on the coat. Beyond him, Molineaux saw a dazed-looking Killigrew being thrown into a chair.

'Shall we tie him up, Cap'n?' asked someone out of sight on the other side of the door.

'Why bother?' Ingersoll stepped out of sight again. A moment later he reappeared with a musket in his hands. 'Be this primed and loaded?'

'Aye, aye, Cap'n.'

'Good.' Ingersoll raised the stock to his shoulder and levelled it at Killigrew's face from almost point-blank range. 'There be only one way to deal with scum like this...'

Molineaux realised that in another second Killigrew would be dead. He had no way of knowing how many other people were in the room, but it seemed reasonable to suppose that Ingersoll was not the only one holding a musket. And Molineaux was armed only with a Bowie knife: intimidating enough to look at, but not when the other cove had a barking iron.

The sensible thing to do was to stay concealed and hope for the best. Killigrew had known what risks he was taking when he had suggested this hare-brained scheme, the same as Molineaux. Staying put was what Molineaux reckoned Killigrew would have done.

No, Molineaux told himself. *That's what you'd like to think Killigrew would do if your places were reversed. But he'd think of something, so think fast.*

But he could not think of anything, except leaping out from behind the door and hoping that there were not too many of them, hoping that Killigrew was not as dazed as he seemed and would come to his aid, hoping that he would have the element of surprise.

Too much to hope for, but he was not going to stand there while they murdered Killigrew. He steeled himself to leap out and...

'*Scheisse!* What do you think you're doing?' snapped a new voice.

'Rat-catching, Reverend,' said Ingersoll. 'I caught this sonuvabitch...'

'I can see that. Do you know who that is?'

'Right enough. This be Killigrew. And if you think I be going to take any chances with him...'

The newcomer stepped into the room and Molineaux recognised him as the Reverend Werner Ultzmann. The missionary knocked the barrel of Ingersoll's musket up. '*Dumkopf!* Don't you know that Zhai Jing-mu wants this one alive?'

'That be Zhai Jing-mu's problem.'

'It will be *our* problem if you kill him now. After

428

Herr Verran so carelessly let him get away, Zhai already suspects we humbugged him. We need Zhai's goodwill if the plan is to work out to our benefit; otherwise all the work we have done will have been for nothing!' Ultzmann turned to someone out of Molineaux's line of sight. 'Tie him up.'

Another man stepped into sight and set to work binding Killigrew's hands behind his back.

'What do you intend to do with him?'

'The next smug boat is due to arrive any moment now. When we've unloaded the tea and put the opium on board, I will take him with me. We'll stop off at Zhai's lair on our way to Swatow and I will hand him over to the pilongs. That way we regain the Triads' trust and we will all be rid of Killigrew. Do not concern yourself, Captain Ingersoll. I shall make sure the *tai-pan* knows who it was that captured Killigrew.'

'And if he escapes? Will you let him know whose fault *that* were?'

'He won't escape. Leave us. I wish to have a word in private with Herr Killigrew here.'

Ingersoll shooed his men out of the office and followed them out. He pulled the door to behind him, exposing Molineaux. Ultzmann had his back to the seaman, but Killigrew was fully conscious now and his eyes met Molineaux's for a fraction of a second. The seaman had to give the young officer credit: his face registered no surprise and he quickly shifted his gaze to the missionary.

'Zhai Jing-mu can kill me if he likes, but he'll be wasting his time,' said Killigrew. 'You think we don't know what the *tai-pan*'s up to? Feeding Zhai Jing-mu all the information he needs about shipping movements, and in return Zhai leaves his shipping alone. Oh, except for one over-insured floating coffin, for form's sake.'

'You blundering young idiot! I warned you once not to interfere in things which were no concern of yours, but you did not listen. Now you will die, and you have done nothing to halt Bannatyne's plan.'

Molineaux still had his Bowie knife in his hand. He started to tiptoe across the deck towards Ultzmann's back.

'What plan would that be?' asked Killigrew.

'You think you'll escape and foil it? Sorry, my friend. I am not a fool.'

Molineaux raised the knife, ready to strike Ultzmann on the back of his head with the heavy haft.

'Whatever it is you're planning to do, I beg you not to,' said Killigrew.

Molineaux froze. Killigrew begging? That did not sound right.

'I'm going to be taken to Zhai Jing-mu's lair?' asked the lieutenant.

'I already said as much, didn't I?' Ultzmann said impatiently, still oblivious to Molineaux's presence.

Molineaux realised that Killigrew was speaking for his benefit rather than Ultzmann's. But at any moment the missionary was going to turn and see him. *What the hell am I supposed to do, then?* Molineaux mouthed at Killigrew.

'You want my advice?' asked Killigrew, his gaze

fixed steadily on Ultzmann. 'If I were you, I would lie low until all this is over. Better still, go to the British authorities in Victoria and tell them I'm being held prisoner.'

'I ... I cannot,' said Ultzmann.

Molineaux tiptoed back to the door and laid his hand on the knob.

'How much is Bannatyne paying you?'

Molineaux turned the doorknob and opened it a crack, praying no breeze would alert Ultzmann.

'You think all I care about is money?' Ultzmann demanded bitterly. 'I am a man of the cloth!'

Molineaux glanced outside. There were no guards in view. He slipped out on deck.

'A man of the cloth who's been aiding and abetting piracy and murder! What sins is Bannatyne using to blackmail you, Reverend?'

Molineaux was curious to know himself, but he closed the door softly. Even then he hesitated, still tempted to go back in and deal with the missionary. Did Killigrew know what he was doing? Molineaux hoped so, for his sake.

He was about to make his way back to the anchor-chain when a door from one of the deck houses opened and light flooded across the deck. Molineaux climbed the companion ladder to the poop deck, grabbed the eaves of the aftermost deck-house and swung himself up on to the roof. A moment later two guards emerged from a door and took up position outside the office where Ultzmann was speaking to Killigrew. There was no way Molineaux could get past them to the forecastle, and if he jumped overboard the splash would alert the guards. He lay flat and waited to see what would happen next.

'Smug boat coming in, Cap'n...' called a voice.

Molineaux glanced to the other side of the ship and saw a boat approaching from starboard.

'They be late,' said Ingersoll. 'All right, the starboard watch can start unloading the opium and bringing the tea on board.'

The oarsmen on the smug boat shipped oars downwind of the hulk and moved into position alongside under sail power alone. When the boat was close enough, ropes were thrown across and it was made fast. Two gangplanks were lowered to the smug boat and several figures ascended to the opium hulk. Molineaux shifted position so he could see what was going on.

'Shall we go inside?' Ingersoll suggested to the two Chinese who had ascended from the smug boat. He gestured to the door of the deck-house and the three of them joined Ultzmann and Killigrew in the office. The door was closed.

Molineaux stood up and tiptoed forward across the roof. He cut loose a backstay and used it to swing across to the next deck house, his feet making barely a sound when he touched down. He spun round and crouched down, expecting men to come pouring out of the deck house and surround it.

'All hands on deck!' A bell was rung, and men came rushing up from the forward hatch to crowd the deck. But they were not looking for Molineaux. They formed two human chains, one down each of the gangplanks. As sacks of opium were passed down one gangplank to the smug boat, sacks of tea were handed up to the opium hulk and thrown down the main hatch. English clerks and Chinese schroffs kept a careful count of the number of sacks passing in each direction.

Molineaux could not move from the roof of the deck-house while the exchange was carried out. He tried to get comfortable. He had a feeling he was in for a long wait.

The men worked quickly and cheerfully, as they might do on a public dockside. They might be working at night, but no one was making any attempt at secrecy: they sang shanties as they toiled in the full glare of the deck lights. And why shouldn't they? They were not doing anything illegal as far as the British were concerned, and the Chinese had already shown a willingness to turn a blind eye time and time again, as long as they received their *cumshaw*.

Bannatyne's massive comprador, Shen, emerged from one of the deck-houses to watch. After a while he called for the proceedings to halt while he weighed a few sacks of tea chosen at random, and opened a couple to examine the quality of the dried leaves. With a nod of approval, he signalled for the sacks to be sewn up once more and the work continued.

The exchange took nearly three hours. Molineaux had to keep shifting his position during this time to stop himself from getting pins and needles. But he could not move while so much activity was taking place on deck.

Eventually all the opium had been brought up from the *Buchan Prayer*'s hold and the smug boat was packed to the gunwales. One of the Chinese called up from the boat in Cantonese, and a guard knocked on the door to Ingersoll's office. 'Laded and ready to go, Cap'n.'

A few moments later the door opened and Ingersoll emerged with Ultzmann and the two Chinese, escorting Killigrew at pistol-point between them.

'Hope you know what you be doing, Reverend,' Ingersoll said as the two Chinese escorted their prisoner down one of the gangplanks to the smug boat. 'Remember: the *Golden Dragon* sails at midnight the night after tomorrow. If you're late, you'll be left behind.'

'You think it wise to use the *Dragon* in this anchorage so publicly?' asked Ultzmann.

'*Tai-pan*'s decision, matey,' said Ingersoll. 'She's got two knots on the *White Tiger*. Don't worry, she'll be disguised. Besides, by that time everyone will have too many problems of their own to worry about the *Dragon* any more.'

Ultzmann took his leave and made his way down to the smug boat. The mooring ropes were cast off and Molineaux watched helplessly as the crew pushed off from the side of the hulk and dipped their oars. As they rowed it towards the Cap-sing-mun Passage, Molineaux wondered where they were going, and what Killigrew's chances of escaping were once he had found Zhai Jing-mu's lair.

Ingersoll and Shen turned and went back inside the deck house while the rest of the crew went below, leaving only one or two guards out on deck. Molineaux realised that the sky had lightened considerably: dawn was less than an hour away.

He crawled across to the forward edge of the roof. A sentry stood immediately below. Molineaux reached down, grabbed the man's neckerchief, and pulled it tight. The man struggled, but the neckerchief which dug into his windpipe choked off his cries. After a moment he stopped struggling. Molineaux jumped down and lowered his body to the deck. The man was still breathing and would wake up in a while with a splitting headache and a very sore throat.

Molineaux climbed back the way he had come on board, shinning down the anchor chain until he was up to his neck in water. He struck out for the shore. His limbs protested agonisingly after the first few strokes: cramp. Hardly surprising: he had been lying more or less motionless on the roof of the deck-house for the best part of five hours. Resisting the urge to panic, he floated on his back until the initial pain had worn off and he was able to strike out once more for the shore, using a less energetic stroke this time.

He had gone two hundred yards before anyone noticed him. He heard shouts behind him. A moment later the first musket balls whistled towards him, but by then he was beyond effective range for sharpshooting. By the time he waded up the shingle beach out of the surf he walked with insouciant slowness to show his contempt. As a final act of defiance, he dropped his trousers and bent over to let them get a good look at what he thought of their marksmanship. Between his own legs he could see the opium hulk upside down, one of the gun-ports amidships opening as they ran out a thirty-two-pounder long gun...

Molineaux swore, hitched up his trousers and broke into a run as the gun boomed. The shot screeched through the air towards him with a sound like canvas tearing. He flung himself flat on the ground as the shot burst over the beach. Pellets of canister showered down on the shingle close by. He quickly picked himself up and ran further uphill before they had a chance to reload.

When he reached the crest of the spine of hills that ran the length of the island he glanced back. On the beach below a long boat had landed and men armed with muskets swarmed ashore. To the east, the sun was just peeping over the horizon. Molineaux turned and ran back to where he had left Mei-rong with the *yolo*.

It was twenty minutes after dawn before he reached the cove where he had left her. She was still waiting for him when he stumbled out of the trees on to the shingle. 'Cast off!' he called to her, breaking into a sprint for the last stretch.

'Where Missee Killigrew?' she demanded.

'He's not coming. Get pushing, Mei-rong, or else we'll have unwelcome guests.'

They put their shoulders to the boat and shoved it back into the water. At last it floated clear and Molineaux collapsed in the bottom while Mei-rong stood on the stern to pole the boat out through the breakers with her sculling oar. 'Missee Killigrew, him spilum?'

'Killigrew dead? Don't be daft. He's got the devil's own luck, that one.' Molineaux hoped it was true.

The *yolo* was a cable's length from the shore by the time the men from the opium hulk appeared behind them. They fired a desultory volley from their muskets but none of the shots even came close.

'You makee someone plenty angry,' said Mei-rong.

Molineaux grinned and glanced ahead. They could see the peaks of Hong Kong island only six miles away.

He pondered what he had overheard. He would have precious little to tell Commander Robertson when he got back to the *Tisiphone*: that Killigrew had been captured and was being taken to Zhai Jing-mu's lair – somewhere between Hong Kong and Swatow from the sound of it – but that only narrowed it down to a hundred and fifty-odd miles of coastline, not counting every creek and inlet. It was hardly calculated to divert Robertson's rage at Killigrew's escape.

Bannatyne and Zhai Jing-mu were planning something, that much was obvious. But what? Molineaux had a feeling it would not be anything good. He hoped Killigrew would find out and then manage to get away and back to Victoria in time to reveal all. But that was too much to hope for, even from a man like Killigrew. Molineaux wished he had knocked Ultzmann out when he had had the chance and rescued the lieutenant. This time Killigrew had bitten off more than he could chew.

They had covered almost half the distance, and Green Island, off the westernmost tip of Hong Kong, was just coming into view, when Molineaux spotted a plume of smoke in the direction of Cap-sing-mun Passage. After a few minutes the base of the plume was revealed as a steamer headed for Victoria Harbour.

'Maybe we catchee tow, catchee Hong Kong,' said Mei-rong.

'Maybe,' Molineaux agreed dubiously.

To his surprise the paddle-wheeler altered direction, a few points to starboard, so that it was coming towards them.

The steamer ploughed through the waves, a bone in her teeth where the foam churned at the foot of her stem. Molineaux expected her to slow or turn when it came within a cable's length, but she did no such thing: she just kept on coming.

'Maybe him no see we,' said Mei-rong, sculling the *yolo* out of the steamer's path.

The steamer changed direction again to follow. It was less than fifty yards away now, and bore down relentlessly on the flimsy boat. The white tiger figurehead seemed to pounce at them.

'She's seen us, all right!' Molineaux jumped up from where he sat and lunged across the stern. He caught Mei-rong around the waist and the two of them hit the water together. He was still towing her clear when the steamer's prow ripped through the boat amidships. There was a great splintering crash which momentarily drowned out the plashing of the paddle-wheels. The bow wave lifted Molineaux up and he was still trying to get his bearings when he saw the steamer's starboard paddle-wheel bearing down on him. He tried to swim out of the way but once again cramp paralysed his limbs. He stared helplessly as the paddles filled his vision, each one slapping down against the water viciously, closer, closer...

438

A strong hand caught him underneath the chin and pulled him clear with only inches to spare. Even so the backwash almost sucked him under, but the same hand grabbed a fistful of his hair and dragged him back to the surface. Mei-rong, God bless her. Like any Tanka girl, she could swim like a fish.

'You oh-kay?' she asked him.

Coughing and spluttering, it was all he could do to nod. As the stern of the *White Tiger* passed them, he saw Shen standing on the rail, glaring down at them malevolently. Molineaux expected the steamer to turn and try to run them down again, but she just altered course slightly and continued on her way. Probably Shen did not think they would be able to swim the last three miles to Hong Kong.

If Molineaux had been alone then the comprador would have been right. But the tireless Mei-rong had enough strength for both of them. She stayed with him the whole way, urging him on when he had the strength to swim, towing him behind her when his limbs finally gave out. At one point he felt his mouth fill with water and he thought he was drowning – he was so far gone he was not sure that he cared – but the next thing he knew she was dragging him on to the beach of Belcher Bay. Then she collapsed on the shingle beside him and they both lay there gasping for breath while the midday sun warmed their bodies.

Molineaux had no idea how long he lay there, but after a while Mei-rong gained strength sufficiently to start complaining in a torrent of

Cantonese. He did not understand a word of it, but it did not sound like the kind of language polite young ladies used. Realising her mother tongue was wasted on him, she switched back to pidgin English.

'Bloody bastard barbarian! My bloody takee them to *yamen*! No *yolo*, no home, no cash; no cash, no rice! My starvum! Mei-feng alla time warnee my 'bout bloody bastard barbarian, she tellee me no mixee *fan kwae*. What for my no listenee?'

'You can take them to the *yamen*, all right,' gasped Molineaux. 'They deliberately tried to murder us!'

'You takee murder charge to Hella, you bloody bastard barbarian devil-slave! My sue him for losum plenty cash!'

'Bring him up on deck,' ordered Ultzmann. Two pilongs – dressed in the same black pyjamy suits and crimson turbans as the Triads who had attacked Killigrew on both of his visits to the joss house on Hollywood Road – seized him and hoisted him to his feet. 'Watch him,' warned Ultzmann. 'He may be pretending to be more badly injured than he really is, to lull us into a false sense of security.'

Killigrew feigned nothing. The Triads on the smug boat had amused themselves on the voyage by beating him, and now he could barely stand. Nevertheless, as he was dragged on deck he tried to observe as much as possible. If by some miracle he was able to escape, he would do so carrying vital intelligence which would serve the

Royal Navy well when it came here to destroy Zhai Jing-mu's fleet.

For there could be no doubt he had finally tracked the pirate to his lair. He counted about three dozen junks in the harbour, most of them carrying nine guns in each broadside. The largest – Zhai Jing-mu's flagship, to judge from the display of steamers and black and red flags – had forty-two guns in total. All in all it was a formidable force. But there was no sign of the *Golden Dragon*.

Killigrew had been kept below deck during the voyage from Cap-sing-mun, but he guessed they could be no more than twenty or thirty miles east of Hong Kong. So close to the seat of British naval power in the South China Seas, yet perfectly safe thanks to their secluded location in an arm of the bay hidden from the open sea.

The smug boat moored against the jetty and while the crew started to unload the cargo of opium, a boat was sent to the flagship to inform Zhai Jing-mu of the arrival of their special guest.

Ultzmann took Killigrew ashore. Even though the lieutenant had both his hands tied behind his back, Ultzmann did not take his pepperbox off him for a moment. The two Triads threw Killigrew to the ground outside one of the huts in the village.

Killigrew watched as the boat from the jetty reached Zhai Jing-mu's flagship. A moment later he recognised Zhai himself, resplendent in his white clothes and crimson sash, climb down into the boat.

He turned to Ultzmann. 'I thought the Triads

wanted to overthrow the Ch'ing Dynasty because they allowed us barbarians to smuggle opium into their country?' he said thickly. 'And yet here they are, helping them to do it!'

'Regrettable but necessary,' said Ultzmann. 'The Brotherhood of Heaven, Earth and Man must have money to buy arms before it can overthrow the Ch'ing Dynasty. Smuggling opium is the quickest way to make that money.'

'Who's going to sell them those arms? Bannatyne, I suppose?'

Ultzmann chuckled. 'Oh, I think you'll find the Triads have a far greater role for us Westerners in the overthrow of the Ch'ing Dynasty than you can ever imagine, Herr Killigrew. And when the Ming Dynasty is restored, this whole country will be made strong enough to resist the bullying tactics of the British. No longer will China be crushed and humiliated by your Royal Navy. With modern shell guns and steam-powered ships, China will be able to defend herself.'

'You think Bannatyne cares about their revolution? He's only interested in making money. You can't believe his promises. It was men like him who urged the British government to go to war with China in the first place, so he could continue to import opium. The last thing he wants is to see China strong enough to defend herself. Even he's not stupid enough to equip Chinese with Western arms. He wouldn't do it for all the tea in China.'

Scrunching up the shingle beach from where the boat had landed, Zhai Jing-mu grinned. He had a crimson eye patch now to match his sash.

442

'That is where you are wrong, Killigrew. All the tea in China is *precisely* what he is doing it for.'

Killigrew stared at him, and then nodded. 'A total monopoly of the tea trade?' That would make Bannatyne the richest man in the whole world; and the most powerful.

Zhai lifted up his eye patch and thrust his face close to Killigrew's. The socket was empty, just an ugly mess of scar tissue. 'Take a good look at your handiwork, *fan kwae*. This was your doing!'

'My heart bleeds for you,' sneered Killigrew.

Zhai kicked him savagely. 'Mock now, while you still can, barbarian. Soon you will be begging me for mercy.' He turned to one of the Triads. 'Bring out a table. Get some coals burning in a brazier and heat up some irons until they are red-hot.' He turned back to Killigrew. 'You think that kick I gave you just now hurt? You do not know the meaning of pain. But you will soon, I assure you.'

XVI:

The *Mœander*

'You think we don't know what it is that you and the *tai-pan* are up to?' Killigrew asked Zhai Jing-mu. 'You're planning to provoke another war between Britain and China.' He was spread-eagled on a table while four pilongs held him down, one at each wrist and ankle. Ultzmann watched while Zhai Jing-mu turned the irons in the brazier. They were already starting to glow red-hot.

'You're insane,' said Killigrew. 'Can't you see? The Chinese can't win, not against steamships and shell guns. You know as well as Bannatyne that if there is a second war, the British won't hold back the way they did in forty-two. British public opinion will demand that this time the Chinese be taught a lesson. What on earth can you hope to achieve by it? Such a war would be utterly ruinous for China...'

Zhai Jing-mu took an iron from the fire and held it up to his single eye to examine its glowing tip. He frowned, and returned it to the fire. 'Precisely so, Mr Killigrew.'

'But of course...' Killigrew could have cursed himself for not realising it sooner. 'That's exactly what you want, isn't it? Another war with the barbarians will be the downfall of the Ch'ing

444

Dynasty. The Manchu administration in Peking will topple, and the Triads will be ready to seize government.'

'A fascinating theory, Mr Killigrew,' said Zhai. 'But of little use to you now. Tomorrow, at the hour of the pig, the first shot in our little war will sound out, heralding a new era in Chinese history. But you, my friend, will not even live to hear that opening shot.'

'You're off your head. You think the British will fight a war to put you in power in Peking?'

'Why not? When my fleets, and my contacts with the Triads, will have helped them to defeat the hated Manchus? You know as well as I do that the British government has no interest in controlling China directly. Much better to install an administration friendly to British trade, which will open more ports to the barbarians.'

'On the condition that only Bannatyne's ships are allowed to deal in tea and opium. And what do you think your friends the Triads will have to say, when they discover that all along you've been planning to help the very barbarians you promised to help them drive out?'

'I have nothing to fear from the Triads. I know their methods, their leaders, their hiding places. Once my puppet is installed on the Dragon Throne, the menace of the Triads will be crushed for ever.'

'Hear that, Ultzmann? You've got to hand it to your friend here, the way he's been playing everyone off against each other: Manchus, Triads, the China traders. Does Bannatyne think that Zhai Jing-mu won't go back on his promise to him, the way he's so willing to go back on his promise to help the Triads?'

Ultzmann looked uncertain, but said nothing.

'Perhaps if the Triads were here instead of you, we'd be hearing a very different story,' persisted Killigrew. 'About how he intends to renege on his promises to the barbarians, to put the Triads in an unassailable position of power in Peking, and to drive all barbarians from the Celestial Kingdom.'

'Herr Bannatyne knows what he's doing,' said Ultzmann. But even he no longer sounded convinced.

'Silence!' snapped Zhai. 'We have heard enough from you, Killigrew.' He took one of the irons from the brazier and approached the table. 'Unless, that is, you wish to scream. That would be music to my ears. An eye first, I think. Do your own Christian scriptures not teach: "An eye for an eye, and a tooth for a tooth"?'

He leaned over Killigrew with the glowing iron and slowly brought it nearer and nearer to his face. The *lao-pan*'s single blue eye glittered as he relished the moment. Killigrew's attention was transfixed by that glowing tip as its searing heat came close enough to warm his cheek and bring tears to his eyes.

'You'd better make up your mind whose side you're on, chop chop, Reverend,' Killigrew called in desperation. 'Help me now, and there's a chance you'll live through this. But don't think neither Bannatyne nor Zhai Jing-mu will betray you.'

'You're not taken in by his foolish chatter, are

446

you, Ultzmann?' asked Zhai.

'Of course not!' stammered the missionary.

'Good. Because you know what will happen if you do not co-operate. You see, Killigrew, there is no one to help you now...'

An excited jabber came from the direction of the jetty. Everyone around the table looked up to see seven more junks sailing up the creek, battered and battle-damaged: round shot embedded in their timbers, masts missing, gaping holes ripped through their mat-and-rattan sails, and scorched paintwork. Someone on one of the junks was signalling.

'What is he saying?' demanded Zhai.

'They have been pursued here by two barbarian ships,' said the man holding down Killigrew's right wrist. While he was concentrating on the signals, he relaxed his hold just enough for Killigrew to raise his arm a couple of inches off the table until the backs of the man's hands touched the red-hot iron held by Zhai. He screamed as his flesh sizzled, and released the lieutenant's wrist.

Killigrew grabbed the iron in Zhai's hand and smashed it against the head of the man who held his left wrist. As the man went down, Killigrew was able to sit up and parry a sword-stroke from the man who had held his right wrist. As the man raised his sword for a second blow, a shot sounded. Surrounded by enemies, Killigrew knew it could only have been aimed at him. He looked down at himself in search of the bullet wound, and then realised he had felt no pain. He glanced up at the swordsman. A bullet-hole had appeared in his forehead. He dropped his sword and sank to the shingle.

'Let him up.'

As the pilong holding Killigrew's left leg backed away from the table, Killigrew twisted. Ultzmann stood with his pepperbox in one hand, smoke curling lazily from one of the muzzles.

Killigrew rolled off the table and snatched up the sword before moving to join Ultzmann. Zhai and the remaining two pilongs – one of them nursing burned hands – backed away, but more pilongs armed with *gingalls* and pistols ran up the beach towards them.

'You betrayed me!' Zhai hissed at Ultzmann. 'It was you who brought the barbarian ships here!'

'No. But since they're here ... it is obvious the Englander is right, Zhai. It is over. The Royal Navy has found your lair.'

'Over?' Zhai laughed derisively. 'My dear Reverend, it is only just begun! But for *you*, it is over. And before you die, I want you to know that Ai-ling will soon die also. Once my men have used her for their entertainment. And I should warn you, some of them have deliciously depraved tastes...'

'You *Arschloch*!' Ultzmann screamed in rage. He pointed the pepperbox straight at Zhai, but the *lao-pan* was faster. Before the missionary could fire, the *lao-pan* drew a dagger from his sash with a movement like lightning and flung it. Ultzmann fell back into Killigrew's arms with the dagger embedded to the hilt in his chest. *'Rettet sie!'* he gasped in desperation. *'Um Himmels willen, passt auf, dass ihr nichts zustößt!'* He

448

coughed, blood spilling from his lips, and lay still.

Killigrew had no idea who Ai-ling was, or what Ultzmann's last words had meant – as luck would have it, German was one of the few languages he did not speak – but there had been no mistaking the anguish in the missionary's final moments.

Killigrew looked up at Zhai.

'Kill him,' the *lao-pan* ordered irritably.

One of the pilongs charged at Killigrew with a sword. The lieutenant snatched the pepperbox from Ultzmann's dead hand in time to shoot the pilong in the stomach. He turned the pepperbox on Zhai Jing-mu, but the *lao-pan* was already running back down the beach gesturing at Killigrew. 'Shoot him! Shoot him!'

Killigrew squeezed off a couple of shots at Zhai Jing-mu's back but missed as the *lao-pan* threw himself flat on the ground. Killigrew fired the last two shots at the pilongs charging towards him, kicked over the table to give himself some cover from the bullets which started to whistle in his direction, and then turned and ran.

He dashed along the side of the creek, leaping awkwardly from boulder to boulder as the bullets spanged amongst the rocks. His only chance was that the pilong who had read the signals from the returning, battle-scarred junk had not been mistaken. If Western ships had pursued a flotilla of junks into this cove, it seemed unlikely they would give up and turn back. If they were close enough for him to swim out to, he was saved. If not...

The wide creek meandered around a headland, and as Killigrew clambered over the rocks for higher ground he suddenly found a wide bay spread out before him. There were two ships at the entrance to the bay: a forty-four-gun frigate flying the white ensign, towed by the Peninsular and Oriental Company steamer SS *Shanghae*.

A ball from a *gingall* ricocheted off the rocks close to his feet and a splinter of rock stung him in the leg. He dropped down behind a boulder as more bullets soughed over his head.

A moment later the first pilong leaped over him. Killigrew jumped up and tackled him from behind. He managed to get on top of the pilong, pushing him face down into the shingle, and pulled the *gingall* back against his throat until he had throttled him. Two more pilongs appeared on the rocks above him, armed with a pistol and sword respectively. He shot one with the *gingall*, bracing the stock against the ground, and then used the heavy gun to parry a sword-stroke from the other before smashing the butt into his face.

The rest of the pilongs were not far behind, nearly two dozen of them. Killigrew picked himself up and ran until he was as close to the two ships as he could get on the land. They were nearly half a mile out to sea, but he could see a gig closer in to shore, sounding the depths over the sand bar at the mouth of the bay. He waded into the surf, waving his arms desperately above his head, hoping the sound of the pilongs' guns would reach the ears of the men in the ships and draw their attention to his plight.

Bullets ploughed into the water around him. A moment later a gun boomed from the side of the frigate and a shot roared over his head, to burst over the pilongs on the shore behind him: canister shot.

He dived into the water and swam out to the gig with a strong crawl stroke, although after his exertions on shore his strength was close to giving out. Seeing he was in difficulties, one of the seamen in the gig jumped overboard and swam to meet him, helping him cover the last few yards. He managed to get his arms over the gig's gunwales and clung there, panting. There were three other seamen in the gig, along with two faces Killigrew recognised: Assistant Superintendent Cargill of the Hong Kong Police, and Captain the Honourable Henry Keppel.

If Killigrew had ever had a surrogate father after his own had died, it was Keppel. It was four years since Killigrew had served on the *Dido* and his old captain was about forty now, but the blue eyes beneath his bushy red eyebrows glinted as mischievously as ever. A younger son of the Earl of Albermarle, he was a small man, less than five feet tall, but he more than compensated for it in terms of personality and strength of will.

'Hullo, my boy!' he remarked with cheerful aplomb, as if he and Killigrew had bumped into one another on Pall Mall instead of at the entrance to a pirate lair in the South China Sea. 'Up to your neck in it as usual, eh?'

'Permission to come aboard, sir.'

'I don't know. What do you think, Haines?' he asked the coxswain, with his customary crooked smile. 'Should we let Mr Killigrew into the boat?'

'He do look kind of bedraggled, sir.'

Aided by the seaman who had jumped into the

water to help him, Killigrew scrambled over the gunwales and collapsed in the stern sheets. Grinning, he ran his fingers through his sopping hair to sweep it back out of his eyes. 'I'm certainly glad to see you chaps.'

'That doesn't make what I have to say any easier, Killigrew,' Cargill said apologetically. 'I'm afraid you're under arrest.'

'I take it you didn't come all this way just to arrest me?' Killigrew asked once he was ensconced in a tub of deliciously warm water in one of HMS *Mœander*'s cabins.

Seated on the bunk, Keppel shook his head. 'We're on routine pirate-hunting duties. Captain Morgan received word that pilongs have been ravaging the coastline in these parts shortly before we arrived in Hong Kong. We set out to give chase at once. Mr Cargill here kindly agreed to come along and act as interpreter.' He gestured to where the assistant superintendent stood in the open doorway, and Cargill inclined his head with a smile.

'When we got to one village, Mr Cargill spoke to the people there and they told us they'd only recently paid money to this fellow Zhai Jing-mu to stop him from torching the place,' continued Keppel. 'We gave chase and a few miles further on found another village; in flames, this time. We crammed on every stitch of sail and sighted a fleet of fourteen junks. When we closed with one of them Mr Cargill hailed them.'

'Naturally they told us they were peaceful trading junks carrying salt to Hong Kong,' said

Cargill. 'But we could see them tricing up their stink-pots and boarding nets, and clearing their guns for action.'

'We got in three broadsides first and managed to sink three of the junks, but then the wind dropped and they drew off with their sweeps,' said Keppel. 'We put the boats in the water to tow us, and gave chase. The next morning found them a mile or so ahead of us, then a light easterly air sprang up and we hauled to the wind on the starboard tack. That was when the *Shanghae* put in an appearance.'

'How did they get caught up in this, sir?' asked Killigrew.

'One of the China traders chartered her to search for the *Coquette*,' explained Cargill. 'Another damned clipper gone missing.'

'Not Bannatyne?' Killigrew demanded suspiciously.

'Bannatyne? No,' said Cargill. 'We signalled that all in sight were enemy, and she gallantly steamed to the attack.'

'That was when things started to go wrong, though,' put in Keppel. 'The *Shanghae* took a shot through her boilers, and while we were chasing one of the junks inshore we ran on to an uncharted reef. My first lieutenant gave chase with the pinnace, cutter and gig and managed to catch another junk, but the rest got away. The *Shanghae* got her engines going and towed us off the reef, and we gave chase and ... well, here we are.'

'What brings *you* here, Killigrew?' asked Cargill. 'When I saw you yesterday, you were

453

supposed to be under arrest on board the *Tisiphone*. Then I learned you'd slipped overboard with one of the hands.'

Killigrew grinned sheepishly. 'Sorry about that. I knew Bannatyne was in with Zhai...'

'What?' exclaimed Keppel. 'Are you trying to tell me that Blase Bannatyne is in league with the pilongs? That's preposterous!'

'That's what I keep telling him, sir, but he won't listen to me,' said Cargill.

'Lucky for us all that I didn't,' said Killigrew. 'I went aboard the *Buchan Prayer* to find proof.'

'And did you?' asked Cargill.

Before Killigrew could reply, there was a knock on the door. 'Enter!' said Keppel.

Cargill withdrew from the doorway to allow the *Mœander*'s first lieutenant to enter. 'We've finished charting the bar, sir,' he announced, saluting. 'It's fairly shallow all the way across, but we think we've found a channel where we can slip through.'

'Good work, Mr Bowyear,' said Keppel. 'We'll cross the bar at high tide.' He checked his fobwatch. 'That's two hours from now. Have the decks cleared for action.'

'Aye, aye, sir.' Lieutenant Bowyear turned to leave.

Killigrew's voice arrested him. 'Hold on, sir. You're not planning to sail after them up that creek, are you?' he asked Keppel.

'I don't see why not. There's only seven of them.'

'Correction, sir. There were only seven of them when you chased them into this bay. But they've

454

just met up with another thirty-five of their friends. Including Zhai Jing-mu's flagship.'

'Zhai Jing-mu is here?' Cargill exclaimed in shock.

Killigrew nodded. 'You've stumbled on to his base of operations, sir.'

'How the deuce did you find it?'

'The Reverend Werner Ultzmann had me brought here after Captain Ingersoll caught me on board the *Buchan Prayer* last night. You want proof that Bannatyne's in league with the pilongs, Mr Cargill? The fact I'm here at all speaks for itself.'

'Hardly proof, Killigrew. Perhaps it ties in Ingersoll and Ultzmann, but ... you understand, I'm only thinking of what a jury will believe after Mr Bannatyne's lawyers have had a chance to work on such testimony.'

Killigrew narrowed his eyes at the assistant superintendent. 'And what do *you* believe, Mr Cargill?'

'I'm a police officer, Mr Killigrew. It's my job to prove, not believe. What I *believe* is neither here nor there.'

'All this will have to be settled later at Mr Killigrew's court martial,' Keppel said firmly. 'If there *is* a court martial, that is, which I'm very much beginning to doubt. When a junior officer finds a pirate nest the navy's spent years searching for, it's damned bad form to court martial him by way of thanks.' Keppel's promotion to post-captain predated Morgan's, so his arrival at Hong Kong made him the senior officer on the station. 'I'd say taking care of Zhai Jing-mu must be our first priority.'

'Killigrew's right, though,' said Cargill. 'You can't take on that many junks with just one frigate and a lightly armed civilian steamer.'

'No,' agreed Keppel. 'But we can try to keep the swine bottled up here until reinforcements arrive from Hong Kong.' He stepped across the tub and bent over the desk, swiftly scrawling a dispatch. When he had finished he blotted it, put it in an envelope and handed it to Bowyear. 'Take this to the captain of the *Shanghae* to deliver to Captain Morgan in Victoria.'

'Aye, aye, sir.'

'And see if you can find the wardroom steward. Mr Killigrew looks as though he could do with a drink.'

A Chinese steward emerged from his cubbyhole, took one look at Killigrew and then ducked out of sight just behind the door. *'Hai?'* he asked Keppel with a bow.

'Be so good as to fetch Mr Killigrew a brandy, steward.'

'Hai.' The steward bowed again and crossed to the drinks cabinet on the far side of the wardroom.

Keppel exchanged bemused glances with Cargill. 'It seems our new steward is shy about the human form, Mr Cargill.'

Killigrew stood up in the bath and tried to get a better look at the steward's face, but the Chinese, as if aware of the scrutiny, kept turning his head away so that all Killigrew could see was the queue which hung down his back. Keppel handed him a towel and he started to dry himself. 'New steward?' asked Killigrew. 'How long's he been aboard?'

'This is his second day. We hired him in Victoria yesterday when our old steward was suddenly taken ill with stomach cramps. Why do you ask?'

'No reason. I just thought perhaps I'd seen him somewhere before. At the Hong Kong races, maybe, or in a joss house in Tai-ping-shan.'

'Entirely possible, I suppose.'

The steward returned with Killigrew's brandy. He had acquired an oilskin hat and wore it ludicrously low on one side of his head so that, as long as he kept his face in profile, it was concealed from the lieutenant. He handed the glass to Killigrew.

'Thank you, Mr Li.'

'Name no Li,' said the steward. 'Name Deng.'

'Of course it is,' Killigrew said with a thin smile.

After his bath, he changed into a spare uniform loaned to him by Bowyear, who was roughly his size, and was given something to eat in the wardroom where he recounted his adventures aboard the *Buchan Prayer* and afterwards to Keppel, Cargill, and the *Mœander*'s officers. After dinner he joined Keppel and the *Mœander*'s master on the quarterdeck for a cheroot and the three of them gazed across to the mouth of the creek in the gathering gloom of dusk. The *Shanghae* had long since headed back to Hong Kong, and the *Mœander* was alone off the mouth of the bay, the only thing between Zhai Jing-mu's fleet and the freedom of the open sea.

'What do we do now, sir?' asked Killigrew. 'Wait

until re-inforcements arrive?'

Keppel nodded. 'Not much else we can do. I've had Mr Bowyear double the anchor watch in case the pilongs try anything tonight, but I expect they'll be busy turning their anchorage upstream into an ambush in preparation for our attack. Should be quite a brisk fight tomorrow, eh?' he added with obvious relish.

Killigrew thought about it. 'Brisk' was one word for it. But he would have been lying to himself if he had tried to deny that he was looking forward to the chance to pay the *lao-pan* back for Peri's murder.

'Zhai Jing-mu's slipped through my fingers too many times, sir, and at terrible cost. It won't happen again.'

The *Mœander*'s master chuckled. 'A regular fire-eater, sir, just like his father used to be,' he told Keppel.

'You knew my father?' Killigrew asked him.

'Certainly, sir. Back in the twenties your father and I were unemployed on half-pay, so we joined Admiral Cochrane in helping the Greeks win their independence from the Turks. But you must know all about that. I can see you've inherited your looks from your mother, but from what I've heard your spirit is all your father's. Always dashing off impetuously, risking his neck in pursuit of one ideal or another.'

None of this matched with the mental image Killigrew had conjured up of his parents. He was astonished. 'I had always assumed my mother was the fiery one. You know, what with her being Greek and all.'

'Your mother? Good Lord, no. No, your mother was always a lady. Demure, softly spoken and kind, she was. Lovely girl. Except when she was killing Turks, of course. She loathed them with a passion. Still, she couldn't match your father when it came to being a buccaneering, jump-first-and-look-later sort of swashbuckler. Hot Celtic blood, I always supposed – but I was always glad he was on our side, bigod! Captain Spitfire, the men used to call him.'

Keppel checked his watch. 'Well, I don't think we'll see much activity tonight. I'm off to bed to get an early night. I suggest you do likewise, my boy. Tomorrow's likely to be a long day.'

Killigrew lingered on deck alone to finish his cheroot and thought about what the master had just told him about his parents. Everything he had previously assumed had just been turned on its head. All his life he had struggled to emulate his father, a man whom he had always pictured as being a staid and proper gentleman. Yet there had always been part of him which found it difficult to control his passions and act in a gentlemanly way; he had always assumed it had come from his mother; it was like being two people at the same time, constantly at war with his inner nature.

He remembered what the Taoist priest had told him at the joss house in Tai-ping-shan: two conflicting influences in his life – *yin* and *yang* – two people he would never meet again who would always be with him. His father and mother, of course; he had been a fool not to realise it sooner. Perhaps it was time for him to stop trying to suppress his passionate nature, but to make the most of it. Instead of trying to be one thing or the other, he would accept that he was both. Perhaps the two combined would be greater than the sum of their parts: after all, he was neither his mother nor his father, but the product of their union.

He chuckled to himself. 'Captain Spitfire, eh?'

The *Mœander*'s gunner overheard him. 'Sir?'

Killigrew flicked the stub of his cheroot overboard. 'I'll show you tomorrow.'

There was a knock at the door to the first lieutenant's cabin. 'Come in,' called Bowyear.

A marine private entered and brought in a couple of jugs of steaming hot water. 'Seven bells, gentlemen.'

'Thank you, Marine Fawcett. You can go first at the wash-basin, Killigrew.'

'Thanks.' Killigrew climbed down from the hammock which had been slung in Bowyear's cabin for him. 'Mind if I borrow your shaving things?'

'By all means.'

'Much obliged.' Killigrew worked up a lather and applied it to his face before scraping at his bristles.

'I wonder if we'll be finished here in time to get back to Victoria for the dragon boat festival?' said Bowyear.

'Christ!'

'What's the matter?'

Killigrew studied the nick he had carved in himself in the mirror above the basin. 'I'd forgotten it was tonight.'

Bowyear grinned. 'Damned inconsiderate,

these pilongs. You should've told Zhai Jing-mu you had other plans.'

Killigrew did not smile. If there was some plot due to be hatched that night, then it was entirely possible that the fact Zhai Jing-mu was holed up in his lair would prevent it from coming to fruition. But if Bannatyne was behind it then Killigrew suspected the *tai-pan* would have taken every eventuality into account.

He dressed while Bowyear shaved and washed himself, and then the two of them joined the rest of the officers for breakfast in the washroom. Afterwards he took his cup of tea on deck and found the Chinese wardroom steward balancing on one leg on the gunwale, performing a sequence of almost balletic movements in slow time.

Killigrew moved to stand in front of him. 'Good morning,' he said in Cantonese.

'Good morning,' the steward replied evenly, neither looking down nor breaking off his sequence.

'Do this every morning, do you?'

'When it is practical. These are my *t'ai chi chu'an* exercises.' Li moved gracefully into a new position: left knee drawn up as far as it would go, right hand raised in a fist above his head and his left hand held level with his stomach, palm upwards. 'This is called "Lion Opening Mouth".'

'I see,' Killigrew said dubiously.

'T'ai chi chu'an exercises focus the mind and spirit, and aid meditation, as well as developing muscles, posture, and correct breathing technique.' Li brought his right hand down and his

461

left hand up until they were level in front of his face, at the same time stretching his left leg out before him parallel to the deck. Then he bent his leg at the knee and stretched his arm out on either side.

'And you find balancing on a gunnel helps?'

'In *t'ai chi chu'an*, as in so many things in life, balance is the key.'

Killigrew shrugged. He was not in the habit of criticising other people's beliefs, so long as those beliefs did not harm other people. He made a gesture with his tea cup that was half-toast, half a motion for Li to carry on, before crossing to where Keppel had emerged on to the quarter-deck.

'You do realise he's a Chinese spy, don't you, sir?' he murmured.

'Good Lord, yes,' said Keppel. 'But you know what the Admiralty's unofficial policy is on letting the Chinese see Western technology.'

'Let them see as much as they like and hope they'll be impressed into acknowledging our superiority?'

Keppel nodded. 'Complete waste of time, of course. Benjamin Franklin obviously never travelled in the Orient, otherwise when he said that nothing was certain in this world except death and taxes he would have added John Chinaman's unshakeable conviction in his total superiority to all other races of mankind. Still, if I'm going to have a spy on board my ship, I'd much rather know exactly where he is—'

'Sail ho!' cried the look-out at the masthead.

It was the *Shanghae*, returning with reinforcements following in her wake; or rather, *reinforcement*, for the only vessel she sailed with was the *Tisiphone*. The paddle-sloop hove to alongside the frigate. Ordinarily it would have been Captain Keppel's privilege as the senior officer of the three ships to ask the captains of the other two vessels to meet him on board the *Mœander*; but since Killigrew had to be taken back to his own ship, Keppel decided to hold his council of war on board the paddle-sloop.

Commander Robertson and Lord Hartcliffe awaited them on the quarterdeck. 'Shall we go down to my day room, gentlemen?' suggested Robertson. Keppel might be the senior officer present, but Robertson was the host and it was up to him to take the initiative.

They made their way below. 'Good to have you back, Killigrew,' Hartcliffe murmured in Killigrew's ear.

'Any news of Mrs Bannatyne or the *Golden Dragon*?'

'Seaman Molineaux says he overheard Captain Ingersoll tell the Reverend Mr Ultzmann the *Golden Dragon* would be in the Cap-sing-mun anchorage at midnight tonight.'

'If Bannatyne hasn't changed his plans,' agreed Killigrew. 'Still, that's one rendezvous the good reverend won't be keeping.'

'He's dead?'

Killigrew nodded. 'Another of Zhai Jing-mu's victims. I persuaded him to change sides at the last moment, not that it did the poor devil much good...'

Hartcliffe coughed into his fist, a quarterdeck

463

signal that Robertson was approaching.

'I shall want a full written report of your activities since the moment you jumped ship the day before yesterday, Second,' growled Robertson. 'When I've seen that I'll decide what punishment to give you for disobeying my orders. That can wait until after we've dealt with these pilongs, mind,' he added, indicating that he expected Killigrew to redeem himself today.

They entered the day room and Killigrew was mildly surprised to find Admiral Huang waiting for them. The admiral rose to his feet and bowed to the British officers.

'Gentlemen, I believe you all know Admiral Huang of the Imperial Chinese Navy,' said Robertson. 'The admiral's fleet of war-junks is following from Canton and should be here in a few hours. Governor Bonham and Governor-General Xu both agreed it would be politic if this was a joint Anglo-Chinese operation.'

The commander did not have to explain further: everyone in the room understood that there would be no arguments with the Chinese authorities about the legality of the operation if a Chinese admiral were party to it.

Keppel got proceedings underway. 'I suggest we start by considering the position,' he said without preamble. 'Since Lieutenant Killigrew has actually been up the creek where the pilong fleet is anchored, he's kindly volunteered to put us in the picture.'

Killigrew unrolled a rough sketch-plan he had drawn up. It showed the shape of the creek as he could best remember it, with the jetty and the village marked on. 'This shows the positions of the enemy's junks as they were when I last saw them late yesterday afternoon,' he explained. 'I think we can rest assured they'll have changed since then.'

'How many junks?'

'I saw thirty-five with my own eyes, not including the seven that the *Mœander* chased into the bay. They hadn't anchored when I was forced to make my rather hurried departure. Most of them carry about nine guns in each broadside but the largest, Zhai Jing-mu's flagship, carries twenty in each broadside and two stern guns. There may be more junks hidden further up the creek; I'm afraid I didn't get a chance to check. There was also a smug boat tied up at the jetty. That's all I can tell you for now.'

'We've sounded the bar and found a channel through into the bay,' added Keppel. 'It's not deep, but the *Mœander* should be able to scrape through at high tide.' Of the three ships in the flotilla, the *Mœander* had the deepest draught.

'When's the top of high water, sir?' asked Robertson.

'Half-past seven this morning,' said Keppel. He had already checked the almanac and had no need to consult his notes. 'And again at five this evening.'

'It's nearly seven now,' said Robertson. 'Do we go in at once, or wait for the Chinese junks and then go in this evening?'

Keppel turned to Huang. 'Admiral?'

'Every moment we delay gives Zhai Jing-mu more time to prepare his defences,' said Huang.

'And the longer we delay, the more time he has to escape overland.'

'Very well,' said Keppel. 'Unless anyone has any objections, we'll go in this morning. Commander Robertson will lead the attack in the *Shanghae*, if Captain Carfax is agreeable...?'

The captain of the *Shanghae* inclined his head. 'What will our strategy be?'

Keppel scratched his head, as if puzzled by the question. 'We go into the creek and shoot up everything in sight.'

Everyone nodded approvingly.

'The *Tisiphone*, under Lieutenant Lord Hartcliffe, will follow the *Shanghae* towing the *Mœander*.' Keppel checked his fob-watch. 'To your ships, gentlemen, and clear for action. We enter the bay in twenty-eight minutes' time.'

They went up on deck. Hartcliffe asked the boatswain to give the order to beat to quarters, while Robertson and Captain Carfax transhipped to the *Shanghae* in one gig and Keppel returned to the *Mœander* in another.

The *Tisiphone* manoeuvred to take the *Mœander* in tow. On all three ships the hands scurried to and fro in the familiar frenetic ballet of clearing the decks for action. Every man knew his post. Netting was strung up over the decks, the anchors raised and the gun crews got into position. Both the *Shanghae* and the *Tisiphone* already had steam up. As soon as the *Tisiphone* and the *Mœander* signalled they were ready, Robertson and Cargill climbed back into the *Shanghae*'s gig and rowed to the prow to lead them in over the bar, sounding out the channel as they went. The flotilla could only sail as fast as the oarsmen in the gig could row, so they moved off slowly at first, the *Mœander*'s sails reefed and the paddle-wheels of the two steamers turning lazily.

Admiral Huang had stayed on board the *Tisiphone* and stood on the quarterdeck with Hartcliffe and Killigrew, who had retrieved his cutlass and pepperbox from his cabin.

With the *Tisiphone* less than half a cable's length astern of the *Shanghae*, Killigrew could clearly hear the voice of the leadsman to the *Shanghae*'s gig as he measured the depth with a lead-line and called out the soundings. 'By the mark, twain ... and a quarter, twain ... and a half, twain ... and a quarter, twain...' The gig moved up and down the bar as the leadsman searched for the channel. The three ships hove to and waited.

'Zhai Jing-mu's flagship must have a draught of at least three fathoms, from the size of her,' said Killigrew. 'If that could get through at high water, then so can the *Mœander*.'

'...and a half, twain ... a quarter less, three ... a quarter less, three...'

'The tide will be turning soon,' said Hartcliffe.

Killigrew gripped the rail tightly. 'Doesn't matter. Zhai's fleet isn't going anywhere, and if we have to wait until this evening then we'll have the added advantage of Huang's junks to help us.'

'And a half, twain,' the leadsman's voice droned monotonously. 'And a quarter, twain ... and a half, twain...'

Hartcliffe directed his telescope across the bay towards the mouth of the creek.

'You won't be able to see them yet,' said Killigrew. 'The main anchorage is a good five miles upstream of that headland.'

'By the mark, four!' the leadsman called out triumphantly, finding the channel where the depth increased to eighteen feet. 'And a quarter, four ... and a half, four ... a quarter less, five ... by the mark, five ... and a half, five ... and a quarter, six...' On the far side of the bar, the bottom plunged away quickly.

'Looks like they're through!' said Hartcliffe, and a moment later the *Shanghae*'s paddles began to turn as she followed the gig through the narrow channel. He turned to Midshipman Cavan. 'Ask Mr Muir to take us ahead, slow.'

'Aye, aye, sir.' Cavan went below to the engine room and soon the *Tisiphone* was towing the *Mœander* in her wake.

Killigrew glanced aft and saw the current before the bar carry the *Mœander* to the left side of the channel. He signalled desperately for the helmsman on the frigate to steer to starboard before they were grounded. Orders were relayed across the frigate's deck and her head began to come around, but it was too late; a moment later a slight shudder ran through the *Mœander* and she seemed to drop astern.

'She's grounded!' warned Hartcliffe, and turned to Cavan, who had just returned on deck. 'Tell Mr Muir to stop all engines immediately.'

'Aye, aye, sir!'

The cable between the *Tisiphone* and the *Mœ-*

ander grew taut. For a moment Killigrew feared it would snap, and the frigate would become grounded. It was touch and go: a moment later the frigate slid forwards once more. 'It's all right, she's free.' Killigrew turned back to where the midshipman was halfway through the after-hatch. 'Belay that last order, Mr Cavan! The *Mœander* is free.'

Then all three ships were across the bar and crossing the deep bay to the mouth of the creek. The *Shanghae* hove to long enough to take the gig back on board and then advanced once more, ahead slow, the leadsman at the channels still calling out the soundings every so often as they groped their way blindly up the uncharted creek.

Killigrew strolled the length of the *Tisiphone*'s deck, inspecting the gun crews and making sure that everything was ready for the coming fight. He paused by the pivot gun in the forecastle, where Molineaux had been appointed to replace O'Connor as captain of the gun. 'I see you made it back all right, Molineaux.'

'Aye, aye, sir. I did understand you right back on the *Buchan Prayer*, didn't I?'

'Perfectly right, Molineaux. I've already commended you in my report to Commander Robertson.'

Molineaux's face fell. 'I'd rather you hadn't done that, sir.'

'Oh?'

'Well, when I got back on board the *Tisiphone* yesterday, Commander Robertson said the only reason he wasn't going to punish me for going adrift with you was because he was certain he'd

469

soon have you yourself to throw the book at.'

'It's nice to know our captain has such confidence in me,' Killigrew said wryly. His inspection finished, he returned to join Hartcliffe and Admiral Huang on the quarterdeck.

'Did you have any success in learning more of the Triads' plot?' asked Huang.

'Some. As far as I can gather, they're trying to start a war between Britain and China. The idea is that the Manchu regime will be so weakened by another war, the Triads will have no difficulty in overthrowing the Ch'ing Dynasty.'

'I suspected as much,' Huang snorted contemptuously. 'The Imperial Grand Council will not initiate such a war, I can assure you.'

'Bannatyne and Zhai know that. My guess is they're planning to commit some atrocity against the Europeans in Hong Kong which will have the people in Britain screaming for Chinese blood.' Killigrew thought hard, trying to remember what little Zhai Jing-mu had told him in the hope it would reveal a clue. 'Zhai said something about the first shot in the war. Perhaps they're planning to assassinate Governor Bonham.'

'The Portuguese didn't declare war when the Governor of Macao was murdered by the Triads,' pointed out Hartcliffe. 'Besides, Governor-General Xu Guang-jin has been invited to sit with Bonham in the gubernatorial stand to watch the dragon boat race. Supposing the assassin missed Bonham and hit Xu by accident?'

'Governor-General Xu has been forced to remain in Canton due to illness–' The admiral broke off and stared at them both in horror.

470

'You think Xu might be a part of it?' asked Hartcliffe.

Huang shook his head. 'Inconceivable. The Governor-General is a close friend of mine. We studied together for the civil service examinations in Peking. He would never be a party to a plot against the Dragon Throne.'

'Perhaps not,' said Killigrew. 'But suppose someone slipped something into his food? Nothing fatal, you understand; just something to give him stomach cramps, like whatever you gave the *Mœander*'s steward to make a place for your man Li.'

Hartcliffe nodded slowly. 'If something happens to Bonham tonight and Governor-General Xu is conveniently absent, no one will believe for a moment that the Chinese authorities were not party to the assassination. The public back home will be howling for Chinese blood. War will become inevitable...'

Killigrew was about to reply when a shout carried across from the *Shanghae*'s look-out: 'Sail ho!'

The *Tisiphone*'s own look-out raised his telescope and peered up the creek.

'What can you see?' Hartcliffe called up through the speaking trumpet.

'Four, five ... no, at least twenty, twenty-five of them! They're anchored in close order across the creek!'

'Trying to bar the passage,' surmised Killigrew. 'The rest must be further upstream.' On an impulse he took the telescope from the binnacle, crossed the deck and ascended the ratlines. He stopped at the maintop and gazed up the creek. The junks were just as the look-out had described them, moored bow to stern across the whole width of the creek. There were twenty-seven of them in all.

He descended to the deck once more and described what he had seen to Hartcliffe. 'Looks like they're ready for us. I recognised Zhai Jing-mu's flagship in the centre of the line.'

'You think Zhai Jing-mu himself is on board? I would have thought he'd be skulking somewhere towards the rear.'

'Not he. He may be a pirate and a murderer, but he's courageous, I'll say that much for him. Besides, his junk has the biggest broadside of them all. They wouldn't want that missing from their ambush.'

'Well, if they're ready for us, that cuts both ways.'

The boatswain's mates piped for silence. It was important for the crew to be quiet when they went into action: soon things would be noisy enough as it was, and they would need to hear orders clearly. But there was more to the silence than that: there was a palpable air of tension on board. Killigrew shared the crew's trepidation. One navy paddle-sloop was more than a match for any junk of war, but three European vessels against forty-two junks? He hoped they were not biting off more than they could chew. And there was always the danger that Zhai Jing-mu had one more trick up his sleeve...

XVII:

A Dragon Throne in Hell

The PS *Shanghae*, HMS *Tisiphone* and HMS *Mœander* rounded another bend in the creek, and then there was less than a mile of water to where the junks were anchored. Zhai Jing-mu had daringly decided to defend the creek at its widest point, so that he would be able to bring more guns to bear on the flotilla.

'*Mœander* is signalling, sir!' warned Midshipman Cavan.

The frigate in the *Tisiphone*'s tow was so close Captain Keppel could easily have called his instructions across to the sloop with his speaking trumpet; but there was a greater chance that someone in Zhai Jing-mu's fleet would understand English than be able to interpret naval signals.

Neither Hartcliffe nor Killigrew needed to raise their telescopes to understand the signal hoist: '*Shanghae* to take left flank, *Tisiphone* will tow *Mœander* to centre three cables from flagship, cast off tow, and take right flank.'

'So we have to run the gauntlet of half their line before we get in place, eh?' a sailor with a Liverpudlian accent grumbled. 'And get into position while we're about it.'

Killigrew did not recognise him at first, which

473

was strange, because he had taken care to get to know the names of all the hands during the voyage from Portsmouth. Then he saw the sailor take out a comb and tidy his hair, as if he were going on a run ashore as opposed to into battle. The gesture reminded Killigrew of where he had seen this man before. 'It's Endicott, isn't it?'

The Liverpudlian turned with a blush. 'That's right, sir. Ordinary Seaman Seth Endicott.'

'When did you come aboard, Seaman Endicott?'

'Yesterday morning, sir, with the other new lads.' He jerked his head at three companions.

Killigrew realised that these men had been brought on board to fill the gap left by the deaths of Dando, Firebrace, Gadsby and O'Connor. Later he would have to find out the names and ratings of the other three newcomers, but now was not the time. 'You don't approve of Captain Keppel's tactics?' he asked Endicott.

'I didn't mean that, sir.'

'I should hope not. I also take it you didn't mean to speak after the boatswain's mates had piped for silence?'

Endicott hung his head.

'You're allowed one mistake in my watch, Mr Endicott, and you've used yours up already. Watch your step.'

Abashed, the Liverpudlian nodded and went about his work in silence.

Smiling faintly, Killigrew studied the line of junks through the telescope once more. They were less than a mile away now, and he was close enough to see the springs which ran from the

474

junks' sterns to their anchor cables, so that their bows did not turn as the tide flowed into the creek. He checked his watch. 'What time did Keppel say high tide was?'

'Half-past seven,' replied Hartcliffe. 'Must be on the turn by now.'

Killigrew nodded and returned his watch to the fob-pocket in his waistcoat. 'Don't you lads fret,' he told Endicott and his companions. 'Captain Keppel knows what he's doing.'

A sound like thunder rolled across the creek, reverberating off the hills on either side, and twenty-one plumes of smoke billowed from the gun ports of Zhai Jing-mu's flagship to merge into one cloud which hid the junk from sight. Even as the first balls hurled up great fountains of water before the *Shanghae*'s bows, the guns of the other junks boomed in quick but ragged succession. About a cable's length ahead of the *Shanghae*, a wall of water boiled out of the creek, momentarily blotting out all sight of the line of junks. Even as the last echoes of the broadside died away, Killigrew could hear the spray thrown up sheeting back down into the water with a loud hiss.

The pilongs had fired first, and their shots had all fallen short.

'Full steam ahead, Mr Cavan!' snapped Hartcliffe. 'Take her three points to starboard, Ågård.'

'Aye, aye, sir!' As the midshipman descended to the engine room once more, the helmsman and his assistant span the wheel, bringing the *Tisiphone*'s head a couple of points to starboard until the paddle-sloop was making for the flagship at the centre of the line.

The paddle-wheels churned with renewed urgency, slapping the water rhythmically. As the two steamers raced to get into position before the pilongs could reload their guns, the *Shanghae* veered off to her allotted position at the left flank of the line.

'We've got the flagship in our sights, sir!' called the gunner. 'Want us to open fire?'

'Hold your fire!' Hartcliffe called back. 'Captain Keppel would never thank us if we snatched the prize from under his nose,' he added *sotto voce* to Killigrew. 'Stand by to alter course to starboard!'

'Aye, aye, sir!' The gunner directed his team to pivot the bow-chaser on its racers until it was ready to fire through one of the gun ports on the port side of the bow.

The *Tisiphone* was less than three cables' lengths from the line of junks now.

'Stand by to let go the tow rope ... let go!'

The cable was dropped in the *Tisiphone*'s wake. Behind them, the *Mœander* glided closer to the line of junks under her own momentum, at the same time putting her helm hard over to bring her broadside-on to the enemy,

'Hard a-port, Ågård!' ordered Hartcliffe.

'Aye, aye, sir!' The quartermaster brought the *Tisiphone*'s head around to starboard so that they sailed parallel to the line of junks. They were only three hundred yards away now, close enough for Killigrew to see the pilongs on deck, barechested and glistening with sweat as they worked to reload their guns beneath the glare of the morning sun. They had almost finished and any moment now the *Tisiphone* would be caught broadside on to the pilongs' guns.

Except that Keppel had timed it to a nicety. The pilongs had almost finished reloading when the ebbing tide suddenly swung the junks on their springs so that they lay in a bow-and-quarter line with their broadsides bearing across one another's sterns. The pilongs on the deck, who only a few seconds earlier had been preparing to sweep the creek with a maelstrom of shot with quiet confidence, now ran to and fro across their decks jabbering in panic as they tried to rectify their new headings. A great cheer went up from the *Tisiphone*'s deck.

'Pipe down!' roared the boatswain. The men at once fell silent.

'Thank you, bosun,' said Hartcliffe. 'Open fire, Guns.'

'Aye, aye, sir!' The gunner turned to Molineaux and the captain of the thirty-two-pounder abaft of the *Tisiphone*'s port-side paddle-box. 'Fire!'

Both guns boomed at once, hurling round shot at the junks ranged to the *Tisiphone*'s left, and both were bang on target, each blowing a hole through the planks of a junk's hull. Then the two gun crews raced one another to be the first to reload ready for their next shot.

Astern of the *Tisiphone*, the *Shanghae* engaged the two junks at the far end of the line, the only pilong vessels which could bring their guns to bear on the *Mœander*. The *Mœander* herself, meanwhile, had anchored three hundred yards from the centre of the line and her port broadside boomed repeatedly as she exchanged shots with Zhai Jing-mu's flagship and the junks around her.

The pilongs on the junks opposite the *Tisiphone* worked furiously, hauling on their springs to bring their broadsides to bear while the paddle-sloop's gun crews had free reign to hammer their opponents unmolested. Within moments two of the junks had been blown out of the water by well-placed shells from Molineaux's bow-chaser, while two more had taken a battering from the thirty-six-pounder and a fifth was in flames.

Then the junks which were still in a position to put up a fight had hauled round their heads until their broadsides had been brought to bear, dashing any hopes of an easy fight. The pilongs kept up a well-sustained fire, hurling shots at the paddle-sloop as fast as they could reload their old-fashioned guns, but their shooting was wild. Some balls flew across the *Tisiphone*'s bow, others fell astern, but most fell short. Only a couple of dozen went home. One ball passed through the signal locker and the gun room; another struck the port-side paddle-box, smashing the bath and harness casks, before landing on the quarterdeck and rolling between Hartcliffe and Ågård, who stood less than three feet apart. The ball ploughed on until it smashed through the captain's skylight and plunged into the cabin below.

Ågård cursed. 'Would you take the helm from me for a moment, sir?' he asked Killigrew. He had to shout to make himself heard above the din, but his voice was otherwise calm.

The lieutenant glanced at him. The passing ball had doubled-up the quartermaster's cutlass and forced the point into his calf. Blood streamed from the wound.

'Of course.' Killigrew helped Ågård's assistant with the wheel. The quartermaster coolly pulled the cutlass-point from his leg – blood gouted – and then bound up the wound with his neckerchief. 'Better get down to the sick berth and let Mr Westlake take a look at that, Ågård. Holcombe can take your place.'

'I'll be all right, sir,' said Ågård, resuming his place at the helm. 'The sawbones is going to have his hands full with properly wounded men to want to worry about a little scratch like this.'

Ships and junks continued to pound one another. The noise was terrific and a thick pall of smoke hung over the creek. On the decks of all three European vessels the gun crews had stripped to their waists to work their guns, while ship's boys scurried to and fro between the guns with powder, shot and shells. Killigrew did not imagine that the scenes on board the junks could be much different.

With so much sweat and energy expended by the Tisiphones, Killigrew was starting to feel like a spare part. He was ready to help the boatswain direct the hands to clear away wreckage or carry the wounded below, but there was little wreckage and no one was seriously wounded; not on board the *Tisiphone*, at least. He was also ready to take Hartcliffe's place if the worst should come to the worst, but thankfully his friend seemed impervious as he dominated the quarterdeck. There was no sign of his usual diffidence.

Wherever there was a space along the port-side bulwark the marines lined up to shoot at the pilongs on the decks of the junks with their muskets, while the pilongs returned their fire with *gingalls*. Killigrew was tempted to blaze away with his pepperbox, but knew at that range he would be wasting shots.

The contest was still undecided, but while all three British vessels had taken a battering, at least they were all still afloat and in action, which was more than could be said for the junks. Of the fifteen or so that were still afloat – with so much smoke drifting across the scene, it was hard to be certain of anything – at least half were ablaze. But the pilongs showed no sign of surrendering, proving that Killigrew's earlier assessment of Zhai Jing-mu applied equally well to the men who followed him. There was no let-up of shots from the crews who were still capable of operating their guns.

Killigrew ducked as another wild shot snatched a spar off the foremast, and it plunged to the netting immediately above his head in a tangle of rigging. 'Everything all right, Molineaux?'

'Just plummy, sir!' Molineaux replied, beaming, and turned briefly to address his men. 'Come on, you idle bastards! Get your fingers out of your bum-holes and get that gun reloaded, damn you! Where's the next cartridge? Ah, there you are. Well don't just stand there like a black slug in a cunny-warren, boy! Pass it to the loader!'

Killigrew smiled. Clearly Molineaux was enjoying himself immensely. The lieutenant lingered by the bow-chaser long enough to see the gun crew put their next shell into a junk, shredding it into so much driftwood in the wink of an eye, and then made his way back across the ordered chaos of the deck to where Hartcliffe stood on the quarter-deck.

Hartcliffe pointed through a break in the smoke torn by a sudden gust of wind to where they could just see a dozen men climbing over the far side of Zhai Jing-mu's flagship into a fast rowing boat. 'Looks like even Zhai Jing-mu thinks he's beaten.'

It was hardly surprising. The flagship was ablaze now, and even as Killigrew and Hartcliffe watched another shell from the *Mœander* exploded inside the big junk's magazine. A great flash lit up all the smoke scarlet with a tremendous boom. A moment later the junk had disappeared in a dense volume of smoke mixed with pieces of junk, masts and men. The very sides of the junk seemed to open out. A cheer rose up from all three British vessels, and Admiral Huang clapped his hands together with a delighted cry. 'How-how-ah!'

When the smoke cleared the junk could be seen to be settling down, with only her lofty stern and the mizzen-mast showing above the water, Zhai Jing-mu's red, black and gold ensign now ragged at the tip of the mast. About a hundred yards away the rowing boat could be seen racing up the creek.

'Damn it, the blackguard's getting away!' exclaimed Hartcliffe.

'Has Keppel seen? Perhaps if we signal...'

Killigrew glanced across to the becalmed frigate and his heart leaped into his mouth. 'Look to the *Mœander!*'

Although stricken, Zhai Jing-mu's flagship had not sunk and its blazing stern now drifted loose of its anchor cable, carried downstream by the ebbing tide towards the helpless frigate.

The crew of the *Mœander* had seen their peril. If the blazing junk ran into the frigate then Keppel and his crew would find it impossible to stop the blaze from spreading through the rigging. What little wind had stirred the air earlier had died altogether and there was no point in the *Mœander* setting her sails, but they had tripped their anchor so they could drift with the tide before the burning junk. But the junk, with most of her hull beneath the water, was moving faster and bore down inexorably on the frigate.

'We'll have to help them!' said Hartcliffe. 'Full ahead, Mr Cavan!'

'Aye, aye, sir!' Cavan set off on another visit to the engine room.

Hartcliffe turned to Ågård. 'Hard-a-starboard!'

While they waited for the engine to start up and give the *Tisiphone* some way, Killigrew realised that the paddle-sloop would never make it. The *Mœander* was almost half a mile away, and with every passing second the ebb tide carried her off further, at the same time bringing the blazing junk closer. Frigate and junk were less than fifty yards apart and the two would be locked together before another minute had passed.

And then a miracle happened. The *Shanghae* suddenly burst forth from the thick bank of

482

smoke on the far side of the *Mœander*. Somehow Commander Robertson had seen the frigate's peril from his own position and steamed to the rescue while the *Tisiphone* had still been getting her engines started. Now the *Shanghae* nosed into the narrow gap between the *Mœander* and the blazing junk. Putting her starboard bow to the frigate's side, she began to push her clear of the fire-raft which the junk had become.

The frigate's weight slowed the *Shanghae* for a moment, and now it was the steamer which was threatened by the blazing junk. The junk came close enough to scorch the paintwork on the *Shanghae*'s sides, and then the steamer's paddles bit at the water once more and won enough momentum to carry both vessels clear of the drifting junk. Killigrew felt relief wash over him.

The *Tisiphone*'s engines started up, once there was no need for them. 'Ah, there you are, Mr Cavan,' Hartcliffe said as the midshipman's head bobbed up through the hatch. 'Ask Mr Muir to stop the engines, there's a good fellow.'

Cavan sighed and went below once more.

Killigrew took stock of the situation. The last of the junks had been silenced. They were all in confusion, the ones that were ablaze drifting into the others and setting those alight as well. Pilongs jumped overboard on all sides, swimming desperately for the shore. Wherever one could see through the thickening smoke, the only sight was that of the heart of Zhai Jing-mu's once-proud pirate fleet sinking in flames.

'*Mœander* is signalling, sir,' said the yeoman of the signals.

Both Hartcliffe and Killigrew could read the signals for themselves: *Go after ZJM. Mœander and* Shanghae *will finish off here.* The frigate was too deep-draughted to risk proceeding any further up the creek.

'Mr Cavan!' called Hartcliffe.

The midshipman was just emerging from the hatch once more. 'Sir?'

'Ahead slow, if you please.'

'Aye, aye, sir.' Cavan rolled his eyes insubordinately and disappeared yet again.

'We should rig up some kind of telegraph running from the quarterdeck to the engine room, so that orders can be relayed instantaneously to the engineer,' remarked Killigrew.

'Nonsense,' said Hartcliffe. 'It's good exercise for the snotties.'

The paddle-wheels churning slowly, the *Tisiphone* nosed forwards between the junks that blazed on all sides. They steamed through the thick smoke, fires showing dimly through the acrid fug. Here and there voices could be heard crying out plaintively in Cantonese as a pilong called out for help to comrades who no longer lived. On more than one occasion a pilong swam towards them only to realise too late it was a British vessel he was turning to for help. When they saw their mistake they would swim off in the direction from which they had come, but one of the marines invariably put a musket ball between their shoulder blades and they slipped beneath the waves.

Killigrew wiped his streaming eyes with his handkerchief and peered through the smoke ahead in case an undamaged junk should suddenly loom in front of them. The gun crews stood by their loaded guns, ready to fire. The smoke thinned out and then the *Tisiphone* had burst through on the other side. There was still no sign of any more junks, and the creek stretched open before them. On either side Killigrew could see pilongs wading ashore and scrambling up the banks to disappear into the trees. Several of the marines levelled their muskets.

'Belay that!' said Killigrew. 'Save your powder and shot for men with fight left in them.' Perhaps the fleeing Chinese might one day return to the sea to renew their careers as pilongs, but Killigrew had bigger fish to fry.

Specifically, Zhai Jing-mu. Whatever else happened this day, Killigrew would see the *lao-pan* punished for Peri's murder, or die himself in the attempt. The fast rowing boat, which had slipped away from the side of the flagship only moments before she had been blown apart, was now half a mile ahead of the *Tisiphone*, disappearing around the next bend in the creek. Killigrew ordered the leadsman to the chainwales to call soundings. Zhai Jing-mu appeared to be getting away, but the *Tisiphone* could not go any faster for fear of running into shoal water; perhaps the pilongs were deliberately trying to draw them into the shallows of the uncharted creek.

Around the next bend they came within sight of the village, where the smug boat was still tied up at the jetty and the four unfinished junks stood in the stocks. 'Those'll have to be fired,' said Hart-cliffe.

Killigrew nodded. 'We'll take care of that on the way back. We can't afford to waste any powder and shot until we know there are no more sea-worthy junks to be dealt with.'

'Ambush?'

'You can be sure of it. Zhai Jing-mu's got fifteen more junks in this creek somewhere, and they'll be waiting for us.'

'All right, everyone keep a sharp look-out!' ordered Hartcliffe. 'If anyone spots a junk, I want to be the first to know about it!'

As the *Tisiphone* moved around the next bend, the creek grew narrower. Everyone on deck was silent, and the only sound to be heard was the throb of the engines and the plashing of the paddles.

Killigrew eyed the tree-lined banks of the creek. 'He's out there somewhere...' he murmured, to himself as much as to Hartcliffe. He frowned. There seemed to be something wrong with the densely packed foliage on the west bank.

He was about to draw Hartcliffe's attention to it when a cry came from the forecastle, 'Two junks, two points off the starboard bow!'

The junks came into view less than two cables' lengths away as the *Tisiphone* rounded a slight headland which jutted into the creek, and a moment later both opened fire with an ear-shattering broadside which hurled round shot through the air towards them. The *Tisiphone*'s fore topmast was snapped off with a splintering crash and plunged through the netting over the deck, narrowly missing the bow-chaser's crew. They worked on, and a moment later scored a direct hit on one of the junks with their first shot, a shell which ripped the junk apart.

Even as the echoes of the explosion were drowned by the cheers of the men on deck, a splintering, crackling sound came from behind them and Killigrew twisted to see a huge fence of interwoven leaves and branches come crashing down to reveal a hidden side-channel. Within seconds no less than half a dozen small, fast junks were propelled from the channel by their sweeps, opening fire on the *Tisiphone*'s stern. Killigrew felt the deck tremble beneath him as a shot smashed through the windows of the captain's quarters.

'Hard-a-starboard!' ordered Hartcliffe, man-oeuvring to bring the greater part of his firepower to bear on where the greatest threat lay, with the six junks which had emerged to cut off their line of retreat. A moment later the *Tisiphone*'s port-side thirty-two-pounder boomed and set one of the six junks ablaze.

'Man overboard!' yelled a voice from the forecastle.

'Who the devil's fallen overboard at a time like this?' Killigrew wondered.

'He'll have to wait until we've got ourselves out of this pickle,' said Hartcliffe. 'Stop engine!'

Endicott ran across to the quarterdeck.

'Why aren't you at your quarters?' Killigrew demanded angrily.

'It's the Chinese admiral, sir,' said Endicott. 'He's the man overboard. He jumped. Molineaux said you'd want to know.'

Killigrew ran to the side and saw the admiral

487

swimming strongly to where the remaining junk ahead of them was moored. Now that the first junk had sunk, he could see what had been hidden before: the fast boat which slipped away from Zhai Jing-mu's flagship moments before it had exploded was tied up beside the second. Admiral Huang had obviously seen it and decided to grab the big fish for himself.

Killigrew cursed. He could not believe his eyes. It was impossible to imagine any Western admiral behaving in such a foolhardy manner, not even Nelson. But then English translations of Chinese words were notoriously inaccurate and Killigrew reflected that it was not beyond the realms of possibility that Huang's title, translated as 'admiral' by the British, actually meant something along the lines of 'escaped lunatic'.

'It's Huang all right,' he called to Hartcliffe as another round shot screeched between the *Tisiphone*'s foremast and mainmast, parting a backstay.

'That's all I need!' groaned Hartcliffe. 'If a Chinese admiral gets himself killed while in the care of the Royal Navy, Bannatyne won't need to start a war between Britain and China; we'll have done his job for him!'

'Want me to go after him while you take care of those fellows?' Killigrew indicated the six junks behind them, now off the *Tisiphone*'s port quarter.

Hartcliffe nodded. 'Take the second cutter.'

Killigrew quickly picked out a crew and they lowered the cutter into the water abaft the starboard paddle-box while the *Tisiphone* exchanged shots fast and furiously with the junks to port.

488

Two more junks had been blown out of the water by the time Killigrew slid down the life-line and landed lightly in the stern of the cutter.

'Bear off and give way with a will! Cheerly does it!'

The cutter skimmed so swiftly across the water that it was only a few yards behind when Admiral Huang hauled himself up the side-ladder on to the junk's deck. The admiral certainly had courage. Killigrew directed the marines amongst the cutter's crew to give him covering fire, and one of the marksmen brought down a pilong who appeared at the entry port directly above the admiral.

'Rowed of all! Watch for stink-pots!'

The cutter bumped against the junk's side and Killigrew rushed up the side-ladder without waiting to see if his men followed. He flung himself over the bulwark, kicking a pilong in the chest as he did so, and drew his cutlass to parry a sword-stroke aimed at his neck. Huang was there, enthusiastically hacking and slashing expertly with his own sword like a man half his age. The pilongs were so tightly packed around Killigrew there was no room for any skilful fencing; all he could do was hack, thrust and shove. Savage, screaming faces surrounded him on all sides. He narrowly avoided being skewered on a sword-point and drew his pepperbox in his left hand. Pressing it hard against a pilong's side, he pulled the trigger and the pilong fell away.

Then the rest of the cutter's crew swarmed on to the junk's deck, and months of cutlass drill paid off as they butchered the pilongs expertly and the deck ran red with blood. The pressure around Killigrew was relieved enough for him to look around and take stock of the situation. A well-aimed blow from Huang's sword saved a British seaman's life: the admiral was clearly perfectly capable of looking after himself.

Then Killigrew spotted Zhai Jing-mu, unmistakable in his white suit and crimson sash, halfway up the companion ladder to the high poop deck. Zhai paused to aim his pistol at Huang. Killigrew raised his pepperbox and fired. The shot narrowly missed, but it was enough to put Zhai off his aim. Scowling, the pilong took his other pistol from his sash and fired at the lieutenant. The bullet splintered the bulwark behind him. Zhai threw the pistol at Killigrew's head and resumed his ascent.

Killigrew ducked and ran across the deck. A pilong moved to block his path, sword raised. The lieutenant brought him down with a shot in the chest. He slid his cutlass back in its scabbard and ascended the companion ladder to the poop. Another pilong appeared above him. He pulled himself close to the ladder to avoid a sword-thrust, and then leaned out to shoot the pilong under the jaw.

'Behind you, sir!' Cavan was busy defending himself with his cutlass against a pilong swordsman, but he was able to draw Killigrew's attention to the man who ran at his back with a spear. Killigrew twisted and shot his would-be assassin, and then shot the man fighting Cavan for good measure. Cavan waved his thanks and then ran to help Molineaux, while Killigrew resumed his ascent of the ladder. He paused just beneath the top rung, and then bobbed up, pepperbox first, sweeping the poop with the muzzle. Zhai Jing-mu was climbing over the taffrail, preparing to jump over the side and swim for the shore.

'Stop right there!' shouted Killigrew.

Zhai Jing-mu twisted and, recognising his nemesis, he jumped overboard. Killigrew climbed on to the poop and ran to the taffrail to see Zhai Jing-mu swimming for the shore, less than thirty yards away.

Huang joined him at the taffrail. 'Shoot him!'

'No bullets.' Killigrew glanced over the deck. The Tisiphones were getting the upper hand wherever he looked and Cavan seemed to have the situation under control. Glancing across the creek, Killigrew saw the *Tisiphone* had sunk all but one of the junks which had appeared astern. He hooked his pepperbox to his belt and scabbarded his cutlass. He was not going to let Zhai Jing-mu get away this time. 'Cover me.' He swung one leg over the taffrail, then the other, and dived into the water.

Zhai reached the shore twenty yards ahead of him and turned with his sword drawn to attack Killigrew as he emerged from the shallows, but a shot sounded behind the lieutenant and he saw an explosion of dust amongst the rocks at Zhai's feet. He twisted in the water and spied Huang at the taffrail with a smoking *gingall* in his hands. Molineaux was also there and he took the empty *gingall* from Huang, exchanging it for a fresh one. As Huang took aim once more, Zhai turned and bounded away from the water's edge, climbing the steep bank like a mountain goat.

Killigrew staggered out of the water and scrambled up the rocks after him. At the top of the bank the ground levelled out and he saw Zhai making for a small farmhouse. He drew his cutlass and charged after him. The *lao-pan* disappeared into the farmhouse and emerged a moment later leading a sturdy pony by a halter. Somehow it did not surprise Killigrew that the pilong admiral had had an escape route planned all along.

The pony was already harnessed and Zhai swung himself into the saddle. He gazed up the track leading inland, glanced at Killigrew, and then at the track again as if trying to make up his mind. Then he tugged on the pony's bridle and charged to meet Killigrew. When he was only a few yards away he drew his sword and aimed a slashing blow at Killigrew's neck.

The lieutenant ran backwards to receive the attack. As Zhai swung, Killigrew tried to duck and parry at the same time. He tripped and fell heavily, narrowly avoiding landing beneath the pony's hoofs. The cutlass skittered from his hand.

He stood up, but Zhai had wheeled the pony for his next charge before he could recover the cutlass. Killigrew instead ran to meet him, dropping on the ground before the pony. The beast instinctively leaped over the prone man. Caught off guard, Zhai had to drop his sword and cling on for dear life to avoid being thrown from the saddle.

Killigrew jumped up and sprinted after him.

Zhai looked about, but the lieutenant had positioned himself behind and to the left of the pilong, in his blind spot. Zhai had to wheel the pony before he saw Killigrew, and by then it was too late. The lieutenant seized the *lao-pan*'s left arm in one hand and his sash in the other. He hauled Zhai out of the saddle and hurled him over his head to land on the ground.

Zhai rolled over and over. As Killigrew approached him, the pilong snatched up a stone and threw it at Killigrew's head. The lieutenant staggered back, stunned. Zhai was on his feet in an instant. He drew a dagger from his belt and hurled himself at Killigrew. The lieutenant caught him by the wrist with his left hand, but the pilong hooked one foot behind his leg and tripped him over. Killigrew went over backwards and Zhai landed on top of him. His face a snarling mask of rage, Zhai tried to force the tip of his dagger into Killigrew's left eye, but the lieutenant refused to relinquish his grip on the pilong's wrist.

With his right hand, Killigrew clawed at Zhai's face and dragged his eye patch down until it was around his neck. Then he reached behind Zhai's head and pushed the thong away, twisting it until the pilong gagged, his one remaining eye bugging from his skull while the empty socket made his face look even more demonic. With his left hand he swept Killigrew's arm away, breaking his grip on the eye patch. He seized the lieutenant's throat in his left hand and squeezed. Killigrew felt himself choking. As his grip weakened on Zhai's wrist, the pilong pulled his arm free and then raised the dagger for a blow to the heart.

Killigrew closed his eyes and braced himself for death. Above him, Zhai's body shuddered violently. When the death blow did not come, he opened his eyes again. Zhai was staring at him with a shocked expression on his face. He glanced down at his chest. Following his gaze, Killigrew saw a bloody hole in the pilong's chest big enough to stick a fist in. He could see daylight on the other side.

Zhai Jing-mu lifted his gaze to stare at Killigrew in bewilderment, and then his one blue eye rolled up in his skull and he slumped sideways.

With a shudder of disgust, Killigrew pushed the grisly corpse off him and twisted to see Huang marching towards him with a *gingall* carried on one shoulder and a beam of satisfaction on his features. Molineaux followed behind him.

'Looks like the goddess T'ien Hou finally won through for you,' Killigrew muttered thickly, rubbing his throat where Zhai had gripped it.

'For both of us, Lieutenant.' As Molineaux helped Killigrew to his feet, the admiral marched across to where the pony stood. The beast shied away skittishly, but Huang calmed it and took the saddle bags from its back.

'You oh-kay, sir?' asked Molineaux.

Killigrew nodded. Zhai was dead, Peri was avenged, but somehow he did not feel satisfied. It was not because he had not had the privilege of killing Zhai himself, but because he could not help feeling that even Zhai Jing-mu had only been a puppet in all of this.

Drawing his sword, Huang marched back to Zhai Jing-mu's corpse and decapitated it with a single blow. He picked up the head by its queue, put it in one of the saddle bags and slung the bags over his shoulder.

'A gift for my emperor,' explained Huang, seeing the expression on Killigrew's face. 'Will you not do the same for your queen when you have killed Bannatyne?'

Killigrew shook his head. 'Somehow I don't think she'd be amused.'

They made their way back to where Huang and Molineaux had left the fast boat they had come ashore in. All of the junks which had tried to outflank the *Tisiphone* were sunk now. Killigrew and Molineaux rowed the admiral back to the junk, where they found Cavan and the others tidying up the mess. There were no prisoners: the pilongs had fought to the last man.

'Everything under control, Mr Cavan?'

Ashen-faced as he wiped blood from his cutlass, the midshipman nodded. His face was streaked with tears. Glancing down, Killigrew saw a large damp patch on the crotch of his pantaloons. 'Don't feel embarrassed, Mr Cavan. No one's going to laugh at you. There isn't a man aboard the *Tisiphone* who didn't do exactly the same thing when he got his first taste of real fighting, and anyone who tells you otherwise is a dammed liar.'

'Even you, sir?'

Killigrew nodded gravely. 'Even me. And even Robertson. Just remember that next time he's weighing you off, and it won't seem so bad.'

Cavan managed a wan smile through the tears. 'What happened to Zhai Jing-mu, sir?'

495

'If he's planning to seat himself on any more dragon thrones, he'll have to find himself one in Hell.'

'Sir!' yelled Molineaux.

Killigrew turned and what he saw filled him with dismay. The remaining seven junks of Zhai Jing-mu's fleet were sailing down from the head of the creek. Several of them opened fire with their bow guns, sending up plumes of water all around the paddle-sloop.

He turned to Cavan and the others. 'All right, let's see if we can't turn this junk on her springs and bring her broadside to bear! You there! Get those guns shotted and run out, chop chop!'

Even as the seamen on the deck of the junk cleared for more action, another shot sounded, the unmistakable boom of a sixty-eight-pounder, and a moment later one of the seven new arrivals was blown apart by a direct hit from a shell. In the same moment, the *Shanghae* came into sight around the spur of land astern.

The *Tisiphone* fired her starboard-side thirty-two-pounder and another of the newcomers received a direct hit which set her poop deck ablaze. Within seconds the rest of the junks had raised white flags.

Molineaux mopped his cheeks with a handkerchief. 'Permission to heave a huge sigh of relief, sir.'

'Permission granted, Able Seaman.'

'Is it over?'

'Not quite.'

XVIII:

Jobbernowl

The flotilla remained in the creek into the afternoon. Zhai Jing-mu's ammunition store was rifled for powder and shot which could be used on board the *Mœander* and the *Tisiphone*, while Killigrew and a team of men set fire to the four unfinished junks in the stocks. Three of the junks which had been captured intact would be towed back to Hong Kong as transports for the prisoners and then auctioned for prize money; the rest would be destroyed so that they could never be used by pirates again.

Cargill came ashore to interrogate the *lao-pans* of the captured junks. 'Ask them if they know anything about a plot due to take place in Hong Kong tonight at the hour of the pig,' suggested Killigrew.

'Zhai Jing-mu's dead, Killigrew,' said Cargill. 'I'm sure whatever plan he and his friends concocted between them died with him.'

'I wish I could be so sure...'

One of the prisoners suddenly broke away from the rest of the group and lunged at Cargill, bawling in Cantonese so rapid Killigrew could not follow a word he said. The others tried to take advantage of the diversion to make a break for it. One of them slipped past Killigrew but he

497

blocked the path of the rest and covered them with his pepperbox. Cargill had dropped his pencil and notebook and was grappling with the *lao-pan*. Molineaux went to help him, but Cargill laid the *lao-pan* low with an uppercut. A moment later more bluejackets had arrived on the scene to surround the pirates.

Killigrew glanced over his shoulder. The pilong who had broken free had almost made it to the corner of a hut when Keppel stepped into view in his path. The pilong tried to side-step him. Keppel quickly assessed the situation, seemed to make way for the pilong, but then tripped him up as he passed. The pilong landed heavily on his face. Keppel picked him up by the scruff of his neck and dragged him across to where the rest of the prisoners were being held. 'Did someone mislay this?'

'Thank you, sir,' said Killigrew.

Molineaux bent over and retrieved Cargill's pencil and notebook from the ground. 'You dropped these, sir.'

'Ah, thank you, Seaman...'

'When I was a kinchin, I always wanted to be a "D".'

'A "D"?'

Cargill smiled thinly. 'Thieves' cant, Mr Killigrew. He means a detective. I shan't ask where he learned such an expression.'

'When you were a child, Molineaux, you were a petty thief,' said Killigrew.

Molineaux shrugged. 'Just the other side of the coin, sir.' He was about to hand the notebook to Cargill, but could not resist opening it and pretended to read a page at random. 'One: do shopping. Two: pick up laundry. Three: beat suspect to death in order to extract confession. Four: tell superintendent the suspect sustained his injuries falling down the stairs.'

'It doesn't say that,' Cargill protested wearily.

Molineaux grinned. 'Just my little joke, sir.' He held out the notebook and the pencil. Cargill was about to take them when a frown clouded Molineaux's features and he snatched it back.

'Could I please have my notebook back?' Cargill protested.

'Give it back to him, Molineaux,' Killigrew snapped irritably.

'Wait a moment, sir.' The seaman reached inside his shirt and pulled out a grimy piece of paper with some numbers pencilled on the back. He stared at the paper, then flipped open the notebook in his other hand and stared at that before glancing back to the paper. 'Sir, I think you'd better take a look at this.'

Killigrew smiled sheepishly at Cargill. 'You don't mind if I humour him, do you?'

The annoyance on Cargill's face was plain to see, but he shrugged wearily as if he could not be bothered to protest.

Molineaux held both the notebook and the paper for Killigrew to see. The paper had clearly been soaked in sea water at some point and was all crumpled and torn, but both the printers' ink and the hand-written information had been fast long enough not to have run too much. The ink was faded but still legible.

It was a receipt for an eight-inch shell gun.

'Where did you get this?' Killigrew demanded of Molineaux.

'On board the *Buchan Prayer*, sir, on Ingersoll's desk. Look at the tails of the Gs, sir, and the capital Es.'

A look of panic appeared on Cargill's face. 'Give that to me!' He tried to snatch the receipt from Molineaux, but the seaman held the paper above his head and took a step back.

Killigrew laid an arm across the assistant superintendent's chest to hold him back. 'I'd say you've got some explaining to do, Mr Cargill,' he said.

'All right, so occasionally I do a little paperwork for Ingersoll,' blustered Cargill. 'That's not a crime, is it?'

'Filling out receipts? Weak, Cargill, damned weak. You'll have to do better than that.'

'Can I say it, sir?' pleaded Molineaux. 'Please let me say it. I know all the words and everything.'

'Be my guest.'

Molineaux stood in front of Cargill. 'Assistant Superintendent Cargill, I am arresting you on suspicion of colluding with pirates and conspiracy to murder.' He reached into Cargill's coat pocket and drew out a pair of handcuffs. 'You do not have to say anything at this time, but anything you do say may be taken down and used as evidence in a court of law.' As happy as a clam at high water, Molineaux cuffed Cargill's hands behind his back. 'I always wanted to say that to a peeler.'

Killigrew smiled thinly. 'That's the biter bit.'

'Surely you don't believe...? The whole thing is preposterous, gentlemen, simply preposterous! I'm an assistant superintendent, for God's sake. What could I possibly have to gain by helping Zhai Jing-mu?'

'How much did Bannatyne promise you?' demanded Killigrew. 'You've been spying for him all along, haven't you? You were the one who made sure that the preparations for Zhai Jing-mu's trial dragged on as long as possible, to give the Triads more time to rescue him. And you were the only one to survive the attack on the gaol when Zhai Jing-mu was rescued. Why weren't you invited to Bannatyne's ball? Because you had to help the Triads rescue Zhai Jing-mu?'

'Damn it, man! I was shot!'

'In the leg. Very easy to shoot oneself there without doing too much damage.'

'I hope you know what you're doing, Killigrew,' said Keppel.

'Doing?' Cargill was livid. 'I'll tell you what he's doing. He's making a big mistake, that's what he's doing!'

'I don't think so, sir,' said Killigrew. 'I should have seen it earlier. Cargill here's been blocking every lead to Zhai Jing-mu every step of the way. The prisoner who was poisoned at the gaol: the bakery had nothing to do with it. You were terrified I was going to persuade him to tell me where Zhai Jing-mu's base was, weren't you?' he asked Cargill. 'The morning we interrogated that poor fellow Chan I noticed you kept looking at your watch, as if you were waiting for something to happen. Then news of Lieutenant Dwyer's

501

death arrived. Was that what you were waiting for? The information which you knew would make me lead Peri Dadabhoy into a trap?' Killigrew struggled to keep his voice calm, but inside he was filled with hatred: Cargill had been as responsible for Peri's death as Zhai Jing-mu himself. 'When you heard I'd survived, you murdered the prisoner in case I came back to renew my interrogation of him. Then there was the Triad I captured outside the joss house on Hollywood Road. You were careful to kill him before he could tell me anything.'

'He was going to stab you.'

'I've been thinking about that. I couldn't work out how you could have seen that dagger from where you stood; even I couldn't see it, and *I* was standing right over him. Now I understand: you *couldn't* see it, could you? Not until after he was dead, when it gave you a perfectly good explanation as to why you shot him.'

Cargill was starting to look pale. 'This is insane. You can't prove any of this.'

'Sooner or later we're going to find Verran. One of you two is going to talk. You both know it's Bannatyne I'm after, so why should you swing for it? Whichever one of you turns Queen's evidence first, wins. The loser goes to the scaffold. You've got a head start, Cargill. I suggest you make the most of it.'

The police officer slumped in total dejection. Then a greasy smile slid across his face and he chuckled. 'You'll have to catch Verran first.' It was as close to an admission of guilt as he was likely to get.

'Don't concern yourself on that account,' said Killigrew. 'We shall.'

'I don't think I have anything more to say until my lawyer is present.'

'Very wise,' growled Keppel.

They put the prisoners in irons aboard the three junks which had not been destroyed and Cargill was taken on board the *Tisiphone* and put in irons in the lee waist with a marine to stand guard over him.

All three of the vessels in Keppel's scratch flotilla had sustained damage in the battle. The *Tisiphone* was the worst hit: both the captain's day room and the wardroom behind it smashed up by the round shot which had penetrated her stern, but Commander Robertson was clearly delighted with a day's work well done and surveyed the damage to his quarters and personal possessions with an uncharacteristically sanguine expression.

The *Tisiphone*'s engineer, Muir, made one of his rare forays from below decks. 'We took a shot in the engine room, sir,' he reported to Killigrew as Keppel explained the implication of Cargill's guilt to Robertson. 'One of the connecting rods is bent out of kilter.'

'Lucky it didn't go through one of the boilers. Can you fix it?'

Muir grimaced. 'I've managed to jury-rig it, sir, but it won't hold for long. It'll need to be replaced as soon as possible.'

'Haven't we got spares aboard?'

'That *was* the last spare, sir. I put an indent in at the dockyard two months ago, but you know

503

what they're like.'

Killigrew nodded. 'Will it hold until we get back to Hong Kong?'

'I'd be happier if we went under sail power only.'

'We need wind for that, Mr Muir.' The breeze had died away to leave the three vessels becalmed.

Molineaux appeared at Killigrew's elbow. 'Sir.'

'That was good work, Molineaux, spotting the similarity of the handwriting on the receipt to that in Cargill's notebook.'

'Thank you, sir. But I still can't help wondering why Cargill should make out the receipt instead of Ingersoll. Unless Bannatyne wanted to be sure there was no way it could be traced back to one of his employees.'

Killigrew stared at him for a moment as the implication of Molineaux's words sank in, and then checked his watch. It was almost three thirty: only five and a half hours until the hour of the pig. He crossed to where Keppel and Robertson were talking on the quarterdeck. 'Sir? We can't waste any more time here. We *must* get back to Hong Kong as quickly as possible.' He explained his theory quickly to both officers. 'If Bannatyne's planning what I think he is, we can't afford to take any chances. He won't know that Zhai Jing-mu's dead; no one in Hong Kong will, until we get there, and that will be with only an hour or two to spare.'

'That's all very well, Second, but the *Shanghae* took a shot in her boilers and ours were damaged,' said Robertson. 'Unless you can whistle up a wind for us, I'm afraid we're becalmed.'

'Sir?'

'What is it, Muir?'

'It's only twenty-five miles to Hong Kong. I reckon there's a good chance the jury-rigged connecting rod will hold out till then.'

'What if it doesn't?'

'If it breaks ... well, it might do some serious damage to the engine. I mean, we could be in dock for weeks.'

'Leaving us stranded, at the mercy of the wind, you mean.'

'We're at the mercy of the wind now,' Keppel pointed out. 'If Killigrew's right – and he usually is – we can't just sit here and do nothing. There are some ponies in the village. I'll send Lieutenant Bowyear and some men overland to Kowloon; they should be able to get a fishing boat there to row across to Victoria.'

Killigrew snapped his fingers. 'That's it, sir! The fishing station at Kowloon! If there's a shell gun lined up at the governor's stand, that's where it'll be.'

'Would it be close enough?' wondered Keppel.

'Extreme range, sir. But firing from a fixed platform, with plenty of time to measure the charge and line up the shot – a good gunner could be bang on target with the first shot.'

'All right. Bowyear will ride for the fishing station at Kowloon to find that gun. Robertson, you take the *Tisiphone* and try to warn the governor. The rest of us will follow under sail with the prisoners, and pray for you. Remember, if Bannatyne can make it look as though the Chinese were behind this atrocity – and with his partner in the House of Commons he shouldn't find that too difficult – then the public will soon be baying for another war with China and anything we say to contradict them won't matter a damn.'

'Do you have any idea how many rumours of plots, assassinations and uprisings cross my desk every week?' Governor Bonham tilted his head back so his valet could tie his cravat. He stood before a cheval-glass in the dressing room of a house he had to rent from one of the China traders; although a site had been chosen and the land had been cleared, building work had not yet begun on an official residence for Her Majesty's governor, plenipotentiary and superintendent of trade. Bonham was obviously used to receiving enquiries from naval officers at all hours of the day and continued to dress for the evening's festivities as he gave them an audience.

'No, sir,' Killigrew said innocently. 'How many?'

Bonham glared at Killigrew. Robertson motioned impatiently for his second lieutenant to be quiet.

'Enough to mean that if I paid any attention to all of them, I wouldn't be able to do my job,' said Bonham. 'In fact, the whole machinery of government would come to a standstill. Did it ever occur to you that that might be exactly what the Triads desire?'

'Sir, I'm not asking you to heed all of them,'

said Robertson. 'Just this one. It's more than a rumour. Lieutenant Killigrew has had titbits from known members of Triad-affiliates – to which Able Seaman Molineaux is a second witness to some – and we've also had it independently confirmed by a Chinese informant.'

Bonham smiled tolerantly as his valet helped him into his coat. 'Listen to yourself, Commander. A Chinese informant? A naval lieutenant with a reputation for being excitable, and a common sailor? Hardly what I'd call reliable sources.'

Killigrew could feel his temper welling up within him like bile, but checked himself. It would be wisest to leave the talking to Robertson.

'A naval lieutenant with a proven track record in getting results, sir,' said the commander. 'And I'm not asking you to halt the machinery of government, just to cancel your attendance at the festivities tonight.'

'And lose face in front of the Chinese? I'm sorry, Robertson, but it will take more than some nebulous notion of a conspiracy to make me do that. You don't even know what it is that these conspirators are planning to do.'

'They've got a gun,' said Killigrew. 'Probably an eight-inch shell gun, by the sound of it; Able Seaman Molineaux found a receipt for one on board the *Buchan Prayer*. My guess is they're planning to fire it at the stand overlooking the harbour. That might put a spoke in the machinery of the island's government,' he could not resist adding. In addition to Bonham, General Staveley and all the island's senior officers and officials had places in the stand, along with their wives.

Bonham's valet adjusted his sash until the governor slapped his hand away in irritation. 'An eight-inch shell gun cannot be an easy thing to conceal, Mr Killigrew. You find me your shell gun, and maybe then I'll listen.' He smirked. 'Of course, once you've done that, I trust you'll attend to the matter so that there will be no need to call off the celebrations.'

'If there's nothing more I can say to dissuade you, sir...' Robertson saluted and motioned for Killigrew to accompany him out of the room. The butler saw them to the door.

'You wouldn't think it would be so difficult to persuade someone to permit you to save his own life, would you, sir?' sighed Killigrew.

Robertson rubbed his temples wearily. 'I don't know, Second. Bonham's got a point. It does sound rather far-fetched. All we've got to go on is cryptic hints and suppositions. If we're wrong about this, we're both going to look pretty foolish come midnight when the celebrations have passed off without a hitch.'

'Oh, I hope we're wrong, sir,' said Killigrew. 'I *pray* we're wrong. If looking foolish is the price I'd pay for that, I could bear it.'

Hartcliffe was waiting for them outside with a dozen bluejackets from the *Tisiphone*, some of them with black eyes and bruises. 'Well?' Robertson demanded impatiently.

'Bannatyne's not at his house or at the factory,

sir. We searched both thoroughly.'

'What happened to your men?'

'Some of Bannatyne's men didn't like us barging into the factory. They tried to stop us.'

'Hope you gave as good as you got.'

'Paid back in full, sir, with interest,' said Hartcliffe. 'The butler at the house said Bannatyne had been called on an urgent trip to Macao for a business meeting. He couldn't tell us any more.'

'I might have known he'd have an ... what are those things called, when you're somewhere else at the time of the crime?' asked Robertson.

'An alibi, sir?' offered Killigrew.

Robertson nodded. 'He's clever, damn him. We know that something ghastly is going to happen tonight, yet all the evidence we have to support our theory could so easily be construed far more innocently.'

'What did the governor say?' asked Hartcliffe.

'Everything's going ahead as planned.'

'Did you tell him about Bannatyne's involvement?'

'Don't be ridiculous! We wanted him to take us seriously, didn't we? "Excuse me, your excellency, but we believe there's going to be an attempt to blow up the gubernatorial stand at the festival tonight, and we think Blase Bannatyne is behind the conspiracy." ' Robertson snorted. 'I'm not even sure I believe it myself.'

'We've still got just over an hour, sir,' said Killigrew. 'I'll take some men across to Kowloon and turn that fishing station upside down.'

'Sorry, Killigrew,' said Hartcliffe. 'I'm afraid Mr Bowyear beat you to it. I bumped into him on

509

the wharf; he'd just come from Kowloon. His men searched every inch of that fishing station and found nothing. He left them on guard there in case Bannatyne showed up with the shell gun, and came across to find us. He went back to join them as soon as he'd spoken to me.'

Killigrew sighed. 'He's wasting his time. If the shell gun isn't there already, then it was never Bannatyne's intention to use the fishing station in the first place. It must be somewhere else. Somewhere behind the stand, perhaps.'

They all turned to where the hills of Hong Kong showed faintly against the night sky. 'Too exposed,' said Robertson.

'Not at night.'

'They'd have wanted to make sure the gun was in place in plenty of time,' said Hartcliffe. 'It needs to be somewhere hidden, but with a clear shot at the stand.'

'What do we do now, sir?' asked Killigrew.

'I don't know,' Robertson said heavily. 'But I've a feeling you're going to be brimming with ideas.'

'Sorry, sir. I'm as much at a loss as you are.'

'Hmph.'

They climbed into the carriage Robertson had commandeered from the harbour master and rode back to Victoria. The house Bonham rented at Spring Gardens was to the east of the town, almost a mile from the centre. Long before they reached the corner of Queen's Road and Pedder Street, however, the crowds became so thick that the carriage was making almost no progress at all.

'We'd be quicker walking,' snorted Killigrew. 'With your permission, sir?' Robertson nodded and he opened the door and jumped down.

'Killigrew!' Robertson called after him.

The lieutenant turned back. 'Sir?'

'You heard what Her Majesty's plenipotentiary said. Find him your shell gun. You've got one hour.'

Killigrew nodded and turned away.

The crowd engulfed him at once. It seemed as if the entire population of Victoria and Tai-ping-shan were out on the streets for the dragon boat festival: Chinese men and women in red clothes, European men in their finest tail-coats and women in elegant ball gowns fanning themselves against the sultry air of the summer night. Every building was bedecked with paper lanterns. Chinese bands played their exotic, twangly music at a frenetic, joyous tempo while dancers twirled streamers and tumblers performed in every open space, spinning plates on bamboo canes or forming human pyramids. Chinese children ran about screaming and laughing, to the delight of the Western ladies and the annoyance of their husbands and fathers. On Harbour Master's Wharf, the oarsmen of the dragon boats performed their *t'ai chi chu'an* exercises to limber up before they climbed into their vessels for the great race. On the roof of his houseboat, Prince Tan was entertaining what Killigrew guessed would be honoured guests; if he had not been otherwise occupied, he would have liked to spend the evening with the mandarin himself. The delicacies would be exquisite, he knew, and the houseboat would provide a grandstand view of the race.

Firecrackers burst like a ragged volley of musketry in a street nearby, startling him. He whirled and came face to face with a dragon: a carnival dragon, its long body supported on a series of bamboo poles, each pole held separately by a man. The men were acrobats as much as puppeteers, following the lead of the one who controlled the head in perfect synchronisation to make the dragon whirl and swoop above the crowd.

Killigrew turned away and bumped into a wizened vendor who tried to sell him a packet of rice wrapped in silk and tied up with brightly coloured threads. He waved the old man away irritably and forced his way through the crowd, disorientated by the whirl of lights, faces, activities, spectacles and noise.

He came to where the governor's stand had been built in the open space in front of the barracks. None of the big-wigs had taken their places yet, and the empty seats looked like one of the few places where he could get some respite from the chaos.

'Excuse me, sahib!' A noncommissioned officer of the Madras Light Infantry, the evening's guard of honour, tried to stop him. 'But those seats are by invitation only.'

'Oh, shove off!' snapped Killigrew.

The soldier hesitated uncertainly, and then saluted. 'Yes, sahib!' The NCO about-turned and marched away.

Killigrew sat down at the centre of the stand and gazed across the sea of faces on the wharf to the harbour beyond. If his tenuous theory was correct in all its assumptions, then the shell gun had to be located within a direct line from where he sat; it would be hidden behind something, but behind something which could quickly be moved aside when the time came.

But there was no shortage of hiding places. Any one of a hundred *yolos* and sampans which crowded the waterfront could have concealed such a weapon; it would take hours to search them all, and there were only forty minutes or so left. The hour of the pig began at nine o'clock, the time the dragon boat race was due to commence, and Killigrew guessed the attack would be timed to coincide with that.

He became aware of a shuffling noise beneath his feet. Glancing down he could just make out a lantern moving around in the empty space beneath the stand. A sudden cold feeling stirred inside him. He had become so fixated on the idea of a shell gun, it had never occurred to him that Bannatyne's plan might be much simpler than that. Taking Guy Fawkes for his inspiration, all he had to do was pack the space beneath the stand with gunpowder and set it off at the appointed time.

Trying to act as casually as possible, he stood up and sauntered to the end of the stand. Then, ignoring the stairs, he vaulted over the rail and ducked under the stand, drawing his pepperbox as he did so.

A shadowy figure played the beam of a bull's-eye about the floor.

Killigrew levelled the pepperbox. 'Stop right there! Identify yourself!'

'Able Seaman Molineaux, HMS *Tisiphone*,' came the prompt reply. 'That you, Mr Killigrew, sir?'

The lieutenant sighed and hooked his pepper-box to his belt. 'For Christ's sake, Molineaux! What the devil d'you think you're doing?'

'I thought maybe Bannatyne might have packed this place with gunpowder, but no such luck. I was jawing with a havildar a while back; he said they checked under here even before they heard the rumours of an attack, and their patrols are pretty regular.'

'Come on, Molineaux.' Killigrew sat down on the front row and took out his cheroot case. He lit one, and then found himself offering the case to the seaman.

'Sir?'

'Go on. Help yourself.'

'Thank you, sir. But I don't smoke.'

Killigrew had his hip flask on him. 'You drink, don't you?'

Molineaux stared at the proffered flask uncertainly, and then accepted it. He took a deep pull and gasped. 'Lumme, sir! That's smooth!'

'John Jameson's finest,' agreed Killigrew. He gestured to the seat beside him. 'Oh, sit down, man, for God's sake! You've been on your feet as long as I have, if not longer.'

'Thank you, sir.' Molineaux sat down beside him, but failed to look comfortable.

'What do you think, Molineaux? Is there really a plot to start a war between Britain and China, or am I just being paranoid?' Killigrew laughed bitterly. 'It's rather rum, when you consider it. All

514

my life I thought I knew all the answers to everything. What was wrong, what was right...'

'You ain't done so bad so far, sir, if you don't mind my saying.'

'Right now, Molineaux, I'd trade the secrets of the universe for the answer to one simple question: where would I put that shell gun if I was Bannatyne?'

'But you're not Bannatyne, sir.'

'That's my point. I'm supposed to be the one with piratical blood in his veins; the one who can think like them, anticipate them, beat them.'

'Not thinking like Mr Bannatyne isn't anything to be ashamed of, sir.'

'It's not a question of shame. It's a question of losing. I don't like to lose. But right now, Bannatyne's got me fairly stumped.'

'I'll wager that Assistant Superintendent Cargill knows, sir. Let me alone with him for half an hour and I'll get it out of him.' Killigrew could tell that the idea of beating the living daylights out of a senior police officer appealed to the ex-thief.

'But that's the catch, Molineaux. We're supposed to be on the side of law and order. We're not allowed to do that sort of thing. Which is why bastards like Bannatyne win every time,' he added bitterly.

'"It was from out of the rind of one apple tasted that the knowledge of good and evil as two twins cleaving together leaped forth into the world. And perhaps this is the doom that Adam fell into of knowing good and evil, that is to say, of knowing good by evil."'

515

Killigrew stared at the seaman. 'Eh?'

'Something I read in a book, sir, that stuck in my memory. John Milton, *Areopagitica*.'

The lieutenant nodded. He had forgotten that Molineaux's choice of reading could be astonishingly highbrow for a common sailor who had grown up on the back streets of Seven Dials. But as Killigrew was starting to discover, Molineaux was a damned uncommon sailor.

Molineaux gestured with the hip flask. 'Mind if I...?'

Killigrew shook his head. 'Help yourself.'

The seaman took another pull, gasped with pleasure, and then screwed the top back on. 'You know what my ambition is, sir? I want to make something of my life. I want to get on in the navy. Maybe even get rated bosun one day; then I can do all the shouting while some other poor bugger does all the graft. I've dedicated the past six years of my life to that aim. But I'll let it all go by the board if it means we can scupper Bannatyne's plans. Just half an hour, sir. I'll make him blab. You don't have to know anything about it.'

Killigrew knew how serious Molineaux was about his naval career. 'You'd throw all that away, just to save the life of Bonham and the other stuck-up bigwigs that will be sitting here in half an hour's time?'

'You mean to tell me you wouldn't do the same, sir? It ain't the guv'nor, it's the Celestials I'm worried about. Damn it, sir – pardon my French – but I *like* the Chinese. Not just Mei-rong, but all of them. They're clever, they're funny, they know how to have a good time when they get the chance ... they're just like us, really.'

'I can't say I'm feeling particularly clever at this precise moment in time.'

'Cheer up, sir. The villains don't always win. Remember the Owodunni Barracoon?'

Killigrew smiled faintly. 'I could hardly forget.'

'We beat 'em then; we'll beat 'em again. You'll see.'

Killigrew stood abruptly. 'Come along, Molineaux. It's time we had a few sharp words with Mr Cargill.'

They made their way to where Mei-rong was living temporarily on board her mother's *yolo* with about a dozen small children. Killigrew could not work out who the children belonged to, but he had the feeling that the mother operated some kind of nursery for working Tanka girls. 'We need you to take us across to the *Tisiphone*, chop chop,' said Killigrew.

'One dollar,' said Mei-rong.

'Here's five.' Killigrew sat down in the stern and Mei-rong quickly cast off and started to scull them out to the paddle-sloop. The children all crowded around Killigrew, demanding that he play with them, until Molineaux came to his rescue by keeping them enraptured with conjuring tricks. They did not understand a word of his monologue, but his funny faces kept them in stitches.

Yolos had never seemed slower than they did now, but at last they bumped against the *Tisiphone*'s side, and Killigrew and Molineaux climbed up to the deck. 'Wait here,' Killigrew called down to Mei-rong.

She had sensed his desperation. 'Five dollar!'

'Five dollars!' exclaimed Killigrew. He sighed. 'All right, five dollars. But you'll have to wait for it. You know, that young lady is going to make some lucky man a fine business manager one of these days,' he added in an aside to Molineaux.

Hartcliffe was on duty on the quarterdeck. 'Any luck?'

Killigrew shook his head. 'We're going to try talking to Cargill.'

'I've already tried, Killigrew, believe me. He's not talking.'

'You just haven't been going about it the right way,' said Killigrew. 'You may want to go below decks for the next fifteen minutes. And the anchor watch, too.'

'I hope you're not thinking what I think you're thinking.'

Killigrew checked his watch. 'We've got twenty-one minutes, my lord. If we don't find that shell gun by then ... I'm going to do whatever it takes.'

Hartcliffe shook his head sorrowfully. 'Fanning! Dismiss the watch.'

'Sir?'

'You heard me. I want everyone below decks. That includes you, Private Barnes,' he added to the marine who was guarding Cargill.

'Don't worry,' Molineaux told the marine. 'He ain't going anywhere. We'll keep an eye on him.'

Killigrew stood over the police officer, who was shackled hand and foot. 'We haven't got much time, Cargill. I think you know I'm right about this shell gun; and I think you know where it is. If you don't tell me where it is, and it goes off ...

if *one person* dies as a result, I'm going to kill you.'

Cargill grinned. 'You wouldn't dare.'

Killigrew shook his head. 'Don't put me to the test, Cargill. Which is it to be?'

Molineaux glanced across to where Bonham was already taking his seat in the stand with the other assembled bigwigs. 'Maybe we should take him to the stand and tie him up next to the governor, sir. I reckon he'd talk fast enough then.'

Killigrew checked his watch again. He was starting to get desperate. 'There isn't time. Look, Cargill: in eighteen minutes dozens of people are going to be killed. If that happens, many more will die over the next few months in the course of a senseless war. Do you really want that on your conscience?'

'Come on, Killigrew. You fought in the last war. What about all those men who died then? What did they die for? The Treaty of Nanking? A treaty that the Celestials are refusing to abide by? Five treaty ports, they said; and now they won't even let us in the walled city of Canton. We should have marched into Peking instead of stopping and making peace when we did. We passed up a great opportunity to teach the yellow-bellies a lesson; if there is another war, it will just put right what was left undone in forty-two.'

Killigrew grabbed Cargill by the lapels, lifted him to his feet and slammed him back against the bulwark. 'My patience is running out, Cargill.'

'You've got no evidence against me, Killigrew. Do you really think I'm going to admit my guilt by telling you where that gun is? What kind of a jobbernowl do you take me for?'

Killigrew stared at him.

Cargill looked uncomfortable. 'What?'

The lieutenant grinned. 'You see? If only you'd said that earlier, you could have saved us all this unpleasantness.'

'Said what? I didn't say anything!' protested Cargill.

'My dear assistant superintendent, you really should take more care about the sort of presents you give – and to whom you give them.'

'Eh? What?' Cargill was bewildered.

But Killigrew was already turning away. 'Come on, Molineaux. We've got work to do.'

'You know where the gun is, sir? I didn't hear Cargill say anything.'

'A little bird told me.'

Killigrew and Molineaux surfaced beneath the bows of Prince Tan's palatial houseboat. Directly above their heads, only a couple of feet above the waterline, a guard armed with a musket stood on the gallery, oblivious to their presence. The two Britons exchanged glances and Killigrew nodded. Then they grabbed an ankle each and pulled the guard's feet out from under him. He fell down and cracked his head on the deck before he could cry out, his musket landing in the water with a splash.

A doorway covered only with a silk curtain led into the houseboat from the gallery and a voice called out in Cantonese from within. Killigrew hauled himself out of the water and on to the gallery, taking up position with his back pressed against the bulkhead by the door.

The curtain was pulled aside and another guard appeared. He saw Molineaux in the water, supporting the body of the unconscious guard, and opened his mouth to cry out a warning. Killigrew's fist smashed into his jaw.

Molineaux handed the cable up to the lieutenant, who tied it in a timber hitch to one of the posts supporting the deck head above. 'That should hold,' he whispered, picking up the guard's musket.

'You sure you want to do this alone, sir?'

Killigrew nodded. 'Prince Tan is – used to be – a friend of mine. He saved my life once. If I can do this without bloodshed, the happier I'll be.'

'And if you can't? You don't know how many men he has on board.'

'You let me worry about his men. Just make sure this houseboat is turned through ninety degrees so that the starboard side points towards the harbour mouth instead of the waterfront.' As Molineaux turned and swam back alongside the cable to where Robertson and Hartcliffe waited on the *Tisiphone*'s quarterdeck, Killigrew pulled aside the curtain and stepped into the passageway beyond. He made his way along it, peeping through the doors on either side as he passed but found no sign of what he was looking for.

A companion ladder led to the deck above. He started to ascend when he heard footsteps above. He quickly ducked back down and hid beneath the steps. He saw feet coming down, thrust the musket's barrel between the steps and swept it to knock the man's feet out from under him. The man fell forward and hit his head on the bulkhead on his way down. Killigrew scrambled over his unconscious body and crept cat-footed up the steps as he heard a voice above call out in Cantonese.

'Chang? Are you all right?'

Killigrew heard footsteps and waited at the top of the stairs. A moment later another guard approached. As soon as he hove into view, Killigrew knocked him out with a right cross. He dragged the body back down the steps and laid it next to the first. Then he ripped down a silk hanging, tore it into strips and used it to bind and gag them both.

Returning to the upper deck, he started to search each of the chambers. The first two he glanced in were deserted, but in the third he found Ai-ling – the Eurasian beauty he had seen talking to Ultzmann at Tan's picnic which seemed like a lifetime ago – tied to a bed. Her eyes widened when he stepped into the compartment. He lifted a finger to his lips, and unfastened the gag.

'Who are you?' she whispered in Cantonese.

'A friend. You're Ultzmann's mistress?'

She looked offended. 'His daughter!'

Killigrew nodded. He should have guessed as much a long time ago. Bannatyne or Tan had somehow found out that the missionary had an illegitimate half-caste daughter. At first they had probably threatened him with exposure; but as their schemes grew more desperate they had kidnapped her and used her as a hostage for the missionary's help and co-operation.

He wondered if she knew her father was dead,

murdered by Zhai Jing-mu; he knew he could not bring himself to tell her now.

'Prince Tan and Zhai Jing-mu are planning to assassinate the governor,' Ai-ling said urgently. 'You must stop them!'

'Don't worry, it's all in hand. They have a shell gun on board; do you know where it is?'

'The upper deck, I think; I heard them manhandling it on board a few weeks ago.'

'I'll deal with it,' he told her. 'Can you swim?'

'A little,' she said.

Glancing down, he saw she did not have bound feet. 'Go down to the stern – you know which way that is?' She nodded, to his relief: he did not have time for lengthy explanations. 'Go down to the stern and swim across to the British warship two hundred yards astern. Use the cable to pull yourself along if you must. They'll look after you there.'

'What about you?'

'I have to have a word with Prince Tan.'

He accompanied her back to the deck below and watched from the bottom of the stairs as she hurried along the passage and disappeared through the curtained doorway leading on to the stern gallery. At his feet, the bound and gagged men struggled powerlessly. He ignored them and climbed back up the companionway to the upper deck.

He peered through a bead curtain covering the entrance to one of the compartments on the port side of the houseboat, facing towards the waterfront. The shell gun was there, pointing towards a door which opened out amidships towards the stand on the wharf. Only a silk curtain, tied down to prevent it from flapping in a breeze, hid it from any prying eyes ashore.

A team of ten Chinese were readying the gun and they had obviously been well drilled. The gun itself was an unfamiliar make, although the operation seemed simple enough: the percussion lock hit a priming tube in the breech to fire a shell. A box of fifty-six-pound hollow shells stood close by, and another of flannel-wrapped cartridges.

Killigrew stepped through the bead curtain. 'All right, gentlemen,' he said in Cantonese. 'That's quite enough of that. This festival already has all the fireworks it needs. Step away from the gun, please.' He gestured with the musket and the Triads backed towards the far partition.

Prince Tan stepped through behind them, flanked by two more guards. 'What is going on here?' he demanded. Then he saw Killigrew, and smiled. 'Ah, my barbarian son. I think, in my heart, I was expecting you to come sooner or later.'

'It took me a while, your highness, but I got here in the end. Tell your men to stand down. It's all over. Zhai Jing-mu is dead, Bannatyne's vanished; we know all about your plan to spark off a war between Britain and China. It isn't going to work. I'm afraid–' Killigrew broke off when he felt the cold touch of a gun muzzle against the back of his neck. 'Ah.'

Molineaux swam back along the length of the cable to the *Tisiphone*'s stern. Robertson and

Hartcliffe waited for him at the entry port. 'Where's Killigrew, Molineaux?'

'He went aboard, sir. Wanted to confront his excellency in person.'

'Damned young fool. Well, as long as we pull the boat clear.' Robertson checked his watch. 'Three minutes to go. Now that's what I call in the nick of time. Go below and tell Mr Muir to start the engines, Molineaux. Full speed ahead.'

'Aye, aye, sir.' The seaman descended by the main hatch to the engine room where the stokers sweated to keep the furnaces burning and the pressure in the boiler just right. It was dark, hot and smoky in the engine room and the air was thick with coal dust. Molineaux would not have been a stoker for – he grimaced at the thought – all the tea in China. 'Turn ahead, full speed, sir,' he told Muir.

The engineer checked the pressure gauge, nodded, and hauled back a lever. Steam hissed and the pistons started to work: slowly at first, then faster and faster. He could not hear the sound of the paddles plashing above the racket of the engine, but he could tell from the motion of the deck beneath his feet that they were moving.

There came a loud snap followed by a clang, and a ghastly screech of rending metal. Something ricocheted past his head and bounced off the boiler casing. Muir swore and hauled on a lever. The pistons slowed and stopped until the engine room was silent but for the hiss of steam.

'What's wrong, sir?' demanded Molineaux.

'Connecting rod's broke. Damn it!'

'You can fix it, can't you?'

'Oh, aye. I can fix it, all right. It'll take a few weeks, but I can fix it.'

'A few weeks! Sir, we've got about one minute. Then it'll be war.' Molineaux sprinted for the upper deck to tell Robertson what had happened, but he knew he would be too late. There was no time to put a boat in the water and send a squad of marines and bluejackets to the houseboat. Now it was all up to Killigrew.

XIX:

Fire and Water

'You think our plan is foiled?' Prince Tan asked Killigrew, who stood with his hands tied above his head to a beam while one of the Triads kept him covered with a pistol. 'Zhai Jing-mu was expendable. He had played his part; he was no more than a pawn. He kept you chasing about the seas while the real plot was taking place right here in Hong Kong, my barbarian son.'

The Triads finished priming the shell gun. 'Is it lined up?' asked Tan.

One of them cut a slit in the silk curtain before the gun's muzzle and peered through. 'Right on target, excellency.'

'Excellent.'

A single pistol shot sounded, startling Killigrew, and a moment later a terrific din went up from the waterfront as the crowd began to beat their drums, cymbals, pots and pans.

The race had begun.

'In just a few moments, as the winning dragon boats cross the finishing line, we shall fire the first shot in the second phase of the great war between Britain and the Celestial Kingdom, and what was started ten years ago will finally be brought to a satisfactory conclusion,' said Tan. 'Two centuries of Ch'ing tyranny will be brought

527

to an end and in time the rightful Ming emperors will be restored to the Dragon Throne.'

Killigrew knew that all he had to do was to keep Tan talking until the *Tisiphone* pulled the houseboat clear of the wharf. He was sure it could not be long now. 'Let me guess. You just happen to be a direct descendant of the Ming Dynasty?'

'A fact my ancestors have kept concealed from their Manchu overlords for over two hundred years. Oh, there are other men with a better claim on the Dragon Throne than mine, but it should not be too difficult to ensure they die heroically fighting the Manchu tyranny in our glorious war.'

'You think the Manchus are tyrants? You don't know the meaning of the word tyranny, Tan. You start a new dynasty drenched in blood, and that's the way it will be for ever.'

'Barbarian blood, Mr Killigrew. Do not think you can dissuade me from this course of action. My whole destiny had led up to this moment.'

'Excellency!' one of the Triads whispered urgently, and nodded to the doorway leading aft. Killigrew followed their gaze and saw Li Cheng standing there.

'Prince Tan? In the name of the Daoguang Emperor I arrest you for high treason,' said Li. 'Tell your men to put down their weapons and release the barbarian.'

Tan stared at him incredulously. 'You came alone? Unarmed?'

Li bowed.

The Triads stared at him, and then burst out laughing. 'Kill him,' Tan said dismissively.

One of the Triads pulled a pistol from his sash

and pointed it at Li's forehead. Li's leg flashed out and kicked the pistol into the air. He punched the man in the throat and then caught the pistol on the way down. He used it to shoot the man who held a pistol on Killigrew.

Two Triads drew swords and charged at Li. He threw the pistol at the head of one, knocking him out, and then caught the other by the wrists to stay the blow. A third Triad came at him. Still holding the second at bay, Li kicked him in the chest and threw him back across the room.

Another Triad drew a sword. Killigrew grabbed hold of the ropes binding his hands above his head and hauled himself up to kick the Triad between the shoulder blades with both feet. The Triad staggered into a man who had been lining up a pistol-shot at Li. The shot went wide, drilling a third man in the head.

'Thank you!' Li wrested the sword from the man he grappled with and knocked him out with a *wu-yi* punch.

'I could be even more helpful if you cut me loose.' As a Triad tried to slash at Killigrew with a sword, the lieutenant kicked him in the crotch and he went down with a howl.

'So sorry...' Li jumped into the air and somehow contrived to kick two men in the face simultaneously. 'I am a little busy at the moment.' He parried a sword stroke from another man and kicked him away long enough to throw the sword across the room. It spun through the air, sliced through Killigrew's bonds and embedded itself in the bulkhead behind him. His hands free, he knocked out one Triad with a right cross, another with a left uppercut, and turned to pull the sword from the bulkhead.

'Fire the gun!' screamed Tan.

'But the dragon boat race is not yet ended, excellency!'

'Fire it *now*!'

Killigrew saw two of the Triads light the fuse of a shell and insert it in the muzzle of the gun: they did not seem to realise there was no need to light the fuse, the firing of the gun did that automatically. In their panic they had not cut the fuse to the correct length – not that a few seconds would make much difference either way when the shell landed on the gubernatorial stand. Why the devil hadn't the *Tisiphone* towed them clear yet?

Two swordsmen attacked the unarmed Li from both sides at once. He side-stepped, grabbed one by the wrist and whirled him around to receive the other on the point of his sword.

Tan picked up the lanyard to fire the shell gun and flexed his fingers around the toggle. Parrying a sword-stroke from one Triad, Killigrew kicked another in the groin. The man staggered back, cannoned into Tan and knocked him across the breech of the gun.

While Li exchanged fast and furious *wu-yi* blows with one Triad, another tried to strike him down from behind. Killigrew flung his sword. It spun over and over and took the man in the throat. The lieutenant turned and found himself staring down the length of a quarrel resting in a crossbow. He had a flashback: it was the same man who had almost shot him at the gaol, the one who had later shown up as the captain of one of the pilong junks which had 'attacked' the *Golden Dragon*.

Killigrew caught him by the wrists and forced the crossbow up towards the deck head. The two of them struggled for control of the crossbow. They bounced against the shell gun and then rolled on the deck beside the gun carriage.

Inside the barrel, the fuse still burned.

Tan steadied himself and adjusted his grip on the lanyard.

The pilong tried to point the crossbow at Killigrew's face but the lieutenant was stronger. He forced the pilong's arm away, into the space beneath the hammer of the percussion lock.

Tan pulled the lanyard. The hammer fell and the pilong screamed in agony. The firing pin failed to connect with the priming tube.

There was no time to draw back the hammer for a second try. Aware of the still-burning fuse in the barrel of the gun, the Triads and the guards fought to climb out of the door and the windows.

Tan was knocked down in the panic. He tried to crawl away but Killigrew grabbed him by an ankle and deftly tied the lanyard in a stout knot around it.

'This way!' Li threw himself feet first against one of the bulkheads. The flimsy partition smashed under his weight. Killigrew followed him through. In the next room he saw Li hurl himself through a window. Killigrew jumped out after him, headfirst. He plummeted twenty feet, hit the water, and a moment later the shell burst in the gun's barrel. Red-hot chunks of metal burrowed through the water all around him. He swam down a fathom, aware of flames lighting up the surface above him, and then struck upwards.

When he surfaced, the houseboat was in two halves and sinking in flames. No one was watching the dragon boat race any longer. A few of the Triads who had managed to escape from the houseboat splashed around, striking out for the shore.

A hand grabbed Killigrew by the scruff of the neck. He twisted and found himself hard against the gunwale of the *Tisiphone*'s thirty-foot steam pinnace. Ågård and Molineaux hauled him on board.

'Are you all right, Killigrew?' Hartcliffe called from the stern.

He nodded. 'Why the devil didn't you just pull the houseboat clear?'

'Engine failure. You seem to have managed well enough without help.'

The marines in the boat were shooting at the Triads who swam for the wharf. A Chinese surfaced on the opposite side of the pinnace. One of the marines whirled, levelling his musket, but Killigrew knocked the barrel up. 'He's on our side!'

Li Cheng was pulled into the pinnace and they rowed back to the *Tisiphone*. When Killigrew had climbed up the side ladder he found Robertson waiting for him on deck. 'Good work, Second.'

'Don't thank me, sir.' He gestured to where Li Cheng was climbing through the entry port after Hartcliffe. 'Chalk this one up to the Celestials. Mr Li just saved my life. And averted a small war.

Miss Ai-ling?'

'The Eurasian girl? In the sick berth, being properly cared for by Westlake and Strachan. Where the deuce does she fit into all this?'

'She's Ultzmann's daughter. They were holding her as a hostage for his bad behaviour.'

'I see. What about Prince Tan?'

'Dead, sir. That just leaves Bannatyne, Verran and Ingersoll to take care of.'

'Except we don't know where they are,' pointed out Hartcliffe.

'There's a slim chance they still plan to make that rendezvous at the *Buchan Prayer* at midnight.'

Robertson checked his watch. 'We'll never make it in time. It's quarter past nine already, and Muir tells me it'll take weeks to repair the engines.'

'Might I make a suggestion, sir?'

'It's your choice, madam.' Blase Bannatyne faced his wife across her cabin on board the *Golden Dragon*. The fire damage had been repaired and cosmetic alterations had been made to the steamer to disguise it from prying eyes on the other vessels in the Cap-sing-mun anchorage. 'Even as we speak, a train of events which will change the whole course of history has been set in motion. When the war is over, a new dynasty will rule in Peking. A dynasty which will be in my debt. A new treaty will be signed: one giving me exclusive rights to all the tea produced in China. I shall be the richest man in the world.'

She stared at him for a moment, and then

shook her head. 'How much money do you need?'

He stared back, as if there were something strange about her question. 'All of it.'

'You're insane.'

'You never understood me, Epiphany. Can't you see my vision? What I'm trying to achieve for us here? When my plan comes to fruition, kings and queens will bow to you. Isn't that what you want?'

'No! Blase, I never wanted kings and queens paying attention to me. Just you. I just wanted you to place some value on the things that interested me, as well as the things that interested you.'

He sighed and stood up. 'I cannot afford the public disgrace of a divorce. You understand that, don't you?'

'Is that the only way you can see to keep our marriage alive? By making veiled threats?' She shook her head. 'It's over, Blase. I just want you to let me go.'

'That I cannot do–' There was a knock at the door. 'Who is it?' Bannatyne called impatiently.

'Cap'n Ingersoll, sir. The look-outs on Lan-tao have reported back.'

'Splendid. I trust everything went according to plan?'

Ingersoll opened the door. His face was pale. 'Something went wrong.'

'What do you mean?'

'Prince Tan's houseboat blew up before the dragon boat race finished.'

Bannatyne stared at him in disbelief. Then his

face hardened. 'Killigrew!'

Mrs Bannatyne laughed. She no longer had any sympathy for her husband. He was deranged, twisted. The only reason she had not realised it before was because he had always kept her at arm's length, emotionally. 'You want to rule the world, and you can't even get the better of a junior naval officer!'

Bannatyne slapped her viciously, knocking her out of her chair. She fell to the deck, but refused to give him the satisfaction of seeing her cry. 'Does that make you feel better, Blase? You can't beat Killigrew, but you can beat me, a defenceless woman ... your own *wife*, for Heaven's sake!'

He scowled, and turned back to Ingersoll. 'Tell Verran to get steam up at once. We're leaving. Fetch all the papers from the safe on the *Buchan Prayer*. And unless you want to be here when the Royal Navy arrives, I suggest you bring your things on board, too.'

'Aye, aye, sir. Where shall I tell Cap'n Verran we're bound?'

'Anywhere but here.'

Molineaux did not recognise the steamer tied up at the landing stage next to the *Buchan Prayer* when Sir Dadabhoy Framjee's pinnace steamed through the Cap-sing-mun Passage. Molineaux manned the tiller while Killigrew and Hartcliffe stood in the bow. 'That's not the *Golden Dragon*!' he protested.

Killigrew raised a telescope to his eyes. '"*Vermilion Bird*", it says. And if you believe that, you'll believe anything. It's the *Golden Dragon*, all

535

right. I'd recognise her lines anywhere.'

Hartcliffe cast his eyes over the squad of marines and bluejackets, and his eyes fell on Li. 'What the blazes is he doing here?'

'He wanted to come,' said Killigrew.

'That's beside the point. This is navy business, and he's a Chinese national and a civilian.'

'I felt we could use all the help we could get,' said Killigrew, and smiled faintly. 'He seems to know how to look after himself.'

'This will be cutlasses and musket-work, Killigrew. There'll be no place for his *wu-yi* skills here.'

'Yes, milord. Want me to have Molineaux put the tiller over and take us back to Victoria?'

Hartcliffe sighed. 'If he gets killed, Killigrew, it'll be on your head.'

Killigrew said something else to Li in Cantonese; telling him to keep his head down and stay out of trouble, guessed Molineaux.

As they closed with the *Buchan Prayer* Hartcliffe raised a speaking trumpet to address the men on the decks of the opium hulk and the steamer. 'This is Lieutenant Lord Endymion Fitzmaurice Berkeley Hartcliffe, of Her Britannic Majesty's Royal Navy. I order you to strike your colours and permit us to board you!'

Killigrew stared at Hartcliffe, who shrugged. 'Never does any harm to use one's full tally in a situation like this. You'd be amazed how many people go weak at the knees in the presence of nobility.'

A shot sounded from the deck of the opium hulk, and a musket ball whizzed through the air above their heads to splash into the pinnace's wake.

'Weak at the knees they may be, milord, but it doesn't seem to have put their aim off by much,' said Killigrew.

Molineaux glanced towards the *Golden Dragon* and saw some of the men on her poop swinging the stern-chaser around to point at the pinnace. 'Pivot gun off the starboard bow, sir!' he called.

'Make for the far side of the *Buchan Prayer*!' ordered Killigrew.

The men on the *Golden Dragon* managed to get one shot off before the pinnace slipped behind the hulk. It screeched over the heads of the bluejackets and plunged into the water on the far side, sending up a great gout of water which almost capsized the pinnace and drenched everyone on board. Then they were protected behind the hulk, and too close in for the men above them to be able to draw beads on them with their muskets.

'Grappling irons!'

Molineaux snatched up one of the grappling irons and whirled it expertly, as he might whirl the lead when sounding. He let go and it flew up to the rail far above their heads, the rope snaking out behind it. Another seaman did likewise, and both irons caught firm on the rail. Molineaux went up one rope and Killigrew the other. Molineaux was halfway up the hulk's side when he saw a man at the rail above him, sawing at the rope with a knife.

Next to him, Killigrew gripped the rope tightly in one hand and braced his feet against the side of the hulk. He leaned out, plucked a pepperbox from his belt and took careful aim. The pistol cracked and the man fell back out of sight.

Molineaux signalled his thanks and went on and up over the rail. He took off the hook and started to fasten the half-severed rope more securely to the rail. He had almost finished when a guard came at him out of the gloom and swung a musket-butt at his head. Molineaux ducked and drove his fist into the man's stomach. He doubled up to reveal another guard behind him, levelling a musket.

Killigrew swung himself over the rail and kicked the musket aside a moment before the guard pulled the trigger. The musket-ball ploughed into the side of a deck house. The lieutenant landed on the deck and laid the man out with a right cross.

Molineaux finished fastening the rope and a moment later more bluejackets swarmed over the side with daggers, cutlasses, hatchets and belaying pins gripped between their teeth or thrust under their belts. They were followed by Li.

'See if you can find Mrs Bannatyne!' ordered Hartcliffe. 'There's a chance she may still be alive!'

'And if anyone finds the *tai-pan* himself, he's mine!' added Killigrew.

If the lieutenant intended to exact his own brand of justice on Mr Bannatyne, that was fine with Molineaux. He ducked between two of the deck-houses and came face to face with Ingersoll. Grinning, Molineaux pulled his Bowie knife from its sheath.

'Oh-kay, you sonuvabitch. Let's hear you call me "nigger" now.'

Ingersoll turned and ran. Molineaux pursued him down the accommodation ladder to the landing stage, and up on to the deck of the *Golden Dragon*. Li was right behind him. No sooner had they stepped through the entry port than the two of them stopped short.

Most of the sailors on the steamer were busy lowering the sails or casting off the mooring ropes, but there were still enough left over to form a semi-circle around Molineaux and Li. Behind the two interlopers, the gangplank was raised as the wind began to carry the *Golden Dragon* away from the landing stage.

On the far side of the deck of the *Buchan Prayer*, Killigrew parried a bayonet thrust from one guard with his cutlass, punched a second in the face with the knucklebow, and then stabbed the first in the throat.

Further along the deck, Ågård glanced at Killigrew and his eyes widened in shock. 'Behind you, sir!'

Killigrew whirled and came face to face with Bully Hayes and Eli Boggs, the two *tindals* from the *Golden Dragon*. Boggs levelled a revolver at Killigrew's head.

'Finish him, Eli!' snarled Hayes.

Endicott stepped out behind them and rammed a musket against the backs of their heads like a quarter-staff. Boggs dropped the revolver and slumped to the deck, while Hayes staggered forward and Killigrew knocked him out with a blow from the hilt of his cutlass. 'Much obliged to you, Endicott.'

The Liverpudlian beamed proudly. 'My pleasure, sir.'

'Killigrew!' Hartcliffe's voice came from the other side of the deck. Killigrew ran across to join him in time to see the *Golden Dragon* move away from the landing stage under sail. Bannatyne stood next to Verran on the quarterdeck, mockingly waving farewell to the two lieutenants. In the steamer's waist, Molineaux and Li were surrounded by Ingersoll and four sailors.

'They're getting away!' Hartcliffe protested.

'The devil they are!' Killigrew slotted his cutlass back in its scabbard and ran back to where he had left a grappling iron hooked over the far rail. He ran to the hulk's poop deck, stood at the taffrail and whirled the iron above his head. It arced up through the air and dropped over one of the yards of the *Golden Dragon*'s mainmast. There was no time to make the rope fast to the hulk's taffrail. The ship's movement pulled the rope tight almost at once, and Killigrew barely had time to swing one leg over the taffrail, and then the other.

He stepped out into space and prayed he had judged the distances correctly.

He plummeted for a couple of feet and then the rope swung him in towards the *Golden Dragon*'s stern. He hauled on the rope to pull himself up, raising his legs beneath them to avoid cracking them on the rail, and then swung across the quarterdeck. He hit the planks and his graceful swoop came to an abrupt and inelegant end as he rolled against the far bulwark. No bones broken, though, as far as he could tell.

He climbed shakily to his feet and turned to where Bannatyne and Verran stood next to Suleiman, the helmsman at the wheel. Killigrew drew his cutlass. 'Hello, Jago. Time for a return match, I think.'

Verran was grinning. He made no attempt to reach for his own cutlass. Killigrew realised what was wrong and began to turn, but he was too late. What felt like a sledge-hammer smashed into the back of his neck. He dropped his cutlass, staggered a few paces and sank to his knees. He flopped on to his back and, through the lights that danced before his eyes, saw Shen loom over him. Then Verran was there, holding the point of his cutlass at his throat.

'Never mind him,' Bannatyne told Verran. 'Shen will deal with Mr Killigrew. You take care of our slant-eyed friend.' The *tai-pan* pointed, and the lieutenant managed to raise his head in time to see Li ascend the ratlines pursued by two Lascars.

Then Shen grabbed Killigrew by the ankles and started to drag him towards the taffrail.

'Three against one,' said Molineaux. 'That's hardly fair.'

Ingersoll and the two sea-cunnies charged as one. Molineaux danced aside, slashed at one of the sea-cunnies with his Bowie knife, dodged beneath Ingersoll's grasping arms, and tripped the second sea-cunny so that he sprawled on the deck.

'Hardly fair to you, I mean,' said Molineaux,

dancing back. He ducked behind the jolly boat stowed on deck as they came at him again. One of the sea-cunnies reached for him across the boat. Molineaux seized him by the jacket with his left hand and dragged him across the boat's tarpaulin cover. He brought the haft of the Bowie knife down against the back of his neck and knocked him unconscious.

He slashed at Ingersoll with the knife, but the captain jumped clear. A moment later the other sea-cunny had dashed the knife from his grip with a *wu-yi* kick. It clattered across the deck. Molineaux tried to go after it, but Ingersoll interposed himself.

Molineaux turned and raced across the deck. Ingersoll and the other sea-cunny pounded after him. He stumbled down the after-hatch and through a door into the captain's day room, illuminated by an oil lantern which hung from a nail in an overhead beam. He waited on the other side of the door, and as it began to open outwards he kicked it with all his might. The door smacked into the first man's face and Molineaux heard his unconscious body hit the deck.

Ingersoll came through the door, dagger in hand. He slashed at Molineaux's chest. Molineaux jumped back and bumped into a table. He rolled over it backwards, accidentally catching the lantern with one of his feet and hurling it into a corner. The glass smashed and a puddle of burning oil spread across the deck. Molineaux managed to get both feet on the deck, and then Ingersoll came around the table at him with the dagger.

Li Cheng paused halfway up the ratlines and turned to stamp on the hand of one of the Lascars who pursued him into the rigging. The man cried out and thrust his knuckles into his mouth. Li stamped on his other hand. The Lascar let go with that hand too and only realised his mistake when the ship, moving out from behind the lee of Lan-tao Island, rolled beneath him. He fell backwards with a cry and plummeted into the sea.

Li continued to climb up to the platform at the foretop where he encountered two Malays who had already been in the rigging. The first tried to kick him in the head as he climbed up through the lubber's hole. Li caught him by the ankle and gave his whole leg a twist. The Malay tried to turn away from the pain, lost his balance and fell to the deck.

Li climbed up on to the platform in time to meet the next Malay, who inched his way in from the foreyard. The man threw a punch at his head. Li ducked, and drove the tips of his fingers into the centre of the man's chest. The Malay doubled up in agony and fell with a scream.

Hassan, the *ghaut serang*, came up through the lubber's hole and slashed at Li's feet with a kris. Li jumped over the arcing blade and backed out on to the yardarm, arms spread wide for balance. Hassan tried to follow him. The more orthodox method for moving out on to the yard was to stand on the foot rope while holding on to the spar, but the *ghaut serang* seemed to sense that would put him at a disadvantage to Li, who balanced effortlessly on the yard itself, in spite of the rolling of the ship.

Holding on to the mast for support, Hassan slashed at Li with the kris. The Chinese skipped back further out on to the yard. The *ghaut serang* swallowed hard and let go of the mast, edging nervously out on to the spar. He faced up to Li and slashed at his throat. His arms folded mockingly, Li leaned back slightly and the wavy blade missed his Adam's apple by a hair's breadth. Hassan overbalanced and fell from the yard without Li having touched him. The Chinese shook his head sadly, amazed that the *tai-pan* should employ sailors with no sense of balance to crew his ship.

Suddenly the yard jerked sharply below him. He almost lost his footing, and his arms flailed wildly as he teetered for a few seconds. He had just regained his poise when the yard gave another jerk, and then another.

He heard laughter as he struggled to maintain his footing. Glancing down to the deck – a mistake: it made him feel even dizzier – he saw Verran directing three sea-cunnies to tug on a rope. Each time they hauled, the yard on which Li stood gave another jerk. Now he could see when each jerk was about to come and brace himself in readiness, it was easier to maintain his balance. He waved mockingly to Verran.

Scowling, the captain went crazy. He drew his cutlass and slashed at ropes left, right and centre. When the third rope parted, the yard suddenly pivoted at the middle and the end on which Li stood dropped down under his weight. As the yard canted he felt his feet slip and the world span around him. He tumbled and fell headlong towards the deck far below.

'What the devil does that idiot think he's doing?' Bannatyne demanded. 'He'll bring down all the sails!' He started to march across the deck.

Shen indicated Killigrew. 'What shall I do with this one?' he asked in Cantonese.

Bannatyne did not even glance over his shoulder. 'Throw him over the side. Suitably weighed down, of course.'

Shen grasped Killigrew by the lapels, hoisted him to his feet and propped him up against the taffrail. He picked up a length of chain and wrapped it about the lieutenant's torso a couple of times to make sure his body would sink. Then he bent down to seize Killigrew's ankles so he could tip him over.

Killigrew had only been pretending to be stunned, and now he seized his chance. He snatched a mahogany belaying pin from a rack and smashed it over the back of Shen's head.

The pin snapped. Shen straightened with an expression of mild annoyance.

Killigrew thrust the splintered end of the pin in Shen's face, but the Chinese caught him by the wrist and stopped the thrust short. He twisted Killigrew's arm, whirled him around and yanked his wrist up into the small of his back.

Killigrew gasped. It felt as if his arm was going to be wrenched from its socket. His hand opened and the broken belaying pin dropped to the deck. Shen pushed him away. Killigrew staggered backwards across the quarterdeck and collided with the helmsman, Suleiman.

The assistant helmsman, a Lascar, seized him in a full nelson and held him fast as Suleiman let go of the wheel long enough to draw a dagger from his belt to finish him off. With no one to hold it, the wheel spun crazily as the waves buffeted the rudder.

Killigrew leaned forward and pulled the Lascar over him so that he lost his balance. Then he whirled round and straightened, putting the Lascar back down in the path of Suleiman's dagger thrust. The Lascar groaned. Killigrew broke free and whirled round again in time to see the Lascar slump to the deck.

Suleiman stared down at what he had done, and then came at Killigrew with a snarl. He thrust like lightning, and before Killigrew could defend himself the blade slammed against his chest.

The two of them glanced down. The dagger's point had caught in one of the links of the chain Shen had wrapped around Killigrew. Before Suleiman could pull back the dagger, Killigrew caught him by the arm. The two of them grappled for a moment. Killigrew forced Suleiman's hand towards the spinning helm. He let go of the arm as the wrist was caught between the spokes of the wheel and the bone snapped audibly. Sobbing in agony, Suleiman sank to his knees.

Another hammer-blow smashed into Killigrew's neck: Shen again. He staggered across to the rail, trying to put as much distance between himself and the Chinese to buy himself enough time just to turn and face his next attack. He turned and braced himself, but Shen was taking his time, his face the epitome of supreme self-assurance.

Killigrew removed the chain Shen had wrapped around him. As Shen advanced on him, he whirled the chain around his head like a flail. He swung it at the comprador. The links wrapped themselves around Shen's head, but the comprador grabbed the chain and hauled on it. Caught off balance, Killigrew staggered towards him and his face met the comprador's fist coming in the opposite direction. He staggered back against the taffrail, dazed, and shook his head muzzily.

Shen unwrapped the chain from his head and tossed it over the side, advancing once more.

The deck heaved violently. With no one at the helm, the *Golden Dragon* was being blown wherever the wind and current would take it; and it only took one glance of Killigrew's trained eye to see that the sea was intent on carrying them to where white breakers betrayed the presence of a reef in the gloom.

Killigrew pointed. 'If someone doesn't take the helm, we'll be run aground!' he said urgently in Cantonese.

Shen did not make the mistake of turning to look. 'First I shall finish you, and then take the helm.'

Killigrew lunged suddenly at the Chinese, raining a salvo of blows against his face: right jab, right jab, left uppercut, right cross and then the *coup de grâce* – that old left hook that came out of nowhere when they were too dazed to see it coming.

Shen grinned. 'Is that the best you can do?' He jumped into the air, kicked Killigrew in the chest and drove him back against the rail.

The fire in the cabin spread swiftly. Molineaux found himself caught between the roaring flames and Ingersoll's dagger. He faced the dagger, the greater of the two perils, first. Ingersoll thrust at his stomach. Molineaux caught him by the wrist and the two of them grappled chest to chest. The captain was stronger, but Molineaux had his arm gripped with both hands. Ingersoll gave up trying to thrust the dagger into his stomach and instead used his weight to push him back into the flames.

Molineaux's feet struggled for purchase on the deck. He could feel the heat of the flames scorch the back of his neck. He threw himself sideways in desperation, and Ingersoll stumbled into the flames. He let go of Molineaux to beat out the flames where his clothes had caught fire.

Molineaux ducked out of the cabin. He heard Ingersoll's footsteps right behind him. He ascended a companionway and turned to kick Ingersoll in the face. The white man avoided the blow and caught Molineaux by the leg. The two of them struggled in the confined space. Ingersoll slammed the seaman first against one bulkhead and then against the other. Molineaux still stood above Ingersoll and he used gravity to his advantage, falling on the captain. Locked together, the two of them crashed back down the steps to the deck below.

They rolled apart, rose to their feet and faced one another. A terrific shudder ran through the ship and there came a groaning, splintering sound from somewhere forward. Even as Molineaux was thrown against Ingersoll, he knew instinctively that the ship had crashed into something.

Unbalanced, the two of them fell down the next companion ladder to the lower deck. Molineaux lay there for a moment, dazed. It felt as if every bone in his body was broken.

Then Ingersoll was on him again, smashing at his face with his fists. Molineaux seized him by the throat and squeezed. As Ingersoll's eyes bulged from their sockets, Molineaux managed to push him off and roll on top, but then Ingersoll lifted his knee sharply into Molineaux's crotch. Fire blazed through his loins. The two of them tumbled over and over on the deck until they fell down the hatch to the orlop deck.

The water broke their fall. Cold sea water: it surged along the deck as it rushed in through a breech in the hull. Floundering, Molineaux and Ingersoll broke apart to find their feet. The water was only waist deep, but it was rising fast. Realising the ship was sinking, Molineaux turned and tried to climb back up the companion ladder, but Ingersoll caught him by the belt and dragged him down. Then he got both his hands around Molineaux's neck from behind and forced his head underwater.

XX:

The Death of the *Golden Dragon*

As Li Cheng fell he braced himself for the bone-breaking impact of the deck, but it never came. Instead something caught his ankle and almost tore out his leg. He found himself dangling upside down thirty feet above the deck, his foot caught in the foot-rope of the crazily canted foreyard.

Below he could see Bannatyne shouting furiously at Verran. The *tai-pan* pointed up to where Li dangled. Verran nodded and began to ascend the ratlines.

Li swung against the limp foresail. He could not get a grip on the canvas to pull himself up. He panicked for a moment, and then his scrabbling fingers found a reef point and gripped it. He pulled himself up with one hand, found another reef point with the other and then disentangled his foot from the foot-rope. His legs swung down and he hung the right way up at last.

As he tried to climb back on to the foreyard the ship juddered and canted suddenly, swinging him out with the dangling yard. Verran, halfway up the ratlines, was almost thrown overboard but managed to hang on. Below, Bannatyne and the sailors were hurled to the deck. On either side of the bows, Li could see the breakers boiling white where they surged over the reef. Her bows impaled on the reef, the *Golden Dragon* began to settle in the water.

Verran resumed his ascent. Li swung himself back on to the foreyard and climbed up to where it was trussed to the mast. Just as he reached the platform at the foretop Verran thrust his cutlass at him up through the lubber's hole. The razor-sharp steel sliced through the flesh of Li's calf. He gasped, jumped clear and caught hold of the shrouds which led up to the cross-trees at the peak of the fore topmast. He began to climb, and Verran climbed up after him.

A series of bangs sounded above the pounding of the waves as they smashed the stricken vessel against the reef. Li glanced aft and saw the panes of glass in one of the skylights below shatter as the flames in the cabin roared against them.

He had reached the cap of the fore topmast. Still gripping his cutlass, Verran continued his ascent. 'No place left to run, my slant-eyed friend!'

Li glanced about desperately. The only other way off the fore topmast was via one of the two ropes that ran from the yard-arm ends of the fore topgallant yard to the main topmast crosstrees. There were only two questions: would one of them be strong enough to bear his weight; and could he make it to the mainmast before Verran sliced through the rope and sent him plunging to the deck far below?

Molineaux was not drowning, but he was not far from it, either. He had managed to get his lungs

551

half-full of air before Ingersoll pushed his head under. Now he floundered about, unable to gain purchase with either hands or feet as Ingersoll kept up the relentless pressure.

His knuckles brushed against something solid: a handrail. He searched for it with his fingertips, found it again, got a good grip, and then pulled himself further under.

It was the last thing Ingersoll could have expected and it caught him completely off guard. His hands locked right around Molineaux's neck, he found himself dragged under the fast-rising water before he had a chance to take any air into his lungs.

Molineaux held on tight to the floor timbers, gambling on there being more air left in his own lungs than there had been in Ingersoll's. The pain in his chest grew tighter and tighter, until he felt he must burst if he did not breathe in now. But Ingersoll's fingers still dug into his neck from behind. Perhaps he had miscalculated. Perhaps Ingersoll still had his head above water.

Molineaux could not hold out much longer. He felt his vision misting, his strength giving out. He allowed himself to go limp, hoping to trick Ingersoll into thinking he was dead.

And then the hands were gone. Molineaux surfaced and banged his skull on the low deck head, but he did not mind that, he was just grateful to whoop that sweet, fetid air into his lungs.

Ingersoll was already wading through the chest-deep water towards the companion ladder. Molineaux went after him, but the water impeded his every step. By the time he reached the ladder Ingersoll had slammed down the hatch cover from above.

Molineaux climbed up the companion ladder and pounded on the underside of the hatch cover, but Ingersoll had made it fast. Molineaux climbed back down to the deck. If he could get forward he knew there would be another way up beyond the hold.

The water was shoulder-high now and he was fighting against the torrent that rushed in. He half-swam, half-pulled himself through the engine room. When he reached the door to the hold he had to duck his head under the water, but there was more headroom on the other side. Chests of opium were stacked high on either side. He swam down the gangway between them until he reached the ladder to the main hatch on the far side. As he climbed up out of the water Ingersoll appeared above him and reached for the hatch cover.

Molineaux grabbed him by the ankle. Ingersoll lost his balance and fell through the hatch. The two of them plunged into the water which swirled furiously between the opium chests.

They turned to face one another in the chin-deep water. Ingersoll's hand came up out of the water and Molineaux realised that the white man had retrieved his Bowie knife. He tried to step back and tripped over some unseen obstruction on the submerged deck. He backed into a stack of chests. Ingersoll slashed at his face with his own knife.

Molineaux ducked beneath the water to avoid

the thrust. He caught Ingersoll around the waist and drove him back. Something – possibly Ingersoll's knee – bumped against his face. The water reduced the force of the blow, but it was still enough to enable him to break free before Molineaux could pull him under.

The seaman surfaced. Ingersoll came at him again, stabbing this time. Molineaux backed into the stack of chests once more and noticed one of the ropes which held the chests in place had been slashed through by one of Ingersoll's thrusts. Then the ship gave a lurch as the next breaker forced it deeper on to the reef. The chests at the top of the stack toppled forward. Molineaux pressed himself back against the chests below.

Ingersoll saw his peril but it was too late. He threw up his arms in a futile gesture and then the uppermost chest smashed down against him and drove him under the water. The chest bobbed up again almost at once. Ingersoll followed a moment later, floating on his back. The Bowie knife had been driven into his heart.

'Time for number-two *wu-yi* demonstration.' On the listing quarterdeck, Shen circled Killigrew. 'Leopard punch!' One hand whipped out and slammed into the lieutenant's chest. He staggered back in agony. It felt as though his ribs had been driven through his lungs.'

'Venomous snake strikes vital point!' Shen struck Killigrew beneath the armpit. The lieutenant sank to his knees.

'Crane drinks alongside stream!' A fist slammed into Killigrew's face, and he sprawled on his back. He rolled over and tried to crawl away.

'Yellow oriole drinks water!' A foot struck Killigrew in the ribs and knocked him on his side. Barely able to see through the waves of pain that swamped him, he crawled over to the taffrail and pulled himself to his feet.

'Are you paying attention?' Shen's face looked demonic in the light of the flames that shot up through the shattered skylight. 'Civilised Chinese pay much money for this kind of schooling. Kicking the sky!' He lifted his foot into the underside of the lieutenant's jaw. Killigrew's head snapped back and he almost went over the taffrail. He steadied himself just in time to receive Shen's next attack.

'Phoenix-eye punch!' A fist smashed into Killigrew's temple. He span away dizzily across the tilted deck. He knew he could not take much more of this beating.

'Double tiger claws!' Two more fists slammed into him with bone-jarring force. He staggered back again on legs like water. Every nerve end in his body was screaming at him to give up and lie down and die.

Bracing his feet in an effort to stay upright on the canted deck, he faced Shen and wiped his sleeve across split lips. 'You know we have martial arts in Britain, too?'

Shen threw back his head and laughed. Killigrew summoned up the last reserves of his strength and grabbed him by the lapels.

'Glaswegian kiss!' Killigrew brought his forehead down sharply against the bridge of Shen's nose. Dazed, the Chinese staggered back with blood gushing from his nostrils.

'Ringsend uppercut!' The lieutenant flicked a boot into Shen's crotch. The Chinese doubled up in agony. Killigrew span him around to face the raging inferno which blazed up through the skylight.

'Naval officer kicks hulking brute in backside!' He slammed the sole of his boot against Shen's buttocks. The Chinese staggered forwards, tripped over the skylight coaming and fell through with a scream.

Holding one arm across his brow against the intense heat, Killigrew squinted down into the flames. He saw Shen in the cabin below. The comprador picked himself up and staggered about for a few moments, but his clothes were on fire and the smoke and flames blinded him. He blundered about for a few seconds, then finally slumped to the deck and lay down to die.

Breathing hard, Killigrew stumbled over to the bulwark and clung on to it for support. A moment later a dripping wet Molineaux emerged from the main hatch and staggered over to join him. Everyone else on deck was either dead or unconscious. 'You oh-kay, sir?'

Killigrew nodded. 'Did you find Mrs Bannatyne?' he asked desperately as the deck gave another shudder.

'No, sir. Where's Li Cheng?'

They both looked about. The only signs of life were in the rigging. Li clung to the fore top-gallant yard at the peak of the foremast. Verran climbed up the rigging towards him, cutlass in hand, but Li seemed more interested in one of the fore topgallant braces.

'He's going to climb across to the mainmast!' gasped Molineaux.

'He'll never make it,' Killigrew said grimly. 'Verran will cut it before he gets halfway...'

Both of them were assuming that Li would haul himself along the brace hand over hand. Both of them were wrong.

Li got his feet on the fore topgallant yard and stood up, spreading his arms for balance. Then he stepped out on to the brace like a tightrope walker. 'Jesus Christ!' exclaimed Molineaux. 'He's crazy!'

Li started to walk along the brace; no, he started to *run* across it.

Muda and MacGillivray ascended the ratlines on either side of the mainmast to meet the Chinese at the other end. 'We'd better go and help him,' said Molineaux.

Killigrew had had more than enough for one night, but he could hardly stand by and allow the young Chinese to be butchered. As Molineaux scrambled up the ratlines to port, Killigrew ascended on the opposite side. The *Golden Dragon* was heeling over to starboard and Killigrew's climb was almost vertical as he pursued MacGillivray, but he forced himself onwards and upwards.

The wind blew Li off balance. He teetered for a moment and Killigrew watched with his heart in his mouth. Somehow the Chinese regained his poise and made it to the cap of the main topmast.

Killigrew caught up with MacGillivray, grabbed

him by the belt and plucked him from the ratlines. The engineer fell with a scream and was swallowed up by the breakers which surged across the reef.

Muda was only a few feet below Li in the main topgallant shrouds, climbing up with a kris between his teeth. Both Killigrew and Molineaux were too far below to catch him before he reached Li. Verran, meanwhile, crawled along the fore topgallant brace after the Chinese, his face twisted in a snarl of hatred.

Li waited for Muda at the main topmast crosstrees. The Malay reached him, took his kris from his teeth, and slashed at his legs. Li kicked him in the wrist and the kris spun high into the air. Li slammed the sole of his slipper into Muda's face and the Malay plummeted to the deck.

Verran was almost two-thirds of the way along the brace. Li deftly caught Muda's spinning kris by the haft. He swung himself around the topgallant mast and slashed at the brace. Verran stared at him in horror as the blade sliced through the rope. Still clinging on, he swung downwards, headfirst. He hit the mouth of the funnel and plunged down it with a hollow, echoing cry which was cut short as he plummeted into the furnace below.

In the same instant his cutlass clattered to the deck.

Killigrew and Molineaux shinned down the backstays to the deck. A moment later Li joined them and bowed. 'I am sorry I killed your friend.'

'That's all right. I never liked him much

anyway.' Mindful that Bannatyne was still loose on board somewhere, Killigrew picked up Verran's cutlass. 'All right, search the ship. We're not going until we find Mrs Bannatyne...'

'Don't bother,' said the *tai-pan*. 'She's here.'

Killigrew, Molineaux and Li whirled. Blase Bannatyne stood behind his wife, the muzzle of a single-shot percussion pistol pressed against the underside of her jaw beneath her right ear. In his other hand he had a second percussion pistol pointed at Killigrew. The two of them were silhouetted by the blaze which now engulfed the whole of the stern. The ship's timbers groaned in her death throes as the waves pounded her against the reef.

'Drop the sword!' snarled Bannatyne. 'Now!'

The *tai-pan* and his wife stood too far away for Killigrew, Molineaux or Li to be able to do anything. Raging with frustration, Killigrew threw down the cutlass so that it buried its point deep in the deck, the hilt quivering.

Bannatyne laughed and took the first pistol away from his wife's jaw to cover both Molineaux and Li. 'You didn't really think I'd shoot my own wife, did you?'

It was Mrs Bannatyne who answered. 'As a matter of fact, I did.' She rammed an elbow into his stomach. He doubled up and dropped one of the pistols. With his free hand he threw her against the jolly boat stowed on deck.

Killigrew lunged for him. Bannatyne fired and a white-hot needle bored through the flesh of the lieutenant's shoulder. A moment later a final shudder threw them all to the deck as the ship was wrenched asunder with a splintering groan. The bows sank almost at once and the stern and midships section canted crazily. Li gave a cry and slipped down the smooth deck to be engulfed by the breakers. Killigrew managed to wrap one arm around the skid beams on which the jolly boat rested, and with the other he caught Molineaux by the wrist as he slid past.

The waves rose slowly up the deck, tilted at an angle of fifty degrees. Above them the blazing stern cast a hellish glow over the scene. As the ship sank deeper the tilt of the deck increased.

Molineaux's weight threatened to pull Killigrew's arm from his socket. 'Hang on!' yelled Killigrew.

Above them, Mrs Bannatyne clung to a grating in the deck while her husband, further up the grating, tried to stamp on her fingers. 'Mr Killigrew!' she screamed. 'Help!'

'Sir!' yelled Molineaux.

Killigrew glanced down. The seaman jerked his head to where Bannatyne's other pistol had wedged in one of the scuppers. 'Swing me over!'

The lieutenant started to swing Molineaux to and fro across the deck. At the furthermost reach of the swing, their grips broke. Molineaux bounced off the bulwark and slithered down the deck. He snatched at the pistol as he went and managed to catch hold of a set of pinrails a few feet above the rising water. One end of the pinrail broke away under his weight. 'You'll have to take the shot, sir! I can't make it from here!'

Killigrew nodded. Molineaux hurled the gun up the deck with all his might. The motion ripped the pinrail away completely and the sea-man plunged down.

The pistol skittered past Killigrew and he caught it even as he saw the water swallow up his friend. 'Molineaux! No!' he screamed in horror.

The seaman did not reappear.

Killigrew turned his attention back to where Bannatyne clung to the grating. He lost his grip and slid down to kick his wife in the face. She cried out and Killigrew braced himself to catch her, but she hung on to her husband's ankles now. He caught hold of the grating further down. She scrabbled against the deck in search of a foothold while he kicked at her face again to free himself.

Killigrew thought of Molineaux, and Peri, Li and Ultzmann, and of all the other people who had died thanks to Bannatyne's machinations. There was no doubt in his mind that the *tai-pan* had lived too long. He drew a bead on him. 'Mrs Bannatyne!' he called. 'Let go!'

'I daren't!' she sobbed.

'Let go!' he repeated. 'I'll catch you, I swear it! Trust me!'

She let go and slid down the deck in a blossoming of petticoats. Killigrew fired and then dropped the pistol in time to catch her. Agony tore at his right arm where it gripped the skids and he distinctly felt the bone pop out of its socket. He cried out in pain.

'Are you all right?' she asked.

He gritted his teeth and nodded. He drew her in closer so she could grasp the skid beams for herself. They both looked up to where Bannatyne lay on his back, still clinging to the grating with one hand. He stared back at them in shock, and with one hand reached inside his coat. Killigrew thought he was reaching for another gun, but when the hand came out it was empty and glistened with blood in the firelight.

Then the *tai-pan* lost his grip, slid down a few feet until his legs struck the first of the skid beams. His body pivoted outwards to roll down the deck to where Verran's cutlass was still embedded. Killigrew buried Mrs Bannatyne's battered face against his chest as the razor-sharp blade sliced her husband's head clean off. Head and body bounced into the foaming breakers.

The water was only a few feet below Killigrew and Mrs Bannatyne now, the deck almost vertical. 'Clasp-knife!' he told her. 'In my pocket. You'll have to cut through the ropes holding the tarpaulin cover in place.'

She nodded, took the knife from his pocket, and clambered up the skid-beams to where the jolly boat was stowed. She sliced through the ropes and wrenched off the tarpaulin cover. Favouring his dislocated arm, Killigrew climbed inside. 'Now cut the mooring ropes,' he told her. 'Leave the ones at the top until last. And make sure you're in the boat when you cut them!'

She did as he told her, climbing into the jolly boat alongside him as she sawed at the last of the ropes. 'Hold tight!' he cautioned her.

The rope parted and the jolly boat shot the last few feet down the deck. The bow bumped sideways off the stump of the mainmast and Mrs Bannatyne was thrown against Killigrew. The prow buried itself in the waves, and then came up again and they drifted away from the ship.

A few inches of water sloshed around the bilges. Killigrew took the bailing scoop in his left hand. 'You'll have to row, get us clear of the reef before the *Golden Dragon* goes down. Think you can manage it?'

'I'll just have to try, won't I?' She fitted the oars in the rowlocks and rowed them until they were clear of both the sinking ship and the reef. Once they were out of danger she stopped rowing and shipped the oars, and the two of them watched as the steamer's blazing stern slipped beneath the waves with a hiss. For a second or two the golden dragon ensign which hung from the jackstaff was still visible, ragged and smouldering at the edges, and then that too was gone for ever.

Epiphany Bannatyne cut off his jacket to avoid twisting his dislocated arm and examined the wound in his shoulder where her husband had shot him. 'You're lucky. It's just a flesh wound.' She did not faint at the sight of blood, but bound up his wound gently but firmly to stop the bleeding.

'One day you'll make some lucky chap a good wife,' he told her.

'He can't be any worse than my last husband,' she agreed. 'In fact, I think I could do a lot better for myself.'

He leaned closer to her. The bruises on her face where Bannatyne had kicked her looked appalling, but Killigrew did not imagine he looked any better. 'Did you have anyone in mind?' he asked her.

'If I think of anyone, you'll be the first to know. Mr Killigrew ... are you a wealthy man?'

'Me? No. Poor as a church mouse. Why do you ask?'

'Perfect.' Her lips slightly parted, she moved her face towards his.

At that moment a figure bobbed up on one side of the jolly boat, and was followed up by a second on the other side a moment later. Killigrew reached for his clasp knife and Mrs Bannatyne snatched up one of the oars, but they were only Molineaux and Li.

'As pleased as I am to see that you're both back from Davy Jones' locker, I must say your timing could have been a good deal better,' Killigrew said ruefully. 'Well, now you're here you can take up those oars and put them to some good use.'

'Don't tempt me,' muttered Molineaux.

'Oars not necessary,' said Li, and pointed. 'Look!'

They all turned to see Framjee's steam pinnace navigating the reef with Ågård at the tiller. Hartcliffe waved from the bows and presently tossed a line across to them. Molineaux and Li let go of the jolly boat and swam across to the pinnace where Seth Endicott helped them on board. 'What happened to Bannatyne, Molineaux?' asked Hartcliffe.

'He's probably trying to bribe Davy Jones into letting him go even as we speak.'

They took the jolly boat in tow and headed back to Victoria. Killigrew tried to get comfortable next to Mrs Bannatyne but something was sticking in his back. He reached underneath him and found a bottle of laudanum. 'Just the thing!' He pulled the stopper out with his teeth and spat it over the side. Before he could take a sip, however, she snatched the bottle from his hand and threw it overboard.

'You don't need that any more.'

'But I only wanted a sip, to take my mind off the pain.'

She moved closer. 'I'll give you something to take your mind off the pain...'

Afterword

Alas, all of Kit Killigrew's efforts to avert a second war between Britain and China were for naught: the two empires were at war within seven years. Once again the British were the aggressors, declaring war on China because of their insistence that British subjects guilty of crimes in China should be tried in British courts. The Second Opium War (1856–1860) is sometimes known as the *Arrow* War, after the name of the ship from which a 'British' seaman (actually a Chinese) was taken by the Chinese authorities. The man was tried for murder and found guilty, prompting another outburst of Lord Palmerston's gunboat diplomacy.

It takes two to polka, and the arrogance of the Chinese in believing that all other races on earth – even those they had never encountered – were subject to the authority of the Emperor in Beijing certainly contributed to this second outbreak of hostilities. But the inescapable fact remains that they were well within their rights both to try people accused of crimes on Chinese soil in Chinese courts, and to forbid the import of opium into China, which of course was the cause of the First Opium War (1839–42) – and also the underlying cause of the second. If the Chinese were beaten thoroughly on both occasions, that is as much a reflection of the pacifist Confucian ethos which had been dominant in China for centuries as of the superiority of British technology. While the cultural and technological superiority that China had once possessed over the rest of the world had by the nineteenth century been long permitted to stagnate, perhaps that was a fair price to pay for centuries of relative peace and harmony. Tragically, that peace was only shattered by the arrival of the barbarians.

While I have no wish to make excuses for the men who smuggled opium into China in the eighteenth and nineteenth centuries – they deserved none – it is only fair to point out that until the mid-nineteenth century it was little understood that opium was addictive; indeed, some tried to argue that opium was beneficial. Uncontrolled before the Pharmacy Act of 1868, it was available over the counter in England, as pills, lozenges, pastilles, liniments, and raw poppy seeds, and as the active ingredient in many medicines. 'Kendal Black Drop' was a particular favourite of Coleridge and Byron, but opium was not exclusively a rich man's vice: it was cheaper even than gin, hence its popularity with industrial workers in Lancashire. The withdrawal symptoms suffered by addicts who tried to quit were supposed by doctors to be unrelated ailments. The cure for these 'unrelated ailments'? More opium-based medicines, of course.

Although Killigrew fought in the First Opium War, I had no wish to write in depth about his experiences at that time: there was no way I could see of salvaging anything noble or heroic out of that shambolic butchery. I was more intrigued by events that took place in 1849, the events which inspired much of this novel. In that year the ravages of the pilongs became so difficult to ignore that the Royal Navy decided to do something about them. The worst of these pirates were Shap-ng-tsai and Chui-apoo – the joint inspiration for Zhai Jing-mu – who divided up the south coast of China between them: Shap-ng-tsai would operate to the west of Hong Kong, while Chui-apoo operated to the east. Shap-ng-tsai was blamed for the murder of *Capitão* d'Amaral, the governor of Macao, early in 1849, and shortly afterwards the murder of Captain d'Acosta of the Royal Engineers and Lieutenant Dwyer of the Ceylon Rifles were ascribed to Chui-apoo, whom they were said to have insulted.

In the autumn of that year Her Majesty's brig *Columbine*, in company with the P&O steamer SS *Canton*, chased a fleet of pilong junks to Bias Bay, to the east of Hong Kong, where Chui-apoo had his lair in Fan-lo-kong creek, an arm of Bias Bay. The *Columbine* kept the pilong junks bottled up in the bay while the *Canton* steamed back to Hong Kong to fetch Her Majesty's paddle-sloop *Fury*. The *Columbine* was unable to enter the bay because her draught was too great, so on that occasion it was left to the *Fury* to go in, and she is said to have destroyed no less than twenty-three pilong junks, although Chui-apoo, despite being desperately wounded, is believed to have escaped.

No sooner had the *Columbine* and the *Fury*

returned to Hong Kong than they were dispatched westwards to deal with Shap-ng-tsai's fleet, in company with the SS *Phlegethon*, a steamer of the Honourable East India Company. Over the course of several weeks they tracked Shap-ng-tsai's fleet ever westwards, into the uncharted islands in the Gulf of Tonquin, until they trapped the pirates in the Tonquin River. In a battle lasting two days, the two navy vessels and the civilian steamer put paid to no less than fifty-eight pilong junks and suffered only one fatality amongst their own crews. Once again the pilong admiral escaped, but his fleet was destroyed. The fates of both Shap-ng-tsai and Chui-apoo are shrouded in uncertainty, but according to one account Chui-apoo was captured by the British and committed suicide while awaiting trial, while Shap-ng-tsai surrendered himself to the Chinese authorities and was given a commission in their navy!

These events actually took place several months after this novel is set. I brought the action forward to set the climax at the dragon boat festival, which also allowed me to feature Captain the Honourable Henry Keppel, who was in command of HMS *Mœander* at Hong Kong at this time, although I also had to delay his arrival by a couple of months for dramatic purposes. Keppel was one of the great swashbuckling heroes of his day and went on to become Admiral of the Fleet in 1877.

Many other characters in this novel were likewise inspired by real people who were in China at this time. Rear-Admiral Sir Francis

Collier did suffer a paralysing stroke in February 1849 – the month Dwyer and d'Acosta were murdered – and died a few months later. There was an Admiral Huang Hai-kwang who took part in the British expedition against Shap-ng-tsai. He arrived with a fleet of six war junks, but knowing they would not be able to keep up he travelled on one of the British vessels. Determined to keep the Chinese end up, on the second day of the battle in the Tonquin River he jumped overboard and swam out to capture a pilong junk single-handed.

Cargill was inspired by Assistant Superintendent Daniel R. Caldwell of the Hong Kong Police. Caldwell also took part in the expedition against Shap-ng-tsai, as an interpreter. He emerges from the pages of this chapter of history as one of the few men who took the trouble to understand the Chinese – he married a Chinese, almost unheard of for a European in those days – for which he was subsequently accused by one of Hong Kong's attorney-generals, T. Chisholm Anstey, of consorting with pirates and being financially interested in brothels. An inquiry cleared Caldwell of these charges, but it was conducted in such a manner – with certain evidence being burned by Caldwell's friends – that though he was never proven guilty, nor was he proven innocent, and in the end it was decided that he was guilty by association with a man discovered to be a pirate and was therefore unfit to hold the office of justice of the peace (a post which by that time he had already quit).

Hong Kong certainly seems to have been a

lively place. Writing of the Hong Kong newspapers in the 1840s, Jan Morris informs us:

We are told of 'astounding rumours implicating certain Chinese residents ... in dark deeds of piracy and crime'. We are told of the 'diabolic procedures' employed by the hordes of pirates infesting the Pearl River Estuary. We hear at length of 'the ruffian Ingood', who specialized in robbing drunken sailors, and who, having drowned one over-protesting victim, became in 1845 the first European to be hanged in Hong Kong. We read of a plot to poison twenty-five men of the Royal Artillery, of a battle in the harbour between junks and boats of HMS *Cambrian*, of an attempt to burn down the Central Market, of a reward offered for the Governor's assassination, of protection rackets, robberies with violence and incessant housebreaking.

Hong Kong was a colony based purely on trade and the *tai-pans* of the trading companies must have set the tone. They were hard, ruthless men who would stop at nothing in the pursuit of wealth. Foremost amongst the China traders was the company of Jardine Matheson. Scottish Presbyterians and the epitome of Victorian hypocrisy, they brought God and opium to China, and by no means in equal quantities. Unlike Bannatyne, both men lived long and died millionaires in comfortable retirement, which was more than they deserved. Such wealthy men were extremely influential – like Sir George Grafton, both

571

William Jardine and James Matheson returned to England to become members of parliament – and there can be little doubt that it was partly the influence of such men that drove Britain to attack China in the first Opium War.

Samuel George Bonham became Governor of Hong Kong, Plenipotentiary and Superintendent of Trade in 1848, after his predecessor was forced to resign by the opposition of the China traders. Bonham was knighted in 1851, made a baronet the following year, and remained governor until 1854.

Ultzmann is a fictional character, but inspired by a real one: the Reverend Karl Friedrich Gutzlaff, known to British sailors as 'Happy Bowels'. He worked for Jardine Matheson for a while and ultimately became Chinese Secretary at the office of the Hong Kong Superintendent of Trade. When he left the colony for France to raise funds for his missionary activities, the French consul at Macao wrote to his government to warn them, describing Gutzlaff as 'a man of considerable inventiveness, who has always sought to enrich himself ... I regret to say that there is not a word of truth in the tales of this Sinologue. Sir Dadabhoy Framjee is modeled on Sir Jamsetji Jeejeebhoy, the first Indian baronet, who was active in the China trade at this time. He made a fortune from the opium trade, but he at least seems to have ploughed vast amounts of money into charitable works in his native Gujerat.

Wu-yi – which simply translated means 'martial arts' – is of course better known in the West nowadays as kung fu (strictly speaking, *gong-fu*).

It was practised by Shaolin monks, whose temples became centres of opposition to the Ch'ing Dynasty in the eighteenth century. Another focus of opposition to the Manchus was the many interlinked secret societies which formed the Triads, of which the Brotherhood of Heaven, Earth and Man was only one. Today the Triads are predominantly criminal organisations, but in the nineteenth century their purpose was very much political. In 1850, however, their efforts were subsumed into the Taiping Rebellion, which the Manchus ultimately crushed in 1864, but only after a bloody war which is said to have cost more lives than the whole of the Second World War. Secret societies continued to be part of Chinese society until Sun Yat-sen overthrew the Manchu Dynasty in 1911: the 'Boxers United in Righteousness' – also known as the 'Harmonious Fists' – of 1898–1900 were one such organisation. If there are still secret societies intent on overthrowing the current regime in China to this day, the Communists aren't telling.

Despite the efforts of the Royal Navy and the Chinese authorities, piracy continues to be a problem in the South China Sea into the twenty-first century. During the 1850s, Westerners seemed to supplant the natives as the foremost pirates in the region for a time. Two of the most notorious were the Americans William 'Bully' Hayes and Eli Boggs. But that, as they say, is another story...

The publishers hope that this book has given you enjoyable reading. Large Print Books are especially designed to be as easy to see and hold as possible. If you wish a complete list of our books please ask at your local library or write directly to:

Magna Large Print Books
Magna House, Long Preston,
Skipton, North Yorkshire.
BD23 4ND

This Large Print Book for the partially sighted, who cannot read normal print, is published under the auspices of

THE ULVERSCROFT FOUNDATION

THE ULVERSCROFT FOUNDATION

... we hope that you have enjoyed this Large Print Book. Please think for a moment about those people who have worse eyesight problems than you ... and are unable to even read or enjoy Large Print, without great difficulty.

You can help them by sending a donation, large or small to:

**The Ulverscroft Foundation,
1, The Green, Bradgate Road,
Anstey, Leicestershire, LE7 7FU,
England.**
or request a copy of our brochure for more details.

The Foundation will use all your help to assist those people who are handicapped by various sight problems and need special attention.

Thank you very much for your help.